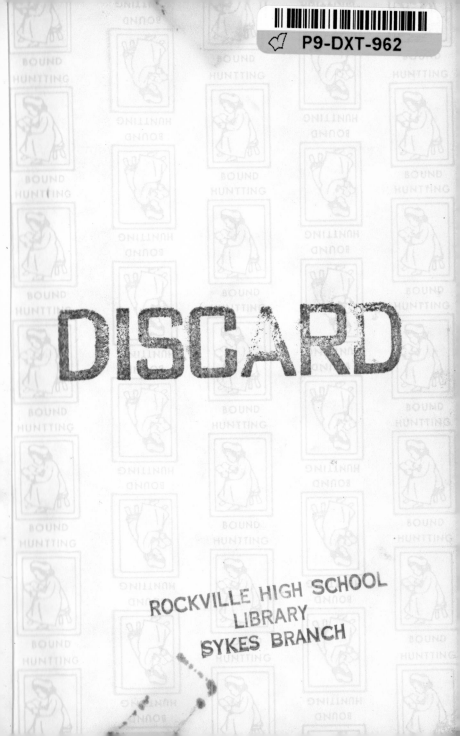

Red Lion and Gold Dragon

Also by Rosemary Sprague

Biography

FOREVER IN JOY: THE LIFE OF ROBERT BROWNING
GEORGE ELIOT: A BIOGRAPHY

Novels

NORTHWARD TO ALBION
A KINGDOM TO WIN
HEROES OF THE WHITE SHIELD
HEIR OF KILORAN
CONQUERORS OF TIME
DANCE FOR A DIAMOND STAR
FIFE AND FANDANGO
THE JADE PAGODA

POEMS OF ROBERT BROWNING (EDITED)

A Novel of the Norman Conquest

REO LION ANO GOLO ORAGON

By ROSEMARY SPRAGUE

CHILTON BOOK COMPANY

Philadelphia   New York   London

F
SP 2/69

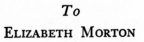

To
ELIZABETH MORTON

◆◇

Foreword

THE year 1066 is one so important in the history of Western Civilization that the researcher is surprised to discover how summarily contemporary sources document it. English chronicles simply record the events between the death of Edward the Confessor and the Battle of Hastings with little commentary, apart from the occasional ejaculation, "Lord, save us all!"; and the Norman chronicles are, naturally, heavily weighted in favor of Duke William. Even the Bayeux Tapestry, probably the most contemporary of all the sources and certainly the most detailed, cannot be given full credence, for it, too, is a Norman creation and devoted to extolling the Conqueror. And, after a lapse of nine centuries, topographical changes on the southern coast of England make the re-creation of the battle itself immensely difficult; expert military histories, written in commemoration of the 900th anniversary, frequently have had to take refuge in the familiar phrase, "It is possible."

Thus, it is in the light of this limited documentation that the actual events must be viewed. For example, "the hasty coronation" of Harold Godwineson, implying that the crown was hurriedly slapped on his head, almost in secret, is mentioned only in Norman sources. Yet, we know from accounts of previous English coronations what an exalted mystique surrounded the kingship, and certainly Harold, whose election had been hasty enough, would not have permitted the order of his crowning and sacring to give rise to question, especially considering the furore over his "broken oath." But the oath, too, must be considered in context, and the charge that he was an oath breaker must be tempered by our general knowledge of English and Norman law in that period. True, an oath was given. It is plainly depicted on the Bayeux Tapestry and is mentioned in both English and Norman accounts. But it was illegal, for an Englishman could not (any more than he can now) so swear to a foreign ruler without being guilty of treason to his own country. In Harold's case, it was pardonable only because it was forced under duress and, consequently, not binding. William of Normandy was well aware of these facts, but a dukedom was not enough for this man who had endured constant opprobrium and even armed opposition because of his illegitimate birth; and he found in Harold's oath—which he knew would have to be broken—a convenient *casus belli* to serve as a cloak for his own ambition to be as great a ruler in his own right as the King of France or the Count of Flanders. And he proved that he could so rule, for, like Harold, he was an inspired leader for those who would follow him. The tragedy of Hastings was that two such men inevitably had to be enemies.

Norman chroniclers, usually writing after the event, created that other myth which has so long dominated popular thinking: that when William was crowned king of England on Christmas Day, 1066, his conquest was complete. We know, however, that one battle has never conquered a nation, then or now. Just as the groundwork for Hastings had been laid a century earlier, when King Ethelred the Unready, of England, married Emma, sister of Duke William's grandfather, and fled to Normandy from the fury of the Danish invasions, so the Norman conquest itself took several centuries to achieve. For the English were not conquered and overwhelmed by their political, cultural, and social superiors. The English of 1066 were not as sophisticated as the Normans; but a nation which had produced the grandeur of a *Beowulf* and the poignant

viii

mysticism of "The Dream of the Rood," which had translated the Bible into its own language, and had given the world a scholar of the caliber of the Venerable Bede can hardly be considered barbaric or uncivilized. Nor were all the English of 1066, without exception, eager for this war which had been foisted upon them, as may be surmised from Harold's difficulties in raising and maintaining his nation under arms for any extended period. Nevertheless, when the crisis came, they fought as Englishmen and, in a very real sense, found themselves as a nation in that October defeat.

A word concerning language: the language spoken in England in 1066 was what academia calls "Anglo-Saxon" or "Old English." It could be compared to modern German, in that it was highly inflected and had the singular and plural forms of the pronoun "you." This singular, þe, metamorphosed in "thee," was retained in the spoken language well into the eighteenth century, and was customarily used by nineteenth century historical novelists. To the twentieth century ear, however, it is artificial; one thing we know certainly—the English of 1066 did not sound to each other as the characters in a Scott novel sound to us! So, even at the risk of some "modern sounding" dialogue, I have decided against strict linguistic accuracy in this instance, and have given some Old English words contemporary spellings as well. French, of course, was the language of the court, having been introduced by Edward the Confessor and his Norman entourage, and educated men, both English and Norman, had some knowledge of Latin. Also, I have called the English people "English," rather than "Saxons," because they were called so by the Normans and by almost everyone else, except the Welsh, Scots, and Irish, who (perhaps as a point of national honor) still occasionally refer to the descendants of their conquerors as *Sassenachs*.

Finally, I wish to thank the Reverend Canon Vivan Albertus Peterson and the Reverend Colin Stephenson, Guardian of the Shrine and Rector of the Anglican Shrine of Our Lady of Walsingham, respectively, for kind and valuable assistance regarding its history and tradition. They may be (I hope agreeably) surprised to find Harold Godwineson among its earliest visitors, since such a visit is not recorded. But it was not an age when every move and thought of a popular hero was set down, and much else about Harold has also been unrecorded. He was, however, a deeply religious man, and he would undoubtedly have taken the opportunity to worship there when in the vicinity. In fact, it is impossible to consider his doing otherwise, since he was aware all his life that the most solemnly observed tradition of an English coronation, apart from the anointing, was that time during the ceremony when the king lay prostrate before the altar of the Abbey Church, his arms outstretched to form a cross.

October 14, 1966
R. S.

Red Lion and Gold Dragon

"Again, Lord Tancred! Again!"

Aelfred Ansculfson looked up from the parchment scroll, frowning at the shouts of the kitchen churls cheering his stepbrother. Quiet and privacy were hard to come by on this busy demesne, and he had hoped that the men's bower—for once empty—would provide both, so that he could read his letter in peace.

"A second hit! *Haele!* All hail, Lord Tancred!"

He sighed exasperatedly and moved his stool across the room, depriving himself of the warmth from the firepit. "I'm to freeze in my own house," he grumbled, "so that Tancred the Norman may show his skill with the bow to churls!"

Then immediately he was ashamed. Time and again he had been told at the monastery that to show impatience at praise of another was the same as being envious, and envy was a sin. But, he thought morosely, he was no longer at the monastery, and by no wish of his own, either. He was atheling of Storches Hundred and had been for over a year. Coventry and the monks were a memory, and this was a different world, where men were more familiar with bows and arrows—and swords—than they were with prayers; a world where he felt lost and a stranger. And since June, when his father had brought home a

1

new Norman wife whose son was everything he himself was not, his life at Storches Hundred had become almost unbearable.

He returned to the letter with a sigh. It was from Edgar, his best friend at Canterbury. They had talked of entering the novitiate together. Now Edgar was on pilgrimage to Walsingham, where the great miracle had come.

"I have seen the Lady Richeldis," Aelfred read with eagerness. "From her own lips I have heard of her vision. They are building a great shrine here, and already the lame and blind have been cured at the holy well. How I wish you were—"

"Lord Tancred! *Haele*, Lord Tancred!"

In sudden rage, Aelfred leaped to his feet. His blue eyes were flashing as he strode to the door and flung it open. "What is the meaning of this?" he demanded. "Why are you churls idling here? Have you no work to do?"

A hush fell over the kitchen churls, who stood with heads hanging. Aelfred raised his chin. They might cheer Tancred's archery, but the atheling of Storches Hundred commanded an immediate respect that they would never show the Norman.

Tancred, however, was debonair as usual. "Ah," he said, bowing with a mocking flourish. "The atheling deigns to join our sport."

Aelfred's lips tightened. "Speak French. I understand it better than your English," he snapped.

"And I, your English better than your French," Tancred replied suavely. "But that is neither here nor there. Come, take a wager with me. The sun is still high and there is no wind."

"I came to ask for quiet," Aelfred retorted. "Their caterwauling over you shakes the house."

"Pardon!" Tancred's dark eyes gleamed with malicious amusement. "I forget—the walls of these English bowers are not as solid as those of our Norman castles. But surely, dear brother—as your father prefers me to call you—you will not refuse a challenge? Say, three shots to split that beam?"

He pointed to a small piece of wood which one of the kitchen churls was holding at arm's length. Tancred's arrogant

2

self-confidence made Aelfred shiver. The slightest move would make a difference: a stray breeze might come, a finger tremble—

Tancred laughed softly. "Perhaps the cheers will be less annoying if they are for yourself," he said, and hurled the bow towards him.

Aelfred, not wanting to disgrace himself completely, leaped to catch it, but a long arm reached past him and snatched it mid-air. He turned to find that Siward, his father's reeve, had come into the court.

"Is this the way Normans amuse themselves?" Siward asked quietly.

"Do you doubt my skill?" Tancred smiled, but his eyes were angry. "I have done this hundreds of times and have never yet missed."

"Strange! I had been told that the Normans were more civilized than the barbarous English. Now you show us that you use men to hold your targets." As easily as he would throw a stone across a brook, Siward tossed the bow the length of the kitchen court.

"How dare you?" Tancred yelped and raced after it.

The churls snickered, but Siward turned a bleak eye on them. "Back to work," he said shortly. "It is late, and there are tables to lay for the feast tonight. If Ecfrith baron's-steward catches you idling here at this hour, he'll switch you all soundly, and I'll loan him the use of my arm to save him time if he needs it. Off with you!"

The boys scuttled away, and Tancred picked up his bow. "It is fortunate for you, my man, that this bow is not my best one," he fumed.

"I am not your man," Siward said coldly, "and you've been told many times not to practice here. The south field is the place for that."

"It's covered with snow," Tancred objected.

"And it does not snow in Normandy? Or do the Normans sleep through the winter like bears and become archers only in the spring?"

"The snow is not deep," Aelfred interposed quickly. He

3

could see that Tancred was ready to explode into one of his rages, which he knew were not only terrible to behold but far-reaching as well. "I practiced there myself this morning."

"Thank you for your kind suggestion, dear brother," Tancred retorted meanly. His face flushed angrily to the roots of his round-cropped hair. "But I think I prefer to hunt now, with your permission." He looked at Siward. "And yours, of course?"

"Hunt where you will," Siward answered civilly, "except, of course, in the west forest land."

"And why may I not hunt there?"

"Because it does not belong to us."

"Baron Ansculf owns all this land—"

"We do not trespass on the west forest," Aelfred interrupted anxiously. How many times had Tancred been told of this rule, too! "It belongs to Mab wife of Wulfric. Wulfric's family had possession of it long before my ancestors came to Storches Hundred, and we do not hunt there without permission."

"Which I believe you have not asked," Siward concluded.

Tancred glared. "When I, Tancred de Belleme, must ask permission of an old witch woman—"

Aelfred's temper rose to meet his. "She's not a witch!"

"She is. Everyone says so."

"She is not." Siward's heavy hand grasped Tancred's shoulder. "Mind your tongue, boy. Never let me hear those words cross your lips again. Don't let me hear of you riding in the west forest, either, or it will be one of the sorriest days you have ever known."

Tancred looked at him defiantly for a moment, then shrugged. "I did not plan to ride there today anyway," he said loftily and stalked away.

"We'll have trouble with him on that score yet, mark my words," Siward said worriedly. "I'm glad you spoke for Mab, Aelfred."

"He made me angry," Aelfred said honestly. "He's always fussing about the west forest, you know."

"Is he? That's interesting. I wonder why?"

"For one thing, he's determined to get the best of Mab. He's

4

been furious with her ever since she did not want to serve his mother." Aelfred sighed. "It was an ill day when he came to Storches Hundred. I cannot understand my father."

"Nor I," Siward agreed bluntly.

"To marry *her!* After my mother!"

"Well, as to that, your mother has been dead thirteen years, and a man grows lonely. Lady Ygerne is beautiful. But she should have left her son in Normandy."

"Or my father should have sent him back." Words came to Aelfred's lips that he had never dreamed he would speak. "I've thought sometimes that perhaps even he wishes that he had not married her." Then he gasped at his own temerity. Sons did not so conjecture about their fathers' affairs.

Siward, however, did not seem shocked. "You have a way of knowing things," he said soberly. "Things that others don't know they know, until you put them into words. It's your mother in you, rest her soul." He crossed himself. "The Lady Ealswitha always knew when people were troubled. It's a rare gift."

"My father would call it a woman's gift," Aelfred demurred, but he was pleased at the praise from this rough man.

"Here I stand woolgathering and forgetting to tell you why I came to seek you!" Siward exclaimed in self-reproof. "Your father wants to see you. He's in his closet."

"Thank you. I'll go at once." Aelfred's heart plunged, as it always did, at that summons. He had been unusually free of it during the past fortnight. His father had ridden up to London on St. Stephen's Day for the winter witenagemot and had returned on New Year's Eve looking very gloomy. Since then he had kept to his closet, only joining the rest of the household for meals. As Aelfred walked towards the little house where the business of the demesne was transacted, he wondered if he would ever lose this nervousness that overcame him at even the sound of his father's voice. He remembered what Prior Wistan had told him when he left the monastery: "Your father is a strong man, and the stronger the man, the greater his need for love." Well, he wanted to love his father. But it was hard to love a man who spoke always as though he were on the battlefield—who seemed to find pleasure only in war and weapons.

If only I were like Tancred, he thought. Siward and I may both be wrong. Maybe his true regret is that Tancred is not his son.

The door to the closet was closed. Hesitantly he raised his hand to the knocker and noticed that he was still holding Edgar's letter. With a sigh he rolled it carefully and put it in his leather pouch. Then he knocked.

"Come in," a loud voice commanded.

He pushed the door open. "It is I, Father," he said diffidently.

Baron Ansculf was a huge man who seemed to fill the entire room. His red wool tunic fitted tautly over his enormous shoulders; his gray homespun breeks did not conceal the strong sinewy legs, which seemed to strain against the leather gaiters. His face and head were in proportion to the rest of him, like a massive piece of rough-hewn rock, crowned with a shock of iron-gray hair. His beard swept his chest like a lion's mane. He was deftly polishing a hunting knife.

Aelfred looked at the huge, dextrous hands that could so skillfully polish a weapon or cleave a man in two with a battle-axe and mentally compared them to his own long slender hands and thin wrists. I've never seen him without a weapon, he thought, coughing as the acrid smoke from the bronze brazier stung his throat and nostrils. No wonder he thinks me a womanish fool! How did it ever happen that I am his son?

He cleared his throat. "Siward said that you wanted to see me."

The majestic head jerked up, and two steel-gray eyes appraised him calmly. "I do." The baron's voice was low, lower than usual, but at the moment it seemed loud and strident to Aelfred. "Well, come in, boy! What are you, in Heaven's name? Atheling of Storches Hundred? Or a churl?"

The edge in those words was as sharp as the knife in his hand. Aelfred stiffened. So, it was going to be one of *those* times! How he wished he could once—just once!—think of a

6

retort for the scathing tone that his father seemed always to reserve for him. Tancred would have known what to say, but then, Baron Ansculf would never use that tone with Tancred.

The baron snorted; then, in a lightning move, he threw the knife towards the door. Instinctively Aelfred reached up and caught it. He held it at arm's length and looked at it distastefully. His father, however, was smiling.

"Siward tells me you're improving." He chuckled.

"It doesn't take much skill to catch a knife," Aelfred said coolly. He laid it on the table and sat down on the empty stool.

"Maybe not. But it could save your life one day," the baron retorted. "I'm glad to see that those monks haven't taken all the spirit out of you."

"The monks have spirit," Aelfred said evenly. "They've had sieges, too."

"Thought they didn't believe in fighting."

"In self-defense, in a just cause, they do. I've told you this often."

"So you have. And it's a good thing they'll fight. They may have to, one of these days. We may all have to, sooner than we think."

The tone was more thoughtful and the eyes had lost their steel. Aelfred breathed more easily, but only for a moment.

"What do you know about the state of the land?" the baron demanded. "Apart from your vigils and prayers, I mean."

"I've been many months from vigils and prayers," Aelfred flared. "I know that King Edward, God save him, is sick unto death in London."

"And who will succeed him?"

"Harold Godwineson, Earl of Wessex, some say. Provided the witenagemot elects him as King."

"And what do others say?"

"William of Normandy. They say that Harold promised him the crown."

The baron had not finished. "And what do you say to all this?"

"I?" Aelfred faltered. "What should I say?"

7

"Heaven help me, I have sired a fool!" Ansculf jabbed the knife into the table so hard that it stood upright, quivering on its point. "You are two years past coming of age. You are atheling of Storches Hundred. One day you will have to take your place among the King's Thanes and vote in the witenagemot yourself. And yet you ask me what you should say?"

"I know that Harold Godwineson is called an oath breaker, Father," Aelfred retorted, stung to the quick.

"He made that oath under duress when he was Duke William's prisoner in Normandy!" the baron shouted. "I was there. I witnessed it. Do you doubt my word?"

Aelfred shook his head. Two years ago it had happened. His father had been on a pleasure voyage with Harold Godwineson when a sudden storm had come up and their ship had been wrecked on the Norman coast. Duke William had given them hospitality but in reality had held them all prisoner until Harold Godwineson had promised that the crown of England would be his when King Edward died.

"An oath under duress is not binding in law," Ansculf continued. "But, even if Harold Godwineson had given the oath freely, he could not honor it. No man in all England, king's son or cobbler's, can be King unless the witenagemot elects him!"

"I know, Father," Aelfred said placatingly. "I'm only remembering that Father Prior said that an oath is an oath. There is a higher law, and Harold Godwineson is bound by it."

"Your Father Prior is a scrupulous priest. But if a Norman takes his place at Coventry, he may be less scrupulous."

"How could that happen?"

"How has it happened? Normans have overrun our country, and do you know why? Because young men like you have let them. Instead of acting like free-born Englishmen, you've become monks!"

The scorn in his father's voice was unendurable and broke the last restraint on Aelfred's temper. "If you think so little of monks," he countered furiously, "why did you send me to

8

Coventry when I was only five years old and keep me there until just eighteen months ago, when you ordered me home for a belated coming-of-age ceremony?"

"You question my judgment?" The baron's face was purple.

"No, Father. I know you must have had good reason for it." Aelfred caught his breath and tried to speak more calmly. "But if the monastery is the only life I've known, you cannot blame me. At this hour every day, for over ten years, I chanted Vespers in the chapel. You told me to obey the Rule, and I obeyed your wish; I didn't know there was anything else to be done at this hour, and every other hour had its duties, too. Now I'm expected to act as though I had always lived as atheling of Storches Hundred. I've been taught to abhor war and violence and killing. Now my father sets me to shooting arrows and puts a knife in my hand."

He stopped short. The baron was staring at him as he would at a stranger.

"I—I'm sorry, Father. I should not speak so," he stammered. Unable to bear that scrutiny any longer, he rose. "May I have your permission to leave?"

Baron Ansculf's eyes flashed. "No, you may not," he said, but his voice was no longer angry. "Sit down."

Aelfred obeyed. There was a long silence; then the baron sighed heavily.

"You speak with reason," he said, as though the words came hard. "I sent you to Coventry, partly to keep you safe when I had to fight in Wales; but also, I wanted you to have some learning. I don't know how to read. I have to have the priest write my name for me, because all I can do with a pen is make my mark."

"All England knows that mark and what it means, Father," Aelfred said with gentle pride.

"True. But the rest of the world does not, and it is not good for England when men say abroad that her barons are ignorant barbarians. The Normans, now—no one can say that of them! And they're good men with swords, too. I know. I've seen them. So, I also sent you to the monastery to learn.

9

And, once you were there, I kept you there. With no mother, it was easier than having you here and worrying about your safety and upbringing when I had to be away."

His father's voice, unaccountably gentle, was more overwhelming than his previous anger. Aelfred looked at him bewilderedly. He loves me, he thought in amazement. For the second time that day he felt deeply ashamed.

"I didn't know what it would do to you," the baron continued after a moment. "I should have called you home sooner—much sooner. Taken you to London with me—let you see the King. Let you know what it means to be heir to Ansculf Aelfredson, the King's Thane. Instead, I've turned you into a monk. And I—" He looked away swiftly, but not before Aelfred had seen the sorrow in his eyes.

"Father"—would the right words never come?—"Father, I should have asked to come home," he said tensely. "Other boys left the monastery. I could have done the same. I think it was easier for me to stay, too."

Ansculf turned to him. "Did you want to become a monk, my son?"

Difficult as it was for them both, he must be honest. "I'd thought of it."

"I see." The baron sighed. "I should have asked you this long ago."

"I even talked to the Father Prior before I left. He said that I might have a vocation, but I could not be really sure because I knew no other life. He also reminded me that I had responsibilities in the world."

A glint of hope came to the baron's eyes. "Then you are not sure?"

There was a moment's pause. Then Aelfred shook his head. "No, I am no longer sure," he said forthrightly. "I love the monastery still. But I have also found in these past months that I love Storches Hundred as well."

"Enough even to fight, to keep it out of another man's hands?"

He recalled Tancred's avid eyes as he spoke of the west forest. "Out of Norman hands? Yes. Yes, I would fight."

10

Ansculf's smile returned. "You grasp things quickly. You're like your mother in that." He nodded at Aelfred's look of surprise. "Of course I mean Tancred. Why else do you think his mother followed me to England with her son?"

"Tancred is everything I am not," Aelfred said painfully.

"Except my son," the baron answered firmly and with a certain satisfaction. "You are my son, Aelfred. Storches Hundred is your inheritance, but the day is past when I can promise that you will possess it when I die. Not as long as Normans with their devious plans and sleights sit and work in places of power."

"But Normans have lands of their own. Tancred has lands of his own in Normandy."

"And Duke William has lands of his own in Normandy. The greedy are never satisfied with their own. Do you know how many good English demesnes have already been given to Normans?"

"But if you feared that," Aelfred said slowly, "then why—" He stopped.

"Why did I marry her?" Ansculf's cheeks reddened. "You have been with monks too long. Lady Ygerne was a guest at Harfleur when I was prisoner there with Harold Godwineson Six months ago, she came to London. Even you can see, I hope, that she is beautiful. It would take a man of stone to withstand her. But I did not know." He shook his head. "I—did—not—know!"

Compassion welled up in Aelfred's heart. He had been right, then. His father did regret the marriage. And here he was, speechless as always, when he longed to say some word of comfort.

"We will speak no more of this," the baron said brusquely. "I called you here for a reason. If the witenagemot elects Harold Godwineson, William of Normandy may decide to contest. That will mean war. I shall be called to the King's standard."

Aelfred reached for the knife, still standing in the table. He pulled it from the wood and studied the polished blade. "I shall be called too, then."

11

"Yes. And if we both die, our line dies with us. Storches Hundred will lie open and free to Tancred de Belleme or any other Norman. His mother's marriage to me will mean that they will be able to take it a little more quietly and within our laws."

Dazed, Aelfred laid the knife across his knees. In the monastery there had been much talk of death, even of violent death. But to have the possibility of a violent death so near was terrifying. He looked at his father's stern face. His father was a warrior born. Death in battle would be his ardent wish. But he, himself? For a moment he longed with all his soul for the sanctuary of Canterbury. He could beg his father to let him return, and he was certain, somehow, that he would not be refused. He had seriously considered giving his life to God; part of him still yearned for the cloister. Why did he hesitate? Why did he feel this surge of pain at the thought of Storches Hundred in Norman hands? Where did his duty lie?

"I want to be sure that Storches Hundred will remain for your heir," the baron continued, "and therefore you must have an heir."

The full impact of those words did not strike for a moment. When they did, the knife fell clattering to the floor. "I must marry, you mean?" Aelfred asked, hardly believing the words as he said them.

His father nodded. "Do you remember Baron Rafe of Birnham? He visited here when you were a child, with his daughter Adelaide. Do you remember her?"

"A little," he murmured. He called the memory out of the past. "We were both very little. She was only three years old. She bit my hand."

"Because you tried to kiss her, only to tease her. No wonder she bit you! You'd better not try that now." The baron chuckled. "She's the Lady Adelaide of Birnham, and very beautiful. Why are you so reluctant? Surely you must have thought of marrying?"

Aelfred shook his head.

"Then it's well that you have a father who thinks for you." The baron's tone was partly jovial and partly anxious. "She

12

and her father will be here tonight for the Twelfth Night feast. Rafe and I have spoken together. We think it a good thing for our children to marry."

"No!" Aelfred protested with sudden vehemence. "No—I don't want to marry!"

"For once I understand you. I said the same thing to your grandfather. So I'll tell you this. Neither Rafe nor I will compel the marriage, if you two really dislike each other. But"—Ansculf smiled—"if you choose not to marry the Lady Adelaide of Birnham, I shall begin to wonder if you are my son."

There was a knock on the door. At the baron's command to enter, it was opened by Siward.

"Lord Ansculf, one of the churls has been taken with the trembling sickness," he said without preliminary. "Two of the boys are carrying him home, but he needs more than just his bed. Will you ask the Lady Ygerne—"

"My lady is resting," the baron said abruptly, avoiding Siward's eyes.

Aelfred looked away, not wanting to see his father's embarrassment. He knew that Siward was remembering how the former lady of Storches Hundred would rise from her bed at midnight to tend any of the demesne people who were ill.

"Tell the boy's mother to send for Mab," Ansculf said after a moment. "Mab nursed me through many an ague when I was a boy."

"I fear Mab will not go to him," Siward answered. "It's Saewulf's eldest, and you know that Saewulf named her a witch in the last folkmoot."

"Witch!" The baron snorted disgustedly. "Saewulf's cows get the mange, and straightway they're bewitched. But Mab will go if I ask her." His eye fell on Aelfred. "You ride over to Mab's cot. Tell her about Saewulf's son, and also that I expect to see her at my feast tonight. You look peaked. A ride will do you good."

"Yes, Father," said Aelfred, obediently getting to his feet.

"Mind you don't stay too long," Ansculf warned. "Be back in time to bathe and dress properly. You want to look your best tonight."

13

"I'll be back by sunset, surely," Aelfred promised.

In his haste, he stumbled over the doorsill, he was so eager to get away by himself. His heart felt like a lump of stone. "It's too quick," he told himself emphatically as he crossed the court to the stables. He could barely manage a smile at the churl who saddled his horse and gave him a boost up. For a moment he had a wild wish to head for the road which would take him back to Canterbury and the quiet surety of the only life he had ever known. But, at the same moment, he realized that his spirit was too divided to find peace there now. He was almost as nervous about meeting Adelaide again as he was about going to war for his country. With a sigh, he turned his horse's head in the direction of the stockade gate.

Just inside the stockade, opposite the great hall, stood the demesne church with its square tower. As Aelfred rode past it, he was tempted to stop a moment and visit Father Owain. When he first came back to Storches Hundred from Canterbury, he had visited the priest almost every day, for Father Owain was the one link with the life he had known for ten years, the one person to whom he had been able to speak freely about his longing to enter the monastery. Now, he realized with surprise that he had seen little of the priest since Tancred's arrival on the demesne. Naturally he had attended Sunday Mass and had been at high table for the Sunday feasts, to which Father Owain was regularly invited, and he had noticed the questioning look in the priest's eyes. Father Owain believed that he really had a vocation and had urged him to follow it. Perhaps he should stop at the church today; there would be time for a short talk, at least, before he saw Mab. Then he realized, with an even deeper sense of amazement and shock, that he really did not want to stop. He knew what Father Owain would say to him, and he also honestly admitted that he did not want to listen.

"What is happening to me?" he asked himself, as he reined his horse away from the church and rode through the stockade gates. He had never felt so miserable and restless in his entire life. As he rode on, he recalled the days at Canterbury, so ordered, so serene, bound into perfect unity by the chapel Offices, the work in the fields, the lessons, the library, the Rule that dictated each hour's obligation. No decisions were required except that initial commitment to God, which gave joy and peace to those who made it. He felt as though he had been flung from paradise into chaos, and his conversation with his father dinned in his ears with an insistence which made him long to escape. A demesne to manage, a war to fight, marriage—these waited for him now. Marriage! Within the monastery, no woman's name was spoken, save only that of Our Lady or some saint. He had been taught to avoid women. They became great temptations, enough even to cause him to lose his soul. Yet, in this environment, he now was told by his own father that marriage was not only advisable but his duty, if there were to be heirs to carry on their line, to work the demesne, to serve the King, and that it could be a much-to-be-desired joy as well. The monks and Father Prior were persuaded that marriage was a lesser state, a barrier to perfection; and perfection, salvation, was man's sole duty in life. How could a man find either perfection or salvation in a way of life so far removed from the limitations of a cloister, where on the one hand marriage was considered the joy of life and, on the other, the comfort of the soul?

Even without marriage, this new world drew him by ties stronger than he had believed possible. He had spoken truth in that moment when he had said that he would fight to keep Storches Hundred from Tancred's hands. Tancred! Had it not been for Tancred, he would be at Coventry now. It was Tancred's presence that had caused him to waver. For a moment he hated Tancred with every fiber of his being; then the fury passed, and he soberly acknowledged that his situation would be the same, Tancred or no. By birth he was atheling of Storches Hundred; by the vows of his ancestors he was bound to serve his King when called. His destiny had been decreed from before his birth. Tancred's coming had only made that destiny more manifest. And he knew, too, that the ancient code of honor, though of the spirit, was bred into his bones. It must be admitted and, moreover, observed. He could not deny that, even if he had already made his vows as a monk. He sighed for a moment to think that, if he had made his vows, he could have been exempt from bearing the weapons he hated. But, since he had not, even the monks at Coventry would undoubtedly feel that God had other plans for him. To turn from his destiny now would be cowardice, and he would be a nithing, a man who was nothing because he had refused to act a man's part.

He had almost reached the forest land. He could see Mab's cot just ahead, smoke rising into the trees from the hole in the roof. The ground immediately before the cot had been cleared, and here, fenced by little wild briar hedges which she kept carefully pruned, Mab had planted the herbs she used in her healing. The plots were barren now, but Aelfred knew that inside the cot large bunches of sweet-smelling dried fennel and parsley and rosemary would be dangling from the roof beams. A small brown hare darted out from the briar and looked at him as if it waited for attention. Aelfred smiled. No animals were afraid in this garden; even the shy forest doe came here in the winter for food, and the birds feasted on dried berries and grain which Mab put out for them every morning. The quiet of the place embraced him, reminding him of the monastery chapel for a moment, and he found comfort in the reminder. Even with chaos all round about, he thought, there could be found an occasional island of peace.

He dismounted, tied his horse to the old wooden hitching post, and started up the path. Suddenly the door was flung wide open, and Mab came hobbling out to greet him, her arms stretched in welcome.

"Aelfred!" she cried. "I thought you'd forgotten your old nurse. It's been weeks since you've come to see me."

"True for you, Mab, and the more shame to me," Aelfred answered, taking her in an embrace.

"Come in, lad. Come in and welcome—a thousand times, welcome!" She led him inside, closed the door, and threw another bundle of twigs on the firepit. "But it's no longer a lad you are," she exclaimed as he emerged from gloaming in the quickening blaze. "A man you are now, Aelfred Ansculfson, atheling of this land, may God bless you. Sit down. Let me give you a cup of milk and a bit of bread."

"You sit too, Mab, and never mind the milk and bread," said Aelfred, firmly guiding her to her stool. He sat down on the ground at her feet. "It's late in the day for eating when there's to be a feast tonight, and my father will take it ill if we do not do justice to his table."

Her musical voice sharpened. "Not I, lad. Do not ask it. I'll not feast at Ansculf's table."

"Now, Mab—"

"No." She shook her head emphatically. "Not as long as that *hiren* queens it over his hall. A grown woman, with a grown son, who traipses about in red gowns with her hair unbound like a maid. It's a disgrace to your mother's memory!"

"But that's Norman fashion. And she's a Norman."

"As who wouldn't know it! But she's married an Englishman. Let her act like a proper wife. I spoke my mind to Ansculf on that first day. You haven't forgotten?"

"Not likely!" Aelfred chuckled. No one in Storches Hundred would ever forget that confrontation between the baron and the woman who had been his nurse as well as his son's. "The Lady Ygerne did not understand how important the nurse is to our families," he said placatingly. "I don't believe she meant any harm. She probably thought she was paying you a compliment."

"By telling me that I was to be her servant and expecting me to be flattered?" Mab snorted. "You always try to give even the devil his due, Aelfred. You're like your mother in that. She always saw good in everyone. But she never had a Lady Ygerne to cope with, nor a Tancred de Belleme!"

Aelfred flushed guiltily. "I admit that I find it difficult to see good in Tancred," he said slowly.

"Why should you, indeed? They mean trouble for Storches Hundred, make no mistake. He rides all around and through this land almost every day without so much as a by-your-leave. Did you know that?"

Aelfred looked his surprise. "But that's been expressly forbidden until he asks your leave," he said indignantly. "Siward told him so again, only today."

"Siward baron's-reeve is a good man. But he is so used to being obeyed that he never thinks to see whether he *is* being obeyed or not. He has never needed to, with our own."

"Why haven't you told my father?"

"What good would that do? Tancred would only deny everything, and his mother would stand with him. But she rides beside him sometimes."

"Where do they go?"

"I don't know. I always see them riding. And talking. Sometimes Tancred stops at Saewulf's cot."

Aelfred's feeling of apprehension grew greater with this news. "How sure are you of this, Mabbie?"

Neither of them seemed to realize that he had called her by the old endearing name. She looked at him somberly. "I'm not as guileless as Siward, and there's not a path in this forest that I don't know. Horse's shoes make marks when snow is new-fallen, and I can walk quickly enough when there's need."

Aelfred frowned. "You must be careful, Mab. You might come to some harm if you were found following them."

"Harm? From them?" Mab laughed scornfully. "That's one thing they would not dare. I have a right to walk where I please on my own land, and your father will uphold me in that."

"My father will not be here all the time, though," he cautioned.

"I know. He will go to London when good King Edward dies, and perhaps to war for Harold Godwineson. But not today." Her wrinkled face broke into a sudden smile that made her seem almost beautiful. "You've news for me. You're to be married."

"Gracious Father in Heaven!" Aelfred exclaimed. "Does everyone on the demesne know what I am last to hear? It was only mentioned to me today."

"Does the idea please you?"

"It horrifies me. I had never given a thought to marrying."

19

"But you must. You are the atheling of this demesne."

"So I am told. But look, Mab—I've always wanted to be a monk. At least, that is what I thought I wanted. Now, though, I don't know."

"If you had really wanted that, you would know," Mab contradicted wisely.

"Father Owain says that my doubts are but temptations of the devil."

Mab smiled again. "Father Owain is a good soul, a holy priest, and Welsh, like myself. But he's a man, and he sees what he wishes to see. Have you ever really looked at yourself, Aelfred? In a mirror, I mean?"

"Yes," he answered with some amusement. "Every now and then."

"And do you think you have the face of a monk?"

He stared at her. "I don't know. I never gave that a thought."

"Well, I say that you do not. You look very like your grandfather, Aelfred Iron Fist. Oh, there's much of your mother in you, too, but more of your grandfather, I'm thinking. You've never had reason to show his spirit, but it's there. Often I glimpsed it when you were a lad."

"Well, whether it's there or no," Aelfred replied, "it would seem that I have no choice. And if my King calls me to serve him, I shall have to obey. But"—now he spoke with grave anxiety—"that means I shall have to kill, Mab. Isn't that terrible? My heart grows sick at the thought."

Mab bristled. "Aye. You will kill your country's enemies in a righteous cause. There has never yet been a nithing at Storches Hundred! Let's talk of that no more. We shall speak of your wedding instead."

"I'd almost rather talk about battles," Aelfred said wryly.

"Why? What's so frightening about Lady Adelaide of Birnham?"

"For one thing, she's a girl."

"Did you expect to marry anything else?" Mab asked amiably.

"Don't joke, Mab. I'm serious. I don't know anything

about girls. At the monastery, they were temptations to be avoided. I've never even talked to one."

Mab laughed. "When you were four and she was three, she bit your hand," she reminded him. "You talked to her then!"

Aelfred laughed with her. "My father reminded me of that this afternoon. I had no business to tease her, and I was punished for it. I can hardly tease her just to annoy her now."

"Nor will you wish to, when you see her."

"Have you seen her? What's she like?"

"Ah, you're curious. That's a good sign." Mab chuckled her satisfaction. "She's tall and slender like a white birch tree. Her hair is brown with golden threads in it, and her eyes are gray, I think, and gentle. I do not think she would bite you now."

"Never mind. No more," Aelfred interrupted a little impatiently. "She is beautiful and she is rich. Heiress to all the lands of Birnham! She will not hate me now, you think. But why should she marry me?" He stopped, aghast, as Mab burst out laughing. The question was hardly a seemly one on the part of a would-be monk. "I mean," he added hastily, "that she doubtless has been among men at court, who can sing and speak and know what to do with a sword."

Mab's eyes glowed with sympathy. "Poor boy. You're like an unstrung bow. Your father should not have told you so suddenly. But Ansculf was always hasty. He should have prepared you a little."

"I wager my grandfather didn't prepare him. He said as much."

"But he had lived as the atheling all his life. You have not, as the Lady Adelaide will know."

"What does that matter?" He could not control the bitterness that surged through him. He jumped to his feet and walked to the door, where he stood for several minutes with his back to her. "Mab, I wish I knew what to do. I'm half a monk and half a man—no, I should not say that. Monks are men. But they are not expected to marry or to find favor in a lady's eyes."

"You are afraid that she may look coldly on you?"

He nodded.

"And you do not wish that, for all your fear of her?"

His voice was barely audible. "No."

Mab smiled. "No. You are not a monk, Aelfred Ansculfson," she said gently. "You are a man meant for the world."

Slowly he turned and looked at her searchingly. "It may be so," he admitted. "But I had a letter today from my friend Edgar. He is at Walsingham, visiting the shrine. He says there have already been many cures there."

"Blessed be God," Mab said, crossing herself. "The vision of Lady Richeldis has brought a holy place to England."

"He wants me to come. When I read his letter, I was afire to join him."

"And now?"

"All I seem to want now is to keep our country and Storches Hundred out of enemy hands." He shook his head. "I know it is a sin to hate. But Tancred makes it so easy for me to hate him. I'm jealous of him—that's the truth of it. He's a soldier through and through. He can split a twig with an arrow at fifty paces and throw a sword I can't even lift. And he can talk, too, and make people laugh. Even my father smiles at him, sometimes. Beside him, I'm a pale, wansick bumbler. I think that Lady Adelaide—"

"Talk no more! You will indeed be wansick, if you do," Mab said vehemently. "Listen to what I say. The Lady Adelaide is no fool. Nor is she a common girl, to be won by fair words and a few tricks with a sword. There are women who confuse force with strength and wed themselves to brutes, but she is one who looks for gentleness and cherishment in the strength of the man she favors."

Aelfred smiled faintly. "Do you speak from knowledge, dear nurse, or from second sight?"

"Do not mock my second sight. It is a true mirror for those I love. And know this, too: gentleness does not mean that a man cannot be strong. You may have great need to be strong." She nodded gravely. "Go home, now. Ready yourself in your finest clothes to meet your promised bride."

"And what do I say to her?"

"When you see her, you will know. Follow what your heart tells you." She paused in an instant of deep thought. "Time can move so fast," she said enigmatically. "Here, now. On the morning after your wedding, give your wife this gift from me." She slipped her hand into her bodice and drew out a small packet. "Take it," she said very quietly. "Open it."

Carefully he unfolded the piece of fine linen. "Oh, Mab!" he exclaimed, holding up a delicate silver brooch in the form of a butterfly. Its wings were etched in gold and studded with garnets and pearls. "Lady Ygerne has fine jewels, but nothing to compare with this!"

"It was your mother's. She gave it to me on the night she died. I've carried it safe with me all these years. She never said, but I know she wanted you to have it for your bride when you had one. Your father had given it to her."

Too moved to speak, Aelfred drew her to him and kissed her. Then he carefully rewrapped the butterfly and put it gently in his pouch.

"You must go now. You'll be late," Mab reminded. "And I must tidy myself, if I am to go to the feast."

"The feast?" he said quickly, then smiled. "Dear Mab! Thank you. I won't feel nearly as frightened if you are there. Besides, it's only fitting that the atheling's nurse should see him meet his bride."

"So? She is already your bride, then?" Mab teased. "Where is your great fear, if you can speak so strongly and certainly?"

His cheeks reddened. "It is still there; I only joke a little."

"Surely, lad. A betrothal is a happy thing, even though King Edward lies at death's door in London town and the world turns faster towards the darkness. We must make no wake at a betrothal." Her voice became a low chant. "And here am I, an old woman with a wrinkled face and no music to sing the bride's praise, only a tongue. But that I can use, to wish you all the joy that life may bring. Yes, I'll come to the feast, though I sit at the foot of Ansculf's table and take the scorn of his Norman wife."

"It will gladden my father's heart to see you," Aelfred said gratefully.

23

"And mine to look on him, if truth were known. Life is too short for enmity. We are bound to each other, he and I and you. May I live long enough to see your first-born son."

Mab's last words reminded Aelfred of the second reason for his coming. He smote his hands together and exclaimed, "I am dully minded indeed. The thought of Lady Adelaide has scattered my wits. My father asks another boon of you." He hesitantly told her about Seawulf's sick son. He expected her eyes to flash with anger, but she remained quite calm.

"Saewulf is an eselbrain, but that is not his boy's fault," she said. "My healing is for all who need it, even for those who hate me without cause. I shall leave a little earlier and stop to see him on my way to the feast."

"Mab, a few moments ago you mentioned Tancred's visits to Saewulf's cot," said Aelfred. "It was after Tancred came that Saewulf named you a witch at the folkmoot. You don't think, do you, that Tancred had anything to do with that?"

"It is possible. Strange things and wicked deeds are in the land, Aelfred. It was not so in the old days. But let us not speak of it." She raised her hand and signed the cross on his forehead. "So. Go with God and my blessing. Take the forest route. It's shorter."

"Until tonight, then."

"I shall be there. And when you meet the Lady Adelaide, just remember whose son and whose grandson you are." She smiled proudly. "And who was nurse to you, too."

The early winter dusk was falling as he unhitched his horse. He mounted and set off at a gallop down the winding path between the great oaks and beeches. Though his fear of meeting Adelaide of Birnham had not entirely vanished, his heart felt lighter because he had persuaded Mab to come to the feast.

At least I've succeeded in doing one thing my father has asked of me, he thought, and he was glad that this was so.

At the end of the path, the forest opened into a large clearing. In the days before the monks came to England, pagan gods had been worshiped here; and while the first Christian baron of Storches Hundred had destroyed the pagan altar, there were still remains of the great stone ring. The trees formed a thick circle around the clearing, and the pale moon, already beginning to rise, barely lighted the darkness. The horse stopped short. Aelfred was not surprised; horses, for some reason, usually shied at crossing here. He patted its glossy mane and was about to murmur an encouraging word when suddenly he saw two dark cloaked figures standing by the center stone.

At his signal, the horse froze almost to rigidity. He waited a moment, but the intruders evidently had not heard his approach, and the dark trees with their mistletoe-hung branches protected him and his horse from sight. As quietly as possible, he slid from the saddle and crept forward, pulling the hood of his cloak over his head. One of the pair turned in his direction. He almost gasped aloud as the fading light revealed the face of Lady Ygerne, who was supposed to be resting for the feast. What was she doing in this place? She said something to her companion, who threw back his head and laughed loudly. Tancred, too! Aelfred strained his ears, trying to hear what they were saying, but their voices were too low. Clearly they were waiting for someone, so while their backs were turned he moved carefully behind one of the huge stones to wait with them.

A rider appeared on the other side of the clearing. He, too, was wearing a cloak, but his bare head was cropped short in the Norman fashion. He hurried to Lady Ygerne, who embraced him; then he greeted Tancred, kissing him noisily on both cheeks. He put an arm around each of them, talking animatedly over their excited laughter. Aelfred tried his best to catch the drift of the words, but his French was not fluent enough for that, though he understood the stranger to say that he had come from London. Then he heard the name "Harold Godwineson," at which Tancred spat on the ground. From beneath his cloak, the stranger took a small packet, which Lady Ygerne thrust into her bodice. He kissed them both again, then ran back to where he had left his horse, mounted, and galloped away. Lady Ygerne and Tancred waited a moment, then crossed in front of the stone where Aelfred was hiding to a thicket on the right where they had hidden their horses. Hardly daring to breathe, Aelfred waited while Tancred assisted his mother to mount. Immediately she wheeled her horse in the direction of the great hall. Tancred vaulted easily into his saddle and set off after her.

Slowly Aelfred got to his feet. He was cold, and not only from his vigil. Mab had said there were strange things and wicked in the land; he realized now that she doubtless knew, or at least suspected, more than she had told him. As he chafed his hands, he tried to fathom the meaning of the scene he had just witnessed. Certainly the stranger was a Norman, and well known to Tancred and Lady Ygerne. He had come from London, with some kind of news that rejoiced them. Aelfred's heart almost stopped. The only news that could rejoice a Norman would be word of King Edward's death.

"The King is dead," he murmured. "I know it. I know it!" And Harold Godwineson must already have been proposed as the new king, which would explain Tancred's contempt. The war, so long anticipated, would be a reality now.

His horse, still standing at the edge of the clearing, whinnied impatiently. Aelfred turned quickly. He must get to the hall at once and tell his father—but what? That King Edward was dead? He had no proof beyond what he had seen, and he knew instinctively that Tancred and Lady Ygerne would deny everything. Also, any word from him would put them on their guard. Better, perhaps, to be silent and watch. He might find out more about their mysterious rides in the forest, and what these boded for Storches Hundred. He might learn what was in the packet that the stranger had given to Lady Ygerne and then, with sure evidence, take mother and son to his father and confront them. For the moment, however, he must say nothing. He had never in his life thought of danger to himself, but now he knew, with deep foreboding, that the meeting he had witnessed could mean only danger, to him and to anyone connected with him. He mounted his horse, crossed the clearing, then rode pell-mell the rest of the way to the demesne.

3

THOUGH Aelfred rode as fast as his horse could carry him, it was already dark by the time he reached the stockade. He galloped through the open gates and into the stable court, where he dismounted quickly and tossed the reins to the stable churl who came running to meet him with a lighted torch, then went directly to the men's bower. Here he found his father waiting for him, standing at the open door in a mighty temper.

"So! My son and heir finally returns!" Baron Ansculf exclaimed with great sarcasm. "My lady is still dressing, my stepson returns late from his hunting, and who is here to greet our guests? Myself. Myself, alone! Unforgivable discourtesy!"

"I'm sorry, Father. I stayed with Mab longer than I intended," Aelfred apologized. "But she will come to the feast."

"Well, so much is well at least," the baron replied, still annoyed, though less vehement. "But you—look at you! Covered with mud! Into the bath hut with you and scrub yourself. Then dress quickly. The feast cannot start without you."

He strode past Aelfred towards the great hall. Aelfred, breathing a sigh of relief that no more speech was forthcoming at the moment, hastened to the bath hut, where he found two kitchen churls waiting with huge buckets of hot water. He smiled at them and stripped off his clothes. Then he got into the wooden tub, which the churls filled, and scrubbed himself with wood ashes and tallow.

"So," he said, clambering out. "The cold water, now."

One of the boys climbed onto a stool. The other handed up a bucket of cold water, which he poured over Aelfred in a shower, then offered a large coarse linen towel. While Aelfred rubbed himself vigorously, the boys emptied the tub into the tile-edged hole in the center of the hut and poured more hot water after it to make sure that the tallow would not stick. Storches Hundred was one of the few demesnes in the district that could boast a real drain. The Romans had built it centuries ago, and it was a great advantage that it could still be used.

"Now the tunic, please," said Aelfred.

A churl handed him a clean white undertunic, which he quickly pulled over his head. Then, wrapping a cloak around him, he left the bath hut and crossed the court to the men's bower.

Tancred, in the small room they shared, was pulling on his Norman chausses. They were of bright red silk and fitted him like a second skin. He looked up at Aelfred with a mocking smile. "Ah, the atheling," he said. "You know, I shall never understand you English. In Normandy, a man about to meet his future bride would show more eagerness."

"My father sent me on an errand," Aelfred replied shortly. He opened his clothes chest and pulled out his best breeks. They were of finest wool and white as snow, but they seemed heavy and clumsy beside Tancred's chausses. The Norman was handsome; he had to admit it. In his overtunic of red velvet, with the short matching cloak lined with gold and his gold sandals, he would be a dazzling sight. But there was no time for envy now. Aelfred finished his dressing in silence, putting on his sandals and lacing the deerskin thongs around his legs. Then he put on his feast-day tunic—blue silk with a dragon embroidered on it in gold thread. He clasped a gold link belt around his waist and fastened the gold collar that

28

his father had given him for his coming of age around his neck. His own mantle was blue wool lined with fur, and its clasp was gold. He put on the heavy gold bracelets that all Englishmen wore on their upper arms. As he dressed, his confidence grew, and when he had put on his gold headband and attached his dagger to his belt, he decided that he could give any Norman considerable competition.

He turned to find Tancred looking at him superciliously. For a moment his confidence wavered, but he immediately determined that the Norman's sneers were not going to make him quail. Not tonight. "Something you don't approve?" he asked.

"The crest of King Harold the Oath Breaker is hateful to me," Tancred answered. "But obviously you feel no shame at wearing it."

Aelfred looked at him coldly. "Why should I? He is no oath breaker. And why do you call him king? King Edward yet lives."

Tancred's cheeks flushed and he looked away. "Harold is king in all but name—your king, I mean. Never mine!"

A smile flickered across Aelfred's lips. That slip of the tongue was proof that the stranger in the clearing had brought the news he thought. His sense of triumph made him eager to press his attack.

"At least my father serves a lawful liege," he said bitingly, "and not a baseborn would-be king."

Tancred's smoldering eyes grew almost colorless with anger. "Take care, Atheling! The day may come, sooner than you think, when you wish you had spoken more courteously of Duke William."

"As Duke of Normandy, I give him all courtesy. But if he tries to take the crown of England, he will wish that he had stayed in France."

"And you will help to make him wish it, I suppose?" Tancred snarled. "Wait—wait, Atheling. You English howl like wolves at an enemy across your channel, but if he sets foot on English soil you will run like curs."

His unsuspected success in baiting Tancred made Aelfred

brash in his boldness. "You are privy to Duke William's plan, then? When does he plan to sail from Normandy? Or have your Norman spies not yet brought that word?"

Tancred blanched. "What do you mean?"

Aelfred's heart leaped. The stranger in the grove had been a Norman. But he must still pretend ignorance. "Norman spies are thick in London as flies around carrion," he said evenly. "Everyone knows that."

"Bah!" Tancred spat. "I know only this: Duke William despises an oath breaker above all other men."

"Men usually detest their own failings in others. Has your Duke William never been known to break an oath?"

"Never!" Tancred shouted. "Why, you sniveling milksop of a monk—"

"Is this the arena where the destiny of nations is decided?" Siward the reeve's sarcastic voice spoke from the door. "Most of the guests have already arrived, Aelfred. Your father thought you might be interested. Or shall I tell him that your interest in politics prevents your feasting tonight?"

Tancred glared. "I'm ready," he snapped.

More tardiness. Aelfred sighed inwardly. Aloud, he said, "I am coming." Siward stepped aside to let him go first, while he and Tancred followed.

The blaze of torches was so bright that it made Aelfred blink as he entered the great hall. At the center firepit his father was receiving the guests. Squaring his shoulders, he moved through the crowd, which parted to let him pass, bowing and bobbing respectful curtsies. His eye caught sight of Mab and he smiled at her. Then he bowed formally to his father.

"Well, at last," said the baron. "Let me look at you." He examined Aelfred minutely from head to foot, then nodded. "Greet my lady properly, and then I'll present you to Rafe of Birnham."

Lady Ygerne, as befitted the lady of the demesne, was seated on one of the carved wooden chairs a short distance from the firepit. She was wearing a yellow gown, cut low the better to display her pearl necklace. Her flowing sleeves were cloth of gold edged with ermine; her long black hair fell unbound to her waist under a headdress of twisted gold leaves. The hand she gave Aelfred to kiss was covered with rings.

Yes, she is beautiful, Aelfred thought, as he murmured a polite phrase, and certainly she knows it well.

He heard his father's laughter and turned to find the baron beside him, Tancred close by. He stifled his instinctive resentment at his stepbrother's ability to make his father laugh and smiled. Ansculf patted his shoulder.

"Come along, the pair of you," he said jovially. "Rafe of Birnham is waiting to greet you. Then we can start the feast."

He led the way to the upper firepit, where a stocky grizzled man with a short cropped beard was conversing with Father Owain. "Rafe, this is my son," he said. "And this is my lady's son, Tancred de Belleme."

"So, this is the atheling?" said Rafe. His eyes twinkled, but he looked searchingly at Aelfred. "Why, Ansculf, you misled me. I had expected a monk. This man is the image of your father, given a little more flesh on his bones. I give you greeting, Aelfred son of Ansculf."

"Thank you. And I bid you most welcome to our hall, my lord," Aelfred replied with his best bow. He liked Rafe of Birnham on sight.

"And here is someone whom you may remember," Rafe continued with a chuckle. "My daughter Adelaide. Daughter, this is your childhood friend, Aelfred Ansculfson. Surely you are neither of you children, now. But may you be friends."

The girl at her father's side smiled and curtsied. Aelfred looked at her in stunned amazement. How could he remember someone he had never seen? Surely she could not have been the little minx who had screeched at him and bitten his hand. Nothing—neither his father's words nor Mab's—had prepared him for such a surprise. In her long white kirtle, her hair bound with a fillet of gems, she seemed almost a reincarnation of the goddess of spring his ancestors had worshiped, or a likeness of one of the saints in the illuminated missal on the high altar at the Abbey. He realized that, in his wonderment, he had not bowed, and he managed to do so, somewhat awkwardly. But he could find no words.

"Since you do not speak, I must," she chided, but her voice was kind. Her smile bedazzled him completely. "Shall I thank you for your welcome?"

He flushed to the eyes. "I humbly beg your pardon, my lady," he said huskily. "Heart's welcome to our hall. I hope you will forgive me. I am—I am so—"

His voice trailed away. Rafe and his father exchanged amused but pleased glances. Adelaide merely continued to smile upon him, and he cast about desperately for something to say—a compliment—anything! Mab had told him that he would know what to say, but surely she could not have predicted this turmoil that beset him.

"You must forgive my clumsiness, my lady," he said. Better to be honest; she'd find out sooner or later what a dolt he was. "I never dreamed that you would grow up like this."

The smile left her eyes and she looked at him gravely. "Nor I you," she answered with equal forthrightness.

"Adelaide," Baron Ansculf interposed, "let me present to you my lady's son, Tancred de Belleme."

Tancred stepped forward as though he were taking the field in an archery contest. He swept into a bow, swirling his cloak, and stood before Adelaide with his left foot turned slightly outward, a maneuver that showed off his chausses to their best advantage. "Had I known that the fairest flower of England awaited me, I should never have delayed my presence here so long," he declaimed extravagantly.

Aelfred waited in utter misery, his eyes fixed on Adelaide. She was curtsying and smiling, murmuring words of thanks which seemed to inspire Tancred to even greater heights.

"How I wish I could carry you from this dreary island to my beloved Normandy," he rhapsodized. "We appreciate beauty there, my lady."

"And would Duke William approve your appreciation of anyone as English as myself?" Adelaide asked.

Aelfred held his breath, hardly daring to believe his ears. Could it be possible that she was not impressed by these Norman flourishes? Her tone had been light; her face was bland, but there was something about her bearing that made it seem as though she was amused at Tancred.

Tancred sensed it, too, and his eyes flickered. But he was not to be put off. "If Duke William once saw you, he would understand my subjection," he answered, sighing gustily.

Rafe of Birnham laughed aloud. "Perhaps you had better consider Lord Tancred's invitation, daughter, as a patriotic duty," he joked. "Your presence at Rouen might persuade Duke William to let us elect our kings in peace."

"I very much doubt that anyone or anything could persuade Duke William to alter whatever he has already decided to do," she replied crisply. She turned to Baron Ansculf, laughing. "My lord, I think your good reeve wishes to give your signal. I know I have interrupted him twice!"

Aelfred wanted to cheer. She was superb! She had deftly put Tancred in his place, and now, as Siward's booming voice requested the company to take their places at table, she was just as deftly placing her hand on his own arm. "Are you not to escort me to high table, Aelfred?" she asked quietly. "And could you not manage to look a little less frightened? I shall not bite you now!"

Miraculously he seemed to find his tongue. "I should not mind if you did," he said laughingly. Proudly he followed his father and Rafe of Birnham, leaving Tancred to walk behind with his mother, who was sputtering at him in French. Evidently Lady Ygerne had expected him to make a conquest, too. The Norman had met his match in Adelaide, and no mistake!

There was silence while Father Owain intoned a long grace in Latin; then the talk and laughter rose again as chairs and benches were drawn back from the tables and the guests took their seats. Aelfred seated Adelaide and took the chair next to hers. He looked about the hall with a sudden rush or pride that he had never experienced before. His grandfather had built this hall, and it was the finest in the shire. Hundreds of torches burned in the iron wall brackets, illuminating the fine tapestries that covered the walls; and an enormous iron ring, suspended from the ceiling, blazed with dozens of candles in its two tiers. The long trestle tables had been scoured to immaculate whiteness; the wooden trenchers were new for the occasion, and the drinking cups had been polished until they shone. For this feast, Baron Ansculf had given each one of his tenants lengths of cloth to make new clothes, and the bright yellow, blue, and scarlet tunics of the men contrasted vividly with the more somber colors of the matrons' kirtles and starched white coifs. The young unmarried girls wore gowns of every color of the rainbow, with wreaths of mistletoe or holly on their unbound hair.

"There could be no finer sight than this in the King's palace," he exclaimed happily.

"This is finer," said Adelaide. "There are fewer Normans here."

Aelfred blushed. He had not realized that, in his excitement, he had spoken aloud, but before he could say as much to her there was a loud blast on a horn. The kitchen door flew open and a troop of musicians entered, playing on flutes and beating small tabors, with an occasional blare of the horn to keep them in harmony. Behind them came the kitchen churls, faces shining, in spotless blue tunics, carrying huge platters of food and jugs of wine. Finally came Ecfrith, the steward, a portly man wearing a splendid gold mantle. He carried the huge salt cellar which he ceremoniously placed on high table. At that moment, Aelfred happened to glance at Tancred. Those whom the host especially honored were always seated above the salt. Whether by accident or design, Ecfrith's placement of the salt cellar had left Tancred quite obviously below it, and the Norman was angry at the slight.

But he could not think about Tancred. He had more absorbing concerns. He looked again at Adelaide. How could she have grown to be so lovely? The ceremony of the wine pouring was beginning. Siward had brought the glass wine jug to the table, and Baron Ansculf rose to receive it. He poured a small quantity of wine into a jeweled cup and handed it to the reeve, who sipped from it and put it back in the baron's hand. The baron drained it, refilled it, and raised it high.

"Welcome, my friends, to these revels," he boomed. "Let us feast!"

At once the kitchen churls began to pass the platters to the tenants seated at the long tables, while Siward and Ecfrith waited on the baron and his guests. Ansculf took Rafe of Birnham's cup and filled it.

"Will not the Lady Ygerne fill the cups?" Adelaide asked in a low tone.

Aelfred shook his head as imperceptibly as possible. By the ancient rite of hospitality, the lady of the demesne always poured wine for the honored guests, but Lady Ygerne would not observe the English ways. Then Siward handed him the wine jug, and he carefully, almost solemnly, filled Adelaide's cup. He was rewarded with a smile that set his heart to pounding again.

"I'm glad you've not cropped your hair, Ansculf," Rafe was saying as he helped himself bountifully to lamprey pie, "nor taken to wearing chausses. Even though our King favors the Norman crop, as does Harold Godwineson, we need not all forsake our English ways."

"Amen," Ansculf replied. "Our King, God save him, is a virtuous and saintly man, but his love of Normans is a great flaw in him. It would have been better for him and for England if he had left the Normans in Normandy when he was elected."

Aelfred could feel the growing tension at high table. Rafe and his father spoke freely together as old friends, but he was aware of Lady Ygerne's scorn and of Tancred's smoldering eyes.

"My lord, you forget." Lady Ygerne spoke in a reed-thin voice that stumbled slightly over the English words. "Your King is grateful to the land that sheltered him in exile when his people elected a Dane to rule them."

Ansculf seemed momentarily at a loss for words. Rafe took a deep draught of wine, while Lady Ygerne looked at them in unconcealed triumph. No Englishman liked to be reminded of the dark time when Canute the Dane had ravaged the land and the witenagemot had finally given him the crown.

Then Adelaide's firm, quiet voice broke the silence. "What else could the witenagemot have done, my lady?" she asked. "King Edward was only a boy when his mother married Canute the Dane. And you surely know that as soon as King Edward was old enough the witenagemot recalled him."

"I find this electing of kings most singular," Lady Ygerne sneered. "No wonder England's government is always in chaos, when every man can think himself worthy of her crown."

"It is a matter of custom, my lady," Adelaide observed serenely, "and, if you will consider history, you will discover it to be a far better and less bloody way than others. We find it singular indeed, for instance, that Duke William had to raise an army and go to war against half the nobles of Normandy to make himself its undisputed ruler."

Lady Ygerne gasped angrily and darted a look at Adelaide so full of venom that Aelfred shivered. But his admiration for Adelaide was increased a hundredfold. Noting that the wine in her cup was low, he gestured to Siward to fill it.

The baron laughed loudly. "Let all the cups be filled," he ordered hospitably.

As the music struck up a lively tune, a troupe of jugglers entered, bounding and cartwheeling into the center open space between the tables. The momentary breach of the revels had passed. "Look at the one in blue, my lady," Aelfred said to Adelaide excitedly. "Three, four—six balls he's juggling. Did you ever see the like?"

"No, never," she answered. But her voice sounded subdued and her smile was forced.

"Please do not mind Lady Ygerne," he said quietly. "She cannot help her Norman prejudices, my lady."

Adelaide smiled again, more naturally this time. "It is strange to hear you call me 'my lady,' Aelfred."

Aelfred smiled back, he hoped not too foolishly. "I didn't think you'd like me to use my old name for you."

"It was no worse than mine for you!" She laughed. "How I hated you! I thought you were the most terrible little boy in the entire world. I'd have tied you in a sack and thrown you off a cliff, if I could."

"Something like that occurred to me for you," he admitted. "Only my thought was a stout wicker cage and bread and water."

"You teased me. No wonder I bit you!" Then she grew sober. "We *were* dreadful, weren't we?"

"Well, I was, at least. Though I hope I've improved a little. You certainly have changed, Adelaide. I'd never have known you."

She made a face at him. "Gallant as ever, I see," she teased. "But my tongue is still unruly, sometimes. I fear I've offended your stepmother."

He dared to put his hand on hers. "She takes umbrage very quickly."

"I know. She's a Norman. Oh, I used to get so angry with them in London!"

"You have been in London?"

"Yes, first at school—All Hallows, Berkynge—and then at court. The town was full of them, boasting and swaggering. You'd think Normandy was Heaven and they'd all been there, to hear them. More than once I asked them why, if they found it so wonderful, they didn't go home."

Aelfred burst out laughing. "You didn't dare!"

"Indeed I did. They were not at all inclined to excuse any of our ways that they did not like, but we had to be so understanding and forgiving. Poor Father was always having to apologize for me, though secretly I think he agreed. Listen to him!"

"No, Ansculf, we have no giants in these days." Rafe of Birnham's voice boomed above the others, making a lull in general conversation. "I remember how your father could split a door lintel with his axe at seven hundred paces. Now, there was a truly mighty man."

"Might may also reside in skill, my lord," Tancred objected.

"What do you mean?" Rafe demanded.

Tancred smiled and pointed. "Do you see the bird carved at the top of that column?"

Rafe squinted at the carving. "I do."

"A wager that I can pierce its beak with an arrow at seven hundred paces."

37

"Done!" Red-faced and smiling, Rafe rapped his fist on the table. "Fifty gold mancusa that you can't."

Tancred beckoned to one of the churls. "Fetch my bow and arrow." Flexing his wrists, he rose and bowed to Ansculf. "Father, will you proclaim the wager?"

Aelfred could hardly contain himself. A hall filled with people, and Tancred aiming at a target hardly bigger than a sheep's eye! Woefully he saw that Adelaide was leaning forward, her eyes bright with excitement. She might dislike Normans, but no girl could be indifferent to such a feat. And Tancred would doubtless succeed. Groaning inwardly, Aelfred clenched his hands below the table.

But just as the baron rather unsteadily stood in his place and raised his hand for silence, an insistent pounding was heard at the outer door. All the men jumped to their feet, knives drawn. Siward left high table and hurried to answer. He opened the peephole a crack and demanded, "Name yourself."

"Guilbert de Belleme and I come in peace," a voice answered.

"My brother!" Lady Ygerne rose quickly and almost ran the length of the hall to greet him. As they walked towards high table, arm in arm, Aelfred studied Guilbert de Belleme intently, trying to decide if he had been the stranger in the grove. The man was panting as though he had ridden hard, but Aelfred's shrewd eye noted that the mud on his boots and cloak was dry. He listened while formal greetings were exchanged, but the words had not been loud enough that afternoon for him to tell whether de Belleme's voice was the same.

"I regret my intrusion upon your revels," said de Belleme.

"No intrusion, brother-in-law," the baron assured him. "All are friends here. Let us be seated again. Siward, a chair for Lord Guilbert and a cup of wine, and serve him food in plenty."

"I thank you for your welcome to me, my lord," de Belleme replied, "but I fear you will not welcome my news." He paused dramatically to gain the attention of the entire hall, then said slowly and clearly, "King Edward is dead."

There was immediate silence. Then the company rose quietly as one man and made the sign of the cross. "God rest his soul," Ansculf said solemnly. "He was a good man."

"Is there other word?" Rafe of Birnham asked intensely.

De Belleme's lips thinned. "Before he died, King Edward named Harold Godwineson as his choice for successor. The witenagemot is called to assemble in London tomorrow."

"The witenagemot will obey," Ansculf answered. He looked over the hall and in that gesture seemed to look at each guest personally as he addressed them. "Friends, we shall drink a cup of remembrance for our good King. Then let us take leave in quiet. It would be unseemly to prolong our revels now."

There was silence while the cups were filled for the toast; silence as they raised the cups, murmuring as one voice, "The King's good honor"; and silence while the cups were drained and set down. A few women sobbed. Then, one by one, the guests made solemn farewells. At a gesture from Baron Ansculf, Lady Ygerne left the hall, Adelaide accompanying her.

The baron turned to Guilbert de Belleme. "Has the hour for His Majesty's funeral been arranged?"

"Noon tomorrow, in the new Abbey Church at Westminster," de Belleme replied.

"Lord Rafe and I leave at cockcrow for London. Will you ride with us?"

"I ride to Dover now, my lord."

"Not tonight, surely," Ansculf said firmly.

"But Lord Baron, a ship waits for me—"

"Your errand in Normandy can be delayed until our King is decently buried," Ansculf said harshly, "and as my wife's brother you will receive the hospitality of my hearth." His eyes flashed ominously. "I do not advise you to decline. The outer gates will be barred by now, and they are opened with difficulty."

De Belleme shrugged and turned away.

"Adelaide shall be our guest this night as planned," the baron continued. "But tomorrow, Siward will escort her safely to Birnham."

Rafe nodded. "My thanks on her behalf."

"Aelfred, you shall go with us to London." Anscuf smiled sadly. "It will be an unhappy time for you to enter the court, but we must do as destiny decrees. And Tancred—" he paused. "Tancred may come to London or accompany his uncle to Dover, as he chooses."

Tancred looked startled. "Who will hold sake and soke here, then, if all the men are away?" he asked ingenuously. "My mother?"

There was utter silence. Sake and soke, the undisputed power of life and death over the demesne, was vested in its ruler, and, while the baron might delegate it to another, it was a power jealously guarded for himself and his heirs. Aelfred knew that, in normal times, sake and soke would be given to him in his father's absence. But these were not normal times. Then his eye caught Tancred's, watching him speculatively, and that glance decided him.

"I shall remain here, Father," he said firmly. "You will not be gone so long that I cannot act in your place, with our people to help me."

The baron's eyebrows shot up in amazement. "You?"

"The boy speaks fitly," Rafe remarked, "but his place is with us."

"Myself, then," Tancred offered.

"No!" Aelfred said sharply. "I am atheling here."

"Neither of you," Anscuf decided. "Aelfred shall come with me. Siward shall hold sake and soke. Next to my son, he is the man I most trust."

"But my lord," Siward protested, his brow furrowed with anxiety, "if you entrust sake and soke to me, I should not leave Storches Hundred. How can I escort the Lady Adelaide to Birnham?"

"With her father's permission, she will remain here," Anscuf replied. "As Aelfred says, we will be gone only a short time." He put his hand on the reeve's shoulder. "Before all assembled here, I charge you, Siward, take and hold sake and soke of this demesne," he said solemnly. "What you say or do shall be as though I myself said and did it."

"Your honor will be as my own," Siward promised.

"To bed, now, all of us," said the baron. "We have a long hard day ahead tomorrow. But one thing is needful before we may rest this night. Come here, Tancred."

Tancred, who had been standing beside his uncle, stepped forward. His face was blandly impassive. "Yes, my father?"

"Kneel and place your hands in mine."

Tancred gasped. "Are you asking me to swear fealty? To *you*?"

The baron nodded gravely. "Of course."

"I protest, my lord! This is an insult!" Tancred cried.

"My own son did not consider it an insult. It is an ancient and honored law with us that sons swear fealty to their fathers."

"But you are not my father—"

"You are my lady's son, and I treat you fairly as mine. You enjoy the protection of my hearth and hall. You will take this oath"— the baron's voice rose threateningly—"or I shall name you enemy to this land. These coming days will not be happy ones for Norman enemies."

"He is right, Tancred." Guilbert de Belleme spoke from the shadows. "Warrants have gone out for all Normans not bound by English law. I made my journey in safety only because I hold a safe-conduct from King Edward, but I do not know how long it will be honored."

"To the end of time, Norman," Rafe retorted, his hand on his knife.

De Belleme raised his hand deprecatingly. "Please do not take umbrage, my friend. I do not consider all Englishmen oath breakers."

"We waste time," Ansculf reproved sternly and turned from de Belleme. "Kneel, Tancred. I treat you as my own blood son, neither more nor less favored. Stand beside me, Aelfred. You must witness this oath, for in swearing to me, your father, he swears fealty to you and to your sons."

Tancred glanced at his uncle. His face was white and his eyes ebony slits. But Guilbert de Belleme only smiled. Slowly

41

Tancred fell to his knees, placed his hands within the baron's, and haltingly repeated the ancient oath to bear true service and to uphold the peace of the land.

"Now, ride where you will, to London with us or to Dover with your uncle, or remain here, if you please," said Ansculf. "Only remember, this oath binds you."

"I am not likely to forget," Tancred muttered. "Have I now your permission to withdraw, my lord?"

The baron nodded. "Aelfred, you will sleep in my bower tonight. Siward, have our horses saddled and ready an hour before cockcrow."

"My lord, if Lord Tancred remains here—" Siward began.

"Rule him," Ansculf said shortly. "You hold sake and soke."

"But if he will not keep his oath?" Rafe questioned worriedly.

"He will break it at his peril," the baron finished grimly. "Why do you suppose I asked it of him? If he breaks it, he will be outlaw. For his own sake, I hope he goes with his uncle to Normandy and never returns." He put his arm around Rafe's shoulder. "A strange end to our revels, but all may yet be well. Come, Aelfred."

"Yes, Father," Aelfred murmured. He was remembering now why these revels had been held, but the thoughts churning in his mind bore no resemblance to the happy ones of a prospective bridegroom. Mab had been right: evil days had fallen upon the land. War was inevitable now. Tancred knew it too, and so did Guilbert de Belleme, with his sinister eyes and blank, constant smile. For a moment Aelfred wondered whether he should mention the episode in the grove to his father, then decided that it would serve no purpose, since he still could not prove that the mysterious visitor had been de Belleme. But of one thing he was absolutely certain—neither Tancred nor Lady Ygerne had shown the slightest surprise or even decent regret at the news of King Edward's death.

4

IN THE chill of dawn before sunrise, the stockade gates were opened and the company from Storches Hundred set out for London. Baron Ansculf and Rafe of Birnham headed the cavalcade; Aelfred followed alone; and behind him came the ten men and boys from the demesne chosen by lot to make up the baron's fyrd, who would serve as soldiers if war came. Neither Lady Ygerne nor Adelaide had risen to bid them farewell, though Aelfred would have liked to have had a glimpse of Adelaide. But, he comforted himself, his father thought the stay in London would be brief, and Adelaide's father had promised to hold a betrothal feast at Birnham as soon as they returned. The wedding would be after Holy Week, at Eastertide. A beautiful time for a wedding! He smiled at himself, remembering how fiercely he had rejected even the thought of marriage only a day ago. Well, Mab had been right, and his father, too. The moment Adelaide's eyes had looked into his, he had known once and for all that he was not destined for the cloister; and, it occurred to him now, the Father Prior had probably been of that opinion, too, all along. Certainly he felt no regret at the discovery; in fact, except for the ominous threat of war, he had never been more joyous in his entire life.

The baron set a brisk pace, and by full sunrise they were only an hour's distance from the city. It was decided to make a brief halt, to water the horses and to eat the food they had brought with them, for breakfast had been hurried and there would be no opportunity to dine until after the funeral.

"Where shall we be lodged in London, Father?" Aelfred asked, as he hacked a slice from the large round loaf of bread with his hunting knife.

"At the King's hall, Westminster," Ansculf replied. He passed the earthenware jug to Rafe. "Wait until you see it. It stands half again higher than our hall, and the King's chair is covered with gold."

"Harold Godwineson will become it well," Rafe said solemnly. "I wonder how soon the election will be?"

"A day or two, at the most," Ansculf answered. "I don't doubt that Harold sent out messengers last night, and none of the witenagemot, not even the lords of Mercia and Northumbria, could have traveled too far since St. Stephen's Day."

"Harold had best wait for the red-bearded brothers, even if it means two weeks' delay," said Rafe. "Edwin and Morcar are touchy concerning the Godwine family, and with reason."

"Why?" Aelfred asked curiously. "I thought all the witenagemot were in favor of Harold Godwineson."

"So they are, boy. But those two will wish to cast their own votes. They remember Tostig Godwineson, you see, and they will probably ask for assurances before the election."

"Assurances?" Aelfred echoed. But before he could be answered, there was a sound of hoofbeats galloping towards them up the road. Immediately the baron's fyrdsmen jumped to their feet.

"Get the horses!" Ansculf shouted to them as he drew his sword. "Aelfred, stay beside me."

Aelfred strained his eyes in the direction of the sound. A company of riders was approaching, led by a man in a red cloak. The cloak, billowing behind him, left part of his tunic visible and showed a glint of gold. "I think they're friends," he said, but he did not take his hand from his sword hilt. "At least, that man is not wearing the Red Lion."

44

"*Haele!*" the leader called. He reined his horse to a halt, leaped off its back, and came towards them at a run.

"Name yourself!" Baron Ansculf demanded.

"Is it possible that you don't recognize me, Ansculf?" the man answered, smiling. He was young and lithe, and he wore his hair in the round Norman crop, but his tunic bore the Gold Dragon.

"Gyrth Godwineson!" the baron exclaimed, holding out his hand in greeting. "What brings you abroad so early?"

"The hope of meeting you," Gyrth replied. "Greetings, Rafe of Birnham. I am glad you were at Storches Hundred when the news came."

"Do you mean that Harold sent that Norman?" Rafe demanded, clasping Gyrth's hand warmly.

Gyrth chuckled. "No, but we knew that de Belleme had left London minutes after King Edward breathed his last. So it did not take much imagination to assume that he would stop at Storches Hundred on his way to Dover."

"He was delayed in continuing on to Dover," said Ansculf dryly.

Gyrth laughed loudly and slapped his thigh. "We were sure of that, too." His eyes fell on Aelfred. "Your son, Ansculf?"

"Pardon me, my lord. Permit me to make my son known to you."

Aelfred bowed. "I am honored, Sire."

"No titles, lad. I am only the King's brother and we are all friends here." He clapped Aelfred on the shoulder in friendly fashion and turned again to Ansculf. "You come in good time. Your vote and Rafe's will make the election a clear majority."

"But what about the northern barons? Will they agree?" Rafe asked. "Or did they remain in London after the witenagemot was dismissed?"

Gyrth shook his head. "No. Our fastest messengers were sent after them last night, but we dare not wait for their return. Guilbert de Belleme was only one of several Normans who left London yesterday to take word of King Edward's death to Duke William. The slightest delay in crowning a new king would give William more chance in advancing his claim."

"Which would throw the entire country into a turmoil while debate raged," Ansculf agreed. "William has supporters in high places, who would not hesitate to use any influence they could on the witenagemot. Your brother must indeed be legally crowned, and quickly."

"He is concerned lest too great quickness show lack of respect for King Edward," Gyrth answered. "But it is planned that he will be declared the elected ruler and crowned and sacrede immediately after the funeral Mass."

"So soon?" Rafe said gravely. "I suppose it must be, but I don't like it. And Edwin and Morcar will like it less. It's not our way of electing kings."

There was thoughtful silence for a moment. Then Ansculf asked, "What about your brothers, Gyrth?"

"Leofwine is in London. As for Tostig—" he sighed. "Tostig is in Flanders. Harold has sent urgently for him, but it is doubtful that he will return."

"He is as great a danger to England as any Norman," Ansculf said decidedly. "Harold is right, as usual. The only way he can deal with Tostig is from the throne. We must delay no longer. On to London, my friends."

"But not at too fast a pace," Gyrth countered. "I've had no sleep, and the day will be long. There is time. The funeral procession need not be ready to enter the Abbey until noon."

Quickly the provision kits were repacked and the fyrdsmen took their places in marching order. "I'll send my escort ahead to the palace and ride with you," said Gyrth. "You and Rafe take the lead, Ansculf. I'll stay with Aelfred. I want to improve our acquaintance."

Aelfred, who had been listening with considerable bewilderment to the conversation, now found himself tongue-tied, as usual. What did one say to a king's brother? Fortunately Gyrth did not seem to notice his silence. He chatted amiably for several minutes about the weather and the condition of the road. Then he looked directly at Aelfred and smiled sympathetically.

"You find all this very confusing, don't you?" he asked.

46

"Very," Aelfred replied.

"No wonder! I'm confused myself sometimes. It's a pity that you have to come to London at this moment. Ordinarily the election of a king is a great ceremony. The witenagemot meets in solemn conclave, people make speeches declaring the candidate's worthiness for the throne, the candidate makes a long harangue, and then there are lengthy deliberations. It's really very impressive, and I'm sorry you must miss it. To all intents and purposes, my brother already is as elected, for some people. Others are going to be quite annoyed, I'm afraid."

"The earls of Mercia and Northumbria? Rafe of Birnham said that they'd want assurances—" The words were out of his mouth before he thought, and he grew fiery red with embarrassment. Assurances, because of Tostig Godwineson, who was Gyrth's brother! "Forgive me, my lord," he mumbled.

Gyrth did not seem in the least perturbed. "My name is Gyrth," he said quietly. "Yes, Edwin and Morcar will want assurances that, provided my brother Tostig does decide to return to England, he will not be permitted to influence Harold overmuch."

Aelfred, trying to remember the snatches of conversation he had heard at his father's table during these past months, wished now that he'd paid more heed to them. "He killed someone, didn't he?" he asked hesitantly. "Is—is he not outlaw?"

"Well, King Edward was ill and never passed sentence on him. But he was deposed from the earlship of Northumbria, and his former subjects elected Morcar in his place. Morcar is the brother of Edwin of Mercia, and he is a very formidable, proud man. So is Edwin, for that matter. They are afraid that my brother might be persuaded to give Northumbria back to Tostig."

"But that would be impossible," Aelfred protested, genuinely shocked. "Harold Godwineson would never do a thing so dishonorable."

Gyrth smiled. "Thank you for your loyalty to a man you do not even know," he said. "I think you are right. But my brother Harold loves Tostig dearly. It broke his heart when he fled to Flanders. Edwin and Morcar know this. They also know that Harold would welcome him home with open arms, if only Tostig would pay the wergild of the man he murdered and promise fealty to the crown."

"And Tostig Godwineson will not?"

"Never. He has had a taste of power." Gyrth sighed. "But that will not prevent Harold from attempting a reconciliation. I only hope that his good intentions will not prove disastrous in the end. Meanwhile, Edwin and Morcar remain aloof at best and hostile at worst. Harold will have a hard task to unite his own kingdom, and he will have to do that before he can meet with the Norman."

"Gyrth, do you think there will be a war?" Aelfred asked bluntly.

"I am afraid there will be. Yes. We must hope that God will give us a little time to prepare for it." Then he smiled. "And we may be lucky. Duke William's fleet will be long in building, and he cannot cross the channel in the winter. Things may change completely in the next few months."

Aelfred smiled too, glad to shake off the sense of foreboding that gnawed at him. If as wise and experienced a soldier as Gyrth Godwineson was optimistic, it was surely safe for him to be.

By now they had reached the shallow stream which separated the Isle of Thorney on three sides from the bleak fields. To the right, the River Thames flowed placidly under the end-of-winter sun. Despite the cold, the river was free of ice, and small boats were moving slowly in the direction of the water gates. For the past hour the road had been increasingly crowded, and Aelfred looked in amazement at the vast company of people, on horse or afoot, converging on the single gate in the massive wall ahead of him. Following Gyrth's example, he urged his horse across the ford, shouting " 'Ware!" at those who were making the passage on foot. When he reached the other side, he looked about for his father and Rafe of Birnham, but they were nowhere to be seen.

"They'll have gone on to the palace to cast their votes,"

Gyrth explained as they rode through the gate. "Business of state comes first, you know."

"Had I better wait for them to come back?" Aelfred asked.

"Heavens, no. They'd never find you in this crowd, and, besides, the witenagemot must march in the funeral procession. So must I." Gyrth thought a moment. "I'll tell you what we'll do. I'll take you into the Abbey and find you a place, and then I'll come to fetch you when the coronation ceremony is over. You'll want to see the fealty ceremony. In fact—you're how old?"

"I will soon be eighteen," Aelfred said proudly.

"Then you are a man full grown, and it is time for you to pledge fealty to your King in your own right." Gyrth turned in his saddle and beckoned to one of the soldiers forming a cordon around the Abbey. "Take our horses to the palace stables," he directed as he dismounted. "Give him your sword and knife, Aelfred. We carry no weapons here."

Aelfred obeyed and followed Gyrth through the crowd already flocking towards the doors. He looked up in awe at the great church with its huge square tower looming like a gray sentinel over him. "I never saw anything so wonderful," he said breathlessly.

"Wait until you are inside," Gyrth replied. "I've seen churches on the Continent, but not one can excel this for beauty."

"I never saw so many people in one place, either."

"There'll never be room for them," Gyrth worried. "Fortunately the soldiers seem to be keeping the way from the palace clear, or the procession would not be able to enter. But here we are, at last."

He pushed the door open. The nave was packed, but the guard on duty ordered the people to step aside and make a path, and soon Aelfred, following Gyrth, found himself in the front, directly before the choir screen.

"This is where you belong, and you'll have a good view from here," Gyrth whispered. "If anyone tries to elbow you out, tell them you're of the King's household. I don't think anyone will, since they've seen you with me." As if to emphasize that statement, he looked challengingly over the congregation. "Remember, now. Stay here until I come. It would be easy to be lost in this crowd and take half a day to find yourself. We haven't the time to spare."

"I will wait here. And thank you," Aelfred answered. Gyrth gave him a friendly pat on the back and strode away.

Aelfred sank to his knees and bowed his head. He tried very hard to put himself into the proper disposition for a funeral Mass, but he was actually too excited to pray. He rose, and keeping in mind as much deportment as his reverence and wonderment permitted, he looked about him with amazement and delight. Through the center arch of the stone choir screen, he could see the monks' choir and glimpse the high altar, vested in black but adorned with cross and candlesticks of gold glistening with jewels. The sun streamed through the slitted windows in the high vaulted roof, glinting here and there on the polished wood of the choir stalls and the bronze braziers, on the carpet on the stone steps leading into the chancel. A little to the left of the altar, a handsome, beautifully carved wooden chair, the coronation throne, stood in readiness. "The King is dead, long live the King," Aelfred murmured. The King would be given his last obeisance, and, almost within the same hour, his successor, annointed with holy oil, would take his place on the throne, wearing the royal crown.

"The King is consecrated to his kingship," he remembered the Father Prior's once saying. "He rules by God's grace. Until he is sacrede, he can claim no authority. But, once sacrede, he must be obeyed in all civil matters, even as Our Lord enjoined his disciples to render unto Caesar his due."

Now a sudden deep hush came upon the congregation, as a company of soldiers, bareheaded and weaponless, wearing black tunics with gold dragons on them, took up positions to make certain that a center aisle would be kept clear. In the distance came the sound of voices. The monks of the Abbey were in procession, chanting, "I am the Resurrection and the Life." Aelfred bowed his head to conceal the tears that started suddenly to his eyes, remembering how he himself had chanted those very words on several occasions at Canterbury. But it was not loneliness for the monastery that made him weep. It was the vivid realization that the great King Edward was being brought to his last resting place with the same words that accompanied the humblest of monks or the least of his subjects.

The procession swept by in solemn magnificence. There were two bishops passing him now, in copes and mitres, and following them, alone, another bishop whose black cope was embroidered in silver. Aelfred recognized him at once: Stigand, Archbishop of Canterbury, who had come several times to visit Coventry. And then, preceded by a crucifer, eight men carried the King's bier on their shoulders. One of them was Gyrth Godwineson; the two others who so closely resembled him must be Harold and Leofwine. As the bier passed, the people knelt and there were sounds of muffled weeping. Immediately behind the bier came a woman dressed in black and heavily veiled; she must be Edith, the Queen and, as Aelfred now remembered, the sister of the Godwines. She walked with royal step alone through the choir and into the chancel, where she knelt at the bier, now before the altar, and then took her place. Behind her came the royal household, followed by the witenagemot. Aelfred caught a glimpse of his father and noticed that he, like all the others, wore a black tunic and was weaponless.

When all was ready, the Archbishop chanted the funeral Mass and burial office. The monks gave the responses. All was performed with great dignity and beauty; no solemnity was lacking, yet Aelfred sensed an air of urgency behind the choir screen. He had been with monks enough to recognize what the Father Prior called "the need for Holy Alacrity" when he saw it. There was no funeral sermon, nor did any of the King's Thanes step forward to give a eulogy. It was as if, in all this throng, neither was needed to emphasize further the love and respect that was so evident. As soon as the rites were concluded, the eight men who had carried the bier in procession lifted it and took it to the altar steps. The Archbishop sprinkled it with holy water, and the bearers slowly lowered it into the open crypt. King Edward had been granted his last wish: burial before the altar of the Abbey Church, which he himself had commanded to be built.

The crucifer, the Archbishop, and his attending bishops now left the chancel, and the congregation watched, hardly stirring, as two monks quickly removed the black altar vestments and replaced them with gold. A number of men left their places in the transepts and moved slowly towards a chapel on the left, where they waited solemnly, silently, until the Archbishop, now wearing a cope and mitre of cloth of gold and carrying his pastoral staff, emerged following the crucifer. Hardly a footfall was heard as the almost breathless congregation watched the two assisting bishops come slowly into the chancel. Between them walked a tall man wearing a red velvet cloak over a white tunic, on his head a gold crown. The monks began to chant the *Te Deum* as Harold Godwineson mounted the steps, removed his crown, and placed it on the altar. As the chant continued, he knelt beside the open crypt, then prostrated himself on the ground.

When the chant was finished, he rose and faced the Archbishop. In answer to the questions the Archbishop asked, he answered in a firm clear voice, promising that he, so help him God, would do all in his power to keep true peace, forbid evil, and temper his justice with mercy and equity, "that England may be ever great." The coronation oath caused a murmur of emotion throughout the Abbey from the still-silent, waiting congregation. Then Harold knelt while the Archbishop intoned the prayers. One of the two bishops who presented Harold took the vial of holy oil from the altar and placed it in the Archbishop's hands. To the solemn yet triumphant chanting of the monks, Harold Godwineson was annointed on the forehead, hands, and breast. Now, sacrede and consecrated, he rose, so that the sword could be girt round him; then he was solemnly escorted to the coronation chair. The tension and anticipation were so great that Aelfred could hardly breathe. The Archbishop blessed the crown, raised it high, then placed it firmly on the head of the new King. At that moment, the entire Abbey rocked as from one voice with the shouts of *"Vivat! Vivat!* May the King live forever!" Then a silence as intense as the shout, while the throng knelt for the benediction and the moment of silent prayer.

The monks began the recessional psalm and the King was leaving the chancel, now carrying the orb and scepter, to show himself to his people. It was a joyous moment, and Aelfred moved forward, shouting his heart out with everyone else. The King was coming towards him, passing so near that he could almost touch him. He saw his face clearly—the high forehead, the deep blue eyes, the look of kindliness but also of command. Now the King was turning in his direction. He raised his hand in a soldier's salute, caught up in an ecstasy of devotion to this man.

"God save Your Majesty!" he cried, hardly knowing what he said, knowing only that he must either shout or weep for joy.

The King slowed his steps. His glance rested on Aelfred for a moment, and he said quietly, "I thank you, Aelfred Ansculfson." Then he smiled and continued on.

Aelfred leaned against the pillar, lest his knees give way. He had seen the King and, moreover, the King had seen him. He had called him by name! To look on royalty newly crowned and sacrede was an awesome thing, but something more had happened to him in that moment of encounter, something as inexplicable as it was momentous. He had expected to give his loyalty to his King. But he had not expected to feel this overwhelming surge of love for him as well. Suddenly he understood his father's devotion to Harold Godwineson. The man himself had a capacity to love that evoked love in others, which made them want to serve him not only as King but as a friend. Yet there must be more. Much more! For no leader could inspire such devotion only for himself. The words of the coronation oath flashed through his mind: "that England may be ever great." That was it. Harold Godwineson's own words proclaimed his secret; he loved England and served her as others served him. And because of this love, others, too, loved England more and served her better.

The people around him were now following the procession out of the Abbey. He could hear their shouts mingling with those of the crowd outside the door. Gyrth Godwineson would come for him soon. He would take him into the King's presence to make his oath of fealty. Aelfred smiled tremulously. That oath he would give, with all his heart, but it would only be the confirmation of one already given. For, in that moment when the King had spoken his name, he had become the King's man.

"He shall be my liege lord as long as I have breath," he murmured, sinking on one knee. "I shall follow him to the brink of death and beyond. May God be witness to my words."

It was not until later, when Gyrth Godwineson again stood at his side, that he recalled for one fleeting moment that this was not the vow he had once thought to take. But it was equally sacred to him.

◆◆◆◆◆◆◆◆◆◆◆◆◆◆◆◆ **5** ◆◆◆◆◆◆◆◆◆◆◆◆◆◆◆◆

TANCRED de Belleme galloped across the south field. His horse moved heavily under him, for he had been riding hard that day. But, he thought irritably, what other amusement was there in this dull place? Siward the reeve had sternly forbidden him to hunt; there was enough meat hung, he said, and to kill more just to shoot an arrow would be wanton extravagance. Tancred snorted. These English! Even their sports would be by necessity. His falcon would lose all her skill if she were cooped up in the mews much longer. Well, that was another score he would settle with Siward one day—the day that Duke William took his rightful place on the English throne.

He slowed his horse to a trot. No use in killing the animal; it was a good one. He sighed impatiently. The baron and Aelfred had been gone for a month. Not that he missed them, but things were livelier on the demesne when they were there. At least there was the satisfaction of baiting his stepbrother. If Adelaide were a little more friendly, he could amuse himself here, but she avoided him. His handsome face scowled. English girls were appalling creatures, if Adelaide was any example. Cold of manner, brusque of speech, no wit, no repartee—and he had used all his wiles to win her. In fact, he had gone out of his way to charm her, and it had been the first time his charm had failed. He had to admit that in some respects she was very attractive, but she ignored his compliments and never laughed at his jokes. He was not accustomed to being scoffed at, nor to being treated with such scant courtesy. So he and his offended vanity had retreated into a lofty silence, which had failed too! Girls in France had lapped up his flattery as cats do milk, but not Adelaide. Once he had made the mistake of trying to appeal to her sympathy, telling her that he was lonely and needed someone to talk to him. And she had replied nicely, but matter-of-factly, "But you have your mother."

I'd like to break that spirit of hers, he thought venemously. I'd like to make her weep. I'd like to strike her until she was welt tracked! But if I did, her father would kill me.

His restless, angry eyes searched the sky. Gray, dreary—he thought of Normandy, bathed in sunshine. Why hadn't his uncle sent for him? He had expected a letter by the time news reached Storches Hundred of Harold Godwineson's coronation. Duke William would be readying his army, and he wanted to be in that army. He had no doubt that he would have all the aid he needed to distinguish himself in battle, and the duke was known to be generous to his supporters. He would, of course, ask for lands in England—perhaps even for Storches Hundred. The thought of Aelfred's being done out of his inheritance made him laugh aloud with pleasure. Then he would no longer be without sufficient funds to operate the de Belleme estate. He knew for a certainty that Baron Ansculf had a fortune in gold and silver. He would demand that, too.

Why hadn't the letter come? The task his uncle had set for him of listing all the people on the demesne and their probable reaction to a Norman invasion had been accomplished. He had already gained much information about Storches Hundred during these past six months, so writing it down had been a simple matter. It had taken a little time to put it into the code that Guilbert de Belleme had given his mother, but that was safely folded into the pouch he always wore during the day and kept under his pillow when he slept. Duke William had asked for this information from all over the south of England, his uncle had said, so invasion must be in the wind. He imagined the Red Lion of Normandy flying from the palace at Westminster and atop Baron Ansculf's hall. Oh, the English would fight, but not all of them. There were some on this very demesne who said openly that they did not care who was in power, as long as they did not need to change their ways; that one king was the same as another.

Well, they'll learn after the war what having a real master means, Tancred thought complacently. And they'll be all the better for a king who holds his power by right and might. How can an elected king have any permanent power, when those who make him king can unmake him just as easily? The Normans would never let go their power, once they had gained it. He was sure of that.

He had reached the stockade, where a churl came running to open the gate for him. The comparative quiet of the court when he had left earlier seemed to have given way to considerable commotion. Kitchen churls were running between the hall and the kitchen with dishes and nappery.

"Has the baron returned?" he asked as he dismounted.

"No, Lord Tancred," the churl answered. "My lady's brother has come."

Tancred's heart leaped. This was his summons! But why had his uncle returned to Storches Hundred instead of simply sending for him? "Rub my horse well, and don't feed him for at least an hour," he said briskly. "Where is my uncle?"

"With my lady, in her bower."

Without further word, Tancred hurried to the small detached house that his mother had taken for her own when she first came to Storches Hundred. Adelaide would not be there; she had slept there only one night, and then, on the plea of "not wishing to discommode my lady," had moved into one of the guest bowers. Tancred knew that her real reason for moving had been because the two women had disliked each other on sight. Dinner tonight would be amusing if Adelaide appeared, he thought ironically.

He knocked on the door, and his mother's voice bade him enter. "We've been waiting for you for over an hour," she said plaintively.

"My regrets, Mother. Had I known, I would not have ridden so late." He kissed her hand, then turned to Guilbert de Belleme, his eyes glowing with unconcealed excitement. "Well, Uncle? What brings you to Storches Hundred?"

"News to gladden your heart, I hope," his uncle replied. "The Duke of Normandy has sent an embassy to Harold, demanding that the oath he gave at Harfleur be honored. If he refuses, William will declare war."

"And I am sent for!" Tancred exulted.

De Belleme shook his head. "Not yet."

"Not yet?" Tancred looked his fury. "All Normandy will be arming for invasion, yet I must sit here, in this godforsaken place, useless and idle?"

"Sit down, Tancred, and don't shout so. They'll hear you as far as the hall," Lady Ygerne warned.

"I don't care if they hear me to Westminster!" Tancred did not lower his voice. "This is a calculated insult on William's part. The de Bellemes are soldiers, not petty English thanes."

"Of course they are soldiers," said Lady Ygerne, "but you cannot leave England."

"What could prevent me? I could take the first ship out of Dover and march into Harfleur and lay my sword at Duke William's feet."

"You'd never reach Dover," de Belleme said quietly. "You swore an oath of fealty to Baron Ansculf."

"A worthless oath!"

"To you, yes. But England will not hold it worthless."

"Ansculf said himself that I might go to Normandy with you."

"That was a month ago. Things have changed overnight. The roads are now guarded by very watchful English patrols. You would be caught and questioned, perhaps imprisoned. And your usefulness at any future time would be completely lost."

"I stayed here at your express wish," Tancred snapped. "Not because I wished it! And I notice that you traveled alone, and no one stopped you."

"I travel under a safe-conduct that is still honored. You

58

would have none. And I have other resources, which I shall tell you about in a moment, if you will be quiet." De Belleme smiled. "Not every soldier fights on the battlefield, Tancred. You will be called to fight, never fear, and I hope you will enjoy it as much as you anticipate. But for the moment there is another task for you, and the duke will be as grateful if you perform it well as he would be for your capturing the enemy's standard. Believe me, the reason I wanted you in England was in your own best interests."

"Very well, I'll listen," Tancred replied sulkily. "What are these interests of mine, and this all-important task?"

"Yes. I shall listen to such news, too," said Lady Ygerne, looking her brother boldly in the eye, "since Tancred is my son."

De Belleme looked at her coldly. "Your attention, dear sister, would be better directed to your embroidery. We meet in your bower because it seems a safe place for a family reunion. Our good reeve Siward could well suspect some conspiracy if Tancred and I talked alone."

"Siward?" Tancred jeered. "Siward sees no farther than the end of his own nose. Storches Hundred is loyal to Harold Godwineson, he says."

"So much the better for us," de Belleme said ironically. "Enough of talk. We have work to do. Where is the list you are supposed to have ready for me?"

Tancred took it from his pouch and laid it on the table. For a quarter hour, de Belleme perused it in silence.

"Excellent," he said finally. "Precisely what I'd hoped. A few outspoken patriots, but we can deal with them in such a way that none of the indifferent ones will want to raise a voice in their behalf."

Tancred frowned. "I'm not so sure of that. One of the most outspoken is Siward, and he is well loved. If you raise a hand against him—"

"There will be no need. We will simply tie his hands."

"What about the priest? Father Owain has preached some violent sermons against the Normans."

"Let him. Words can't hurt us. Priests are controlled by

their bishops, and we will control the bishops, once William obtains the Holy Father's blessing."

"The duke will take his cause to Rome?"

"Certainly. He can't invade England until late summer, so he will employ his time wisely. He has a powerful weapon in Harold's broken oath, and he can get the Holy Father's ear before Harold sends his own embassy."

"Duke William is a very shrewd man."

"And very watchful. No detail escapes his eye. That is why he will win."

"And what is my part in all this?" Tancred asked impatiently.

"William will win over Harold Godwineson in a pitched battle. So much is certain. But one battle does not conquer a country. His way will be easier if some of England is already in friendly hands. Which brings me, finally, to you." He smiled nastily. "Baron Ansculf has only one heir. If that heir should fail to accede to the demesne, the way will certainly be open to you as the Baron's foster son."

"But how is that possible?" Tancred stopped short, his spine tingling. "Are you suggesting murder?"

"Only as a last resort," de Belleme said suavely. "Outlawry would do as well, or an accusation wherein he could not prove himself innocent."

Tancred burst out laughing. "Uncle, you are baying at the moon. Aelfred spent eleven years in a monastery. What accusation could you make anyone believe?"

De Belleme grinned, showing his pointed teeth. " 'Thou shalt not suffer a witch to live.' " He pointed at the list before him. "Mab wife of Wulfric was Aelfred's nurse. He is devoted to her, no?"

"Excessively."

"And Mab was accused at the last folkmoot of sorcery by one"—he scanned the list—"Saewulf. These horrible English names!"

"She was acquitted, though."

"Of course. The baron was here, then. But I have learned
60

that Harold Godwineson plans to ride north very soon. The earls of Northumbria and Mercia are angry that the witenagemot acted without them and must be placated. Baron Ansculf rides with him, and so does Rafe of Birnham."

"Won't Aelfred go as well?"

"That, I admit, is a matter for delicate handling. If the baron is led to believe that his own presence is required here, he will not be able to come because of his duty to the King, so-called. But you could, in your letter, suggest that he send Aelfred."

"In *my* letter? Uncle, I wish you would speak more plainly."

"And I wish you had more finesse." De Belleme sighed. "But, since you do not, I must draw a chart for you. First, Saewulf must be encouraged to revive his charge of witchcraft against Mab."

"That won't be easy. Mab just cured his son, and he is grateful."

"His son could fall ill again," Lady Ygerne suggested from the shadows.

"Excellent, sister! Would that your son had inherited such perceptiveness. Then Mab will be arrested."

"Never, with Siward in charge," Tancred scoffed.

"If the case is sufficiently grave, and if others threaten her—as can be arranged—Siward will arrest her and bring her to the stockade for her own safety. Then, we bring Aelfred home."

"Who immediately goes to Mab's defense," Tancred said excitedly. "I'm beginning to see. Then he is accused of aiding a sorceress."

"Precisely. Then, there is a trial by ordeal for Mab—"

"In which she dies?"

"Few survive the hot iron. And Aelfred will be tried at the folkmoot."

"But Siward will be judge. He'll never give sentence against the atheling."

"If the people are sufficiently aroused, he'll dare do nothing else. We may even be able to convince him that the charge is true. Aelfred, then, is outlawed or perhaps returned to his

61

monastery for discipline. Either way, he is no longer a threat to us. A condemned sorcerer has no right of appeal except directly to the King. But Harold Godwineson will be on his travels and will hear no word of this for a long time. Neither will Anscuf. We'll see to that. By the time they both return to London, Duke William may have landed. You, meanwhile, will have taken control of Storches Hundred. What else can you do? You *are* the baron's foster son."

Tancred laughed softly, then stopped. "But suppose word of this does reach Anscuf? Suppose he returns before Duke William comes? He won't accept Siward's judgment against his own son without question."

"I told you that I have other resources, nephew. I hold a royal patent as King's High Reeve of this district."

Tancred was astounded. "How on earth did you get it? And where?"

"Never mind. My methods need not concern you. The important thing is, I have it and can override all other judgments. Anscuf will be helpless to oppose me." He nodded triumphantly. "I think I've covered every possible contingency."

"You certainly have," Tancred said admiringly. "It's strange, Uncle. I was thinking just today that I would ask Duke William for Storches Hundred as a reward for battle service. And now—"

"Now it is a ripe plum, ready for shaking," his uncle replied. "You will have Storches Hundred, I promise. And something else has occurred to me, as well. I think you would be wise to consider marriage."

"To whom?" Tancred's tone was a mixture of amusement and condescension.

"To Adelaide of Birnham, and as quickly as possible."

"No!" The vehemence of Lady Ygerne's objection startled them both. She put down her embroidery frame with an emphatic gesture. "I will not have such a marriage! My son marry a whey-faced little nobody—and English to boot—when he can have his choice in Normandy?"

"Dear sister, before you make other objections, consider

the advantages of the match," de Belleme said quietly. "The girl is rich. Birnham would be a fine addition to Tancred's fortune. And if, by some mischance, our plans for Storches Hundred should miscarry or Harold Godwineson should win, Tancred as her husband would at least hold her lands. One must be practical."

"But she is so gauche and unattractive," Lady Ygerne protested. "Though she does embroider exquisitely," she added grudgingly.

De Belleme laughed. "She is unattractive to you, perhaps, but is her fortune to your son? What do you think of her, Tancred?"

Tancred, for the moment, was speechless, dazzled by the unlimited prospects that had suddenly opened before him. It was an effort to turn his attention to his uncle's question. "The idea is not displeasing," he admitted. "But you forget: she is Aelfred's betrothed. And she seems to dislike me."

"Women often conceal their true feelings," his uncle said sagely, "and it would not be the first time that a lady changed her mind. So let us consider the matter settled." He yawned loudly. "I feel the need to rest."

Tancred rose. "I'll take you to my bower. I feel the need of rest, too."

"But first you must write a note to the fair Adelaide and implore her presence at table this evening." De Belleme smiled. "Ladies like to feel that they have sway over a man's destiny, so you must cloak that arrogance of yours until after you're married."

"Very well," Tancred agreed. "One last question: suppose the baron sends Aelfred home with power of sake and soke?"

"H'm." De Belleme grew thoughtful. "I don't think it likely. But if he should"—he raised one eyebrow—"it will be highly amusing to see the atheling sit in judgment, unaware that I am King's High Reeve." His laughter, low and insulting, was joined by Tancred's uproarious mirth as they left the bower.

In the guest bower, Adelaide sat beside the window working industriously at her embroidery. She paused to contemplate one of the threads left in her needle, then selected another green strand from the cut lengths on the table beside her. The hanging was almost finished, for she had had considerable time to spend on it, but she did not mind that, since Aelfred was not at Storches Hundred. On the contrary, if they were to be married at Eastertide there would scarcely be time enough to finish what she needed for her dower chest. At least, her father said they were to be married, so she assumed matters were settled. A smile flickered across her lips at the thought of her father's surprise if he should ever learn that, as far as she was concerned, matters had been settled long ago.

She threaded the needle and set to work again, frowning a little as she carefully matched the stitches. She wondered what Aelfred was doing at this moment and why he had not written to her. For that matter, she'd had no word from her father, either, though that was not unusual. From earliest childhood she had been accustomed to his long absences on mysterious "King's business." But Aelfred was her betrothed. It was strange, she thought. At Berkynge Priory School she had met a number of her schoolmates' brothers, and, when she went to court, Westminster seemed to be filled with handsome young men. At least three had proposed to her. But when her father had told her that he had spoken with Baron Ansculf, she had known in a lightning flash that she would marry Aelfred, and that knowledge had been confirmed in one evening at the Twelfth Night feast. Yet, if anyone were to ask her at this moment if she loved Aelfred Ansculfson, she would have to admit that she did not know. Their brief time together had given little opportunity for her to discover whether she did or not. As for him, he seemed to be pleased with her, though Tancred had been the one who had paid the compliments. She chuckled. Tancred certainly could turn a phrase, and she had to acknowledge him handsome. But Tancred was a Norman, and she despised Normans. She ought not even to be thinking of him.

"And I'm not, really," she murmured. "Only I do wish Aelfred would write. It's lonely here."

The door opened and she looked up with an affectionate smile at the girl who stood there. She and Ellen had played together as children, and when she grew up Ellen had become her maid. But they were more like sisters than mistress and servant.

"Is it time to lay the table?" she asked. She had been taking her meals in the bower to avoid dining in the hall with Lady Ygerne and Tancred. Especially Lady Ygerne, to whom she found it difficult to be even civil.

Ellen shook her head. "I've a letter, mistress."

"A letter!" Word from London at last. "Oh, give it to me, Ellen. Quickly!"

She opened the parchment, paying no attention to the seal, her eyes darting at once to the signature. Disappointment overwhelmed her. It was not from Aelfred. The flourishing letters formed the name of Tancred de Belleme. In most beseeching words he was begging her to dine in the hall tonight, saying that he was waiting suspended between Heaven and the pit for her answer.

"What shall I tell him, my lady?" Ellen asked, her eyes dancing. "He is most anxious."

Adelaide wavered. A little while ago, Tancred's exaggerated self-abasement would have made her laugh and she would have refused. But she found herself now suddenly provoked at Aelfred's silence. Westminster was a busy and interesting place to be. Why should she stay night and day quite alone in this little bower? It was pleasant enough, but lonely. She scanned the letter again. Tancred wrote that his uncle had come for a visit. Hospitality demanded that all guests be treated with courtesy. If she did not appear, she might be considered rude. For Aelfred's sake, she did not want that.

"Tell him I shall be pleased to dine tonight," she answered. "Ask him to greet his uncle for me. Then return quickly to help me dress."

As Ellen closed the door behind her, Adelaide went to her clothes chest. It was rather exciting to be wondering what to wear after so many solitary evenings. The white gown she had

65

worn at the Twelfth Night feast lay on top in its linen wrappings, but she would not choose it. It belonged to her meeting with Aelfred, and she would save it for her betrothal feast. There was her red wool, but Lady Ygerne might decide to wear red. Finally she decided on a blue wool kirtle with long fitted sleeves banded in silver. Her blue fur-lined cloak went well with it, and she could wear her hand-wrought silver necklace and brooch.

An hour later, she was seated at table between Tancred and his uncle, surprised to find herself glad to be there. The two men were charming and gallant. Their witticisms kept her constantly laughing. Even Lady Ygerne was pleasant to her. After dinner Tancred sang for them; his glowing eyes never left her face. Adelaide was conscious that Siward, standing nearby, was not altogether approving of her presence; but she also remembered how she had dined alone every night for the past month. True, it was due to her own choosing, but when Tancred asked her to ride with him next day, as he bade her good night, she agreed.

The days which had seemed to drag so slowly now seemed hardly long enough. She rode regularly with Tancred every afternoon. He taught her hawking, even letting her carry his falcon on her own wrist, promising her a fledgling when the birds nested in the spring. In the evenings there was music, and Tancred taught her to dance, vowing that no lady in Normandy could surpass her in grace. She still laughed at his extravagance, but she had to admit that she enjoyed his compliments. Any pricks of conscience she silenced with the thought that to ride with a man signified nothing, and that Tancred's mother and uncle were always present when they danced. She gave herself completely to the enjoyment of the moment.

It was Ellen who gave her the first inkling that all was not as pleasant as it might seem. Three weeks had passed when the girl came in one morning, her eyes wide with bewilderment.

"Have you heard what they're saying, my lady?" she asked breathlessly.

"Who?" Adelaide had been looking out the window at the snow which had come suddenly in the night and thinking there could be no ride today.

"Saewulf's son has been taken with the trembling ague, and Saewulf says that he is bewitched."

"Bewitched? Nonsense," Adelaide scoffed.

"He says that Mab has bewitched him. He was talking to Siward this morning and making a fearful pother. Siward told him to be quiet, but Saewulf shook his fist at him and said that he would not be silenced this time. I wonder you did not hear them, my lady."

"I did hear voices." Adelaide frowned. She placed Saewulf, now. He seemed to come to the stockade frequently, a shaggy man with ferret's eyes. Once she had noticed him talking with Tancred. "What a dreadful thing for him to say!"

"Even more dreadful if it is true, my lady, and I fear it is."

"Hush, Ellen. You must not speak so," Adelaide reproved. "Mab was Aelfred Ansculfson's nurse, and the baron's, too."

"But have you seen her? I did once, and that was enough. Old and ugly, with a glittering eye. Oh, she is a witch, my lady!"

"Hush," Adelaide repeated. She did not believe a word of Saewulf's accusation, but there was a chill in the air, and not altogether from the cold.

The snow stopped about noon and the sun broke through the clouds. Adelaide had just finished midday collation when there was a knock at the door. She opened it herself, knowing that Tancred would be there. He was dressed for riding.

"Come out with me," he said gaily.

"In this weather?" she objected, but she smiled. It was impossible not to smile at Tancred these days.

"It will be beautiful," he promised. "A world all in white. Come and see it with me."

"All right," she agreed. Ellen was already beside her with her cloak. She wrapped it around her closely and pulled the hood over her head. Then she drew on her gloves. Tancred took her arm as they walked down the slippery path. He had

67

never touched her before, except in a dance, and she found the pressure of his hand more than a little exciting. For a brief moment she had second thoughts about the ride, but their horses were ready at the stable, and she was mounted and away before she could put any thoughts into words.

"You're right. It is beautiful," she said, after they had gone a short distance. "I'm glad you made me come."

"How I wish that we might always ride so together," Tancred answered. "But alas, it may not be."

His tone, usually so bantering, was deeply serious, and there was no mistaking his meaning. "No, it may not," she said firmly, deliberately keeping her voice cool and level.

He was silent, and Adelaide looked away, her thoughts in a turmoil. Here she was, a girl betrothed, listening to a declaration from another man! She ought to be heartily ashamed of herself, and she was, but not altogether from a sense of disloyalty to Aelfred. For, in her heart, she had to admit guiltily that she did not find Tancred's avowal at all unpleasant.

"Forgive me, Adelaide." He was speaking again in the same serious tone. They were riding very close beside each other now. He placed his hand over hers on the reins and slowed both horses. "It would take a man of stone to see your beauty every day and not speak. I shall not again."

"There is nothing to forgive," she answered, her voice high and strained.

"Thank you." Then he smiled. "Shall we ride faster?"

"Yes," she replied, relieved that the moment had passed.

He dug his spurs into his horse's flanks and took the lead. She rode after him, her cloak streaming behind her. The little mare went like the wind. She could feel her cheeks glowing with the cold; she panted in the winter air until she thought her lungs would burst. Tancred was leading her through a circular clearing filled with strange broken stones, then on into the forest, when he suddenly stopped.

She reined in beside him. "What's the matter?"

"I hear shouting," he said. "Listen!"

The roar of angry voices broke the white stillness. "It's over there," said Tancred. "Wait a moment. I'll see what it is."

"I'm coming with you."

"Follow at a distance, then. It may be some trouble, and you must not be hurt."

Obediently she rode behind him. The shouts grew louder, and there was a smell of burning. Now she could hear the words "witch" and "sorceress." She made her horse go faster until she came to the edge of another clearing, where she stopped in shocked dismay at the sight before her. A throng of men had surrounded a small cot and were hurling stones at it. The turf roof was already smoking.

"Witch, witch, burn the witch!" the voices chanted.

One man, whom she immediately recognized as Saewulf, raised a torch and howled, "Thou shalt not suffer a witch to live!"

Horrified, Adelaide remained where she was. Tancred, however, rode straight into the middle of the crowd, his horse rearing on its hind legs and neighing shrilly. He stopped right beside Saewulf who, seeing him, dropped the torch. The others grew ominously quiet. Tancred spoke, too low for Adelaide to hear, but some dropped the stones they were carrying and began to move away. The last to go was Saewulf. Tancred waited a moment, then returned to Adelaide.

By now she was shaking in every limb and near tears. "That was horrible!" she cried. "What was happening?"

"Saewulf's son died this afternoon," Tancred said gravely. "Mab put a spell on him, Saewulf says, and he was—well, you saw."

"But what can we do?"

He considered. "I think I've quieted them for the moment. I told them that there'd be a folkmoot as soon as the baron returned. Perhaps we'd better send word to him to come at once."

"Yes," Adelaide agreed. "I'll write to my father, too."

"I wonder if Mab will be safe? Saewulf is after blood, and witch or not I can't let her be burned alive in her own house. After all, I am bound to uphold the peace on this land." He paused, then said, "Adelaide, I'm going to stay here. You ride back and tell Siward what has happened. Tell him that Mab had better be brought to the stockade or she may not be here to face her accuser at the folkmoot. Saewulf is a violent man."

She nodded. "Yes, that would be best."

He put his hand on her arm. "You are not afraid to ride alone?"

"No," she answered, glad that her hood shielded her face.

"Tell Siward that we must act quickly."

She set off at a gallop, feeling the warmth of Tancred's eyes still following her. It was not for several hours afterwards, after she had told the story to Siward and he had ridden out to the forest land, that she was struck by the curious fact that Tancred had not seemed at all horrified or even surprised by the episode. In fact, despite his concern, there had been a certain satisfaction in his attitude, as though things had gone exactly according to his expectation. She remembered, too, how Saewulf had immediately dropped the torch, and the crowd had quickly dispersed. And where was Father Owain, who should have been there to attend to Saewulf's son? Also, Tancred's disposition of Mab had been almost too glib. The more she pondered, the more troubled she became. She could not frame her suspicions into words, for there was really nothing to suspect. Tancred had behaved perfectly in the circumstances, but that perfection seemed somehow flawed.

"My lady, dinner will be served in a few moments. Should I not help you dress?" Ellen had come in so quietly that she had not even heard her. And she remembered Ellen's talk only a few hours before Tancred had asked her to ride. Had it been coincidence? She shook her head. She must not let these strange happenings unnerve her so that she lost trust in everyone.

"My lady?" Ellen spoke again.

Adelaide looked at her searchingly. The girl's face indicated nothing but concern for her mistress. Still, Ellen had known about Mab early that morning. "I shall dine here tonight," she said calmly. "You go and find Siward. Tell him quietly that I must speak with him."

"He has just returned," Ellen answered. "He's brought the witch with him."

"Do not speak of Mab so," her mistress reproved. "Of course he brought Mab here. You forget: he has power of sake and soke over Storches Hundred. You just give him my message."

Ellen left, a little crestfallen at her mistress's unwonted sharpness. But Adelaide was in no mood for gossip. I must write my father, she decided firmly. Siward will know who can be trusted to take a letter to London. And I'll write to Aelfred, too. Surely Siward himself will send word to Baron Ansculf.

AELFRED was standing guard in the Court of Request at Westminster Palace. The door to the Painted Chamber, where King Harold was meeting with his council, was closed, but occasionally the reverberation of a loud voice raised in protest or dismay penetrated the heavy oaken door. A Norman embassy had arrived this morning, bearing Duke William's latest ultimatum, and Leofwine Godwineson, the King's brother, had sent word from the continent that the Normans had already begun preparations for war. Gloom hung heavily over the palace, save only in the apartments where the Normans were lodged, and that laughter was boisterous and mean, not mirthful.

Through the slitted windows, he watched the sunset. At a time like this, he reflected sadly, the sky should be sympathetically dark and lowering, but nature seemed unconcerned with a kingdom's anxieties. Vivid red, purple, and gold streaked the sky; the sun looked like a fiery orb. He crossed himself and murmured the *Jubilate Deo,* hoping that this display of glory would be a good omen for the King he served. "Let nothing happen to him," he pleaded. "Harm to him would shatter the world."

He paced slowly up and down, blowing on his hands to

warm them. There was no fire in this room, and he was cold, despite his warm cloak. He would be glad when the time came to go into the hall for dinner and he hoped that the King would dine with them; the meal was always more festive when Harold Godwineson was there. Berdic, the King's gleesman, sometimes had a new song for these occasions. But of late the King had kept to his chamber, even for meals, dictating endless dispatches to his secretary, Dom Regembald. Aelfred knew about the dispatches. It was strange, he mused, how useful his studies with the monks had been here in the royal palace, in ways that he had never dreamed they would or could be. Because he could read and write, one of his assigned duties was to assist Dom Regembald by making pens and mixing ink. Occasionally he was even asked to write out a dispatch himself. In fact, he had learned, within twenty-four hours of the coronation, that the King would be a tireless worker, and a month at Westminster had greatly increased his admiration for Harold Godwineson as a ruler.

He resumed his post at the door, thinking how long the time seemed since he had seen Storches Hundred and Adelaide and yet how quickly that completely occupied month had really passed. From the moment of his arrival at Westminster, he had hardly had a moment to himself. He had immediately been placed in the company called the Young Men, which was really a kind of preparatory school for the company of the King's Thanes. The Young Men were easily recognized; like himself they were sons of thanes who had yet to prove themselves in battle and were serving at court to learn the arts of government, defense, and soldiering. They had to attend the King at stated times each day, and one of their most serious and time-consuming occupations was the drilling and military exercises conducted in a field outside the palace walls, under the eager eye of their drillmaster, Thurlkill the Dane. Thurlkill was a giant of a man with fierce black mustaches; he had lost one eye in battle, but the one remaining, pale blue and glittering, was as sharp as an eagle's when it came to an imperfect sword thrust or a bungling shield defense.

All the Young Men, with the exception of the eldest ones who had progressed to double-handled swords and battle-axes, were terrified of Thurlkill, and Aelfred was no exception. He blessed the time he had spent with Siward—more than once it had saved him from a whack across the back of his legs with a broadsword, Thurlkill's favorite method of reproof. Also, much to his surprise, he did very well at knife throwing. Once the drillmaster had even deigned to smile bleakly at him and say, "You've some of your father's blood in you, I see." And then he had made Aelfred do the overhand throw again, while the others watched. That afternoon in the Young Men's quarters he had been cheered by his comrades, most of whom he still knew only by sight. He had not yet made any special friends among them, not even with Brand son of Halnoth, his swordmate. He liked Brand, however. He wished that Brand were on watch with him now. It would be pleasant to exchange a word with someone during the long hours of standing guard.

But standing guard over the Painted Chamber was an honor not often given to the Young Men. Usually the thanes had that duty. But when the thanes were in council, none could be spared, and this time Aelfred had been chosen. In all modesty, he had to admit that his luck was probably due to the fact that, in assisting Dom Regembald, he was under the King's eye almost every day. However, when Harold had named him as the standing guard over his council, his father had told him, with hardly concealed pride, there had been little objection. Thurlkill had grunted affirmatively, and Esegar of Middlesexe, who carried the royal standard, had nodded approval. Baron Ansculf's eyes had glowed with pleasure, and that pleasure had made up for much of the loneliness of the past month. Even—almost—for not having given him the time and privacy to write to Adelaide.

"You must serve the King well," Ansculf had told him solemnly after he had informed him of the honor given him.

"With all my heart," Aelfred answered, amazed to discover that his throat felt tight, as though he was going to weep.

But his father had not chided his emotion. "There are two

kinds of men, Aelfred. Builders and destroyers. Our King is a builder. May he be spared long enough to build us into a strong nation."

Those words recurred to Aelfred now, as he waited for the council meeting to adjourn. Building a nation was a difficult task, he knew, but far more difficult and complicated than he would ever have dreamed. Who, for instance, would have thought that Duke William would be so obdurate? Or that the barons of Mercia and Northumbria would have remained stubbornly aloof for so long, and that either or both situations could affect the welfare of an entire country? He heard footsteps sounding along the corridor and he grasped his sword. Thanks to Thurlkill, he could now draw it on the instant, but weapons were not bared in the palace except against declared enemies.

"Who comes?" he called sharply.

"A friend to this house," came the answer, and Aelfred recognized the voice of Gyrth Godwineson.

"Gyrth!" he exclaimed joyfully. "Welcome! I hope your news is good. We've had our share of ill today."

"So I've heard," Gyrth replied, but he was smiling. He looked Aelfred up and down. "Great heavens, man, I hardly knew you! You're no longer the sapling you were a month ago. You've become a sturdy oak. How do you like being a soldier?"

"Better every day." Aelfred clasped hands with him. Gyrth had ridden north a few days after the coronation, and he was glad and relieved to see him safely returned. "The King will be overjoyed. He has spoken of you often and anxiously."

"I'm glad I bring good news, then," Gyrth said heartily. "The good barons of Mercia and Northumbria are eager for the King's visitation. They will meet him at York when he arrives there."

"Good! I'm glad to hear it," Aelfred exclaimed. He had copied several letters to the red-bearded brothers, but this was the first indication that they had been received. "But should we be speaking of this before the King hears you?"

"Oh, as to that, Edwin and Morcar have already proclaimed their intentions, so the word is abroad. It's probably already reached Normandy." Gyrth's eyes twinkled. "Nothing like a threat of war to bring the most stubborn men to their senses! All I regret is that time has been lost. Those two could have recognized Harold at once. But, no! They had to sit on their dignities for a month. I very nearly told them to stay sat—that we'd fight the Normans without them."

Aelfred laughed, then became serious. "Why do they want to wait until the King rides north? Why don't they come to Westminster?"

"Because Harald Hardrada, the King of Norway, is getting his fleet together and will begin his spring harrying as soon as the ice melts. They are afraid that, if they leave their lands, Hardrada may seize the occasion for an invasion. _I_ say that Hardrada is Duke William's ally, and that he'll move when William tells him to, whether they're away or not, but they only mutter in their beards about the Norsemen. Stubborn mules!" Gyrth sighed.

"Well, it's known abroad, then, that the King plans to ride north."

"Yes, it's considered a good tactic." Gyrth smiled again. "So, announce me to His Majesty."

Aelfred knocked on the door. Upon command he opened it and said formally, "Gyrth Godwineson asks leave to enter, Sire."

Without answering Aelfred, Harold fairly leaped from his chair at the end of the long table. "Gyrth!" he exclaimed and hurried to meet his youngest brother. He grasped him by the shoulders and embraced him, then stood quietly for a moment, his eyes searching his face. "Is it good news you bring?"

"The best," Gyrth answered triumphantly. "The lords of Mercia and Northumbria will meet with you at York."

A shout of approbation rang through the Painted Chamber. Aelfred moved to close the door, but Harold stopped him. "No need, boy. We are adjourned." He returned to his chair, his face radiant. "The council has finished its business. Our decision to ride north tomorrow will stand, but, happily, we now ride with the good will of our northern brothers. I thank you for your help, my friends. The King will join the feast tonight."

The thanes pushed back the benches and rose as Harold Godwineson left the Painted Chamber. Then they crowded around Gyrth, smiling, talking excitedly, congratulating him. Faces that, an hour before, had been drawn and anxious now broke into laughter. Among the last to congratulate Gyrth was Baron Ansculf, but as he started to leave, Gyrth detained him.

"On my way in, I was stopped by a man who said that he was Osric son of Osric, from your demesne," he said quietly. "He had letters for you and Aelfred. I told him to give them to me, since I would be seeing you immediately, and sent him off to the kitchen for food." He took the packet from his leather pouch. "Here they are. There's one for Rafe of Birnham, too."

Baron Ansculf took them and glanced at the writing. "I don't recognize this hand," he said, frowning. "Aelfred, come here."

Aelfred, who had been setting Dom Regembald's desk in order, came to his side. The baron thrust the packet into his hands, demanding, "Whose writing is this?"

"I don't know. But it's French script," Aelfred replied.

"No trouble, I hope?" Gyrth asked.

"Can't say until I've read it," Ansculf answered shortly. "Here, Aelfred, give them back to me. Finish as quickly as you can with pens and ink, then find Rafe. Tell him there's a letter for him and to meet me at our quarters." He glanced at the letters casually and added, "There seems to be one addressed to you, too, so you'd better come with him."

"Yes, Father," Aelfred replied, truly admiring the way in which his father always managed to put to use the little reading he could do. Quickly he returned to his task. Never, it seemed, had there been so many pens to mend, and the inkpot was empty. He was consumed with curiosity over the letter for himself. It was not possible that Adelaide—he swallowed and felt his face burn. No, it was not possible. He had not written to her. But—could it be, anyway?

77

He found Rafe of Birnham enjoying a cup of mead in the Princes' Chamber with some of the other thanes. The moment he walked through the door, Rafe hailed him, and someone thrust a cup into his hand.

"We're drinking the King's health," Rafe said jovially.

"Death to all his enemies," Aelfred promptly answered, and drained the cup at one draught while everyone applauded. "Rafe, my father wants you. There are letters for us from Storches Hundred."

"Letters? Nor for me." Rafe refilled his cup. "Who'd write to me?"

"I don't know. He said only that we must come as quickly as possible."

Rafe grinned at him. "There's one for you, too?"

"That's why the boy's so eager," one of the thanes crowed. "Does a sweeting wait for you at home, Aelfred?"

"You're a deep one, Aelfred Ansculfson," another chuckled.

Aelfred, a little embarrassed at their laughter, still hoping for word from Adelaide, looked imploringly at Rafe, who pulled himself from his chair. "I'll not be long," he told his friends. "Don't broach the new cask until I return."

Baron Ansculf was pacing up and down the thanes' hall when they arrived. He had sent for candles and drawn three stools up to a small table. "Good, you're here," he said and handed the first letter to Aelfred. "It's in French, confound it, so you'll have to read it to us. Here's yours, Rafe."

Rafe sat down and broke the seal of his letter. "It's from Adelaide," he said, surprised. "Something must be amiss. She never writes to me."

"Who's mine from, Aelfred?" Ansculf asked impatiently.

"Tancred," Aelfred replied. "He writes very strangely. He says there's grave trouble at Storches Hundred and respectfully urges that you return as quickly as possible. He conveys to you his most filial sentiments—"

"Never mind his sentiments! Does he say what the trouble is?"

"No, he doesn't."

"Neither does Adelaide," said Rafe. "She says that she's writ-

78

ten Aelfred as much as she—" He squinted at the line. "She says, 'As much as I dare.' That's a strange word for her to use."

"Nothing more?"

"No, only that you must come at once."

Ansculf sighed. "Read your letter, Aelfred. I hope she tells us what is wrong."

Aelfred took it from the table and carefully broke the seal. The sight of Adelaide's handwriting made him tremble, and he hoped they would not notice. A man should be able to read his betrothed's letter in private, he thought wistfully, but nothing was as it should be in these times. He began to read, then gasped.

"She says that Mab has been accused of sorcery and that the people are demanding that she be put to trial by ordeal," he cried. All thoughts but the need to get to Adelaide quickly and to help her were swept out of his mind. "She says that Mab was nearly burned alive in her cot."

"Not by our people?" the baron asked incredulously.

"Yes. Saewulf was leading them, and only Tancred's happening to be there stopped them."

"Merciful God!" Ansculf sat down. "They've gone mad. And how did Tancred 'just happen' to be there? And Adelaide, too? I must go home at once."

"Ansculf, you cannot." Rafe shook his head emphatically. "The King rides north tomorrow. What is your reeve doing? He is a good and trustworthy man."

"Adelaide says he is doing all he can," Aelfred replied, "but that the anger of our own people is being inflamed to the point of violence." He paused, then added in a low tone, "She says that she is terribly afraid."

"That settles it. I go home tomorrow," Ansculf decided.

"No," Rafe insisted. "No, Ansculf. Let your reeve take care of it. You know how women exaggerate."

"But you said yourself that 'dare' was a strange word for Adelaide to use. Something is very wrong, Rafe."

"But surely nothing that calls for you to change all your plans. The King has commanded you to ride with him."

"Father—" Aelfred began, then fell silent. The thought of

79

Mab's life being endangered made him angry, and Adelaide's fear made his blood run cold. There was more to this than met the eye, and his suspicion had immediately fixed upon Tancred. But the enormity of what he was about to propose made him quake.

"Father, send me," he said, glad that his voice did not tremble, but that it gained in steadiness as he continued to think and speak. "Send me with the power of sake and soke. Our people have been aroused against Mab somehow, and they will not listen to Siward because he is really one of them. But they will listen to me." He clenched his fists. "I will make them listen to me."

"You were to ride with the Young Men," Ansculf said slowly.

"I know. But I shall not be missed in the company as you would be. And once the folkmoot has met and Mab is safe, I can ride north and join you."

Rafe nodded his head. "It sounds like a good plan, Ansculf."

"But we don't know yet where the King will go after he leaves York," Ansculf worried. "He may think it wise to visit all the northern thanes while he is there. Aelfred could be chasing us for weeks."

"Didn't His Majesty say that he plans to visit the shrine at Walsingham on his return south? Aelfred could wait for us there."

"So he could." Ansculf pondered for several minutes; then he rose and looked searchingly at his son.

"I am not easy about your going, and I'm not going to pretend that I am. I have a foreboding—but no matter." Solemnly he put his hands on Aelfred's shoulders. "Take and hold sake and soke of Storches Hundred. And beware of Saewulf. He's an ugly one—a destroyer."

"He'll do me no harm," Aelfred assured him, though his own forebodings were strong and his heart felt like lead.

"Osric son of Osric who brought the letters is in the kitchen. Seek him out. Maybe he can tell you more. But both of you leave here as early as possible tomorrow. I'll make your farewells to the King."

"Yes, Father. And we'll meet at Walsingham." Those words gave some comfort.

Ansculf nodded. Then, quite unexpectedly, he clasped Aelfred in his arms. Aelfred embraced him, blinking back his tears, then turned to Rafe, who took his hand.

"Commend me to Adelaide. Say I'm well," he said gruffly. "And follow us soon."

Before dawn the next morning, Aelfred was on his way to Storches Hundred. Osric son of Osric rode at his side. Aelfred questioned him closely, but the churl could or would tell him no more than he had already known from the letters. His stolid face showed neither concern nor guilt when he spoke of the attempted burning; clearly, Aelfred thought, Osric was the sort who neither questioned nor answered as long as he was not bothered, and he evidently had little to bother him. Or perhaps he had been ordered to say nothing about the grave situation on the demesne and was afraid to disobey. As Aelfred listened to the boy's brief words, he realized that it was useless to expect anything from him except comment about the state of the demesne fields. He became eager only to reach Storches Hundred, hoping and praying, if fate could be so kind, that somehow, miraculously, the storm over Mab had subsided. But this hope was a faint one, and his heart beat heavily with dread.

A little less than a mile from the stockade, he saw the figure of a horseman waiting in the middle of the road. Hand on his dagger hilt, he slowed his pace a little, motioning to Osric to ride alongside him. But the horseman made no effort either to come forward to meet them or to leave. Then, as Aelfred recognized Siward the reeve, he raised his arm in greeting.

"*Haele!*" he shouted, digging his heels into his horse's flanks. A few moments later, he had reined beside Siward. "How did you know I was coming today?"

"I didn't," Siward answered, "but I prayed. I've been praying every day. Thank God my prayers were heard. Had you not come today—" He shook his head.

"Siward, what *is* happening?"

"Not yet." The reeve gave him a warning look, then let his eyes flicker towards the churl who waited near them. "You ride on ahead, Osric," he said. "I'll escort Lord Aelfred to the hall."

Osric nodded and rode past them, then turned in at a by-track and disappeared. Aelfred watched, dumbfounded.

"Don't tell me you're afraid to speak before Osric?" he protested.

"I'm afraid to speak before anyone," Siward replied tartly. "Answer me one question. Do you hold sake and soke?"

"Yes, I do. Rafe of Birnham witnessed it."

"That should help matters. And you're the atheling, which ought to mean something to them, too. I've tried to make them see reason, but they won't listen. It is all that I can do to keep their violence in check. I've managed thus far to protect Mab, but what would have happened if you'd stayed away much longer, I would not want to guess."

"I can't believe it, Siward. It's like a nightmare. What sent them off against Mab?"

"I don't know, but I have my suspicions. How much did Lady Adelaide tell you in her letter?"

"All she knew, I think. She said all she dared. Siward, you're quaking like an aspen."

"It's partly relief at seeing you alive, I guess." The reeve drew his hand across his brow. "There's something afoot here, Aelfred. Ever since Guilbert de Belleme came a month ago—"

"He came here?" Aelfred's intuition leaped to bridge the gap. "I suppose he and Tancred talked much together?"

"Constantly, hours at a time, in Lady Ygerne's bower. He's not here now, though. He took himself off on the day of the burning."

Aelfred shivered. "You think he may have started the trouble?"

"Yes, though I can't prove it. So does Lady Adelaide, now. She was blind at first, too. We have all been blind."

"What do you mean about Lady Adelaide?" Aelfred asked sharply.

"Oh, she did nothing against Mab. But she and Tancred rode together often. Ever since the burning, though, she's locked herself in her bower and has refused even to speak to him."

He dismissed the flicker of jealousy. Tancred had not won Adelaide over, and that was what mattered. "She wrote to me that she was afraid."

"So she is. So am I. The entire demesne listens only to Tancred. He rides out every morning, visiting the cots. And the people have come every day, demanding that Mab face a trial by ordeal. I've refused and said there had to be a folk-moot. They tried to shout me down, but I would not give into them. Finally they agreed to wait, but only after Tancred had spoken to them."

"And they listened to Tancred? A Norman?"

Siward sighed heavily. "I've learned a lot these past weeks about our people, Aelfred. I once thought they were loyal to your father and you. I've changed my mind. They are loyal to those who promise them what they want, or think they want. They've never liked Mab because she's Welsh, and she can speak better than they can and knows things they don't. They feel she is a favorite of your father's, and they resent it. They forget that she was his nurse and yours, and that she cared for your mother. They don't care. They have the chance to hurt her now, and they're taking it, thanks to Tancred."

"But surely they hate Normans more than they resent Mab!"

"Oh, yes, some do. They might even fight, if called upon. The rest—" Siward sighed bitterly. "You may as well hear it first as last. They've been promised that these lands will be theirs outright when Duke William becomes King."

In spite of himself, Aelfred trembled. But he spoke bravely. "Duke William will find the road to Westminster a long, hard one. And he may not reach it. Has Tancred told them this?"

"I have, but they will not listen. They're fools, especially Saewulf. Even if his son is dead, that's not to say that Mab is responsible."

"Wait, wait!" Aelfred drew to a halt. "Mab cured his son. Now you say the boy is dead?"

"That's why Saewulf led the burning. Tancred stopped them; I'll give him that much. It was horrible, Lady Adelaide said."

There was a long pause while Aelfred tried desperately to think in orderly fashion. The situation was more tangled and sinister than he had believed possible. "Saewulf is accusing Mab of murder, then, as well as sorcery?" he asked, his indignation growing with every word. "That's monstrous. What proof does he have?"

"None. What could he have? Saewulf is being influenced by Lord Tancred. Mab isn't guilty."

"Of course she isn't." Aelfred started to ride again. "In the absence of proof, the verdict will be no guilt. The law is explicit. We have nothing to fear."

A faint smile came to Siward's lips. "It gladdens my heart to hear you say it. And with you sitting in judgment, they'll have to listen."

The stockade was just a few feet ahead. Suddenly Aelfred turned to Siward. "Father Owain!" he exclaimed. "He surely doesn't believe that Mab is guilty. He'll help her at the folkmoot."

"Didn't Lady Adelaide tell you?" Siward looked his grief and dismay. "Father Owain is in Wales. Family illness, the message said. He's been gone for three weeks."

A cold chill again struck Aelfred. "Merciful Heaven deliver us! Have we no priest, then?"

Siward shook his head. His voice was almost inaudible. "I feel as though the devil has us at his mercy."

"No!" Aelfred cried violently, quelling the fear that rushed over him like a wind. "Things will be harder, that is true. But with the help of God, right must prevail." He raised his head high, and his voice rose in defiance. "Now!" He drew to a halt. "Call out my name, Siward. Proclaim me at the gates! Let the whole world know that the atheling of Storches Hundred has been sent by his father to see that justice is done on this demesne!"

THE great gates had scarcely closed behind him and Aelfred had just dismounted when Adelaide came running towards him across the court. She was not wearing a cloak, and her hair was flying in the wind. With a cry of "Thanks be to Our Lady that you've come!" she ran into his outstretched arms, weeping as though her heart would break. Aelfred clasped her to him tightly, and, when she did not stop crying, kissed the tears as they fell on her cheeks. At last she raised her face and his lips found hers. In that instant, all else was forgotten in the surge of joy that welled up in him as he felt her heart pounding against his own.

"Adelaide," he whispered, "I love you! Oh, my sweeting, my dear one, I love you more than life itself."

He held her a moment longer, then reluctantly released her. She was no longer weeping, but her lips were trembling and her tense fingers clutched at his arm. "Aelfred, we must talk about Storches Hundred at once," she said urgently.

"Of course, my darling. But had I better not see Mab first? She should know that I've come."

"No—*no!* That above all else you must not do," she answered. "Siward will tell her. You must listen to me first."

He saw the reeve at the far end of the courtyard, walking towards the little huts where the demesne prisoners were kept on the rare occasions when there were any. "Very well," he agreed. "We'll go indoors. You can't stay out here." He tried to make her smile. "You are shaking with cold. Even your teeth are chattering."

He wrapped a fold of his own cloak around her and drew her to him.

"I told you that I loved you a moment ago. Did you not hear?"

"I heard." She smiled gravely. "It made me stop weeping. But now we must speak of you. You are in terrible danger, my dearest."

They walked swiftly to the little bower, and it was not until they were inside with the door bolted that she spoke again. Then she said ruefully, "It is about as cold here as outside. I'm sorry. I'm not very good about fires."

"I am." Aelfred put some sticks and moss from the metal container into the firepit, struck the iron on the flint, and blew. "We'll have it warmer presently. Doesn't your maid tend it for you?"

"I have no maid. I dismissed her"—she shuddered—"on the day of the burning. I was afraid. I did not think I could trust her any longer."

"Did she return to Birnham, then?"

"No. She's still here. I see her sometimes, with *him*." Her emphasis left no doubt that it was Tancred she meant.

Aelfred led her to a chair near the firepit and knelt beside her. He took her cold hands in his. "Now tell me all you couldn't write, Adelaide. Why are you all so frightened?"

She swallowed hard. "On the day of the burning, I was riding with Tancred."

"I know. Siward told me."

"Oh, I've been very foolish. You hadn't written and I was cross. So, when Tancred asked me to ride—"

"You had the right to ride with him, if it pleased you," Aelfred said gently. "He *is* my stepbrother, and foster brother, too."

"It was not especially to give me pleasure that he invited me," she said bitterly. "He had paid little attention to me, really, until his uncle came, and I less to him. Then, after those two talked together, he was very insistently attentive. I realize that, now." She looked at him intently. "Aelfred, would you think me mad if I told you that I think he deliberately planned to have me see the burning?"

"That would mean that he also arranged the burning," he said slowly.

"I think he did. Afterwards I remembered seeing him talking often with Saewulf in the courtyard. Oh, I have no proof, but I'm sure Tancred is at the bottom of everything. I am sure he is!"

"So am I. But why should he want you to see such a thing?"

She clung to his hand. "Because he wanted to bring you to Storches Hundred."

"But his letter was to my father."

"He knew that your father would hold his duty to his King above even his love for Storches Hundred. Quite probably Tancred's uncle told him that your father could not come. Siward is certain that de Belleme is a spy."

"I see. At least, I think I see. He was counting on my father's taking his letter seriously enough to send me in his place. But why does that put me in danger? I am the atheling. I hold sake and soke. At the folkmoot tomorrow, the final judgment will be mine and Mab will be released. I promise you that."

She shook her head. Her eyes darkened and her face became white as chalk. "Aelfred," she said, "what is the punishment for one who aids and defends a witch?"

He gasped. He felt as though an iron claw were clutching his throat. "The punishment is death. But there is no question of that. Mab is not a witch."

"Aelfred, please listen!" Adelaide cried vehemently. "I'm horrified about Mab, but it's you I care for. You! If you defend Mab, or even see her, Tancred will be able to accuse you of defending witchcraft—or worse."

"How do you know?"

87

"I don't." She clasped her hands tightly. "That is, no one has said it in so many words. But it would take someone much less shrewd than I not to know from Tancred's smug look and the smiles he exchanged with his mother and uncle that they are planning some devilment against you. What easier way could there be to dispose of you and for Tancred to take over Storches Hundred?"

"Oh, Adelaide! Darling!" He put his hand on her shoulder. "You're hysterical. You forget the law. If there is no proof of Mab's guilt, and I'm sure there is none, she'll be freed. I'm not aiding anyone. I'm merely the judge."

She buried her face in her hands. "You won't see," she moaned. "You're blind." She looked up at him again and said hopelessly, "If I tell you that he tried to lead up to a proposal of marriage to me, will you still believe that he is not using every ounce of his wit to be rid of you?"

He stared at her incredulously. Anger began to burn in him. "He didn't dare do that?"

"He dared. Oh, I blame myself. I should never have gone riding with him. But I told him no, and plainly, too."

Before Aelfred could answer, there was a sharp rap at the door. Siward called his name, and Aelfred unbarred it to admit him.

"I must speak to you, Aelfred Ansculfson," he said quickly. "I've seen Mab. She's rejoiced at your return, but she says that you must not come to her."

"Adelaide has been telling me the same thing," Aelfred replied.

"For the same reason, I'll wager. You must not seem to defend a witch."

"She is not a witch!" Aelfred cried impatiently. "I'm tired of listening to that senseless accusation."

"Mab says further, and you had better heed her. She says that Tancred de Belleme is determined to have her judged a witch so that you will defend her, and then he will have an excuse to attack you. To save your own life, you must let a guilty verdict stand."

"But there's been no verdict yet," Aelfred retorted. Then he stopped short as he realized the horrible import of Siward's

88

words. "Do you mean that the men of Storches Hundred have already decided?"

"Enough of them stand with Saewulf to make a majority in a vote. Mab begs you to decree for them."

"She's gone mad. She knows what that means!" Aelfred paced frantically up and down. "So do you. Trial by hot iron! She'd never survive it."

"If you defend her or judge in her favor, it will mean the same for you," Adelaide said hollowly. "You must do as we ask. Mab does not want you to die."

For several minutes he was too stunned to speak. Fear left him shaken and spent. When he could finally open his lips, he hardly recognized his voice.

"You are telling me that for me to live Mab must die," he said tautly. "Well"—painfully he drew a deep breath—"I don't believe it. I can't believe it. It would take a fiend to frame such a plot. I loathe Tancred, even more since you've told me of his effrontery, Adelaide. But I don't think the devil has taken complete possession of him."

Again there was silence.

"But even if that were true," he continued, "I could not do otherwise than defend Mab. I could not look my face in the mirror if I let her be judged guilty when I know her innocent. Can you understand that?"

He addressed his last words to Adelaide, who looked at him mutely. Finally she nodded. "Yes, I understand," she said. "I think I could not love you so much if you did anything else."

He bowed his head and kissed her hand, then held it to his cheek. Siward cleared his throat.

"Very well," the reeve said brusquely. "As I said on the road, they ought to listen to you, so have it your way. But do us one kindness. Keep away from Mab until the folkmoot. You are the judge and must be impartial. No use in giving opportunity for tongues to wag."

"I'll concede that much," Aelfred agreed.

"I think you had better keep to yourself until tomorrow, too. Do not see either Tancred or Lady Ygerne. Where will you sleep tonight?"

"In the baron's bower. Have it made ready." Aelfred raised

his head proudly. "Tonight I shall dine in my own hall. I've come home in honor, Siward, not skulking like a fugitive. Adelaide will sit at my table, and so shall Tancred and his mother, if they wish. Tell them so for me."

For the first time that morning, Siward laughed. "By the Rood," he said, nodding vigorously, "I never thought it possible, but you're behaving exactly like your grandfather as I remember him. Shall I tell Ecfrith baron's-steward to summon musicians as well?"

"Please do. Then go to the stable and have fresh horses saddled. I must ride out, and I want you with me." He bolted the door after Siward had gone, then turned to Adelaide. "You will dine in hall tonight, won't you?"

She smiled and, in a movement swift as lightning, kissed his cheek. "Wild boars could not keep me away," she promised. "You almost make me believe that my fears are foolish, and that all will be well."

Her kiss sent the blood racing through his veins. "When all this business is settled, we shall talk properly," he promised. "What a way for a man to have to treat his betrothed!"

"I am not complaining," she answered. "We have said that we love each other. Is more talk needed?"

"No—but this." He drew her to him in a tight embrace, then hurried from the bower.

The next day broke clear and cold, and the sun was shining when Siward came to fetch him. Aelfred, weaponless, wrapped in a heavy cloak, walked beside the reeve to the Tree of Justice, an old oak just outside the stockade. Though the baron was judge of all disputes on the demesne, ancient custom decreed that trials might not take place in his hall. There must not be the slightest indication that the impartiality of the law would not be scrupulously observed. With the exception of the baron's reeve, no member of his personal household might attend. For that same reason, no man might come to a folkmoot bearing arms. Evidence and proof were the only weapons admitted here.

Aelfred was confident as he took his place on the stool of

justice under the tree. The men of Storches Hundred were making their way across the field, Saewulf and three others in the lead, the rest following. The women, of course, were at home. No woman ever attended a folkmoot; it had been with great difficulty that he had persuaded Adelaide that she must observe that custom. He smiled, remembering her insistence, how she had said, "I'll dress as a boy, then. But I want to come." She had been most disappointed at his firm refusal, but he was glad that she seemed to have recovered from some of her fear. Never again, he vowed, would she be frightened, as long as he lived.

He looked up at Siward, standing solemnly beside him. "Have you seen Tancred this morning?"

"No. But I heard that he rode out early," the reeve answered.

"Really? He drank so much wine last night, I thought he'd still be abed," Aelfred commented, putting aside a slight uneasiness at the news.

"Arrogant young whelp!" Siward's eyes flashed. "If he had any sense of what was fitting, he'd have dined with his mother in her bower."

"I must admit that he has more gall than character," Aelfred said disgustedly. "Few men we know, if any, would have had the gall to come, under the circumstances. He must know that we suspect him of having some part in this fracas."

"He's a brazen Norman, and I trust him less when he's quiet than when he speaks." Siward frowned. "I was going to advise you to hold the folkmoot within the stockade, but I knew it would be no use."

"Certainly not," Aelfred said sharply. "Only in time of war or siege may that be done."

"Well, we might as well be under both. Tancred has declared war on us."

"We cannot break the law, Siward."

The men were almost within speaking distance. Aelfred's eyes narrowed as he watched them. He noticed how the expression of dogged determination on Saewulf's face changed slightly when he saw who occupied the stool of justice.

Good! His presence was a surprise. Siward had been right in his insistence that no one but himself and Adelaide should know who now held sake and soke.

He looked at the group ranged in front of him. His steady gaze went from one man to the next, holding each man's eyes with his own. He knew them all, and he thought he could count on the friendship of a few: Elred, the head shepherd, and his son Wilnoth; Dodda, who had charge of the stables; Thored and Thurgood, the blacksmiths; Osric son of Osric, attending his first folkmoot since his father's death a year ago. Not many, but they were sensible men. They might be enough.

"You have come seeking justice. Justice you shall have," he said formally. "Who wishes to speak?"

"I do." Saewulf stepped forward. He was a big man with an untidy mane of black hair streaked with gray. "I accuse Mab wife of Wulfric of sorcery."

"The law decrees that an accused person has the right to meet his accuser face to face and hear him." The centuries' old formula came smoothly from Aelfred's lips. Not for nothing had he sat in the King's presence and copied his dispatches. "Where is Mab wife of Wulfric?"

"She may not appear," Saewulf protested. "No woman appears at a folkmoot."

"She is accused of a crime," Aelfred said sternly. "The law I have just spoken applies to her. Where is she?"

"They are bringing her now," Siward answered quietly.

Aelfred looked towards the stockade where the gates had opened wide enough to let two men pass. Between them walked Mab, huddled in a cloak, her gray head uncovered. His heart welled up at the sight. He could not keep from showing his sympathy, despite the whispering of Saewulf's supporters.

"Who is with Mab?" he asked Siward quietly. "I don't recognize them."

"Beorn and Eshern, sons of Thurgood blacksmith," Siward answered. "Home from border guarding for spring plowing. Both good sensible lads."

"I hope so," Aelfred murmured. Mab stood before him now, and the look of her cut him to the quick. She was so frail among all these burly men, but the air of pride had not left her, nor the flash in her eyes.

"Mab wife of Wulfric, you have been summoned to hear accusation against you," he said over the lump in his throat. "Saewulf, you may speak."

Saewulf stood boldly. "My son is dead by her bewitchment," he declared in a voice as raw as the wind.

"How do you answer, Mab?" Aelfred asked.

"What does it matter how she answers?" A voice spoke from the rear. "She is guilty. Let her die."

"No, the hot iron first," another said gleefully.

"Silence!" Aelfred thundered. The men stopped their murmuring and stared at him. "We shall act like men freeborn, not savages. As long as I sit here, we proceed according to the law. Now, Mab, how answer you?"

"I am not guilty," Mab replied firmly. "His son was ill of an ague, but I cured him of that with proper medicines within five days." She turned to face the men. "He was walking and well. You saw him yourselves."

"That is true. I did." The speaker was Thored. "He did not fall ill and take to his bed in death until—"

"Until when?" Aelfred asked. He had been right about Thored, though now the blacksmith seemed to falter.

"I—I don't remember," he mumbled.

"I remember." Osric son of Osric stepped forward. "It was the day before the burning. We were in the kitchen together when he said he had a monstrous pain about his vitals. Then he fainted."

"That's not true!" Saewulf cried furiously. "He'd been ailing for days before that. It was Mab's medicine that poisoned him."

"Are you changing your accusation, Saewulf?" Aelfred asked. Things were proceeding better than he'd dared to hope. Osric should be commended for his honesty and plain speaking. His words had visibly disconcerted some of Saewulf's friends.

"What do you mean?" Saewulf asked truculently.

"First you accused Mab of causing your son's death by be-witchment. Now you say that she poisoned him."

"What difference does it make? The boy is dead and she killed him."

Saewulf's firm supporters drew nearer to him, but others looked at him uncertainly. Aelfred pressed his advantage.

"What evidence do you have of poison?" he asked. "There's not a poisonous herb within miles of Mab's cot, though I noticed yesterday that her garden had been trampled and her house almost torn to pieces. You searched them, didn't you? What poison did you find?"

"None," Mab said in a clear high voice. "There was none to find."

"*He* must answer, Mab," Aelfred said gently. "Well, Sae-wulf? Any poisonous herbs? Toadstools? Serpent's fangs? Bat's eyes?"

Some of the men were smiling, and Osric laughed aloud. Saewulf glared at them. "No," he muttered, "but that doesn't mean she didn't have them hidden."

"That's right." The man who had spoken so gleefully of the hot iron raised his voice again. "She could have bewitched them away."

"The law says that if two accusations come at once, they must be considered separately. We'll get to bewitchment presently. Let's dispose of the poison first. Saewulf, you've heard two men declare that your son was cured of the ague he took sick of on Twelfth Night. Do you dispute them?"

Saewulf looked for a moment as though he would dispute the world, but then thought better of it. "No," he said surlily.

"Good. Now, answer me this. To your knowledge, did your son see, meet, or talk with Mab between the time she cured him of his first ague and the time he fell ill of the second? To your knowledge, remember, and as you hope to see salvation."

"No," Saewulf answered reluctantly, obviously cowed.

"Does anyone else here have such knowledge?"

There were a few whispers, then all the men shook their heads.

"There is no evidence of poison, either by its being found at Mab's dwelling or by her having sight or voice of your son. I think we can rule that she is not guilty of murder by poison."

"She bewitched him, then!" Saewulf shook his fist. "I say she bewitched him, just as she bewitched my cows last year."

"You put your son and your cows in the same category?" Aelfred asked blandly. "As I recall, the folkmoot acquitted Mab of poisoning your cows for lack of evidence."

"There was evidence," Saewulf insisted. He pointed a thick finger at Mab. "But she bewitched—"

"My father?" Aelfred interrupted. "Your words are foolish, Saewulf. Let us keep to the point. What evidence have you that Mab bewitched your son?"

"She bewitched him because she's a witch!"

"What evidence do you have of that?"

"Hang your evidence and all your fine words!" Saewulf was beside himself with rage. "I say she's a witch."

Aelfred surveyed the group calmly. "Does anyone else say so?"

There was no answer. Then Thored the blacksmith cleared his throat. "I never held she was," he said brusquely. "I think no one here held so, except Saewulf and some he persuaded. There are some of us, Lord Atheling, who like no part of this. I was not at the burning, nor was my brother."

"Nor was I," said Dodda the stablekeeper.

"Nor I, nor my son," said Elred the head shepherd. "We came here today minded to tell you so."

"I thank you," Aelfred said gravely. Inwardly he rejoiced. He glanced at Siward, who nodded approvingly. Yes, the people of this demesne—his people—were listening to him. And he was no longer afraid to act as their atheling. He turned to Saewulf. "All men here are not of your opinion. Does your accusation stand?"

"Yes!" Saewulf shouted. "The law holds—you see, Atheling, I know the law, too—that a person accused of witchcraft must submit to trial by ordeal. I demand that Mab wife of Wulfric be compelled to walk the hot iron. We'll soon see whether she's a witch or not." He looked about him triumphantly, but clearly a majority of the others did not agree, so he stared defiantly at Aelfred. "The hot iron," he repeated. "That is the law."

Aelfred shook his head. "Not exactly. The law says that one accused of witchcraft and judged guilty may ask for trial by ordeal to prove his innocence." He looked at Mab and permitted himself to smile. "There has been no judgment, because no evidence of guilt has been brought into this folkmoot, and without evidence there can be no judgment. For the last time I ask, is there such evidence? Whoever has it, let him speak now."

No one said a word. Aelfred drew a deep breath. "Then the accused, Mab wife of Wulfric, is released, to go freely as she will."

Mab, unable to restrain herself any longer, threw herself on her knees before Aelfred. He put his arms around her. "The folkmoot is concluded," he said. "Go your ways, my people, with God's grace."

"Not yet!" A cold voice with the hardness of iron in it came from the back of the group. Through them, almost sauntering, walked Guilbert de Belleme.

Aelfred rose. "You have come unexpectedly, my lord," he said civilly, though he felt as though an icy hand had been laid on his naked shoulder.

"And in time," de Belleme answered. From the pouch at his belt he drew a parchment. "I hold here a warrant, declaring me King's High Reeve of this district. Do you recognize this seal?"

Aelfred took the warrant and glanced at it. The seal was the late King Edward's. "I acknowledge the seal. I do not see the King's signature, however."

"Do you imagine that King Edward signed every document personally?" de Belleme asked suavely. "The warrant holds his seal. That is enough to empower me to pass judgment over all affairs in this district."

Aelfred stared at him. Of all the possibilities, this was one he had never remotely anticipated. He looked at the men of

Storches Hundred, who seemed as bewildered as he. "Surely not in simple domestic affairs," he said in a tone much like de Belleme's, though his gorge rose within him. "There is nothing here of sufficient moment to warrant the attention of the King's High Reeve."

"It would be interesting if this discussion could continue, but there is no time," de Belleme replied and, raising his voice, called a few words in French. Before Aelfred or any of the others could move, a company of soldiers appeared—seemingly from nowhere—and surrounded them. Two laid hold of Mab, who screamed pitifully as they dragged her towards the stockade.

"Stop! What kind of devils are you?" Aelfred cried as he started after them, but more soldiers fell on him and threw him to the ground. In a blaze of fury, he rose sufficiently to flail at the Red Lions on their tunics. Red Lions! Norman soldiers! He could hear the shouts of the men of Storches Hundred, not one of them armed, as they fought barehanded against Norman swords and daggers. He caught a glimpse of Saewulf, hurtling himself against a Norman. There was a flash of steel and Mab's accuser lay on the ground, blood welling out of a wound in his throat.

"You killed him—he was unarmed—" Aelfred shouted. "Cowards!" Strong arms dragged him to Guilbert de Belleme. The other men had stopped fighting and were looking dazedly down at Saewulf.

"Let the rest of these English swine go back to their sties," de Belleme said, as though nothing whatever had happened. "Aelfred Ansculfson, you are hereby arrested in the King's name for the crime of harboring and aiding a witch. But we are merciful." He smiled hatefully. "We shall not execute you until you have had the opportunity to prove your innocence. You and the witch woman shall walk the hot iron at midday tomorrow."

Aelfred stared at him. The soldier next him seized him by the arm. Then he heard laughter, low, malicious, triumphant. Under the oak tree, on the stool of justice, sat Tancred.

Aelfred, with a strength born of rage he did not know he

possessed, broke from his captor and went straight to the grinning Norman. "You—you man without a name!" he cried. "You have done this. And before God, you shall suffer for it!"

The soldiers seized him again and Tancred's laughter grew louder. Aelfred looked at him with all the pent-up loathing he had tried so long to suppress; then, slowly, deliberately, he spat at him full in the face. Tancred, furious, leaped to his feet and cracked his riding whip around Aelfred's shoulders.

"This is only the beginning of *your* sufferings, Atheling," he taunted.

Tancred's laughter, which Aelfred had so often heard in the hall and to which he had paid little attention, rang now in his ears as Norman soldiers, shouting vile French words, marched him into the stockade.

AELFRED's prison was a stone hut about five feet square inside, with a slitted window through which he could see the head of the Norman soldier stationed there to guard him. The door was barred on the outside, and the stone walls were about two feet thick. When his captors thrust him inside and drew the bolts, he had thought dazedly, This cannot be happening! Not here, in Storches Hundred! But as the hours crawled by, he knew increasingly that he was indeed a prisoner with no means of escape, guilty of nothing but rightly and justly ordering the affairs of his demesne, which Tancred de Belleme coveted. He could hear the voices of Tancred and Guilbert de Belleme directing the Norman soldiers swarming about the court, telling them how to lay the iron plowshares they had gathered, from Heaven alone knew where or how, in a straight line. He heard them discussing how the faggots were to be laid, had even seen them fan the embers to light the fires which would be kept going all night so that the iron would be red hot by midday tomorrow. Over that iron he would be driven. It was unlikely that he would survive. His heart contracted in fear. It was death that he must face, without even the comfort of a priest to pray with him or to give him absolution.

He sat down on the floor, drawing his cloak closely around him, for it was bitter cold. He thought of Mab alone in her prison, facing the same frightful doom. They would make him watch her walk the iron, hear her screams of pain, see her die before they compelled him to the ordeal. If only they could be together now, he might comfort her a little. "The devils," he muttered between clenched teeth. "They have thought of everything and omitted nothing." And Tancred would watch, too, as an important personage, with that horrible smile on his face, certain now that Storches Hundred would be his. He would sit in the great hall on the high seat. True, Baron Ansculf would ultimately hear and return. Aelfred's heart quickened in hope for an instant, but as quickly slowed down. It might be months before word reached his father, and, in those months, Tancred could make the demesne safe for Duke William. The people could not fight him with Norman steel at their throats. Even Saewulf, who had so briefly allied himself with de Belleme, had not escaped. Tancred would have everything his way. He might even force Adelaide to marry him. Aelfred groaned aloud. Hatred for Tancred, black and murderous, swept over him like a gale in a storm. He leaped to his feet and paced up and down the tiny hut, shouting every curse against him that he knew.

A snigger outside the window brought him to his senses. The guard had been watching. Aelfred stared coldly at the grinning face and turned his back on it. Above all things he must not let the Normans think him a coward. That would be too great a shame. If the line of Aelfred Iron Fist, the old baron, must die, it must die honorably. And he must forego this hatred. It could not harm Tancred, but he could surely damn himself by it. He fell to his knees. At Canterbury he had often chanted the prayers for the dying. He forced himself to be quiet, then whispered his last confession and prayed that his sins would be forgiven. He prayed for Mab. Then he recited the Psalms. Gradually he grew calmer. Destiny had decreed his death tomorrow, and if destiny could not be thwarted, it could be met with courage.

He did not know how long he had stayed on his knees. He

knew that it was dark outside the prison when he heard a strange sound at the door and something fall with a dull and heavy thud. Then the bolts were drawn back and the door opened a little way. A man in a dark cloak slid into the prison hut, whispering, "Lord Atheling, come with me."

"Who are you?" Aelfred thought he recognized the voice even in a whisper.

"Osric son of Osric," the answer came. "Hurry! Don't ask questions. The Normans are in the hall, except for a few watching the fires."

"And the guard?" Aelfred asked, breathing deeply as he stepped gratefully into the open air.

Osric pointed to the ground.

Aelfred stared, first relieved, then appalled. "Is he dead?"

"I hope so," Osric said grimly, replacing the door bolts. "Keep in the shadows. Don't talk."

They kept walking swiftly, softly, at a distance from the horrible fires, hardly daring to breathe until they stopped at the bath hut. Here Osric scratched at the door, which was opened part way.

"Inside," he said urgently. "They mustn't see the light."

The light was a wick burning in a clay saucer full of oil. It revealed Thurgood, standing before a gaping hole in the floor.

"You've done it!" Osric said breathlessly. He turned to Aelfred. "Thurgood and his brother have been in here all afternoon, opening the drain. Wilnoth and I kept watch."

"But what—" Aelfred began bewilderedly.

"The drain goes to the river. Thored's been and back," Thurgood explained. "He said it was a tight squeeze for him, but that you and Osric should be able to manage without much trouble. You'll be outside in half an hour."

Aelfred began to shake. "Where is Thored now?"

Thurgood chuckled. "Gone to get some mortar, so we can patch the floor after you've reached the river."

Aelfred shook his head. "Thurgood, I can't let you. They'll kill you if they find out."

"They won't find out," the blacksmith said calmly, rubbing

his huge hands on his thighs. "Between their carousing in the hall and their fires, they've no time for anything else. They thought they'd frightened us! 'English swine,' he called us!" His eyes blazed. "Better English swine than Norman jackals! Did you think we'd let you walk the hot iron?"

"I—I can't find words." Aelfred's voice shook with emotion. "But I must not go. There's Mab. I can't leave her alone with them."

Osric and Thurgood exchanged glances. Then Osric said, "Mab is dead, Lord Atheling."

"Dead? Did they—"

"No," Thurgood said quickly. "It was the fright at what had happened to you. She was half dead when they brought her into the stockade, poor soul. Lady Adelaide found her. When she heard what had happened at the folkmoot, she insisted on going to the prison hut. But Mab was already dead."

"Rest her soul in peace." Heartbroken, Aelfred crossed himself. "But—"

"Lord Atheling, you must not wait a moment longer." Osric spoke quickly. "Siward is waiting. We have a plan. You must hurry."

"But Lady Adelaide—I can't leave her. I can't," Aelfred insisted.

Thurgood shook his head. "There are others to care for her," he said. "Never fear. She would want to help you save yourself if she could. For herself, if for no other reason."

Aelfred put his hands on the blacksmith's shoulders. "You have done what few men would dare to do. If ever I am able—" Words failed him for an instant. Then he said, "Please take care of Lady Adelaide!"

"We will, Lord Atheling, never fear," said Thurgood. "Now go."

Osric had already preceded him down the gaping hole, saying, "Come, Lord Atheling. Come quickly!" Aelfred followed him, crawling into the drain. It was dark and very cold, but he could hear Osric just ahead, so he continued to creep after the sound on his hands and knees, as fast as he could. Occasionally something swished across his face, probably a root that had grown through the breached tiles. Once he felt something run over his hand and he shuddered. There were old tales of strange creatures who lived underground, and these were easy to believe now. The air was foul; it stifled his nostrils. But he continued, doggedly, automatically, until finally he saw a little light ahead through the murkiness and caught a whiff of cold clean wind. Minutes later he had pulled himself through the opening and was standing beside Osric, knee deep in the icy river.

"This way," Osric whispered.

They waded the short distance to the bank and clambered out of the water. Osric put two fingers in his mouth and whistled two low notes. When an answering single whistle came, he nodded to Aelfred.

"Siward is there," he said. "Follow me. Make no noise."

Again he led the way and Aelfred followed to where Siward waited in the shadow cast by a ring of beeches. When Aelfred saw him, his eyes so filled with tears he could hardly see his face.

"Siward!" he whispered, embracing him. "I never hoped to see you again. How did you manage to get out of the stockade with the soldiers there?"

"By putting the fear of God into Tancred," the reeve answered. "I reminded him of his oath of fealty to keep the peace. Told him he'd suffer worse blame from Saewulf's death if I were kept from making arrangements for Christian burial, especially since we have no priest. I've been making arrangements of many kinds today!"

"And his uncle let you?"

"He had no choice. His warrant does not include such matters," Siward said brusquely. "I think he was glad of the offer. He saw how our men fought today, and he wants as little of that as possible. So he agreed that what happened to Saewulf was an unfortunate mistake, and that I must naturally do what was customary."

"Double-tongued adder!"

"Yes. But never mind him. We'll attend to him, too, one day. I've brought you a change of clothes, some food, and a little money. You must be well away from Storches Hundred before morning dawn."

Aelfred looked at him despairingly. "Where can I go? How can I leave my lands? And the Lady Adelaide—what of her?"

"She will be cared for, I promise," the reeve said with deadly quietness.

"But how? Tancred will never let her leave. Siward, my blood runs cold at the thought of what he'll do to her, if I go."

"My blood runs cold at the thought of what he'll do to both of you, if you don't go—and at once," Siward retorted. "What good would you be to the lady after the hot iron?"

Aelfred shook his head. "Do you think Saewulf realized what the outcome of his cry for the hot iron would be?"

"He knew before he died. And it was why he died. I saw his face when de Belleme spoke the words against you. He was like a man rousing himself from too much mead. Stop talking, now, and get out of those wet clothes. Put on these I've brought you. They probably won't fit, but at least they're dry and warm."

Without more words, Aelfred stripped and put on the dry undertunic that Siward handed him. Then he put on the coarse wool breeks and bound the leather thongs around his legs.

"You will have to wear your own wet boots." Siward sighed. "I hope they dry out on the way. Now put on this tunic."

Aelfred slipped it over his head and put the black cloak around his shoulders.

"Here is a knife." Siward took his own from his belt. "You'd best hide this money pouch. You've got to look as much like a churl as possible. A few days' dirt will help. The roads are crawling with Norman spies, and de Belleme's arm is long, apparently, so keep away from people as much as possible. Your one hope is to reach the King."

"The King?" Aelfred stared at him. "He is in the north, no one knows where. How can I possibly reach him?"

"You told me that you planned to meet your father at Walsingham shrine, so strike out in that direction. If the King is delayed, you can take sanctuary at the Holy House. Even de Belleme would not dare to touch you there."

Aelfred stood immovable. The prospect was appalling. To travel alone, in a direction unknown to him, when de Belleme's spies would be looking for him? He had been frightened in the prison hut, but that fear was nothing compared to the desolation that gripped him at this moment.

"You will not walk alone, Lord Atheling." Osric, who had been keeping watch, came to his side. "I do not know the way to Walsingham, either, but I know the stars and the way the sun rises and sets each day. And I know the land, as you do not. Together we shall find it."

Aelfred turned to him. How could he ever have considered this man only a stolid churl? At the moment when his own life hung in the balance, Osric knew ways and means of action better than he did himself and gave his help willingly.

"I am everlastingly grateful to you, Osric, but are you sure that you want to face such a danger?" he asked. "I shall be a condemned fugitive. De Belleme will no doubt declare me outlaw when he finds I've gone."

"He will do the same to me, then," Osric said calmly, "and you cannot go alone."

"No, that I cannot," Aelfred admitted. He looked again at Siward. "I go with a heavy heart, my friend. Will you tell me once more, surely, that you will watch over Adelaide carefully —that she will be safe?"

"As far as human wit can devise, my lord, she shall be. But the less you know, the better," Siward said firmly. "God willing, she will meet you at Walsingham. If I know her, she'll not rest or give anyone else rest until she does!" He put his hands on Aelfred's shoulders. "Go with God, Aelfred Ansculfson. Have no fear. Your people will never betray you or your father. Even those who thought they did not care are raging now against the Normans."

"Tell them they must keep the land. One day we shall all be avenged."

"We'll go now, Lord Atheling," Osric urged. "The moon is

beginning to rise, and Siward must be returning before he is missed."

"Call me by name, Osric," Aelfred said slowly, as he turned to go with him. "It is more fitting. I am lord of nothing, now." He looked towards the hall in the distance and raised his arm in farewell. Then he followed Osric out of the grove.

In her bower, Adelaide huddled by the dying fire. She had drawn the curtains across the window to keep out the sight of the iron, but nothing could silence the noise of the carousing in the great hall. The Normans had been feasting since before sunset, and the lateness of the hour seemed only to increase their shouts and laughter and drunken singing. Tancred had boasted that he would sit in the baron's chair, and, had she not managed to drive him from her presence and bolt the door, she would have been forced to sit at table next him and watch him lord it over Storches Hundred. He wanted to humiliate her.

She closed her eyes and held her hands tightly against her head, but she still could not erase the terrible memory of those few moments after she had found Mab dead in the prison hut. After what had seemed to be an eternity of waiting this morning, she had opened her door at the shouting from the gates, thinking that Aelfred was returned in triumph, only to see Norman soldiers dragging Mab between them. Probably she should have shut her door at once; she would never know why, without a moment's hesitation, she had run frantically toward them, forcing her way to the prison hut, knowing that she could do nothing, but still furiously demanding—to their raucous laughter—that the door be opened. Finally she had managed to pull back the heavy wooden bar herself and had gone inside, to find Mab crumpled on the floor. Tancred, of course, had followed her, had forcibly brought her back to her bower, she fighting every step of the way until he had roughly picked her up in his arms. Then she had screamed like a mad-woman, but he had only laughed and told her that now he was master here. She could still hear his voice exulting, "You will obey."

"I will never obey you nor any other Norman," she had

106

cried, and drawn the nails of both hands down the length of his face. He had been so overcome by his own rage and surprise that she could push him out the door, slamming and barring it after him. He had fallen, sprawling in the mud; she had laughed and wept hysterically, drowning out his curses and the jeers of his compatriots who watched.

This was in broad daylight, however. Now, in the cold night, she was afraid. She had taken great satisfaction in driving Tancred away, but she knew that her victory had given her only short respite. Tomorrow Aelfred would surely be forced to walk the hot iron. For a moment she thought wildly of leaving the safety of her bower and going to Aelfred's prison. She could unbar the door and release him, let him try to escape. But he would not escape. The soldiers would seize and kill him, and her, too. No—they would not kill her, she thought bleakly. Tancred de Belleme wanted her alive.

She looked frantically about her. If only she had a knife! Though in that same instant she knew that she would be too fearful ever to turn a weapon on herself. Tears streamed down her cheeks. She had always been strong enough to cope with any situation, and it terrified her to discover that she was so weak and helpless against a force quite outside herself and her experience. Who would have thought it possible that Tancred and his uncle could have accomplished so much evil in so short a time? She mechanically threw another stick onto the fire and stretched her trembling hands over the embers. She was cold, so very cold. She remembered now the surging of her heart when Aelfred kissed her. Would she ever know such joy again?

There was a faint scratching at the door. Cautiously she went to the window and lifted the edge of the curtain a very little. The iron was glowing cruelly in the darkness, but she could see no one. Again she heard the scratching, followed by two light taps. She was frightened, but she quickly decided that, whoever was outside, it could not be Tancred, and there were no soldiers near. She slipped back the bolt and opened the door a crack.

"Who is it? What do you want?" she asked.

"Let me in, my lady. I beg of you, let me in." The face of her visitor was hidden by the hood of her cloak, but Adelaide recognized Ellen's voice.

"Why do you come?" she said harshly. "How do I know that you have not come from *him?* To spy on me—kill me, perhaps?"

"No, no, my lady!" Ellen fell on her knees and clutched at Adelaide's skirts. "I swear by the Holy Rood that he does not know. Let me speak to you."

That desperate plea seemed genuine. "Come in, then," said Adelaide. She re-barred the door, then repeated in a more kindly tone, "Why do you come?"

Ellen threw back her hood and undid her cloak, displaying her bright scarlet kirtle.

Adelaide looked at it with distaste. Once it had belonged to Lady Ygerne. Her momentary sympathy for the girl vanished. She eyed her coldly. "Well?"

"My lady, I come as a friend, no matter what you believe of me," said Ellen. Her lips were trembling so that she could scarcely speak. "I know, may Heaven forgive me, I have given you cause for suspicion. But I swear that I did not know that we harbored snakes here. None of us knew, until today. My lady, Lord Tancred deceived even you for a little while."

"Yes," Adelaide admitted, "but what has that to do with it?"

"You are in terrible danger—"

"I don't need you to tell me that," Adelaide said bitingly.

"You must leave here. Now. At once!"

"Are you mad?" She stared at her. "How can I possibly? I am as much a prisoner as Lord Aelfred."

Ellen came very close to her and whispered, "He is free, my lady."

"*What?*"

"Yes. Siward and the others helped him. They have sent me to you. They will help you, now, if you will do what they have told me to tell you."

The news of Aelfred's escape made her lightheaded. Trembling, she took Ellen by the arm. "You are telling me the truth? He is really free?"

"Yes, my lady."

"Thanks be to God," Adelaide whispered.

"And now, we must free you, too. You and I must change clothes—"

"Change clothes? Why?"

"I was very careful, but some one of them may have seen me come here. If anyone did, then it will be well to let him think that I am the one who is leaving. We are the same height, and under the hood of my cloak no one will recognize you. The soldiers have not seen enough of you to know how you look."

"Lord Tancred knows. So do his mother and uncle."

"Lady Ygerne is asleep," Ellen replied. "I gave her her posset myself. As for the others, they have drunk so much that they will probably sleep in the hall tonight. Most of them are almost insensible already."

"Their natural condition." Adelaide grimaced. "Very well. We will change clothes. What then?"

"You must go to the stable gate. Siward will be waiting, or, if he cannot come, someone he trusts. There is a plan, my lady. I do not know what it is. I am only to follow orders. It is better that I should not know more than that."

Something in Ellen's tone made Adelaide stop short. The girl's eyes were huge and black with shadows; her face was pale as death. "And you, Ellen?" she asked. "What will you do?"

"Stay here. With your permission, my lady, I will sleep in your bed tonight. I think I can imitate your voice if anyone should come. I'll keep the door barred so that no one will know that you've gone."

"But tomorrow!" The complete realization of what Ellen actually meant to do started Adelaide to trembling even more. "Ellen, I can't let you. He'll find you here instead of me, and with Aelfred gone, too—you know what he's like when he's angry. He is uncontrollable. He may kill you."

Ellen's eyes remained unwavering. "He could do nothing that I could better wish. He has already killed me, my lady."

"Ellen!" Adelaide covered her mouth with her hands lest

she scream. Then she put her arms around the girl, holding her tightly. "Forgive me," she sobbed. "I am to blame, not you. If I had not dismissed you—I was supposed to protect you. We were raised together."

"I gave you reason to distrust me," Ellen said softly. "When Siward asked me to help them, I nearly cried for joy, because I knew it would be a way I could try to make up for my wrong against you."

Adelaide kissed her. "You are braver than I."

"No, my lady. But I am bound to serve you." Ellen pulled herself away. "We must not talk any more. Let me unlace your dress for you."

Quietly, swiftly, the two exchanged kirtles. Then Adelaide went to her jewel chest. She could not carry it, but her mother's rings and her own pearl necklace would fit in a little bag that she could hide inside her dress. She put on the cloak and pulled up the hood. Then she faced Ellen. Tears came to her eyes. She put her arms around her and kissed her again. "God bless you," she whispered. "I have not heard of an act so loyal as yours, not even in the songs of the heroes."

"Our Lady guide your steps," Ellen answered. "Walk quickly. Let no one see you. Do not speak. Remember—the stable gate. As for Lord Tancred, he may be merciful."

She opened the door and Adelaide stepped into the court-yard. For a moment after she heard the bolt slip into place behind her, she was too frightened to move. She stared in horrified fascination at the row of red-hot iron. Some soldiers were standing watch over it, but they were drinking, their backs to her. With every ounce of will she possessed, she forced her legs to move. She must try, at least, to be as brave as Ellen and the others who were risking their lives to save hers. She darted from shadow to shadow, praying at every step. She passed the prison huts; the knowledge that both Mab and Aelfred were now out of reach of cruel Norman hands gave her enough courage to run toward the stables. The gate was ajar. She slipped through it quickly and peered into the darkness, whispering, "Siward?"

A figure loomed before her. "No, my lady. I am Wilnoth

son of Elred shepherd." His voice was low. "I am to take you to my father's cot."

"Will it be safe for you?" she asked. "Suppose the Normans discover I've gone and start to search?"

"They won't," he assured her. She could sense that he was smiling. "They are sure that we're too afraid to do anything but lie down and let them put their foot on our necks. But they don't know us, my lady."

"No," she agreed vehemently.

"Saewulf and Mab are to be buried one hour after Terce tomorrow," Wilnoth continued. "Siward will be at our cot early, and he will tell you his plan. I do not know anything, except that we shall shelter you tonight."

"It is better that you should not," Adelaide said tremulously. Ellen had used those words. She felt her knees give way and she stumbled.

"So Siward told us." He put his hand firmly under her arm. "I mean no disrespect, my lady, but the ground is slippery."

"Thank you for your help," she responded automatically, thinking, at the same time, I must not disgrace myself by fainting. But her head was reeling, and after a few steps she stumbled again, sinking to her knees.

Dear God, please help me, she prayed and tried to rise. Then Wilnoth's strong arms lifted her as easily as though she had been a child, and darkness, blacker than the night and more merciful, overcame her.

TANCRED rolled over in the great bed and opened his eyes. He didn't remember how he had gotten there. Then he heard his uncle snore on the pillow beside his and remembered. He made no move to wake him. For one thing, his head was throbbing, and for another he was only half awake himself. He must have drunk too much wine last night.

He yawned prodigiously. Well, after all, the feast had been a celebration. He was no longer only a stepson or a visitor. He was the owner of this demesne! A man did not often acquire wealth and lands so easily. The thought of Baron Ansculf flitted through his mind, but he dismissed it. The baron was in the north and would not guess at anything amiss. Even if he had made some arrangement to meet Aelfred, roads were treacherous in these times, and men fell prey to robbers every day. It would be simple to devise some reason for Aelfred's disappearance; and perhaps no reason would be needed. In a few weeks it would be spring, and Duke William would cross the channel. The country would be in such a turmoil that a simple-minded English baron would have no time to concern himself with his lands or his son. He would be fighting Normans or fleeing to save his own life. Tancred smiled exultantly. Storches Hundred was his! And Adelaide of Birnham would be his. One prospect pleased him as much as the other.

Too excited to want to sleep more, he threw back the cover, wrapped a cloak around his nightshirt, and went to the door. A soldier standing nearby came to him and saluted.

"Breakfast," Tancred commanded. "And water. I want to wash."

"At once, my lord," the soldier answered and hurried away.

Tancred walked round to the other side of the bed. *"Allons, mon oncle,"* he said, shaking him by the arm. "Do you plan to sleep all day?"

De Belleme turned away from him. "Let me sleep," he muttered. "What time is it?"

"Long past Prime. I've sent for breakfast."

"Breakfast!" The other groaned. "It is too early for breakfast. Why don't you sleep? Our festivities won't begin until noon."

Tancred pulled back the window curtain. "It is a nice day," he said. "The iron has a lovely color."

"Your aesthetic taste is charming," his uncle retorted sarcastically.

Tancred laughed. "Aelfred's color will be even more charming after he's crossed it." There was a rap at the door. "Come, Uncle, get up. Some hot meat and bread are what you need."

"The very thought revolts me," de Belleme answered.

He got up, however, and slipped into his velvet bed gown as Tancred called in English, "Come in."

The door was opened by the soldier carrying a large wooden tray. "What's this?" Tancred asked. "Where are the churls? A Norman soldier wait at table?"

"The churls have gone to the funerals," the soldier answered. "The only person in the kitchen is someone who calls himself Ecfrith."

"He's the steward," Tancred said shortly. "What kind of breakfast is this? Bread and cheese, and a pot of"—he dipped his finger into it, put a gop in his mouth, and grimaced—"mush! And cold! You go back and get us a hot meat pie."

"Oh, I asked for one," the soldier assured him. "Ecfrith said we'd eaten all he'd baked last night, and the ovens have not heated enough yet to bake more."

"They had all night to heat up to this hour," Tancred

113

stormed. "English pig! He'll learn a lesson from this, make no mistake."

"Please, nephew, my head," de Belleme said plaintively. "The food isn't bad. I've eaten worse on the battlefield and so will you."

"But I will have respect!"

"Not by raging, you won't," his uncle reproved. "How many times must I tell you that that attitude will gain you nothing? Sulky anger is childish. And by the way, when you speak of the hot iron, don't act so pleased. Your stepbrother's ordeal is a regrettable necessity, forced on us by his own actions. A look of grave concern will be more impressive."

"You may go," Tancred said curtly to the soldier, who was still waiting and enjoying what he heard. "Try to have the water hot."

"There's fire enough for that," the soldier said cheerfully and left them.

Tancred took his knife from the table and attacked the loaf. "Have you any more helpful little suggestions, Uncle?" he asked irritably.

"Everything must be kept calm," de Belleme said emphatically. "Duke William will not be pleased at any disorder."

Tancred looked at him, outraged. "And who caused the disorder? Your men killed Saewulf deliberately. I saw that soldier stab him."

"Is the pot calling the kettle black? Why didn't you intervene? Your oath to Baron Ansculf bound you to care for his people." De Belleme spooned some mush onto his trencher. "Saewulf had to die because he knew too much about you, and he finally understood what you had done. Alive, he was dangerous. The others followed him once against Aelfred, but after yesterday he'd have turned on you, given the chance. If that answers you, you might give me that piece of bread you have cut."

"Here." Tancred handed it to him on the knife point. "Do you think it a good idea for all the demesne people to be going to Saewulf's funeral?"

114

"And Mab's. Don't forget her. In a way, I'm glad her heart failed her. I really did not want to see a woman walk the iron." He sighed. "Yes, it is a good idea. It is one way of keeping the peace for a while."

"I suppose you're right." Tancred shrugged. "But I think they are too afraid to make another disturbance."

De Belleme raised one eyebrow. "Don't underestimate them, Tancred. You never know what an enemy is capable of doing under stress."

"I discovered that yesterday," Tancred admitted. "Why, some of those who seemed to care least whether William or Harold rules fought the hardest."

"They were attacked on their own land. Duke William will be interested. This may be a foretaste of what he can expect. If those men had been armed yesterday, I would not have wanted to wager who would win."

"Well, we did. And we always will," Tancred said complacently.

"That remains to be seen. One thing more—under the law, a condemned sorcerer is given a final opportunity to recant before he faces the hot iron. So, when we've eaten and dressed, you must call Aelfred to the great hall."

"Uncle, you're too scrupulous," Tancred objected. "Why waste time? You know what he'll say."

"Then we can proceed with a clear conscience. He will have proved himself obdurate," de Belleme said suavely. "At times like these, nephew, it is best to observe all proprieties. It's a pity that we had to send the priest away, but he was too great a danger. Besides, confessed sorcery is punishable by secular, not ecclesiastical, law. Nevertheless, the opportunity to repent and recant must be given."

"Very well," Tancred agreed. "After breakfast."

Half an hour later, freshly washed and dressed, they crossed the court to the great hall. The curtains of Lady Ygerne's bower were still drawn; doubtless she was still sleeping. Adelaide, apparently, was asleep, too.

"Women!" Tancred snorted. "How could anyone sleep on such a day?"

The hall was in disorder from the feast. Benches were overturned and a few soldiers still slept on, their empty wine cups beside them. There were stains on the carpets, and the hangings were blackened in places by soot from the torches.

"Incredible!" Tancred exclaimed. "Why wasn't this place cleaned?"

"The churls are all at the funerals. They would have needed to work all night to put it in proper order, and we gave no orders," de Belleme replied. "Call the captain and have him get his men out of here."

Tancred obeyed, and the sleeping soldiers were rudely wakened. Grinning foolishly, they staggered out of the hall. Then more soldiers came and righted the benches. When a semblance of order had been restored, Tancred sat down on the high seat and said imperiously, "Fetch the prisoner."

The soldiers left, and Guilbert de Belleme smiled. "You become the high seat, Tancred, I must admit."

Tancred did not answer. He was too absorbed in his own sense of power. All his life he had longed for such a moment; since coming to Storches Hundred, the longing had become an obsession. He clasped the arms of the chair and pushed himself against its back, until the more delicate places in the carving almost split under his strength. He had won. Only Aelfred's death was necessary to give him possession of the demesne and make his victory complete.

There was hubbub in the courtyard, a sound of running feet, a scuffling outside the door, and almost simultaneously the captain rushed into the hall. He knelt before Tancred, his face ashen. "My lord, the prisoner is gone!" he cried.

It took a moment for the words to make sense. Even de Belleme seemed stunned. Then Tancred jumped to his feet. "That is not possible!" he cried. "Who is responsible for this? Who let him escape?"

"None of us, my lord," the captain pleaded. "The door was barred when we went to the prison hut. We took down the bar ourselves, but the hut was empty."

"I don't believe you!" Tancred struck him a hard blow. "You did not guard him well enough. *You* shall walk the hot iron for this!"

116

"Be quiet, Tancred. You're wasting time," de Belleme interrupted. He turned to the captain. "Where is the guard who was assigned to the prison hut?"

"He—he was lying on the ground," the captain stuttered. "He did not move when we called him. But the door was barred. I swear by all the saints, the door was barred!"

"All right," barked de Belleme. "Turn out all your men. Let them search the stockade. Leave the ladies' bowers for the last. Then you come to the prison hut. There's some explanation for this, unless our atheling really is a sorcerer, who can walk through walls and bars and fly through the air."

"Do you really believe that, Uncle?" Tancred sneered.

"About as much as you do," de Belleme said evenly. "Follow me."

But Tancred could not follow. He stood in the middle of the hall, dazed with disbelief. Was his golden dream to be destroyed now, at the very moment he had it within his grasp? Cold fury welled up in him. He knew the one who could tell them where Aelfred had gone. "And she will tell," he muttered between clenched teeth, as he strode out of the hall and straight to Adelaide's bower.

He rapped sharply; when no one answered, he pounded. Two soldiers ran by and he stopped them. "Help me break down this door," he commanded.

"But Lord Guilbert said—" one of them began.

"Never mind Lord Guilbert," Tancred retorted. "I am master here."

The door gave way under their combined weights, and Tancred went immediately to the bed. He pulled viciously at the hangings. "Wake up, Adelaide of Birnham." Forgetting even a pretense of courtesy, he shook the girl roughly. Slowly she turned and faced him.

"Ellen!" he gasped. "What are you doing here?"

She did not answer. She merely looked at him with eyes filled with loathing and not a trace of fear. A hammer beat at his temples; he had used her shamelessly in his attempt to gain Adelaide's sympathy. Now his hatred for both of them filled every fiber of his being.

He tore back the covers and dragged Ellen from the bed. She

made no resistance, not even when he pushed her onto a stool and stood over her, his hands around her throat. "Where is your mistress?" he demanded.

"I don't know," Ellen said coldly.

"Where is the atheling?"

"In prison."

"He is not. He's gone. I think you know where he is. He and your mistress went together."

Ellen shook her head violently. He put a hand on her shoulder and gripped until she cried out with pain.

"So, you don't like being hurt," he said with a mean smile. "Very good. Now I know how to make you tell me what you know."

"I know nothing," she insisted.

"Do you want to walk the hot iron?"

"No!" she shrieked.

"Then tell me! Tell me or you shall! Now!" He increased the viselike grip.

Her whole body writhed in agony. "I know nothing," she whispered.

"We shall see." He turned from her to go to the door where the soldiers still waited, but before he could speak, Ellen, in a lightning move, followed him. Her hand reached the dagger in his belt. A moment later, before his horrified eyes she fell to the ground, blood welling from a wound over her heart.

Simultaneously Guilbert de Belleme came panting to the door. *"Nom d'un nom!"* he exploded. "You fool!"

"She did it herself," Tancred protested, "The knife was in her hand. These men saw—they'll tell you."

"I believe you. Millions would not," his uncle retorted. "This is all we need: one more death to make Storches Hundred infuriated against us. A splendid peacekeeper you are! I suppose you'd have Adelaide do the same thing, if she'd been here."

"She knew where Adelaide is," Tancred insisted.

"Heaven save me now and forever from fools, especially my relations. You—you, there—take the girl away," he commanded the soldiers. "Bury her somewhere. She must not be found."

They were his own men, but they looked at him as they would an enemy as one of them held the door open while the other lifted Ellen's body in his arms and carried it out of the bower. Tancred sank onto the chair and bent his head to his knees. His uncle closed the door again and barred it.

"I've given orders to let the fires go out," he said. "No one will walk the iron today. The entire countryside would be aroused."

Tancred looked at him helplessly. "What shall we do? What *can* we do?"

"I said this morning never to underestimate the enemy. Well, you can't be blamed too much. I did the same thing myself. So, our birds have flown. We must get them back. They can't have gone far." De Belleme looked moodily out the window. "I've sent our own men out in pairs to search the demesne for them."

"Do you think they're together?"

"I don't know, that's the devil of it. If they are together, they may be hiding somewhere here at Storches Hundred. But if we can't find them here, then, my dear nephew, you'll have a mission." His eyes gleamed like a ferret's waiting to scent its prey. "Aelfred will doubtless try to reach Harold Godwineson. You must prevent him."

"Prevent him?" Tancred laughed. "Harold Godwineson is in the north, no one knows where. How can I possibly find him, much less Aelfred?"

"You'll find Aelfred. I have information that Harold will stop at Walsingham on his way south. It's my guess that Aelfred will try to meet him there."

"Then I go to Walsingham?"

"Yes. With Norman soldiers, and a safe-conduct signed by myself as King's High Reeve. Even at that, you must intercept the atheling before he reaches the town, and, above all, before he takes sanctuary at the Holy House. You may possibly overtake him on the road. And, when you do—"

Tancred did not change expression. "I will kill him," he said steadily. "But what about Adelaide? She may be with him."

"I doubt it. Aelfred would never allow a girl to make such a journey."

Tancred grimaced. "You don't know Adelaide."

"If she is with him, you'll have to trust to the inspiration of the moment—hoping you'll have one," de Belleme added skeptically. "She will probably try to return to Birnham, however. There will be ways to deal with Adelaide. We'll find them."

"I have a strong suspicion that Siward is at the bottom of all this," Tancred said angrily.

"I am sure of it. And I am keeping close watch on him, never fear. I don't trust these strong, quiet men."

"Perhaps you ordered the fires put out too soon, Uncle?"

"Perhaps. But we need Siward, at the time being, to keep the people in order, if nothing else. These English! They don't fight like civilized men. Well, do you understand what you are to do?"

"Perfectly." Tancred rose. "I wish I were starting now."

"All in good time. See to it that you succeed, too. Duke William has little patience with failure."

The warning note in his voice was unmistakable, but Tancred chose to disregard it. "You'll find me a good bloodhound, Uncle," he said confidently, though he was aware that, inwardly, he was more shaken by Ellen's suicide that he cared to admit. It could so easily have been Adelaide, and he intended to have her alive. Marriage would be a little thing to pay for that advantage. But he had more important things to consider at this time. After a moment he stretched out his arms, then walked out into the courtyard with his usual firm stride, his hatred against Aelfred Ansculfson burning in his heart more fiercely than the irons, which would cool of themselves.

At Elred's cot, Adelaide, dressed in a boy's breeks and tunic, waited impatiently. She had slept well, much to her surprise, and had shared the family breakfast of bread, porridge, and ale. Then she had put on the clothes which Wytha, Elred's wife, had brought to her. As she twisted the leather thongs around the breeks, she had remembered fleetingly that she had threatened to attend the folkmoot in boy's clothes, and she thought that fate indeed worked strangely. She wondered where Aelfred was. Far from Storches Hundred, she hoped, and she whispered a prayer for his safety. She slipped the tunic over her head; it was much too large, but she must not be too well clad. She was supposed to look like a common churl, and she might just succeed if she kept her hands hidden.

It was when she pulled the hood over her head that she realized that her disguise would have its difficulty. "Too much hair!" she exclaimed. And she could not wear it pinned on top of her head. "Wytha?"

The shepherd's wife came to her. "My lady?"

"Bring me some shears, please."

"Oh, my lady." Wytha clucked. "Not your beautiful hair?"

"It will grow again," Adelaide said quietly. "I'll cut it just to my shoulders. Where is Siward? I thought he'd be here by now."

"He will come soon." Wytha handed her the heavy shears. "You'd best give me the hair you cut off, my lady. We'll hide it with your clothes."

"Yes. They must not know that I've been with you." She cut the long, wavy strands with firm strokes, letting them fall to the ground. "There. That's better. Now I can wear the hood and hide my face a little."

"If I might suggest, my lady," Wytha said hesitantly, "a few streaks of dirt on your face would be good."

"Of course." Adelaide smiled, bent down, and picked up a handful of ashes from the firepit, which she rubbed on her cheeks. "Now do I look like a churl?"

"You could never look like a churl, my lady. But, as Siward told us, this way no one will notice you enough to tell whether you are a churl or not."

There was a moment of quiet. Adelaide watched the shepherd's wife as she gathered the strands of hair, and the thought assailed her that this family was placing itself in terrible danger. "Wytha," she said earnestly, "let me tell you this. If you or your husband or your son are threatened by helping me,

I'll give myself up. I could not bear to think of your suffering on my account."

"Give yourself up? To the Normans?" Wytha's eyes flashed. "We would all die first. And I do not think we will suffer. Lord Tancred cannot manage the flocks by himself."

"That he cannot," Adelaide agreed.

"I think I hear Siward," said Wytha, and hurried to the door.

The reeve came in, wearing his ordinary breeks and a leather jerkin under a heavy cloak. "Good morning, my lady," he said quietly. "Did you sleep well?"

"Yes, and breakfasted well, thanks to these good people," she answered. "And I'm dressed, too, as you see. When do we leave?"

"This is the plan. In a quarter hour, I'll walk over to Saewulf's cot. It's best that we not be seen together. Some of our people will come down the road just then, bound for the funerals. Elred and his family, and you, will join them. Keep yourself in the midst of them. They know, and they'll protect you."

"I will. Yes."

"At Saewulf's cot, the funeral procession will form. We will walk towards the Tree of Justice, but there's a little side road just before we get to it. I'll turn off there, and you follow me. Dodda will be waiting with horses."

"Dodda?" she exclaimed in amazement. "How did he manage that?"

"He managed. There are many ways in and out of the stockade." Siward smiled. "Then we ride as fast as we can. With a little luck, we'll be well away before we're missed."

"Where do we ride, Siward?"

"I thought of Birnham at first, but the same idea might occur to de Belleme and he might follow us. So we'll ride to London, to the convent where you went to school. The nuns will surely give you sanctuary, if need be."

"Will Aelfred be in London?" she asked eagerly.

"I hope not!"

"Then why can't we go wherever he is?"

122

"Perhaps later—"

There was pounding on the door and a voice called loudly, "For the love of Heaven, open!"

Wytha slipped the bolt to admit Ecfrith baron's-steward, who rushed in, panting for breath. Adelaide looked at him in surprise. Ecfrith was usually composed, almost solemn. Now he was distraught.

"Siward, they've discovered that Aelfred and Lady Adelaide are gone," he gasped. "Lord Guilbert has sent his Normans to search the demesne."

Adelaide began to tremble. "Ellen?" she asked, grasping Ecfrith's arm. "Did Tancred find her in my bower?"

Ecfrith nodded. "Tancred threatened her with the iron. She was afraid that she might speak, so she—she killed herself with his knife. It was quick, my lady."

Her hands flew to her mouth. "Ellen!" she sobbed. "Oh, Ellen—"

"Hush, my lady. Hush, now. There's no time for weeping, God help us," Siward said urgently. "Where are they searching, Ecfrith?"

"Everywhere. I was lucky to get away without being seen. It won't be long before they're here. We must get the lady to safety."

"But how?" For the first time, Siward, too, looked desperate. "If she could reach Dodda, she could ride to the ring of stones, perhaps, but even that would be a risk."

"No, I'll go back," Adelaide moaned. "We can't have any more killing."

"Siward, there is one place where she could hide." Elred and his son had come into the cot while they were talking, and now the shepherd spoke. "The cave in the high pasture. Wilnoth and I often sleep there during storms. It's protected by a mass of shrubs, so that it can't be seen unless you know it's there."

"She couldn't find it alone," Siward protested.

"I'll go with her," Wilnoth answered.

"Suppose the Normans start counting heads and you aren't here?" Ecfrith demanded.

"Is it strange for a shepherd to be mending the pasture wall?" Wilnoth grinned. "I noticed some bad holes in it, yesterday. Mother, put some food in a sack and give Lady Adelaide my heavy cloak." He bowed to Adelaide and said respectfully, "It is a rude shelter, my lady, but it is the safest spot I know. And, though it is dry, there is a brook nearby. You could stay there a month and no one the wiser."

"God grant it will only be a few hours," Siward said fervently. "My lady, I think Wilnoth's plan is good. If you ran back to the stockade, Lord Tancred's wrath would not only fall on you but on all of us. Keep yourself well hidden, and I will come for you as soon as possible. Ecfrith, can you run another race?"

"What's to be done?" the steward asked.

"Dodda is waiting with horses at the side road near the Tree of Justice. Get to him as quickly as possible and tell him what has happened. He'll think of something to do. Meanwhile, I'll walk over to Saewulf's cot, as planned, and warn them. Elred, you tell the others when they come."

He looked sympathetically at Adelaide, who stood dazed, almost numb with grief and fright. "Your leave-taking has just been delayed a little," he said gently. "Be brave, as your father would wish you to be, my lady."

"I'll try," she faltered.

"You would not want to be in Tancred's hands," Ecfrith said firmly.

She shuddered. "Never." She raised her chin and blinked away her tears. "I'll wait until you come, Siward. But please don't be long."

"We must go, my lady. It's a long climb to the cave," Wilnoth prompted. He threw the provision bag over his shoulder. "Let me look at the road, first." He opened the door and peered up and down in both directions. "No one in sight," he said. "But we'd better make a run for it."

"I'm coming," Adelaide answered. She looked at the anxious faces around her and tried to smile. But she was afraid that she might start to weep again, so she only trusted herself to murmur, "God be with us all." Then she followed Wilnoth, running as fast as her legs would carry her.

IN A high ditch concealed from the by-track by a mass of small scrubby trees and shrubbery, Aelfred waited for Osric. It was nearly noon and he had been alone since early morning. For the first days after leaving Storches Hundred, they had traveled through the by-tracks, mostly by night, away from the villages connected by the old Roman road, but there had been enough scattered houses to provide the bread that Osric had begged for them. Now their route had taken them deep into the fen country, where houses were few and far between.

To add to their troubles, Aelfred had cut his foot. It had not been cleaned properly, and it pained him so much that he could hardly walk. The last few miles on the preceding night had been agony, and he had fallen into the ditch at dawn exhausted. When Osric left him at sunrise to search for bread and ointment of some kind, he had dozed fitfully for a time but had not really slept. His forehead was hot to his touch; beads of perspiration were running down his back. And, though he did not want to admit it, he was terribly afraid lest Osric lose his way and not return. He might die there, alone, and no one would know.

"But Osric won't get lost," he told himself, trying to keep

up his courage. During the week they had been together, he had acquired a tremendous respect for this churl who had found their way so surely by the stars, who knew what plants were safe to eat and when water was fresh. Osric was a quiet man, who spoke little, but of the two of them he was stronger and better able to stand the rigors of their hand-to-mouth existence. Aelfred had taken comfort in the thought that he would surely reward Osric handsomely when this ordeal was over, provided—he added bitterly—he was ever again in a position to reward anyone.

Tancred de Belleme! He clenched his fists and gritted his teeth. The hatred in his heart for the Norman rushed over him like a raging fire. He *must* reach Walsingham so that he could repay his enemy in kind for the deprivation he was suffering now. His feverish mind gloated on the punishments he could inflict on Tancred, once he had reached the King and was restored to his rightful place. He recalled having been warned that hatred was a sin, but that thought, in his present hazy condition, was not enough to overcome his rage, for that rage served to give him strength to go on.

He heard the thicket above him crackle and looked up in alarm. Relieved, he saw that it was Osric, climbing down beside him.

"I'm sorry I was so long, master," Osric said anxiously. "I had to walk far. But I found a place where a woman gave me bread and a pot of herb salve for your cut. Does it pain you very much?"

"Horribly," Aelfred admitted. "I don't know if I can get off my boot."

"Let's try, anyway." Aelfred braced himself and Osric slowly drew the boot off the now-swollen foot. He looked at the festering gash and shook his head. "The woman said this salve is good. What can we use for a bandage?"

"Tear a strip off my undertunic," Aelfred gasped.

The bandaging was accomplished and the boot replaced, an even more painful process than its removal. Aelfred lay back limply, his hand over his eyes.

"Here, master. Try to eat something," Osric urged.

"I couldn't," Aelfred moaned.

Osric put a rough hand on his forehead. "I think you have a fever. Perhaps we'd better rest here until night."

"No." Slowly he pulled himself into a sitting position. "We must go on. How far are we from Walsingham?"

"At least seven days' journey," Osric said reluctantly.

"It will take us longer, I'm afraid, and we can't travel by night in the fens. Help me up. I'll be all right."

With Osric's help he climbed out of the ditch. Every move was like a touch of fire. "This is as bad as the hot iron," he said grimly.

"Perhaps it will be better after you've walked a little." Osric put an arm around his waist to steady him. "If only we could travel the high road."

"No. We don't dare." He took a few limping steps. "I'd feel easier in my heart if I knew Adelaide was safe. Are you sure that Siward and the others could get her away in time?"

"Siward promised, and he never breaks his word," Osric replied. "Who knows? The lady may already be at Walsingham herself."

The thought gave Aelfred courage, and he walked on, groaning occasionally when the pain grew too intense. For several hours they picked their way over the marshy ground. Then Osric stopped and looked him full in the face.

"Master, I can't let you go on. You'll kill yourself," he said emphatically. "We must take the high road. Bury St. Edmunds is not far away, and we'll find a leech there, surely."

"We may be caught, too," Aelfred reminded.

"We must chance that."

Too exhausted to object, Aelfred limped on for what seemed an eternity. Several times he might have fallen into a hidden bog, had Osric's strong arm not been around him. At last the by-track widened, a sign that the high road was near.

"We're almost there," Osric encouraged.

"I don't think I can go any farther," Aelfred gasped. "It's like all the fires of Hell. Perhaps you'd better leave me and go on alone."

"I'll never leave you, master," Osric said quietly. "Please, never say that again. I'll carry you on my back if need be, but we go together."

To Aelfred's amazement, there were tears in Osric's eyes. "My words are poor thanks," he said tautly, over the lump in his own throat. "I had thought once of becoming a monk, Osric. But I am glad now that I did not. I would never have known how precious a thing the land bond can be. Each to his own."

"And to all of us," Osric said stoutly. "We are bound to you, and you to us, for as long as our generations last."

He was about to say more when suddenly the sound of marching feet broke the silence. Before their startled eyes, a company of soldiers appeared, led by a man in a bright green cloak who seemed as surprised to see them as they to meet him.

"Halt!" he barked. "Name yourselves and go no farther."

"We walk in peace," Osric answered.

"No one walks the roads without proper authority in these times," the leader retorted.

"Are you a Norman, who speaks so to free Englishmen?" Osric demanded.

"Norman?" For a moment the soldier looked as though he would draw his sword. "We are Welshmen from the border marches, going to join King Harold. Now name yourselves, or as sure as my name is Gryffin ap Gryffin ap Llewellyn I'll take you both for Norman spies and kill you where you stand."

Aelfred started to speak, but Osric flashed him a warning glance. "I am Osric son of Osric, of Storches Hundred," he said. "My friend is called Aelfred."

"Is your friend dumb that he cannot speak for himself?" Gryffin waved a long skinny finger in front of Osric's nose. "Who is his father—or is he baseborn? Answer me!"

"His foot is hurt and he suffers great pain," Osric parried.

But Gryffin would not be denied. "What are you doing here?"

"It's no use, Osric. We shall have to tell him," Aelfred said

128

quietly. He drew himself to his full height. "I am Aelfred son of Ansculf, son of Aelfred Iron Fist." Swiftly he told the story of their escape from Storches Hundred, while the Welshman listened intently, his eyes narrowed, his lips pursed.

"We seek King Harold at Walsingham," Aelfred concluded. "If you will let us go our way in peace, my father will reward you richly. I promise."

Gryffin looked at him impassively. "A strange story," he commented. "Am I to believe this thing?"

"You must believe it." The pain in Aelfred's foot was so great that it made him dizzy. "We are not Norman spies—I swear it. Let us go." Then his knees buckled under him.

"You'll go nowhere in that condition, unless to the church-yard," Gryffin said brusquely. "We march to Walsingham. You may join our company. I'll decide on the way whether I believe you or not."

He turned to his men and gave a few swift commands in Welsh. Two soldiers stepped forward and made a chair of their arms.

"I'll carry him," Osric offered.

"You're as weak as he is, by the look of you," Gryffin retorted. "Walk by his side, then, if you don't trust Welshmen."

"We trust them," Aelfred said weakly. "Mab was Welsh."

"The woman that the Normans wanted to walk the hot iron?"

"Yes. She was my nurse. I told you."

"You told me," Gryffin replied succinctly.

The field camp was in a clearing not far away, and there Aelfred and Osric spent the rest of that day and night. One of the soldiers who knew leechcraft dressed Aelfred's foot, shaking his head gravely as he did so, but Aelfred was too ill to notice. All he wanted to do was sleep for a year, but his dreams would not let him. The hot iron appeared before him again and again; he cried out brokenly for his father and for Adelaide. He was dimly conscious of someone wiping his face with a cool cloth, but the face was sometimes Osric's and sometimes Mab's. By daybreak, when the soldiers were dousing the campfires, his fever was raging. He felt himself being lifted into a litter and carried, but where he neither knew nor cared.

It was not until several nights later, when the company had camped in a field just off the high road, that he opened his eyes and recognized Osric's anxious face bending over him. "You're still with me," he murmured.

"Always, master," Osric replied.

"Where are we?"

"Not far from Walsingham. Captain Gryffin says we will be there tomorrow."

"Thank God." Aelfred closed his eyes for a moment, then opened them again. "Does he believe me yet?" His voice was half anxious, half affectionate.

"He has not said. But he has been most kind. He told the leechman to give you special tending and has never let the fire near you go out at night. There is hot broth for you now, master, if you would like it."

"I think I could take some." He pulled himself up on his elbow. "My foot still pains, but not as badly."

"Good. Then you'll be able to march like a man, instead of lying abed like a child." Gryffin moved out of the shadows. "Get the broth, Osric. I want a few words with him alone."

"I cannot tell you how grateful I am, Captain," Aelfred faltered.

"Gratitude, as your Norman friends say, butters no parsnips."

"They are not my friends," Aelfred flared. "Do you still not believe me?"

"Well, more now than I did at first. You spoke freely in your fever. You were fairly in the wheel there, for two or three days. I decided that some of the things you said must be truth, for no Norman could know them. But an Englishman, turned traitor, could."

"I am not a traitor," Aelfred said evenly, but firmly. "I am not. And if you believed that, then why did you let your leechman cure me?"

"Because I wasn't sure. You see, there's been a small company of Normans following us these past three days."

"Normans?" Aelfred started to tremble.

Gryffin nodded. "Horsemen. They were definitely looking for someone. So tonight I camped by the high road to give them the chance to visit us. And"—he cocked his ear—"I think I hear them now."

There was the unmistakable sound of hoofbeats on the road.

"Yes, they're coming. Were you expecting them?"

"I was afraid they might follow me," Aelfred admitted. "Guilbert de Belleme, the Norman I told you of, is crafty as Lucifer."

" 'Tis a young man leading them."

"That would be Tancred."

"Do you want to see him?"

"Only if we meet knife to knife," Aelfred said coldly.

"H'm." Gryffin stroked his beard. Then he moved to the center fire, shouting commands in Welsh. His men quickly formed ranks around him, while Aelfred, in an agony of dread, watched the horsemen approach, the Red Lions on their tunics plainly visible in the torchlight. He could see Tancred. Would Gryffin betray him?

"Halt. Name yourself," Gryffin called.

"Tancred de Belleme, emissary of the King's High Reeve of Storches Hundred." The suave, hateful voice rang clearly in the cold night air. "I demand that you surrender one Aelfred Ansculfson to me. He's a condemned sorcerer, declared outlaw and dangerous."

Aelfred held his breath. Then Gryffin answered, "I know no sorcerers."

"Don't pretend with me," Tancred threatened. "I know he's with you, and I have a warrant to search and take him by force if necessary."

"Search?" Gryffin snorted. "Now we hear it all! I wouldn't try it, if I were you. My men are rough lads from Wales. Mark you, they've not had a good fight since St. David's Day last."

"How dare you bandy words with me?"

"Very well. In plain words, then, we're a hundred and fifty to your eleven." Gryffin's voice could not have been more conversational. "I've never heard that Normans excelled at night fighting, and while I don't like to refuse my men a chance for practice and exercise, as a Christian I don't want to see murder done, either."

There was a definite pause. Then Tancred said blusteringly, "You've not heard the last of this. Next time we'll meet by day." With that, he called a command to his horsemen and they galloped out of the clearing.

Aelfred lay back on his pallet, drenched with perspiration. Gryffin ambled over and squatted down beside him. "Well, now," he said cheerfully. "That was an interesting encounter."

"I have no words," Aelfred answered faintly. "You do believe me, then."

"My last doubts were gone when I saw the Norman." Gryffin spat. "And did you see the way he turned tail and ran?"

"I saw. But he will return."

"Yes, and treacherously, too. I know his kind. The only difference between him and a snake is that you recognize a snake when you see it. But *his* kind!" He spat again. "However, I doubt he disturbs us any more tonight. Here's Osric with your broth. Drink it and sleep soundly. You'll need all your wits tomorrow."

The sun was high when Aelfred awoke to find that camp was broken and Gryffin's company ready to march. The captain was standing beside him, his green cloak swirled over his shoulder. "So you've decided to face God's light?" he asked humorously.

"You should have wakened me," Aelfred apologized.

"No need. I sent out two of my lads to do some scouting and they only returned half an hour ago. Here's Osric with meat and ale. Make a good meal. You'll want your strength."

Aelfred looked at him apprehensively. "Tancred?"

"Up the road a bit, waiting to greet us. Friendly, isn't he?"

Though he realized that his situation was most serious,

Aelfred could not repress a smile, and he bit into the meat with real appetite. "Would he be such a fool as to offer a fight?" he asked.

"Not a real fight. He couldn't. But he can create enough confusion to fulfill his real purpose, which seems to be to kill you."

Aelfred shuddered. His brief time at Westminster had not been long enough to accustom him to the way that soldiers spoke of killing.

"Not that he'll succeed, if you're a clever lad who can follow directions," Gryffin continued.

"I'm not sure that I'm clever, but I can follow directions. I spent eleven years in a monastery."

"Will wonders never cease? I'd never have guessed it." For the first time in their acquaintance, Gryffin smiled. "Well now, let me tell you. My lads report that the demesne of Lady Richeldis de Faverches is not far from where Tancred and his Normans are waiting. You can see the gates just over the top of the hill. If we keep the enemy busy, can you slip out of the line of march and run like all the fiends of Hell are after you to that gate?"

"I can."

"Even with your bad foot?"

"I'll go with him," said Osric, who had been listening quietly. "I'll stand between him and them."

"You have the makings of a real soldier, Osric." Gryffin nodded approval. "My plan is to give them a fight they don't expect."

"But that will be a danger to you," said Aelfred.

"Not at all. It's they who'll be breaking the peace of the King's high road if they draw swords on us, and my lads will enjoy rebutting them. When I call 'Now!' you run. There's a cross on the gate. Take hold of it and keep calling 'Sanctuary!' until someone answers."

"The Holy House," Aelfred murmured. "I had not thought to see it this way."

"Be thankful if you're alive to see it at all," Gryffin advised. "May the Blessed Mother protect you until you reach it."

"And the King? How will he know where I am?"

"Leave that to me. He'll be told. I speak to any king alive as an equal, and don't you forget it."

Aelfred smiled. "I'm not likely to forget it, or you. In my father's name and my own, I say that whatever you ask in reward you shall have."

"Don't make rash promises. I might ask the hand of the fair Adelaide." Gryffin's eyes twinkled. "You called for her constantly in your fever. She must be the beauty of the world."

"She is, and more than that," Aelfred said gravely.

"Well, she'll have a good man in you. Finished eating? Then let's march. You and Osric follow close behind me."

Sternly willing his knees not to shake, Aelfred fell in as he was told. The Welshmen were already in marching order, and, at a quick command from Gryffin, they proceeded out of the field into the high road.

"Does your foot pain you, master?" Osric asked.

"No," Aelfred said shortly, steeling himself against a wave of weakness that nearly overcame him. The Welshmen had started to sing. "What's that song they're always singing?" he asked Gryffin.

"The song of the great King Arthur and his twelve victories over you Saxons," Gryffin answered with a broad grin.

"Let us hope they do as well against the Normans," Aelfred replied. They had begun to climb up the hill, tension growing with every step. Still the Welshmen sang, their voices blending in glorious harmony.

"You'd think we were on a hunting trip," Aelfred said to Osric.

"It is a hunt," Osric answered grimly. "There are the Normans."

"Keep your eyes on me, now," Captain Gryffin said over his shoulder, signaling to his men to form closer ranks. "And keep away from their horses when the trouble starts. We'll hit them first."

Slowly, deliberately, the column moved forward to where the Normans barred the road. Aelfred could see their drawn swords. Then came the command to halt. The voice that spoke was Tancred's.

Gryffin raised his hand, and his men slowed their pace but did not stop. "Who breaks the peace of the King's high road?" he asked calmly.

"We own no king but William of Normandy," Tancred answered haughtily. "We are not bound by other laws."

"We own no king named William," Gryffin retorted. "Let us pass."

"Give us the traitor sorcerer in your midst, and you shall pass."

"There are no traitors with us. Look to your own!"

"We waste words," Tancred said harshly. "Forward!"

The horsemen started towards them. What happened next, Aelfred would never have believed, if he had not seen it with his own eyes. As the Normans moved to encircle them, the Welshmen dispersed to all sides of the road, some dropping into the ditches on either side, some scrambling up the banks. The horses were trotting too fast to be stopped quickly; before their riders could turn them, the Welshmen had aimed their bows. One arrow found its mark, and a black horse lay kicking and thrashing in the road, his stunned rider beside him. In vain Tancred tried to rally his men; the Welshmen, shouting their battle cries, were everywhere at once.

"Now!" Gryffin suddenly shouted at the top of his voice.

Aelfred had been standing beside him, watching in dazed disbelief. Now! He remembered his orders and started to run. The road seemed to stretch before him into infinity. He heard Osric's footsteps pounding behind his. He felt as though his lungs would burst. Still he ran, his eyes searching frantically for the gate with the cross. Then, just as he glimpsed it, he heard the sound that made his heart almost stop with fear: the thundering hoofbeats of a horse pursuing him.

"Run, master! Run!" Osric shouted.

The galloping came nearer. The gate was fifty paces away. There was no sound from Osric—had Tancred ridden him down? He must not stop to think. Osric might have given his own life to save him, and that sacrifice must not be wasted. With a last burst of effort, he reached the cross and flung himself on it, crying "Sanctuary!" as loudly as he could.

Tancred reined in, leaped from his horse and came after him with drawn sword.

"Sanctuary!" Aelfred screamed. Would Tancred dare attack him when his hand was on the cross? Would no one come? "Sanctuary!" he cried a third time, but his voice seemed only a whisper, and Tancred was near, so very near.

Then, miraculously, the gate swung open, and Aelfred fell on his knees at the feet of a woman dressed all in gray. She looked at him in silence, a silence that enveloped him like a velvet cloak. Even Tancred paused uncertainly, then withdrew a pace from her.

"What do you seek?" she asked quietly.

Aelfred knew now in whose presence he was. "The sanctuary of the Holy House, Lady Richeldis," he gasped.

She frowned. "The Holy House welcomes all who come in peace—"

"I come in peace," Aelfred said urgently. Fumbling at his belt, he unfastened his knife and threw it aside.

At this, Tancred moved forward. "He is a criminal, my lady," he said roughly. "I have a warrant for his arrest."

Lady Richeldis' eyes held his for a moment in a penetrating look; then she shook her head. "He asks for sanctuary and comes in peace," she said. "You—you come with drawn sword. It is not lawful arrest you seek, but unlawful revenge."

Tancred started to protest, but she silenced him with a gesture.

"Go," she commanded.

To Aelfred's amazement, Tancred slowly turned from her. He seized his horse by the bridle, sprang onto its back, and rode away from the gates.

Aelfred looked up at Lady Richeldis as though to the Madonna. "How—how did you know that of him?" he whispered.

"It is given to some to know," she answered. She bent down

136

to help him and raised him to his feet. "As I know of you that you hate him."

"Yes, I hate him." Aelfred's mouth and eyes were grim.

"You must not," she said, in the same quiet tone. "You see what hatred has done to him. It will do the same to you."

He looked at her uncomprehendingly, and she smiled.

"The Holy House gives sanctuary to hurt souls as well as broken bodies," she said. "There will be time for you to learn before you leave us. Come with me, now. Your foot is bleeding."

He looked down. Blood was seeping through the leather, but he could not yet obey her gentle command. "There are others," he said huskily. "A company of Welsh soldiers and their captain who helped me. And another—a friend. I think *he* rode him down."

"I shall send my servants after him. And the others also shall have hospitality here."

"With all my heart, I thank you," Aelfred answered. Trembling in every limb, he forced himself to stand upright. But the effort was too great. A wheel of light seemed to swirl before his eyes, and then he fell into darkness.

◆◆◆◆◆◆◆◆◆◆◆◆◆◆◆◆◆◆◆◆ I I ◆◆◆◆◆◆◆◆◆◆◆◆◆◆◆◆◆◆◆◆

AT THE convent of All Hallows, Berkynge, just within the great London wall, the bell was ringing the noon Angelus. Adelaide let the kneading rest while she said the prayer. Actually she was not required to stop in the midst of bread-making, but she always did so, adding a word of thanksgiving for being safe within these walls which, a month ago, she had never thought to see again.

Sister Winfred, the cook, an energetic woman who looked as though that energy might at any moment burst her habit, came from the stove to see how the dough was progressing. "Good," she said, washing her hands and dusting them with flour. "You're improving. Let me have it now, child. I need to get the feel of it."

Adelaide smiled and stepped aside. "I need to get the feel of it" was Sister Winfred's phrase for everything from hands on dough to spoons in sauce. She watched the dough grow smooth and elastic under those expert fingers. Would she ever be able to do as well herself?

"It's practice you need," Sister said quietly, as though reading Adelaide's mind. "You'll learn in time. And even if you never have to bake, yourself, you'll know when it's rightly done. Or, what's more important, be able to teach someone

138

to bake it for you. No man wants ill-made bread. The crock, now."

Adelaide brought her the large warmed stone crock, carefully greased with butter, and placed it on the wooden tray. The dough was put inside, a clean linen cloth laid over the top, and between them they carried it to the warm place beside the oven to rise.

"What shall I do now, Sister?" Adelaide asked.

"Well, there are the dried peas to be picked over," Sister Winfred suggested, and she turned to the simmering fish stew on the stove.

Adelaide went to the storeroom and fetched a sack of peas. She sat down on a three-legged stool, a kettle on one side of her, a small bowl for discards on the other, and soon was absorbed in her task. She would have enjoyed a little conversation, but Sister Winfred observed the Rule strictly and spoke no more than was absolutely required. And, Adelaide thought, there was much to be said for the Silence. As a pupil she had not appreciated a number of people being restricted from chattering as much as they liked, but her time away had made her see its benefits. Especially in comparison to those last days at Storches Hundred, the long wait in the cave, and her escape in boy's clothes. She had arrived at Berkynge wearing them, like a fugitive seeking sanctuary.

And, in a sense, a fugitive she still was. Oh, she had broken no laws, and she could hardly make herself believe even now that her life had actually been in danger, though when she remembered the cruel preparations and the terrible hot iron, she realized it had been possible: Tancred, deprived of one victim, might easily have turned on her. At the worst, he could have used Aelfred's life to bring her to marry him—have married her by proxy, if nothing else—and then claimed his full dower rights as her husband. She still trembled at the memory of how Ellen had taken her own life to save her. "May she rest in peace," she whispered.

But certainly, she mused as her hands worked busily, she had never expected the few hours in the hillside cave to stretch into nearly three weeks! Had Wilnoth not come each day, she

139

might have lost her wits. From him she learned that Tancred had left the demesne in great haste on the day after Aelfred's disappearance, with ten Norman soldiers riding after him. She had been terrified, thinking that Aelfred would surely be captured; Wilnoth had reassured her, telling her how cleverly Osric son of Osric would elude pursuit. Her intense anxiety had led her to tell Wilnoth that she neither knew nor cared about Osric, but that if Aelfred should be killed, she herself would die! She had begged to leave her hiding place and start after her betrothed and was brought to her senses only by Wilnoth's calm inquiry, "But what could you do, my lady?" Then she had wept at her own helplessness, face down on the rough sack that served her as a bed, remembering Aelfred's kindness and gentleness to her, sobbing over the destiny that seemed bent on thwarting them both. And of a certainty she dared not leave the cave; Guilbert de Belleme was still at Storches Hundred and daily sent out Norman soldiers to look for her. But no one betrayed the cave in the hills, and, finally, after what seemed an eternity, Siward came early one morning before she was half awake.

"My lady, we ride to London at once," he said, while she was still rubbing the sleep out of her eyes. "Tancred returned yesterday, and he and his uncle left before dawn by the Dover Road."

"What's happened?" she asked apprehensively.

"I did not stop to question. The soldiers have gone with them, so you can go freely. I've brought a horse for you. We can be at Berkynge by midmorning."

"But I want to go to Walsingham, where Aelfred is," she objected.

Siward shook his head gravely. "Too great a risk, my lady. I don't know whether Aelfred Ansculfson has reached Walsingham. If we take that road, we may be stopped. Guilbert de Belleme is still King's High Reeve, you know."

"We could be stopped on the London Road, too." She would not even let herself think that Aelfred had not reached Walsingham.

"Not as easily. I know all the by-tracks."

140

"Why can't I just stay on the demesne? Someone of Aelfred's family should be there, and I'm his betrothed."

"Lady Ygerne is still there, and she is the baron's lady, remember. Nor do I trust her not to do you an injury if she can. And there is the chance that Tancred and his uncle may return. You will be safest at the convent. In London we can find someone to take a message to your father."

She touched his arm. Siward was exposing himself to great danger for her. "And you, Siward? What will you do?"

"What I have always done. Look to my master's lands. I have no fear of Lady Ygerne." He smiled. "Life goes on, my lady. The land must be plowed; seeds must be sown; the flocks must be tended. To keep this land is my trust. But I must see that you are safely away. That was my trust, too."

Her first few days at Berkynge had been almost harder to endure than the fear for her life at Storches Hundred. In the cave she had worried incessantly about Aelfred, but she also had the question of her people's safety, as well as her own, to place before all else. Now that she was safe within these walls, with good food, proper clothes, and a good bed to sleep in, the possibility that he might not have reached Walsingham became a constant source of anguish. More than once she had unburdened her heart to the Mother Abbess, who had been most sympathetic—at least, for the first few recitals of woe. But the day had finally come when Mother Abbess had frowned.

"Adelaide, you must stop this," she said firmly. "You are making yourself ill. Your betrothed would certainly not find any comfort in that. It would only add to his own difficulties. A certain amount of worry is natural, but this—this would not please him, I am sure."

That Aelfred might be displeased had never occurred to her. In fact, she was not at all convinced that Mother Abbess was right, but she blinked back her tears and tried to speak calmly. "I know I should have more faith, Mother," she said, "but the more I pray, the more I seem to cry."

"That is because you have nothing to occupy you apart from prayer," the abbess said briskly. "You are neither a pupil nor a novice, so you have no regular tasks. But idleness is one of

141

Satan's own handmaids, and even prayer can be a form of idleness. We shall find some occupation for you. From now on, in the mornings you will help with the household tasks. It will be good for you. You've had no mother to instruct you, and you are to marry a young man of great estate. You know no more about managing a demesne than a babe new born."

"That is true," Adelaide admitted humbly.

"In the afternoons, you will assist Sister Hildegardis with the poor, at our gates and when she goes into the city. You will need to know how to minister to the sick, and charity is a virtue a great lady must possess. And remember this, too, Adelaide." Her ring of office on her raised forefinger glinted in a stray sunbeam. "Wars may come and wars may cease, but life goes on. In large measure, it is a woman's part to see that the children are tended and the old comforted; that food is cooked and clothes are woven and sewn. Above all, it is a woman's part to be patient. Patience," she added humorously, "was never one of your most salient characteristics."

"No, Mother," Adelaide agreed, smiling in spite of herself.

"Well, one acquires patience by practicing it. God usually gives opportunity to practice the virtues we need to acquire. You will find no lack of opportunity, my child." She rose and extended her hand in blessing, indicating that the conversation was ended.

For almost a month, now, Adelaide had been given all the occupation—and opportunity—that Mother Abbess had promised. The kitchen, the brewhouse, the weaving house, the sewing room, all had welcomed an extra pair of hands. True, she had been awkward at first and was still not the most skillful help they had known, but the nuns had taught her willingly —"suffered a fool gladly," she had thought to herself more than once, but without resentment. Her anxiety for Aelfred became no less, but she felt a strange comfort in the thought that her work at Berkynge might in some way be helping him. Sometimes she pretended that she was already mistress of Storches Hundred, a housewifely lady of the demesne, managing the estate while her husband was away at the wars. She knew full well that it was a foolish fancy, for she knew too well that Aelfred might never return. She tried desperately to be patient and to trust. But why—*why* had there been no word?

"Why so long a face?"

She started, then realized that Sister Winfred had spoken. "I was thinking that it is nearly Lady Day, and there's been no word from my father," she said. "Do you think he may not have gotten my message?"

"Who can tell? Happen the messenger has had to wait for him, or even to follow after him," Sister Winfred answered. "Your father rides where the King rides. Perhaps they've not yet reached Walsingham."

"But I know that the King plans to keep Easter at London."

"Easter is over a month away. Are the peas done?"

"All but two handfuls."

"Finish, then, and get yourself something to eat. Sister Hildegardis wants to go into the city today."

Adelaide hurried to finish. She liked to go into the city; it offered a change from the convent, and there was always the chance that a messenger might come, even be waiting for her when she returned. She set the kettle on the table, took the discards to the door and scattered them for the chickens in the kitchen court, then cut herself a slice of brown bread and poured a mugful of milk. She always had her breakfast and dinner with the nuns, but midday collation was easier in the kitchen. She looked across the room to see that Sister Winfred was smiling at her.

"Happen this time next year, you'll be in your own kitchen," the nun said. "And it may be a child will be in the cradle by the fire."

Adelaide had never let her pretending go that far. It seemed to be tempting fate. "If God wills," she said quietly. Then, on impulse, she asked, "Sister Winfred, do you really think I'll ever see Aelfred again? Please don't bid me be patient—I am trying to be. But it's been so long. I sent a letter to him at Walsingham with the one to my father."

Sister Winfred wrinkled her brow. "He left before you, I think you said?"

"Yes, nearly three weeks before."

143

"And you came here a month ago. And it would take two weeks at best for a message to reach Walsingham to tell him that you are with us. Perhaps longer. And at least that long for a message from him to come to you."

There was a pause. Then Adelaide said, "Sister, I've been very foolish."

"Not foolish. Just young. You'll hear soon. I feel it in my bones."

"Bless you," said Adelaide. Swiftly she went to the nun and threw her arms around her. "I'll say an extra prayer at Vespers for you."

"Say one that the hens will lay better," Sister Winfred said practically.

Adelaide laughed and hugged her, then went to her room in the guest hall for her cloak. She glanced at the little mirror and smoothed her hair, which had begun to grow again. I look different, she thought. Her cheeks seemed paler than she remembered, and her eyes looked back at her with a gravity that had not been in them before. "I must be growing up," she murmured. She was not sure that the change was an improvement, but she must not take time to consider that now. Sister Hildegardis would be waiting, and, besides, looking in mirrors overlong was vanity. She draped her cloak around her, fastened the clasp, and walked quickly out of the hall.

Sister was waiting for her at the convent door. "Well, child, and how are you?" she asked. She was a tiny woman, and, though she had been thirty years in London, her voice still carried an Irish lilt.

"Well, thank you." Adelaide smiled affectionately. She loved Sister Hildegardis.

"Take the panier, then, and we'll be going."

Adelaide put the wicker basket full of bandages and medicine on her arm, and they walked side by side to the main gate. Sister Hildegardis paused long enough to tell the portress when they would return; then they started up the road.

"Where do we go today, Sister?" Adelaide asked. "Can't I carry your panier for you? It looks very heavy."

"No, thank you, child. I can manage," Sister answered.

"There are meat jellies in it that Sister Winfred made, and she's set them just so. She'll have my head if they're upset. And I"—she paused dramatically—"I should have to confess to negligence in the Chapter of Faults."

Adelaide chuckled. Sister Winfred's meticulousness was well known. "I should not want to be the cause of penance to you. Where are we going, though?"

"To the blacksmith's by the wall. He came to see me this morning. Everyone in London came to the infirmary this morning." Sister threw her eyes to Heaven. "The novices and I were running our legs off for two hours, nearly. There was one boy with a boil the size of a lemon on his nose. His mother brought him, and I don't know which of them was more frightened when I took the knife to lance it. Then a sailor came. He'd been at sea for over a year. He was full of rare tales—the novices hadn't had so much entertainment in all their lives. His ship touched last at Harfleur, he said, so he had all the latest news about Duke William."

"What about Duke William?" Adelaide asked, as Sister paused for breath.

"May God put the curse of Cain on him! The sailor said that all up and down the coast you could hear the ring of hammers. He's building the greatest fleet the world has ever seen. I asked if he'd have men to fill them, but the sailor had no word on that. He did say that we could expect some excitement this summer—why, child? What's the matter? You're white as a ghost."

"I was thinking of my father," Adelaide answered. "And of Aelfred. And how terrible war is!"

"Oh, there'll be no war," Sister Hildegardis scoffed. "King Harold, God bless him, will stop it in an hour. You wait. The Normans will take one look at his army and run for their ships."

"I hope so. Oh, I hope so!"

"You'll be married long before then, I'm thinking. And besides, something may happen to Duke William. I'm praying to the dear Lord to throw a thunderbolt at him."

"Sister!" Adelaide burst out laughing.

"Oh, Blessed Mother, another sin to confess." Sister Hilde-gardis sighed contritely. "And I'll have to confess to hating him, too. But I'll tell you something." Her eyes twinkled. "The whole community is constantly doing penance for hating Duke William. Even Mother Abbess!"

"I'm glad," Adelaide said fervently. "I hate him, too. I hate all Normans—especially Tancred de Belleme."

Sister Hildegardis looked at her reprovingly. "No, you don't, child."

"I do! I hate him so much, it frightens me. I can't forgive him. I can't!"

"I don't blame you," Sister answered sympathetically. "But you must try, for your own sake. Your hatred won't hurt him, but it *will* harm you. Not that your forgiveness will do him any good, either, if he does not repent."

"He'll never repent."

"Then on him be the guilt. Leave him to God, child. He's out of your hands. One day he'll meet his guilt face to face, but that day may be long in coming. Meanwhile, don't waste your life dreaming of a revenge that may not be yours to take."

"I don't think I'm dreaming of revenge," Adelaide said soberly. "At least, I try not to, Sister. Truly, I do."

"I believe it. And I'll tell you something. You'll need to put your own hatred by, to help Aelfred Ansculfson deal with his."

"That would be hard. I know what he feels."

"Of course. If you love him, you would. But hate is worse for men than for women, because men have simpler natures. For instance, if you saw Tancred in pain, you'd try to ease him."

"Yes, I suppose I would. But only because it would be my duty."

"Certainly you would. You're a woman. Every instinct you had would tell you that it was your duty. You'd see anyone ill, or hurt, and you'd think at once of helping him, even if it were the Devil himself. But a man does not do that by nature. So hatred turns him to cruelty more quickly than it does a woman."

"Aelfred could never be cruel," Adelaide protested.

"He could. I've seen it. Or, what's worse, the wansickness could take him, just out of despair that he could not have what he would call his just revenge. You must not let that happen. God help us, there's little help for wansickness."

"I know." Adelaide swallowed hard. Her father had told her once of a man he himself knew, who had gone so far in wansickness that he had finally taken his own life. "He thought too much," her father had said. "Men who think too much are more likely to fall prey to it than are simple eselbrains."

"Ah, well, by God's grace it will not happen to Aelfred Ansculfson," Sister Hildegardis said reassuringly. "Now, then. The blacksmith's wife has an ailing baby, did you know that? Says the poor little one can take no food."

"What do you think is wrong?" Adelaide asked, glad to be diverted.

"If it were a dog, I'd say distemper, but as it's a baby, I shall have to see. Here we are. And will you look at the house! Blessed Brigid save us, I think there are as many here as came to the infirmary."

The next two hours passed swiftly. The baby was dosed with a mild posset of vermifuge and weak wine, wrapped warmly in flannel, and soon was sleeping peacefully. The blacksmith's old mother smiled in toothless pleasure at the wine jellies. Adelaide lost count of the number of children with assorted cuts and bruises who were salved, bandaged, and comforted with sweet patties from Sister Hildegardis' pockets. She helped the nun to set a broken arm for one man and to change the dressing on an ulcer for another. The last task made her feel quite faint, but her sympathy for the moaning victim sustained her; and, as always, she was lost in admiration for Sister Hildegardis, who seemed to be everywhere at once, clucking, comforting, and giving advice. When the last patient had been ministered to, she herself was exhausted, but Sister was as fresh as a daisy. Taking one final look at the baby and promising to return the next day, she left the house talking as animatedly as though she had done nothing more arduous that afternoon than seam a pillowcase.

147

At Berkynge, the portress was waiting for them impatiently. "My lady," she said breathlessly to Adelaide, "your father has come. He's waiting in the guest hall."

Adelaide's heart leaped, then sank to her shoes. Had he been ill? Wounded? "How does he look?" she asked tensely.

"Well, my lady."

"God be praised," said Sister Hildegardis. "Give me your panier. Run, child."

"Thank you." Adelaide started to run towards the guest hall, then slowed to a more decorous pace. But she was too happy to keep her eyes downcast. Her father had come to fetch her, to take her to Aelfred! Perhaps the wedding would be at Walsingham. She no longer was minded to wait to be married at Birnham. The long corridor seemed endless, but at last she came to the door. She opened it without knocking and, a moment later, was clasped in her father's arms.

"Father! Oh, Father," she cried. All the pent-up emotion of the past month came out in a burst of weeping. Rafe held her tightly until she grew calmer, then led her to a chair.

"Sit down, daughter," he said quietly. "I'll pour some wine for you. The Mother Abbess very kindly had some refreshments sent to me."

"Thank you," she said gratefully, accepting the cup. "I'm sorry I cried. But it's been so long, and so much has happened."

"I know. Siward told me."

"Siward? You've seen him?"

"Yes. I had to ride to Storches Hundred. That is why I am so late."

"Is Siward all right?"

"He is all right. Everything goes well there, and will go better. I brought Lady Ygerne to London this morning and put her aboard a ship leaving for France on the midnight tide. Ansculf has declared himself parted from her. King Harold has ordered her to leave the country. Tancred and Guilbert de Belleme have been declared outlaw. So that is the end of them, and good riddance."

"I'm glad," Adelaide said emphatically.

Rafe's eyes smoldered. "I'd kill the pair of them myself, one with each hand for what they did to you! Are you all right, daughter? He did not—he did not dare lay hands on you?"

"No. The people of Storches Hundred kept me safe." She trembled a little, as if with chill. "Are you sure that Tancred will never return?"

"Only if he comes with Duke William's army, and he'll face a shield wall if he does. That's the reason we've been north for so long. King Harold is calling out the largest army England has ever seen. He plans to muster on the coast, on the first of May." Rafe smiled exultantly. "William of Normandy will turn about and sail for home at the sight."

Adelaide looked at him searchingly. There was something in his manner not wholly natural, as though there was something he did not wish to say. She drew a deep breath. "Aelfred?" she asked, trying to keep her voice steady.

"He is at Walsingham."

Relief made her lightheaded. But why did her father not smile? Her heart began to pound. "He is ill?"

"Yes." Slowly Rafe got to his feet and turned his back on her. "His foot was injured. He took fever—but that is not what is wrong."

She went to him and put her hands on his arms. "Tell me."

He turned, and she was shocked to see the grimness of his face. His eyes were completely blank. "Daughter, you are betrothed to him no longer," he said roughly. "Put him out of your mind as fast as you can. You cannot marry such a man."

"What has he done?" she cried. "Nothing to bring disgrace on him! You could not make me believe that."

"Is it no disgrace when a man sits staring in front of him, speaking to no one, doing nothing?"

"But he had a fever—"

"That was gone weeks ago. He acts like one already dead. If he and his wits were parted, he could be pitied, but this! He will listen to no one. He will do nothing to help himself. He's no husband for you. Why, when I told him I'd break the betrothal, do you know what he did? Such words would have sent my hand flying to my sword, in his place, but he—he looked at me blankly and said it might be best."

For a moment, she was stunned. That Aelfred could agree so easily was beyond belief.

Her father's eyes grew milder. "I'm sorry, child, but you *would* hear it," he said quietly. "I'm to take you to the palace. The King will return soon, and you'll find enough distraction to make you forget all this."

"Forget?" Adelaide said dully.

"Of course. You're young. It's not as if you'd seen much of him."

Her eyes swam with tears. "Sometimes love does not take much seeing."

"You love him, then?" Rafe sighed. "By Heaven, I'm sorry. I'd have given my right arm to have spared you this."

"I know, Father." Then a thought darted through her mind. "Tell me, does he always act so? Does nothing anger or excite him?"

"Yes. Mention Tancred, and he's a raging bull. I don't blame him for hating that Norman, but it's a foolish, useless hatred. He's lost nothing. His lands are safe, and so are you."

"Then it's the wansickness that's taken hold of him."

"Wansickness?" Rafe drew her to him gently. "Poor child— and poor Aelfred, too. If it's that, I pity him. There's no cure for wansickness."

Her father's flat statement should have discouraged her completely, but it did not. Sister Hildegardis had said that there was *little* help for wansickness. She had not said there was no help at all. "Father, I must go to him."

"Saint Mary, help me!" he exclaimed. "Have you lost your own wits?"

"No. But I must go to Aelfred. I must try to help him."

He shook his head. "You cannot. His own father cannot. Even Lady Richeldis, who is as holy a woman as ever lived, can do nothing. What could you hope to do, except make yourself more unhappy?"

"I shall be unhappy for the rest of my life, if I do not," she answered. "He is my betrothed. I know what he feels. I found Mab, but I could not save her from the horrors of the de Bellemes. And you did not see the hot iron. It was horrible." Tears streamed down her face. "I know how stunned my wits were when I could not save Ellen. Please, Father—take me to Walsingham!"

She could see him wavering, and she looked at him beseechingly.

"Father, you told me that you would not betroth me to Aelfred without my consent. Well, you cannot break my betrothal without my consent, either. And I do not consent."

Rafe sighed heavily. "Girls! I've been wondering this past quarter hour what your mother would have done."

"She'd have done as you wanted her to do. She always did. Particularly if it concerned me. And you always agreed that she was right."

Rafe smiled. "You were the rose of her heart, and mine," he said softly. He put his arms around her. "Suppose I said no to this wish of yours? Suppose I forbade you ever to think of Aelfred Ansculfson again?"

"What would you do, Father, if someone forbade you to do a thing that you felt with all your heart was right?"

"Run him through, probably. If I felt certain that I was right."

"And whose daughter am I?" She smiled at him tremulously.

He shook his head. "From the day you were born, you were able to twist me around your finger," he said gruffly. "You are certain that you want to do this?"

She nodded. "I gave my betrothal promise in honor. More cannot be said."

"Well, heaven knows I would not want any man to die of wansickness—nor do I want to be run through," he added dryly. "Very well. We go to Walsingham."

She threw her arms around his neck and kissed him. "If it is as you say, and I cannot help him—if he is so changed as to be no longer the man to whom I plighted my troth," she said gently, "I will do as you ask." She gave him both her hands. "I promise."

"We'll start tomorrow," her father answered. "I must go to the palace, now. Give my respects to Mother Abbess, and tell her I'll fetch you after Mass." He looked at her for a moment, then said, "He's a fortunate young man, this Aelfred." He cleared his throat noisily, kissed her, and strode out of the room.

She stood there, listening to the sound of his footsteps receding. Her mind was in a turmoil. Her wish had been granted, but she was suddenly afraid. Suppose the wansickness had taken such hold of Aelfred that she indeed could do nothing? Would there be any comfort, then, in her having tried?

She stared unseeingly before her and shook her head. She must not consider such a possibility. She must try. The bell rang for Vespers. She looked at the empty wine cups, thinking that she should take them to the buttery, but the call to prayer was insistent within her. She was praying even before she pulled the hood of her cloak up over her head and hurried out into the cloister, where the nuns were gathering for evening procession into chapel.

In the guest bower, Aelfred was listlessly finishing his noonday meal. He dutifully sopped his wooden trencher with a piece of bread, ate it, then drank the ale in his cup to its dregs, though he tasted nothing. Through the open window he could see a tree covered with pale green leaves. A bird was trilling in one of its branches. The April sun was warm; in a few days the sowers would go out into the fields, and the shepherds would bring out the flocks, carrying the lambs that were weak from their long winter penning. Spring had come, and here, in this place of all places in the world, his own spirit should be quickening. But he felt nothing; he was like a man imprisoned in northland ice that no sun would ever melt.

He wished—oh, how he wished!—that he could cast off this bleakness that had for so many days possessed him, but even his father's urgings could not rouse him. What could his father know of failure and despair, he who had experienced neither? There was no use in trying to explain his own feelings to a simple soldier, who lived by the code that a man was either a man or a nithing. Aelfred smiled bitterly. Could a man be considered a man who had been so foolishly credulous as to trust such a one as Tancred de Belleme, when many things had pointed to the fact that the Norman could not be trusted? Instead of sitting under the Tree of Justice, unarmed and unprotected, he should have held the folkmoot in his own hall. The law provided for such a procedure in extraordinary circumstances, and Tancred's very presence at Storches Hundred could have been sufficient warrant to invoke it. Instead, he had insisted upon fulfilling the law to its very letter. Often since he had asked himself what was the use of holding to the law when a Tancred de Belleme could, by treacherous means, use that same law to win over honest men.

Yes, he had failed. He had been driven from his lands like a common criminal and forced to cry sanctuary while his enemy pursued him. He had not saved Mab. A sob rose in his throat as he remembered the sight of her being dragged away by the Norman soldiers. He'd have walked the hot iron himself, six times over, to have her safe. And Adelaide—he dared not think of her. Even her letter remained unopened, though he touched it often, wistfully and gently. Why did he not read it? What kind of nithing had he become? He was certain that it only confirmed her father's statement that their betrothal was broken. He could not blame her. He should have fought Tancred when he had the chance, then and there, with his bare hands, if necessary, instead of stealing away by night, leaving her to face the chaos alone. He might have been killed, but at least he would have behaved like a man. And then, Osric. He shut his eyes. He could hear still the terrible sound of those hoofbeats, and Osric's cry to him to run. And he had run, leaving a friend helpless and broken in the road, while he had sought safety for himself.

Now Tancred had escaped to Normandy and was laughing with his Norman friends at an English weakling. Aelfred clenched his fists. That his lands were safe meant little, when his enemy was free. "One day, one day," he murmured. Anger followed by hatred welled up within him and engulfed him. Forgive his enemy? No. Not he. He would never forgive Tancred de Belleme, nor the evil woman who was his mother, nor his uncle, the treacherous snake. The time would come when he would have his revenge against Tancred, and it would be sweet. For a moment his eyes flashed and his cheeks grew hot; then he slumped back into his chair. He was a fool. He could do nothing to Tancred. The Norman had simply eluded him. Aelfred's hands relaxed slowly and lay limply on his knees. He was powerless to do anything. For days, now, he had been unable even to pray, and he knew the reason. He could not forego his hatred, though it was killing his spirit within him. He was appalled at some of the thoughts that came to him, thoughts that once would have sent him flying to a priest for confession but which now only fed the hatred consuming him. He knew that if he were to die in this state, he would surely lose his soul; and, in a flash of frightening insight, he realized that he almost did not care.

His head began to throb. Had the wansickness taken him, then, that could make a man die while he still lived? "No!" he whispered in horror. He must not give way to that final despair. Slowly he got to his feet and opened the door. The sun streamed down upon him, but it warmed him very little. He pulled his cloak tightly about him and walked out into the courtyard. His breath came in short hard gasps, and he was glad that no one was there to see.

Unsteadily, for he had moved little except from his chair to his bed for weeks, he walked towards an open gate in the stockade and found himself in a neatly patterned garden. Not a sprout was showing, but the beds were carefully planted and edged. Tears came to his eyes. The garden reminded him of Mab. Obeying some hidden instinct, he reached down, scooped up a handful of earth, and let it run through his fingers. It was good land. Things would grow in it. He glanced at a rose-bush and saw that the buds were already swollen. The sun seemed a little warmer, now, and he was strangely glad to be under it.

"I am happy to see you better," a gentle voice said behind him.

He turned to see that Lady Richeldis had followed him into the garden. "I thought a walk might do me good," he said lamely, though he knew that no such thought had brought him out of his solitude.

Lady Richeldis, however, accepted his remark as quite reasonable. "I, too, was about to walk," she said. "I would be glad of your company, unless you had rather be alone?"

"No," he answered. Then he added, "I think I have been too much alone these past days."

Her brow furrowed anxiously. "I am sorry. Had I known, I would have come to you. You had only to speak."

"Yes." He flushed a little at his tactlessness. "But it seemed that I could not speak"—some old habit of courtesy evidenced itself—"until this moment."

She smiled and put her hand on his arm. "I was on my way to the Holy House."

He stopped short. The Holy House! Not once had he asked to be taken there. How could he, riddled with hatred of himself as well as of his enemy, enter a place where love had manifested itself in great miracles? Yet, at the same time, it was the only place he longed to see. He felt as though his feet were weighted with lead.

"You are afraid." It was a statement, not a question. "Why?"

"I—I do not know." He could not bring himself to speak the truth.

Her piercing eyes looked into his. "Let me tell you. You are afraid because you refuse to forsake the hatred and vengeance in you that keep you chained, though you long to be free."

He began to tremble. She was so amazingly right that it terrified him. That there could be no pretense with her frightened him even more. "My lady, what can I do?" he asked, his voice barely audible.

"Let us walk, as we speak together," she said, moving towards the path. "You know what you must do. You must learn to stop this hating before you die of it. You must learn what love is again."

She was a great lady, but she was a woman nonetheless. What could she know of men's minds? He looked at her challengingly. "I cannot love Tancred de Belleme," he said flatly.

Her eyes never wavered. "No one asks you to, at least not in the way that you consider love. Your affection for him,

156

even if you had any, would be useless, for he wants none. Tancred is no prodigal son. The prodigal son loved his father before he went away, and it was love that made him return." She nodded emphatically. "Your love for Tancred will be no more than absence of hatred, but it must be that. You must not wish him harm."

"I must forgive him, you mean?" His voice was hard.

"You do not understand forgiveness, either, I see. You think it is overlooking wrong. It is not that. Neither is forgiveness condoning another's wrongdoing, Aelfred Ansculfson. It is giving over the desire for vengeance to the One who has said 'Vengeance is mine.' Can you not do that?"

"No!" he cried. But he could not leave her with that answer, for in honesty it was not completely true. Bending his head, he murmured, "I wish that I could, my lady."

"Why can you not? Is God working too slowly for you?"

He gasped; then, seeing the glint of amusement in her eyes, he burst out laughing for the first time in weeks. "You make me feel very foolish," he admitted.

"And so you are, doing nothing all this time but brood over impossibilities," she said sternly. "Suppose Tancred were before you, unarmed, as you've so often dreamed. Would you strike him down?"

She knew of his dreams, too! Aelfred swallowed hard and said, "No."

"Why not? It would be the answer to all your hopes."

"I don't know why not. I only know that I could not." He sighed. "But don't you see, my lady, how that feeling only makes it worse for me? Suppose I were to meet him face to face in battle?"

"You'd do your duty as a King's man against an enemy. Did they teach you nothing in that monastery?"

Her voice was as astringent as vinegar to the tongue. "I can see that a battle would not be like taking private vengeance," he said slowly, "and I might not be the one who killed him."

"And that grieves you? Don't let it," she said succinctly. "Tancred de Belleme will receive his just deserts. Do you

157

think he is happy now? His magnificent plot has gone up in smoke. He is an outlaw, despised by those he despises, distrusted by those who flatter him."

"That will not matter to him, I fear."

"It will one day," she insisted. "I saw his face."

"But still, I ran from him. And I could not save Mab."

"More objections? Have done, Aelfred. You did all you could, decently and honorably, at the time. That counts for much. Mab had been acquitted because of your presence at the Tree of Justice. Tancred was the trickster. But you are alive, and he does not hold your lands. It seems to me that you should be grateful for that, instead of sending your father nearly out of his wits."

"Was my father really worried?" he asked, surprised.

"Naturally! He thought his only son had the wansickness, and that it was his fault because he had not let you enter the monastery. I told him that you did not have wansickness, and that a monastery was no place for you. As for Osric—"

"Osric?" He stopped and steeled himself for her reply to his question. "What of Osric?"

"He is alive and well."

"Why did no one tell me?" His whole being vibrated in relief and joy. It was so long since he had felt anything but hatred that he was weak.

"We tried to tell you, but you refused to take notice. Osric came twice to see you and was heartbroken at the sight of you."

"I think I thought it was his ghost. I really think I did," Aelfred whispered, amazed at his own indifference to all life around him. Then he said urgently, "My lady, pardon me, but I must go to him at once. Where is he?"

"He went with your father to Norwich this morning in the King's train. They'll be back in three days, and I imagine you'll ride south with them then."

He walked on beside her, hardly knowing that he walked. Osric was alive! It was a miracle—but why should there not be miracles in this lovely place? His own sudden awakening was surely miraculous; the thought filled him with joy and then with shame. How could he have brooded so long in silence, causing distress to those who loved him? He looked up at the sky and filled his lungs with the warm clear air.

"You must stop hating yourself, too, Aelfred Ansculfson," Lady Richeldis said after a moment.

"How can I do otherwise?" The thoughts that had filled his mind all these weeks struggled to be spoken. "In vanity I trusted where I should not, and I failed miserably in the trust my father gave me."

"Do you think that you are the only man who has ever failed?"

"No. But I added cowardice to failure. I ran away. I could not save Mab. And Osric was hurt because of me."

"Don't deprive Osric of the grace of his sacrifice. He wanted to save your life. And you thought of him when you yourself could scarcely stand. As for Mab, I repeat—the folkmoot had already acquitted her because of you. You could not have foreseen what the Normans would do to her."

Her words, measured and solemn, gave him strength. "And Adelaide? What of my leaving her alone on the demesne?"

"She was not alone. She was in the care of your own people. What better could you have done? A grand heroic act is something for poetry, perhaps, but it does not always serve the purpose in immediate life. Your duty was to live. And, as I am a woman, I know Adelaide's mind. She wanted that, too."

"Perhaps." He could not accept her words completely, but some of the searing pain had left his heart. "I cannot help but wish, though, that I had acted more like the man my father expected."

"Your father is more than satisfied with you," she said quietly.

He looked at her gratefully. "Thank you for telling me so, my lady."

They had reached a clearing. Before them stood a little stone chapel; nearby a spring circled with the same rough stones bubbled out of the ground. "You are here," Lady Richeldis said, her eyes burning with exaltation. "Within that chapel is the Holy House, as Our Blessed Lady showed it to me in my vision—exactly like her own in Nazareth where the Angel came to her. And the spring rushed forth out of the ground, as she promised. It has mysteriously brought healing to many sick and sad of heart. Do not try to know why," she warned. "Accept some blessings without question. Only with gratitude."

She dipped her hand into the spring and held it out to Aelfred. He took the water from her finger tips and signed himself with the Cross.

"Go in peace, Aelfred Ansculfson," she said, smiling joyously. "May you find there what you seek."

He was hardly conscious of her going, so intent was he on the chapel before him, and she went quietly. One day there would be a great church here; stone for the building lay all about him under straw, ready for the masons to resume their work when the weather was warm enough. Now there was only a rough shell with a small, square tower, but through the low, open doorway he could see an altar with a magnificent gold and jeweled cross. He had to bend his head to see it, and that was fitting. No one should enter such a sanctuary with head unbowed.

But dared he enter? With all his heart he wished it, but the sense of unworthiness of those past weeks held him back as strongly as his yearning pulled him forward. He wavered, then started to walk, then found himself praying for forgiveness, for release from his hatred, for peace for Mab, for Osric, for Adelaide. "God help me!" he moaned again and again. He was trembling so that he could no longer stand; he fell on his knees, tears streaming from his eyes. All consciousness of time left him. He did not know how long he remained there, nor when something drew his eyes to the shrine again that made him rise to his feet, crying out in mingled amazement and terror.

Someone was standing in the open door, a woman wrapped in a blue cloak. For a moment he thought he might be seeing a vision and covered his face with his hands. The woman spoke his name. He tried to answer, but his voice would not obey him. He looked at her dazedly; now the hood of her cloak fell back to her shoulders, showing hair that shone in the sun. She was smiling. Slowly he took a few steps towards her.

"Adelaide!" he cried, and all his heart was in his voice. An instant later she was in his arms, gently weeping but crying at the same time. He held her tightly, hardly daring to believe that it was she. But her arm about his neck was no illusion. Gently he kissed her. No, this was reality itself.

Suddenly he held her at arm's length. "We forget," he said tautly. "We are no longer betrothed."

She looked at him soberly. "Is that your wish?" she asked.

"No! No, of course it is not," he answered, his hands tightening on her shoulders. "How could it be? I love you, Adelaide. That you surely know."

"If you do, then why did you tell my father that you thought it would be best to break our betrothal?" she asked with her old forthrightness.

"Because I was a fool," he answered. "I had no thoughts left. I'd brooded so long on my own troubles that I could think of nothing else. I despised myself for my weakness. I thought you must despise me, too."

Her eyes widened in genuine perplexity. "Why?"

He let her go, his arms dropping helplessly to his sides. "At the time, my leaving you at Storches Hundred seemed the only thing to do." He spoke with difficulty. "But I think now that I should have stayed and protected you."

"How could you have protected me if you had stayed? You were a prisoner."

He quailed before her honesty as he had before Lady Richeldis. "That only makes things worse. I *had* to take the coward's way." He smiled ironically. "You should have seen me running up the road and clinging to the gates with Tancred lowering over me on his black horse. It could not have been an inspiring sight."

"You did what the Welshman told you to do," she said quietly. "And you are alive."

"Yes. But I should like to have been a little more heroic for you."

She looked at him for a moment, then took his hand in hers.

161

"Aelfred, you are alive. That was all I wanted. Why, do you think I would have lived long, if you had been killed?"

"Adelaide—"

"No, I would not." Her voice rose. "I could not. Not even in the convent."

"Hush," he said, putting his arms around her. "You must not say such things. Your life is precious to me. We should enjoy our lives, my dearest, and not spoil this present by foolish threats." He could not make her understand, and he knew that he never could, but that did not seem to matter. Now that she was here, he was not sure that he understood himself. As she had said, he was alive. Perhaps that was the one thing needful, after all.

She looked up at him, tears glistening in her eyes. "Father said that you had the wansickness. Did you?"

"I was very near it, I think. But, thank God, it did not take hold of me completely."

"When he told me, I thought my heart would break. But I would not let him break our betrothal, for all that."

He looked at her in amazement, scarcely able to believe his ears. "What did you say?"

"I told him that he could not break it without my consent and that I would not believe that you wished it to be broken unless you, yourself, told me so."

"Oh, my dearest one!" He clasped her tightly, his heart pounding. "I shall never tell you that."

"And I shall never consent," she answered.

He kissed her again and again and then reluctantly released her. "I shall speak to your father tonight," he said firmly. "Mine has gone to Norwich with the King, but he will rejoice when he hears."

"So will mine. He likes you, Aelfred. And he was truly sorry about everything, especially when I told him that I had not changed—that I love you."

He could not keep from smiling. "You really told him so? You have never told me."

"I did," she said indignantly. "Don't you remember that day in Storches Hundred?"

"Yes, I do," he said, smiling more. "I was only trying to make you tell me again. Your telling me this is what has kept me alive, I think. Will you not say it now?"

She had never looked more beautiful. "I love you, Aelfred Ansculfson," she said clearly.

He raised her hand to his lips. "And I love you," he answered. "Adelaide, we must be married at once. I'm afraid to let you go from me again. I don't want to wait until Easter."

"Nor do I," she said honestly. "But it is Lent, Aelfred."

"There are times when a rule can be dispensed," he reminded her. "In extraordinary circumstances the letter of the law is put aside. I've learned that. Would you not rather be married here and ride south with the King as my wife?"

"If he will permit it."

"He will. I shall persuade him."

She smiled. "You are very confident, aren't you?"

"Could I be otherwise, now that you are here?"

"I think he may agree. He is a new-wedded man himself, you know."

"No, I had not known that."

"My father told me that he married Earl Morcar's and Earl Edwin's sister, Edith. That is another reason why he has stayed so long in the north. A wedding takes a little time, even in these strange days." She shook her head. "I hope it will be a happy marriage, but Father thinks he was in love with someone else and only married the Lady Edith to satisfy the anxieties of the red-bearded brothers."

"What a sad reason for a marriage!" Aelfred shook his head. "I've been out of the world too long. Adelaide, will you marry me as quickly as it can be arranged?"

"As quickly as it can be arranged, yes. I should like to be married here, at the Holy House, if Lady Richeldis will agree— and if that is your wish."

He looked at the chapel. "I think I had rather it be here than anywhere else, if it is to your liking. It's strange. Once I dreamed, dear love, of coming here as a pilgrim. Never in my wildest imaginings had I thought that my pilgrimage would end this way. It is a miracle."

"One is ending," she answered. "But the greater miracle is that ours is beginning, Aelfred."

"You are wise beyond your years, my love."

"I seem to have become wiser in these past weeks."

They stood for a moment in silence, then Aelfred asked, "Shall we enter the Holy House together?"

"Yes, if you wish."

"I do wish it. And I must tell you this, Adelaide. Perhaps it is because love drives out all hatred, but suddenly I no longer hate Tancred as I did."

Her eyes were shining. "I am glad."

"Oh, I can't let you think I have lost all hatred," he admitted honestly. "But in some strange way I can almost pity him. He not only lost the lands he wanted, he lost you, too, and I think he wanted you more than the lands."

"That was one thing he would never have won," she said simply.

"I know." There was pride in his voice as he said it. "Oh, Adelaide, help me not to waste myself in hatred of him. Dark days are coming. We have so little time. I want to live in the sun, with you, as long as possible."

She put her hand in his. "Perfect love casts out fear," she said. "There will be sun for us, even in darkness."

TANCRED strode up the stone stairs, his bow slung nonchalantly over his shoulder. It was long past sunset, but Duke William's hunting party had only just returned to the palace adjoining Fecamp Abbey, where the nobility of Normandy had gathered for the annual Easter court. The day had been long and the riding hard, but Tancred whistled a tune as he walked, for his day had been completely successful. His arrow had brought the giant stag to earth at such an incredible distance, that Taillefer, the minstrel, had promised to compose a ballade about the feat and to sing it at the feast tonight. Even more important, Duke William's cold blue eyes had looked at him for the first time with something like real approval. His luck had turned; he was sure of it. His three months of patient strategy were about to be rewarded. And, if he won the archery contest on the next day—

"*Sainte vierge,* let me win," he prayed, but the words were a gesture, for he was sure that he would win. His only real competition was the marshal, FitzOsborne, captain of the archers. But FitzOsborne was getting old. His arrow had missed the stag by two full yards.

He opened the door to his chamber—no men's bowers here in Normandy, he thought scornfully. Here he received what his rank as a de Belleme deserved, though he had arrived, more or less, under a cloud. Duke William had received his uncle and himself with great coldness on that first audience and had not minced words in expressing his displeasure, not—to Tancred's amazement—because they had failed to take and control Storches Hundred but because they had attempted to do so at all.

"My war with Harold Godwineson, when it comes, will not be piecemeal. It will be declared openly and honorably," he had said bitingly. "I'll have no one besmirch my name with intrigue and treachery." And he had summarily ordered Guilbert de Belleme to join a diplomatic mission to Rome, while Tancred was suffered to remain in the palace as a squire.

"All the same, Duke William would have been pleased if we had succeeded," Guilbert de Belleme had told Tancred at leave-taking. "However, use this time well, nephew. You'll be under his eye, and he can be generous when he pleases."

But, apart from having a personal chamber and a page to serve him, he had been the recipient of little ducal generosity these past three months. Still, it was pleasant to know that Denis would be waiting for him with hot water and fresh linen after his long ride. He smiled at the boy and wished him a friendly good evening, as he tossed the bow on a chair and sat down on the boot box for Denis to remove his boots for him. He was glad that Denis was not a chatterer; usually the boy had little to say, as was proper between master and page. Yes, it *was* good to be in Normandy, where churls knew their places. Tonight, however, the boy seemed bursting to speak, so Tancred indulged him.

"What's been happening?" he inquired.

"You've not seen the star?" Denis asked excitedly.

Tancred yawned. "What star?"

"You can see it through your window, *mon seigneur*. Look at it! It is the brightest I have ever seen."

Tancred pulled himself up and went to the window. The boy was right. There *was* such a star in the heavens, the like of which he had never seen, either. He gazed at it in astonishment; it seemed to grow brighter, more dazzling with every moment. He felt great excitement for some reason.

"It's a good omen," he said. "It means good fortune."

"For Duke William?" Denis asked eagerly.

"For all of us," Tancred answered, inwardly exulting. "For me!" He tore himself away from the window. "Bring water, boy. Hot, remember."

"I have it here," Denis answered, filling the basin.

In silence, Tancred stripped and washed himself. First the stag, he thought, and now the star! His fortunes had begun to rise. He might even be called to serve at the duke's table tonight, so he had better put on his best clothes. He had been constantly "in attendance" upon the duke since his arrival in Normandy, but he had not yet been called for personal service and he longed for this special mark of approval. Still, he had used the time well. His eyes gleamed. One look at Duke William had told him that this man was honest, not double-tongued like his uncle. He wanted his nobles honest, too, so Tancred had made himself appear so. He had not even scrupled to drop a few hints here and there that he had been his uncle's victim in the Storches Hundred fiasco, and, since no one at court could possibly know what actually had happened, he had been believed in several instances. He had cultivated the acquaintance of a few powerful men who were in the duke's special confidence, like William de Warrene and Marshal FitzOsborne, and he knew that he had been mentioned favorably. Today he had been summoned to join the hunt, and he had won a smile. Those late afternoon hours he had spent practicing in the archery field, with Denis to hold the targets, had been amply rewarded. He smiled triumphantly. How easy it was to hoodwink honest men!

He was dressed, now. With a wave of the hand he dismissed Denis to clean the basin and returned to the window. The star was rising in the darkness; its brilliance now was almost unnatural. Nevertheless, he thought, it was a portent of his own success. Like this star, he would rise suddenly out of the darkness to dazzle all beholders. When the time came, he would sail with Duke William to England. He would fight well in the battles—that is, well enough to be noticed without being injured—and then he could claim his reward. "The demesne of Storches Hundred and the hand of Adelaide of Birnham," he murmured, and with Adelaide, of course, came all the lands of Birnham. He would be rich beyond all calculating. And he would have Adelaide, despite her efforts to elude him, for he wanted her. Not because he loved her; love was unimportant. The man who married for love alone often found himself left with only love, and what was that worth without money and influence and power? He turned from the window and paced up and down the room, striking his clenched fist on his palm. Possession of her—yes, that he must have. Possession. And she had better comply. If she did not, he would master her. But, he thought complacently, she was not likely to protest overlong; he had nearly won her at Storches Hundred. He was quite willing to forgive her running away, he decided magnanimously. Girls, he had discovered, were impetuous creatures, and they never knew what they wanted until someone told them. Well, he was the one who could and would master Adelaide of Birnham.

"What a life will be mine!" he chuckled, sinking into his chair. Of course Adelaide would be agreeable: Duke William's generosity would probably include a title of greater consequence than "my lady." What woman could resist the possibility of being addressed as "Madame la Comtesse?" He could restore the property at Belleme with her dowry and be a true *grand seigneur*. And, when his uncle died, he would be the Comte de Belleme, as well. He closed his eyes and leaned his head against the chairback, his lips curved in a sleek, gluttonous smile.

A knock at the door aroused him. "Come in," he called lazily, thinking that Denis had come to summon him to the feast. "Is it time to go down?"

"Not quite," the voice of Guilbert de Belleme answered. "Duke William was delayed in his dressing. We have time for a talk."

Tancred jumped to his feet. "Uncle! Don't tell me you're back from Rome so soon?"

"Surprised? So am I, and decidedly saddle-worn," de Belleme answered. "His Grace, the Archbishop of Lisieux—may the Lord save him—rides like an old campaigner, but I am not as well upholstered as he."

Tancred laughed at his uncle's grimace. "Take this chair, then. The cushions are soft." He pulled up a footstool for himself. "How did the embassy fare?"

"Both embassies fared excellently."

"Were there two?"

"Of course. His Grace the Archbishop's, and mine."

"Well!" Tancred looked his surprise. "Duke William sent *you* on an embassy?"

"Assuredly," de Belleme said quietly.

"But he was angry with you!"

"Oh, yes. At least, he convinced himself that he was. But that would not prevent his making me useful to him."

Tancred shook his head. "He was angry. He is an honest man, Uncle. Do you know, the first notice I've had from him in all these weeks was when I killed that stag today?"

"Yes, I've heard about that. Your name is being praised all over the palace. The first man I met insisted that I pause to drink your health."

"I'm going into the archery contest tomorrow."

"Let's hope you win. The duke says there will be a triple prize. Money, which I believe you will find useful—"

"Indeed yes," Tancred said ruefully. "You should have warned me that dice throwing was in fashion here."

"As it is with soldiers the world over." De Belleme shrugged. "The second prize will be his own gift to whomever wins, which I have an intuition will be a captaincy among his archers. FitzOsborne is growing old, and someone must be trained to replace him."

"And the third prize?"

"Whatever the winner wishes to ask." De Belleme's eyes gleamed in the candlelight. "You'd better give some thought to your choice. Meanwhile, let me tell you about our success at Rome. Or aren't you interested?"

"Yes—yes, of course," Tancred protested, but his mind was filled with his own imaginings that, moment by moment, grew to exceed the star in brightness.

"Well, the Holy Father has blessed the Norman cause."

"Wasn't that expected?" Tancred asked impatiently. "Especially after all the money that Duke William has given to Norman monasteries."

"Your cynicism pains me, nephew. Unlike yourself, I have some doubts as to our liege's honesty. But none whatever about his devotion! Naturally Pope Alexander took that devotion into consideration, but his decision was based on the broken oath."

The peculiar emphasis in his uncle's tone made Tancred a trifle uneasy. "Did Harold Godwineson send an embassy, too?" he asked.

"No, strangely enough, he did not. That made our task all the easier, of course. Duke William had apprised him of his intention long ago, and Harold's neglect in taking his own cause to Rome was easily interpreted as a confession of guilt. Or of indifference to the Holy Father. It is a toss of the coin which is the worse."

"And your own mission, Uncle? What was it?"

"To raise a mercenary army in Italy."

Tancred whistled. "The duke is leaving nothing to chance. Did you get many volunteers?"

"Several thousand men are on the march right now from Sicily and Calabria. On our way back from Rome, we learned that the Duke of Burgundy is sending men, and that Count Aimeri of Poitou is leading a huge force personally. The duke's banner has been raised in Anjou and Sicily, and Count Brian is coming with his Breton slingmen, the best in the world." De Belleme smiled. "You wanted a battle, Tancred? Well, you'll see the greatest army ever mustered, provided the duke can get his ships finished in time."

Tancred's heart was pounding. "Harold won't dare stand against him."

"You have much to learn about wars," de Belleme said tolerantly. "Never underestimate your enemy, nephew. I told you that once before, I think. You, of all people, should know its truth."

"Bah! Any man can be outwitted. Duke William will have an army."

"True. But still, be advised. Harold Godwineson is an experienced commander, and he will have the advantage of being on his own ground. Of course, it is being rumored that Duke William has entered into a treaty with Harald Hardrada of Norway to attack Northumbria and draw the English army from the south. Also, Tostig Godwineson is said to be much in evidence in Flanders these days."

"I know. Tostig was here, two weeks ago. All very secret, of course. The duke doubtless sent him to Flanders."

"So? You know something I did not. Then we can probably count on the help of the duke's father-in-law, as well."

Tancred nodded. Count Baldwin of Flanders, the father of Duchess Matilda of Normandy, had one of the finest armies in Europe. "And he has ships, too."

"And builders. Flemings are already at work on our fleet at the mouth of the River Dives."

"It's glorious!" Tancred exclaimed. "I cannot wait for it all to begin. When do we invade England?"

"When all is prepared. When the wind is right." De Belleme threw his eyes to Heaven. "*Mon dieu,* what it is to be young! How do you think you will comport yourself in battle?"

"As bravely as any man." Tancred bristled. "Do you doubt that?"

"Can you follow orders? Take discipline? Keep your head when arrows and javelins are flying about it?" his uncle asked sternly. "Wait until your horse is killed under you and you lie there, wounded, perhaps, with no one to help you rise and the cavalry charging over you. Believe me, you'll discover in that moment that courage is nothing. In battle, survival is all that matters."

"I shall survive," Tancred said proudly, eyes flashing, "and claim my just reward as well."

"Indeed? And what reward do you consider just?"

"The demesne of Storches Hundred and the hand of Adelaide of Birnham." He stopped short and glared. "Why do you laugh at me?"

De Belleme stopped his laughter. "Be assured, I do not laugh at you," he said. "I'm merely amused to find that you are almost as shrewd an intriguer as I am. It must run in the blood."

"Do you think my choice unreasonable?"

"Not in the least. Ask it as your third reward when you win the archery contest tomorrow, provided, of course, that Duke William is victorious in England. It might be good strategy to delay your request until that happy event is certain. Meanwhile, I have some information that should lend spice to your venture."

"Oh? What?"

"I stopped at Belleme a week ago. Your mother is there."

Tancred stared at him dumbfounded. "Impossible!"

"I assure you, I saw her with my own eyes. Baron Ansculf has separated himself from her, and Harold Godwineson has pronounced her banished."

"How dare they?" Tancred leaped to his feet. The blood rushed to his head, dyeing his face an ugly crimson. "This insult is not to be borne!"

"Of course not. So, naturally, I think your choice of reward a most appropriate one."

"I'll demand Ansculf's death, as well. My mother married him honorably. He shall redeem this dishonor with his life—or Aelfred shall—or both shall!"

"Provided they survive the battle," de Belleme said dryly. "They may not. However, take comfort. There will still be the lands and the fair Adelaide. Nothing like a good glow of vengeance to put zeal into a man."

"Don't mock me, Uncle! You should be saying the same thing. Have you no care for my mother's honor? Your own sister?"

"Oh, Tancred, don't be childish. Talk of honor from either of us sounds like what it is: talk, and false at that. Your mother will manage; she always has. After all, we both know full well that *she* married Ansculf."

"English cur!" Tancred spat.

"Well, you pretended sufficiently to help her decision when she asked. We both knew that you very much enjoyed the idea of living comfortably. You were not at all happy at Belleme. The marriage was convenient for all concerned, and would have remained so, had you handled Aelfred with a little more finesse."

"Finesse? Who made the plans so that Aelfred would be stripped of his inheritance?" Tancred flared.

"Oh, I admit to making the plans. But do you deny that the thought was also your own? And that you could hardly wait to carry it out?"

His uncle's bland face so infuriated Tancred that he could hardly speak. "All right, I thought of it," he said thickly. "But your plan was not good enough, or Aelfred Ansculfson would have walked the hot iron that high noon."

"Enough! You bore me." De Belleme's eyes were like arrow points. "Sit down, nephew. You're as guilty as Lucifer. You wanted Aelfred out of the way, and I undertook to gratify you."

"With a long story about how Duke William wanted loyal supporters in England."

"*Bien,* we were both guilty of misjudgment. Or mismanagement, rather. Others have been more successful in the attempt. Let us not be guilty of either, now—or, perhaps I should say, let *you* not be so now."

"Is that likely?"

"Very likely. Or don't you remember an oath of fealty that you made to Baron Ansculf on Twelfth Night?"

Tancred sank onto the footstool. This, then, was the reason for his uncle's visit—to emphasize Harold Godwineson's broken oath, and his own. "I took it under duress."

"I think not." De Belleme's voice was smooth as silk. "Ansculf offered you a fair choice: to go with me, or to remain under a son's pledge of loyalty. You chose to stay."

"Only because you told me to."

"I never uttered a word."

"You looked at me," Tancred insisted. "It was meant as a signal."

"Perhaps you mistook my look. You have been mistaken in other things. Why not in this?"

"Others were there. They witnessed," Tancred cried, grasping at straws.

"Do you think they would witness in your favor, even if they were called upon to do so?"

Tancred stared at him in dumb dismay. Was his magnificent dream to be destroyed so quickly? "Why do you speak of this?" he asked tensely.

"Because Duke William will speak of it."

"There's no reason why he should," Tancred faltered.

"No? Let us consider. The duke, as you have observed, is an honest man. Also, he has promised the Holy Father that, if he is victorious over Harold, he will rule England by English law. He's not coming as a conqueror, you see. He is merely pressing a just cause against an oath breaker." De Belleme paused. "Of all men, he despises most an oath breaker."

Tancred quailed. "What do you want of me?" he asked helplessly.

"Very little. Only that you stop posing as the innocent victim of a wicked uncle. I've heard a little of your attempt to put a sheep's fleece over your head, but I want no more of it. Let me tell you, the man *I* most despise is the one who lies to himself and others about his own desires."

There was a long silence. Then de Belleme continued.

"When you demand Storches Hundred, the duke will ask whether you swore fealty to Baron Ansculf. What will you tell him?"

"I shall tell him no," Tancred cried violently. "A forced oath is no oath under English law."

"So says Harold Godwineson. And so you may say, as long as you stop these whisperings and complaints and intrigues against me. Otherwise, I shall be forced to tell the truth—that you swore of your own free will, and that you intentionally broke your oath as soon as it was made."

174

Tancred felt as though he were being pulled into the center of a whirlpool. Frantically he made one last protest. "Did you not tell me that, if Aelfred Ansculfson were to be condemned for sorcery, my oath of fealty would give me the right to assume control over Storches Hundred?"

De Belleme drew his lips into a slit of a smile. His white teeth gleamed. "I may have. Unfortunately, I've forgotten."

"My mother heard you!"

"I can assure you that she has forgotten." His smile grew more sinister. "Behave, nephew. Keep your clever schemes for your own help. You will need them. You are not yet quite as clever as I. And after all"—he shrugged deprecatingly—"is it so much that I am asking? Think of what you stand to gain— Storches Hundred, Birnham, the fair Adelaide. That should be worth more to you than the petty satisfaction of villifying me."

He rose and stretched.

"We shall be summoned very soon, so perhaps I had better leave you to compose yourself. The duke has asked me to feast at his table tonight." He moved towards the door. "As I have told you, he is very generous in his rewards."

The door closed behind him, leaving Tancred spent with impotent rage. That his uncle could so easily have found him out was not only infuriating, it was humiliating. How vain he is! he thought. I had not known that he was so vain. Then it occurred to him that his uncle's vanity might be very useful. He thought quickly. *Bien,* if the duke now smiled on Guilbert de Belleme, he too would smile—and work for his own advancement at the same time. Once he had received his reward, he could settle matters to his own satisfaction, and in more than one way. Let his uncle enjoy his place in the sun. He would not have it long.

And there were other matters, much more important, to occupy him now. No matter what his uncle had said, the insult to his mother must be avenged. And it would be. Indeed, it would be, and easily. If fate deprived him of both Baron Ansculf and Aelfred, there was another object on which he could wreak his hatred, which would hurt them more than any hurt to themselves. "The fair Adelaide," he sneered, through clenched teeth. Yes, she would marry him, and he would take her lands; and then, after he had gotten all he could from her and humiliated her expertly, he would cast her off without a shred of remorse. He hated her. He hated all of them, but Adelaide above the rest because she had been so loyally cared for by the people of Storches Hundred and had put herself—for the moment—out of his reach. But not for long! Under the protection of William of Normandy he would demand her as his wife, and she would be subject to him. She could have nothing that it did not please him to give her, and he would give her little and make her pay dearly indeed for that little. When Denis came to tell him that the duke was ready to dine, he was smiling diabolically, thinking of the pleasure he would take in humiliating her, in breaking that fine spirit of hers, and the sheer delight it would be to hear her weep.

AELFRED slowed his horse to a walk. The London road lay like a broad ribbon in the sunlight; in the distance he could already see the towers of the Abbey Church. He turned to smile at Osric, who followed close behind him, and at the twenty Storches Hundred men, chosen by lot to serve in King Harold's army, tramping along at a quick march.

"We're almost there," he called, motioning to Osric to come beside him.

"It's a fast pace you set, master," Osric remarked. "The others are tired, they say."

"They'll rest in London. When the King says come at once, he means yesterday, not tomorrow," Aelfred replied with an attempt at humor.

But Osric sighed plaintively. "It's a pity to have to leave our lands now. They are so beautiful in June. Master, will we really be home before harvest?"

"So the King says. Duke William will certainly attack as soon as the wind is right, and I hope that's soon. All I want, Osric, is to have this battle over and done, so that we can go home and stay there."

"Amen," Osric said fervently.

Aelfred looked at the green fields along the road. The

trees were in full leaf and the sun was warm. In that moment, the memory of Storches Hundred smote him so fiercely that his eyes burned. He had been bravely reassuring to Osric, but within himself he was far from that brave. Would he ever see his lands again? Yesterday he had ridden the boundaries of the demesne, and the somber thought had intruded constantly that it might be his last time. The great fields, already green, the orchards, the forest land had never seemed so compelling in their beauty, though the sight of Mab's empty cot and neglected garden had made his heart ache. Yet the pain was not as great as it might, for Adelaide, his beloved wife, had been with him and had understood why he could not speak. Then she had spoken herself, quietly and gently, but with a firmness that amazed and delighted him.

"Wilnoth is thinking of marrying," she had said. "The girl has good hands for a garden, he says. Shall we give this cot to them?"

"You are the lady of Storches Hundred," he answered gratefully. "It grieves me, though, to think of anyone else but Mab here."

"Mab would wish it, Aelfred. The forest land must be tended, and Wilnoth will be faithful." She put her hand on his arm. "Life must go on, my dearest."

"Yes," he murmured now on the London Road, well in sight of the Abbey. And his own life these past weeks had been glorious beyond belief. He had married Adelaide at Walsingham, they had kept Easter with the court at Westminster, and the King had given him leave to return to his lands, from which only yesterday the royal messenger had summoned him. He had been a whole month at Storches Hundred with Adelaide, trying to put from him the knowledge that war would surely come, wringing from each day, each hour, every possible joy. The demesne had prospered; Siward had done his work well, and the departure of the de Bellemes had seemed to lift a curse from the land. The fields had already been plowed and sown, but his people had delayed the land blessing for his return. Father Owain, aged by the grief he had suffered from the de Bellemes and their treachery, was once more in his church; he had said the requiems for Mab and Saewulf. Aelfred had seen to putting a stone cross on Mab's grave, and Adelaide had planted rosemary and fennel on it. There was peace now at Storches Hundred, and he prayed only that peace could be kept.

Again he thought of Adelaide. Not that his thoughts were ever far from her, for in his wildest imaginings he had never anticipated the happiness that she would give him. Her beauty had enchanted him from the beginning, but in those quiet days on the demesne he had discovered with delight her perceptiveness and enthusiasm, which renewed itself with every sunrise. Whether she rode beside him across the fields or sat quietly embroidering while he discussed business with Siward, her heart and mind were one with his. Not that they agreed on everything, and she was a witty piece, indeed. He chuckled, remembering a spirited argument over a particular grove of trees that he had wanted felled and she had been determined to keep. Life, he decided, might not be precisely placid with Adelaide, but it would never lack for interest. He longed for her now; he felt like only half a person without her. Yet at the same time his joy was great, for he knew the depth of her love for him. He had seen it in her eyes, when they parted, and had blessed her doubly because she had not wept. Was she weeping at this hour, he wondered, in the solitude of their bower? His heart twisted; then he smiled proudly. Adelaide would find much to do for their people, who already loved her as much as they had his mother. She would hold his lands while he was away and bear well the power of sake and soke which he had given into her hands. She was not one to spend her days altogether in lonely tears.

They had passed the Abbey and now were approaching the palace. The sentry looked familiar, and, as they came nearer, Aelfred discovered to his delight that it was Captain Gryffin who was on duty. "Aelfred Ansculfson gives greeting!" he called.

"Well! Behold the bridegroom cometh," the Welshman laughed. "It's a fine world when a man must be called from his new-wedded wife to fight a war."

"Duty, Gryffin, duty," Aelfred answered soberly, but his eyes danced.

"You could have stayed home. I asked Gyrth Godwineson, full and fairly, what need of you does the King have when I am here?"

"True." Aelfred smiled. "Is Gyrth at the palace?"

"He'll be at this gate directly. He asked to be told the moment I caught sight of you. And so he was. The very moment. Your men are to go to the barracks."

"All but Osric. He stays with me."

"Quite right." Gryffin bawled a command, and a soldier came out of the sentry hut for orders.

Aelfred turned to his company. "Go with this man," he said. "He'll see that you have food and rest. We'll meet again at Wight."

With murmurs of "God be with you, master," the Storches Hundred men marched away. Aelfred dismounted and gave the reins of his horse to another soldier who had appeared at Gryffin's bellow, gesturing to Osric to do the same.

"How is it that you're still here, instead of at Wight?" he asked.

The Welshman grinned. "I'm in charge of rounding up bridegrooms and other stragglers," he said jovially.

"Are there that many?"

"Bridegrooms? No, not nearly enough. Stragglers, too many! And the greatest are the earls of Mercia and Northumbria. But here's Gyrth Godwineson. He'll tell you everything that I am too busy to tell."

Aelfred looked beyond Gryffin to the tall figure moving swiftly towards him. "Gyrth!" he shouted and ran to greet him at the double quick.

The two men clasped arms, then pounded each other on the back. "So! Let me look at you," said Gyrth. He scrutinized Aelfred from head to foot. "Marriage evidently agrees with you. How is the fair Adelaide?"

"She is all my joy. She sends greetings to you."

"Mine to her, when you write." His glance fell on Osric. "Who is this?"

"Permit me to make known to you Osric son of Osric, my friend," Aelfred said formally. "He saved my life, Gyrth. I stand eternally in his debt."

Gyrth looked at Osric for a moment, then extended his hand. "And I am Gyrth Godwineson," he said quietly. "As friend of my friend, I bid you welcome."

Osric took his hand. "Thank you, master."

"We'll go into the palace," Gyrth continued. "I've so much to tell you, I don't know where to start, but it can wait until you've had a cup of ale."

As they entered the palace court, Osric following, a small dog darted from behind one of the arches, yapping fiercely. A little boy followed in hot pursuit and, behind the boy, as quickly as his dignity would permit, strode a tall spare man in a black cassock, whom Aelfred immediately recognized as Stigand, Archbishop of Canterbury. The dog wheeled around Gyrth's legs, and the boy made a lunge for it, sprawling in the dust.

"Whoa, Edgar," Gyrth said humorously, bending to pick him up.

"It's my new brachet," Edgar cried. "She mustn't get into the street."

"She won't. The gates are closed," Gyrth reassured him. "Ah, Your Grace, your pupil has escaped you, I see," he remarked, as the Archbishop joined them.

"It's that wretched dog," His Grace said severely. "Edgar, return to the study at once. You have not yet finished your Latin translation."

Crestfallen, Edgar turned and walked into the palace. "I'll see that your brachet is kept safe," Gyrth called after him.

"Poor child," Stigand said after a moment. "It's hard for him, being penned up here at Westminster."

"I know. But he must be guarded carefully," Gyrth warned.

"He shall be. Never fear," Stigand answered, and, with a benevolent smile, he hurried away.

"Who is that child?" Aelfred asked curiously.

"When we're safe in my closet, I'll tell you," Gyrth said in an undertone.

Not another word was spoken until they were behind closed doors. Gyrth sat down in the armchair.

"Sit there, Aelfred," he said, pointing to another chair. "Osric, fill the cups. One for you, too."

"Thank you," said Osric, picking up the jug.

"You wish to be a soldier, I take it?" Gyrth continued.

Osric looked at him with glowing eyes. "With all my heart."

"What weapons do you use?"

"The bow and the knife, master."

Gyrth nodded. "Very well. You will be the personal guard of my friend, Aelfred Ansculfson, and your duties will begin now. Take your cup and sit on that stool by the door. If anyone comes, ask his name. Admit no one without my leave."

"Yes, master," Osric replied, with a brisk salute.

"Where did you learn to do that?" Aelfred asked.

Osric smiled proudly. "I've been practicing."

"One thing more," Gyrth said impressively. "Whatever you hear spoken, you will never repeat, even under pain of death. Your eyes, your ears, your tongue—above all, your heart, belong to England and the King. Swear to remember this."

Osric dropped to his knee. "I swear," he said, his voice shaking a little.

"Rise, Osric son of Osric, soldier of his majesty. Go to your post." As Osric saluted and obeyed, Gyrth smiled at Aelfred. "Are the other Storches Hundred men as stouthearted as he?"

"There is only one Osric," Aelfred answered. "But the others are eager."

"We shall make soldiers of them, then." Gyrth's eyes blazed with excitement. "Wait until you see the encampment at Wight, Aelfred. It's the greatest army ever raised in England."

"Before you tell me about it, please answer my question about the little boy. Who is he?"

"Edgar, grandson of Edmund called Ironside. Surely you remember him?"

"Good Heavens!" Aelfred cast his mind back over what he had heard about those turbulent days, long before he was born, when Canute the Dane had ravaged England. The king's eldest brother, Edmund Ironside, had been killed by the

Danes, and Canute had hounded his family into exile. Edmund's son had been recalled after Canute's death but had died himself within a few months of his arrival in England, leaving two daughters and an infant son, Edgar.

"Edgar was born in Hungary, in exile, wasn't he?" Aelfred recalled. "I confess, I'd forgotten about him completely."

"He is easy to forget," Gyrth said soberly. "Yet if the succession to the throne was determined by blood, Edgar would be the rightful heir. Not my brother."

"I'm very glad our law calls for election, then. What could that child do against William of Normandy?"

"As William knows." Gyrth looked at him piercingly. "That was why he tried to maneuver King Edward into declaring that child his successor. That was why he accused Harold of murdering Edgar's father."

"How could that be possible?" Aelfred exclaimed.

"Oh, the Norman has his little ways. He even had King Edward believing that my family were traitors."

"Not for long. Surely not for long?"

"No, but it was dangerous there, for a time. You see, William has wanted the crown of England ever since he could walk, I think. He is ambitious, and the crown would be a great prize for a baseborn man." Gyrth smiled ironically. "The odd thing is that, apart from his obsession, he really is very likable."

"You have met him?"

"He visited England once. A tall, very handsome man. He doesn't smile much or say much, but you sense his power the moment he looks at you. Certainly he deserves great credit for what he has done in Normandy. He is a builder, I think, not a destroyer. But he is like certain others of his kind. He identifies the will of God with what he himself wants. And he wants to be King of England! That is why little Edgar is being so carefully protected. Harold has made known to the witenagemot that, should he fall in battle, his own vote for his successor is Edgar."

Aelfred shuddered. "God grant that such a vote will not be needed."

"Amen to that. But, as Harold says, the fight must go on, if not under his command then under another's. But we won't anticipate that. Wait until you see our army!" Gyrth's voice regained its enthusiasm and he finished off his ale. "If Edwin and Morcar will leave their precious earldoms, we'll be invincible."

"Yes, Gryffin mentioned them. What's wrong?"

"They won't march south," Gyrth said exasperatedly. "Harold has sent a dozen messages, but they still will not move. A week ago he sent your father and Rafe of Birnham, hoping their old comrades-in-arms might persuade them."

"I can't understand why they won't come. Don't they know they're needed?"

Gyrth sighed. "Oh, yes, but they think that their own lands need them, too, and, in a way, they're right. You see, my brother Tostig has been up to his tricks again. Last month he sailed sixty ships up the Humber River. Edwin and Morcar met him and he had to fly for his life. The reports say that it was the greatest rout since King Athelstan beat the Scots at Brunanburh."

"A health to Edwin and Morcar!" Aelfred raised his cup. "It's the first I've heard of it."

"Bridegrooms are spared certain worries." Gyrth chuckled.

"Do Edwin and Morcar feel that their armies must rest, then?"

"After one single day's battle over a month ago? No, they're waiting it out to see whether Tostig will persuade King Malcolm of Scotland to attack them. Malcolm, for reasons best known to himself, has given Tostig shelter."

Aelfred shook his head. "But surely Malcolm would not attack? He owes his crown to England. Why, it was Morcar's father who fought for him against King Macbeth."

"Yes, but Tostig can be overpersuasive," Gyrth said gloomily. "Oh, I wish Harold would declare him outlaw, once and for all. He's broken his heart over him for years. And the red-bearded brothers can never completely trust Harold, as long as Tostig is free." He looked at Aelfred sharply. "But say nothing about this. Especially to the King. It's better not to dwell on it. We'll win without Edwin and Morcar, and that will be to their shame, so don't you be dispirited." **Gyrth** rose. "Come, now. I'll show you and Osric to your quarters."

"When do we leave for Wight?"

"Tomorrow, on the morning tide."

At dawn, they boarded the warship with its gold beaked prow for the journey downriver to the channel. It was the first time that Aelfred had actually seen the great port of London, and the array of ships, each strategically anchored to afford maximum protection to the city, fascinated him. He had known that Harold's army was enormous, but he had not realized that His Majesty commanded so mighty a fleet in addition.

"Wait until you see Wight," Gyrth told him, laughing at his amazement.

"Wait until Duke William sees it, you mean," Aelfred replied proudly.

"Yes. No matter how fast he builds, we'll outnumber his fleet. Harold has called out the ship fyrds from all the port cities."

"Ship fyrds?" The term was new to Osric, as was the roll of the ship under him.

"The governors of the ports have a certain number of ships under their command. In time of war they are called upon to serve the King." Gyrth looked at Osric quickly. "Are you all right?"

"I—I think so," Osric replied uncertainly.

"Better go into the cabin until you get your sea legs." Gyrth smiled sympathetically. "No disgrace, Osric. You're a landsman, after all."

"They're raising the sail," Aelfred said excitedly.

"And the oarsmen are taking their positions." Gyrth pointed to the deck below them. "Look at that fellow running along the oarlocks."

Aelfred watched in consternation as the sailor progressed along the outside of the ship, stepping from oarlock to oarlock as steadily as though he were on dry land. "He'll fall into the water!" he cried.

"Not he," Gyrth assured him. "See, he's at his bench now. There's the steersman at the far end, and the chief oarsman is ready to begin the count."

Slowly the ship started to move; the deck seemed to shiver under their feet. "I think I'll go into the cabin," Aelfred said suddenly.

"You'll be all right in a few hours," Gyrth promised. "By the time our escort ships meet us, you'll be running the oar-locks yourself."

"Never!" Aelfred assured him.

Nonetheless, by the next day he was on deck and thoroughly enjoying the journey. The ship now moved like a solid island over the glistening water, surrounded by the seven escort ships with their brilliant sails and gilded prows. Sailors called from ship to ship; sometimes they joined in a rousing song. The convoy proceeded slowly, for Gyrth had orders to inspect the Cinque Ports—Sandwich, Dover, Hythe, Romney, and Hastings—towns which from earliest times had formed the bulwark of England's coastal defense. All was well; all was in order. Each one of the five garrisons seemed to be ready and waiting for William to attack there instead of meeting the royal army at Wight.

Two weeks later, the ships anchored at the island citadel where Harold had decided to wait for the Norman invasion. Aelfred thrilled to the sight of the Gold Dragon standards rippling in the breeze atop the sentry towers. In the harbor, ships of every possible kind rode at anchor: royal warships greater even than the one in which he had sailed from London, and merchant ships converted to battleships that could move swiftly under an arrow or a javelin barrage. He walked with Gyrth past the sentries and up the main camp road, hearing the noise of hammers clanging on anvils— swords and arrows being tempered at the smithy fires. He could smell the huge roasts which the cooks were basting over gigantic firepits. In one field, he glimpsed black-bearded Thurlkill, putting the Young Men through their drill with the same concentration on both sides as had prevailed at Westminster; and he smiled ruefully at what Thurlkill would probably say to him when he appeared for practice. He'd had very little of drill in these past months. Then they were at Harold's scarlet tent, and the King himself was giving them welcome.

"And how goes Storches Hundred?" he asked Aelfred, after he had greeted his brother.

"Well, thank you, Sire. My wife commends herself to you," Aelfred replied.

"How proudly we speak those words, 'my wife,' " Harold chuckled. He turned to Osric. "And who is this?"

Aelfred presented him, and the King smiled.

"Welcome, young man. Inasmuch as you serve Aelfred Ansculfson, you shall serve me. We'll have a tankard in my tent." He indicated that they should precede him. "There's someone here who's been waiting your arrival with great impatience, Gyrth."

The words were hardly spoken when Gyrth cried, "Leofwine!" A tall, broad-shouldered man, his hair cropped Norman style, clasped Gyrth's arms, then slapped him on the back with considerable enthusiasm.

"Didn't expect to see your brother, did you?" he asked with a grin.

"I never know where I'll see you," Gyrth answered. "Aelfred, this is the wandering son of the house of Godwine."

"*Haele!*" Leofwine took Aelfred's hand firmly and cordially. "Don't believe a word Gyrth tells you. When I wander, Aelfred, it's on the King's business."

"Sit down, sit down, all of you," said Harold. "Osric, pour us a round of ale, then stand guard at the door. Leofwine has news—not happy, I'm afraid. But we'll reckon with it."

Aelfred drew a stool up to the long table. "How has Dom Regembald managed for pens without me?"

"Appallingly," the King answered. "He'll put you to work the minute he sets eyes on you."

"Mending pens?" Leofwine asked incredulously. "Can't you find anything better for him to do?"

"Aelfred can read and write his name, which is more than can be said for you," Gyrth quipped.

All three brothers laughed, and Aelfred thought how handsome the sons of Godwine were. But, of the three, Harold was the kingly one. His was the face that won men's hearts.

"What is your news, Leofwine?" Gyrth asked.

"King Harald Hardrada of Norway is massing his fleet for spring harrying," Leofwine answered.

"As he does every spring," Gyrth scoffed. "That is no news."

"Yes, but rumors are flying that he plans to strike at the Humber." Leofwine's eyes were grave. "And when I left York, word was out that Tostig had sailed to join him."

Aelfred, sitting opposite the King, looked down at the table, unable to bear the look of naked pain on Harold's face. Gyrth stirred uneasily.

There was a moment of silence, then Harold said quietly, "That is only rumor, however."

"But well founded, my brother. And the prospect is doubly grave, because Tostig was in Normandy in early April, and later in Flanders," Leofwine answered.

The King rose abruptly and walked to the rear of the tent. Keeping his back to them, he said tautly, "If only Tostig would let me speak with him! Why will he not come?"

Gyrth swallowed hard. "Because the only thing he would accept in return for his good will is Northumbria," he said gently, "and that you cannot give him."

"He's your enemy, Harold, open and declared," Leofwine said flatly.

"I know." The King returned to his chair. He looked un-utterably weary. "But he is also our brother, though he has always favored the Normans."

"You are King, now, Harold," Gyrth reminded.

"I know that, too. But will the good of England be served by a ruler who shuts his doors against his own blood? Tostig was always hotheaded and impetuous, and too stubborn to admit that he was wrong until circumstances forced it of him. I keep hoping—" He sighed, then looked earnestly at his brothers. "It may be that he will yet change. So, promise me—"

"If Tostig asks for peace, he shall have it," Leofwine answered. "But I don't think he will. Ever! His ambition will not let him."

188

Harold sighed again, then looked at Aelfred. "Forgive us for imposing family matters upon you," he said. Once more he was the King. "You think, Leofwine, that the earls of Mercia and Northumbria fear an attack from Harald Hardrada?"

"Yes, and with considerable reason," Leofwine answered.

"Bah!" Gyrth retorted. "Hardrada is Duke William's man. He is probably massing his ships only to frighten Edwin and Morcar from joining us."

"And then, again, he may be serious," said the King.

"Sire, what will we do if Hardrada does attack?" Aelfred asked hesitantly.

"We shall defend the south against William. The red-bearded brothers must take care of their own earldoms."

"But you need them here," Leofwine objected.

Harold smiled wanly. "I also need them there. It's six of one and half a dozen of the other. I'm gambling on the hope that Tostig's defeat will make Hardrada think twice about sailing into the Humber; but if he does attack, I'm hoping that Edwin and Morcar can stop him. I'm hoping that William of Normandy, when he sees the entire south of England arrayed against him, will decide not to attack. But if he does attack, I'm praying that Edwin and Morcar will get to us in time, for, believe me, we shall need every man in England in arms on that day."

Again there was silence. Then Gyrth asked suddenly, "Why don't we cross the Channel and strike at William ourselves? Wouldn't that be better than sitting here and waiting his pleasure?"

"Yes," Leofwine agreed. "We have the men and the ships. And the wind is right for us."

"Don't you think I've considered that?" Harold demanded. "But we cannot! Defending our own land against an attack is just and right. Striking at Normandy would brand us as conquerors, seeking lands to rule. So, my brothers, we wait."

"Yes, we wait." Gyrth sighed exasperatedly. "Let us hope that waiting does not prove more disastrous than the battle itself."

With these words, he rose and took his leave, Leofwine following. The King looked at Aelfred and smiled kindly. "My brothers are good men, but they are soldiers," he said. "They see the glory of England through the clash of iron. But we must see more than that. Do you understand?"

"Yes, Sire," Aelfred murmured. But Gyrth's last remark had sent shivers down his spine.

"You had best sharpen Dom Regembald's pens. The glory of England may be served with a pen, as well as with a spear."

For a moment, Aelfred wanted to throw himself on his knees. Then he felt as though he must weep. Never before now had he realized how lonely the King must be, how burdened with care. He had aged since that day—was it only six months ago?—when he had stood crowned in majesty at the Abbey Church. We have all changed, Aelfred reflected. I myself have grown older, even in this hour. He longed to speak some word of comfort but could find none. Finally he said, "Thank you, Sire. I shall mend the pens well."

"Good. Our daily tasks will save us, I think," Harold answered.

Within a few days, Aelfred had settled down to the routine of camp life as though he had known no other. He heard Mass with the King in the chapel tent; then, after a hearty breakfast, joined the Young Men in the drill ground. Afternoons he sat beside Dom Regembald, mending pens and copying dispatches, and he even composed dispatches himself from the notes the secretary gave him. Sometimes he was called upon to carry messages from His Majesty to the various camp commanders, and always he stood guard during council meetings.

As the weeks went on, he came to realize how vast and complicated the defense of the realm was. It was not only a matter of levying troops; soldiers had to be provided with barracks and arms and food. Men were constantly sent to the mainland to buy more provisions, or to ask why promised meat and grain had not been received. Raw recruits, fresh from the plow and sheepfold, had to be drilled in the use of sword and javelin, for the King's Thanes, the Young Men, and the House Carls—the king's personal bodyguard—represented only a very small part of the army assembled at Wight. The task of whipping the churls into a fighting force was a formidable one, and, to Aelfred's amazement, even some of the clergy acted as drill masters. Abbot Aelfwine, the King's uncle, came with twelve monks from Winchester, wearing coats of mail over their habits and swords buckled at their waists.

"The King must expect a mighty battle," Aelfred remarked to Dom Regembald on the day that the Winchester monks arrived.

"Not all monks will come to Wight," the secretary answered. "But they will hold their own abbeys against the Norman. As for Abbot Aelfwine, he is a Godwine, and his nephew is his King. He stands with him."

But as July passed and August came with its searing heat, Aelfred noticed that the atmosphere at Wight had changed. The change came so gradually, so subtly, that no one could say when it had begun. The enthusiasm ebbed, and now the men who had been first to shout their loyalty were complaining of the long delay, for Duke William had not moved from the mouth of the River Dives. Churls who had volunteered with the understanding that victory would be swift, and that they would be home for harvest, openly voiced their resentment. Even the House Carls demanded to know of what use to have the greatest army the world had ever seen, if they were to sit like nesting hens on a tiny island and never strike a blow? And time and again the question was raised, where were Edwin and Morcar? If the danger was so great, why had the armies of Mercia and Northumbria not come to join them? Why must worried farmers wait until their grain had rotted in the fields?

Council meetings in the scarlet tent grew stormy, as one commander after another begged the King either to attack Duke William or to disperse. Aelfred, sick at heart, listened to Harold try to cajole and placate them. He himself was anxious about his own land. He knew that Siward would do his best, but Storches Hundred was short of men. He was concerned, too, about his father; he'd had no word from him all summer. Yet he knew that the King's worries were greater by a thousandfold. As August wore on, the food supplies were less, and fear of hunger increased the demands to disperse.

"We dare not disperse," the King said repeatedly. "William of Normandy is depending on your impatience. We must wait. Any day the wind may change in his favor. We must wait!"

But the only answer he received was a cry of "How long?" The more he warned of danger, the more the army insisted that they be allowed either to attack or to go home. Aelfred watched in anguish, feeling the King's pain as his own, for, deep in his heart, he knew what the end would be. The men were now as united in this wish as they had once been united to stand against Duke William. King Harold, leader of men though he was, could not hold out indefinitely against the thousands of personal considerations with which they beleaguered him.

The end came on the eighth of September. Aelfred was alone in the scarlet tent when the King came in from a last fruitless attempt to persuade the army to stand. He looked exhausted, and he did not even try to smile. "Write an order," he said, white-lipped and hollow-eyed, "the order disbanding the army and fleet of England."

Aelfred stared at him dumbly. Though he had steeled himself to hear those words, he had not expected the desolation that swept over him at the hearing. He could not even take up a pen. "Oh—Sire!" His voice broke. "This is tragedy."

"No," Harold said tonelessly, "this is folly. The tragedy is yet to come." He looked at Aelfred wearily. "And you, Aelfred Ansculfson? Will you return home, when the others do?"

Aelfred trembled. He longed to return to his lands as much or more than any man in the camp. But how could he leave his King to face what must be faced? It would be treachery and cowardice—the act of a nithing. The oath he had sworn on the coronation day must not be broken.

"No, Sire," he answered, as steadily as he could. "You are my liege and my loyalty is yours. Much as my lands call me, I shall stay."

The King smiled faintly. "I thank you," he said formally and left the tent. Only then did Aelfred, in complete emotional exhaustion, fall to his knees grieving for Adelaide, for Storches Hundred. Then, when the storm had spent itself, he rose, picked up a pen, and proceeded to obey the King. Harold had said, "Our daily tasks will save us." This one almost broke his heart.

◆◆◆◆◆◆◆◆◆◆◆◆◆◆◆ 15 ◆◆◆◆◆◆◆◆◆◆◆◆◆◆◆◆

It was a dejected company that rode through the gates of Westminster Palace a few days after the order to disperse had been issued. King Harold retired at once to his apartments, leaving his brothers to see to the billeting and provisioning of the House Carls and the small group of Young Men who had remained with him. Most of the King's Thanes had taken leave to return to their demesnes until summoned for the winter witenagemot, for there was no urgent business to hold them at court; and no date could be set for the army to reassemble, since no one knew when or where Duke William would strike. Adverse winds continued to hold the Norman forces locked in the mouth of the River Dives, and this was the only ray of comfort in the general gloom.

"If only he is held there for a few more weeks, we shall be safe," Gyrth said grimly to Aelfred. "Let us pray that the winds hold until October. William won't dare risk crossing the Channel then."

Aelfred nodded. He knew that Gyrth was far from reassured. The dispersement of the army had seemed the height of foolhardiness at the time, and, as the days wore on, more and more an ominous foreboding took possession of him. He be-

194

came convinced that the destiny of England had hung in the balance on that day at Wight, and impatience had weighted the scales in William's favor. It would be most indiscreet of him to speak such words to anyone, but he knew that Gyrth shared his feeling, and so did the King, who moved like a man of stone about the quiet palace. Aelfred did his work conscientiously; there were many dispatches to write and pens to mend and other tasks regularly performed, and he drilled daily with the Young Men. But whatever he did, however well he did it, he felt that same sense of futility. His only inspiration were the letters from Adelaide, giving home news of herself and their people, telling him of the bountiful harvest and the beauty of the land, and he blessed her for her complete comprehension of his reasons for remaining at the palace with the King. There had been one letter from his father, too, telling him that the fear of a Viking attack had lessened and that he would soon be returning to London. They would all keep Christmas together at Storches Hundred, and that thought gave him joy. But he could not seem to rid himself of an odd sense of depression and a premonition of doom which hung over them all. It was like that great sword in the Painted Chamber, which hung suspended over the King's chair from a heavy chain, a chain that was only as strong as its weakest link.

Day after day, the wearisome waiting continued. Then, on the eighteenth of September, a company of men galloped wildly into the palace yard and stormed past Aelfred, standing guard as usual, into the Painted Chamber, crying the King's name. Their clothes were covered with mud, and their hair and beards were tousled and matted. One had a blood-stained bandage about his head King Harold, who was conferring with Gyrth and Leofwine, rose with his brothers to greet them. Gyrth and Leofwine drew their swords and tried to stand in front of the King, but he pushed them aside.

"They bear no arms," he said quickly, then asked the company, "What is it? Who are you?"

The man with the bandage stepped forward. "We are from

Holdernesse," he answered. "Harald Hardrada of Norway has harried us. He burned our orchards and houses and stole the wheat we had harvested. Now he's sailing for the Humber."

All color left Harold's face. "When?" he asked.

"Two days gone, Sire." The second speaker was a young man, barely come of age. "I come from Scarborough and he stopped there first. He climbed the hill outside the wall and his men threw burning brands on our houses. We were caught like rats! The whole town went up in flames; it wasn't even given a chance to fight. I was lucky—I was in the fields outside the walls and escaped to the woods when I saw that I could do nothing. My mother and sisters—" his voice broke.

"The same thing happened at Cleaveland," the leader continued. "They brought us warning, so we could fight, but it did no good. The whole coast is ablaze from Tees to Spurn Head."

The King looked as though he had been seized with a nervous chill, but he managed to control his voice. "And does Hardrada come alone with his Vikings?"

There was an awful moment of silence. Then the leader fell to his knees. "Sire, forgive us," he said huskily, "but we must speak truth. Tostig Godwineson marches with him."

Harold turned away, his head bowed in grief. Gyrth and Leofwine looked helplessly at each other, and Aelfred's heart twisted with pain. Not only had an enemy raised a standard against the King but there was treachery added to the evil.

Then the King roused himself. "And where are the earls of Mercia and Northumbria?" he asked.

"On march with their armies to defend York," the leader answered.

"How great is Hardrada's army?"

"Upwards of five thousand men, Sire."

Harold raised his head proudly. His eyes flashed and his voice cracked like a whiplash. "Hardrada the Land Waster will regret this expedition. It will be his last." He smiled grimly. "Leofwine, send out the summons to the thanes to reassemble the fyrds. Those who can reach Westminster by noon tomorrow will march with us. The others will join us en route. Send out your riders at once."

"Yes, Sire," Leofwine answered just as proudly, immediately on his way to carry out the order.

"Gyrth?"

"Yes, Sire? Yes, my brother?"

"Start north within the hour! Ride with all possible speed to Edwin and Morcar. Tell them they must *not*, no matter what the means used, allow Hardrada to draw them into battle. They cannot possibly win, outnumbered as they are. Tell them to hold York at all costs and wait until I come."

"I will, Sire," Gyrth replied. He paused, then asked, "And what are our plans regarding Duke William?"

"We will pray that the winds hold against him until we have settled with Hardrada," the King said steadily. Then he added, in a voice barely audible, "And our brother." As Gyrth left him, he turned to Aelfred. "Take these men to the soldiers' hall and see that they have food. Then find Dom Regembald and bring him to me. I must send letters to Edwin and Morcar with Gyrth. Be quick as possible. There is much to be done."

By noon the following day, King Harold led the House Carls and such other troops as had been hastily assembled from the districts near London up the North Road. His face was white under his gold helmet and his mouth set in a grim line. Aelfred rode with Leofwine, immediately behind the battle standards—the red banner bearing the Gold Dragon of Wessex and the king's Golden Man, a figure of a warrior made of beaten gold and studded with jewels. He wore full armor and a long sword was buckled at his side. His heart was pounding, and he knew that he was suddenly, overwhelmingly, afraid. He looked at Leofwine, envying his stern self-command. He was glad that his helmet covered at least part of his face so that no one could see what a poor soldier he really was. He glanced at his sword; his hands trembled on the reins. He would have to use that sword very soon, and he wondered if he would even be able to draw it. Yet he dared not disgrace himself by so much as a sigh. Osric and other Storches Hundred men were marching in the ranks behind him, and they looked to him for proper leading. He had seen Osric that morning and wondered how he could look so cheerful and excited. At that moment, he envied Osric, too

Leofwine now looked at him penetratingly. "Ride easy," he said gruffly. "We're on a forced march, you know. You'll never reach York if you clutch the reins so tensely in the first hour."

Aelfred tried to relax his grip.

"That's better," Leofwine approved. "Let your back be more easy, too. Let your horse carry you. That's what he's for."

Aelfred managed a smile. "Thank you. I'm a little nervous, I guess. It's my first time, you know."

"You're not nervous. You're quaking with fear, just as we all are."

"All?" Aelfred looked at him incredulously.

"Of course. Do you think you ever grow accustomed to battles?" Leofwine shook his head. "Never as long as you live! Courage isn't not being afraid. Courage is doing what must be done, no matter how afraid you are."

Leofwine's words comforted Aelfred so greatly that he dared to ask, "What is a battle like?"

"Like all the horrors of Hell," Leofwine replied simply, "whether you win or lose. In fact, you might say that in a war everyone loses. But you must also understand that there are worse things than war. Dishonor, slavery, seeing your land destroyed by a ruthless Viking like Harald Hardrada—" He paused a moment, then added, "Treachery. I think treachery is the worst, especially when it's your own flesh and blood who's the traitor."

"The King will hate to fight against his own brother."

"So shall I. But it will be like the tortures of the damned for Harold. He loves Tostig deeply. He's always taken his part. But they do say that there is always one no-good in every family. I suppose we should be content that we have only one." Leofwine sighed. "I keep hoping that when they meet face to face a miracle will happen. That's why Harold prayed at Walsingham, you know. I'm afraid, though, that Tostig will not let even God change his heart."

"It may happen," Aelfred said quietly. "They have not yet met together."

"I pray so," Leofwine answered, "for if it does not, Harold will do his duty. But his heart will break. And, though Tostig is my brother, I say that he is not worth the sorrow that he has caused my brother and King. If we meet in battle, he will feel the edge of my sword. I swear it!"

Aelfred shuddered and said no more. During the days and nights of the march, stopping only an hour at a time when rest was absolutely necessary, he found himself unable to speak much, and he tried hard not to think of things which would interfere with what he must do. He had a duty to perform. That was all he knew. His eyes were burning from lack of sleep; his body was so heavy that he wondered more than once why he did not fall out of his saddle. The messengers who met them along the road brought only evil tidings: Hardrada had sailed into the Humber and landed at Riccall; he was marching towards York; Edwin and Morcar, with the forces of Mercia and Northumbria, were hurrying to intercept him.

Then, six days after they left London, Gyrth Godwineson met them outside Tadcaster.

"I was too late," he told them. "Edwin and Morcar met Hardrada at Gate Fulford and were completely overwhelmed. York surrendered, and the Vikings despoiled it."

King Harold's face was terrible to see. "By the power of Heaven, Hardrada shall know the edge of my sword before another day passes," he said furiously. "Where is he? At York?"

Gyrth shook his head. "He knew you were coming and feared a siege. He has not provision enough for that. But he's a sly fox, as well as an evil one. He is camped on the other side of the river at Stamford Bridge."

"Tomorrow night he will camp in Hell," Harold answered. "Where are the red-bearded brothers?"

"At York. Hardrada allowed them to enter the city after they promised not to raise their arms against him."

"I see. We can look for no help from them."

"We could not anyway. Their armies were cut to pieces. Hundreds were killed, and there were many wounded."

Aelfred had been listening with a sinking heart. "My father, Gyrth? And Rafe of Birnham?" he asked hoarsely.

Gyrth's face was white. "Rafe escaped with a shoulder wound. But your father—" He spoke again to the King. "Sire, Aelfred Ansculfson must ride at once with me to York."

Harold nodded. "Go with him, Aelfred. Ride hard."

Dazed, Aelfred turned his horse out of the line of march. Gyrth set off at a gallop and he followed, urging his horse forward, his mind and heart set on only one thing: to reach York before it was too late. Gyrth's eyes and the King's immediate permission had given him the answer to the question he dared not ask.

He was hardly conscious of the devastated land around him and the smoking fields. It seemed a century before the city gates loomed up before him. Gyrth shouted to the guards, who let them pass without question, and led the way to the palace court. Here they both dismounted and ran into the great hall, where Rafe of Birnham, disheveled and distraught, hurried to meet them.

"Thank God you've come!" he cried.

Aelfred took his arm. "My father?"

Rafe put a firm hand on his shoulder. "An arrow wound in the throat. He cannot speak," he said brusquely. "It's a miracle that he's lasted this long. He's kept himself alive only to see you. Come with us, Gyrth. Witnesses are needed."

On leaden feet Aelfred walked with him into the small dark room where Baron Ansculf lay on a rude oaken bed. Tears burned his eyelids. Even now, at the point of death, his father's presence was overwhelming. Love for him tore at Aelfred's heart; he could hardly bear to see the mighty warrior lie so rigid, his powerful hands gripping the harsh blanket.

"You must not weep," Rafe warned. "Go and speak to him."

Hardly knowing what he did, Aelfred knelt beside the bed. "Father," he whispered. Then, louder, "Father, I've come."

Slowly the massive head turned towards him. The bleak, unseeing eyes suddenly became alive as the baron held out his hand. Aelfred took it in both his and held it tightly. Then Ansculf moved his arm and painfully began to twist the heavy gold ring off his finger. It was evident that the effort was agony to him, and Aelfred looked up at Gyrth.

"May I not help him?" he pleaded.

Gyrth shook his head. "It must be his free gift," he said. "Hold your right hand out to him."

Aelfred obeyed, and the baron slipped the ring halfway onto his finger. It was the one that his grandfather, Aelfred Iron Fist, had worn.

"Now put it on the rest of the way," Rafe directed.

Aelfred did so, acknowledging by this act that he accepted the responsibility as Baron of Storches Hundred. Ansculf looked intently at the two other men.

"We are witnesses," Rafe and Gyrth intoned solemnly.

Painfully Ansculf smiled and placed his hand on Aelfred's bowed head. His breathing rasped in the silence. The heavy hand fell.

"Father!" Aelfred cried. He leaped to his feet and looked wildly down at the still form on the bed. Then, by what instinct he could never have explained, he drew his sword and held it aloft. "Father, I swear you will be avenged!"

Once more Ansculf opened his eyes and looked at his son. Again he smiled and his lips moved a little. Then his head slumped on his chest.

"He is gone," Rafe said quietly.

The sword clattered to the floor as Aelfred fell to his knees in a paroxysm of weeping. The others waited until he grew calmer, then Gyrth raised him to his feet. "You are Baron of Storches Hundred now, and the King's Thane," he said gently. "Bear yourself as he would have wished."

Slowly Aelfred wiped his eyes. "He must be taken home," he said.

"I shall see to it," Rafe promised. "The King will give me leave. My wound will not let me fight again, so you must fight for both of us."

"Yes," Aelfred answered, struggling against his tears. "I shall fight. Though I have never wished to fight, I shall do so now, with every drop of blood in me." He looked pleadingly at them. "Am I wrong to feel so?"

"No," Gyrth answered firmly. "Your father was good and honorable. He had done no harm to those who killed him. For you to feel otherwise would make you a nithing. Besides, like him, you are fighting for something greater than vengeance. You are fighting for our land."

"With all my heart."

"Sometimes swords are the only answer." Gyrth took his arm. "Come, you are exhausted. You must rest now."

"Yes." Aelfred picked up his sword and looked once more upon his father. Then swiftly he raised his sword in a last salute and followed Gyrth into the hall.

The next morning, he took his place once more behind the standards and rode between Gyrth and Leofwine behind the King through the silent city streets and out the gate. Not a word was spoken. Suddenly the trumpets sounded. The broad Derwent River lay before them, and Stamford Bridge. A company of armed Viking soldiers stood guard on the near side. Across the river, Hardrada's main force was camped.

Harold raised himself in his stirrups. "Now, God guide our weapons," he prayed. Then he leaped from his horse, threw the reins to a stable churl, and shouted, "Forward, men of England!"

With a mighty roar, the first salvo of arrows and slingstones was fired. Aelfred dismounted, leaving his horse to the churl to lead to the rear, and pressed forward. He had no company to command; though he was now a King's Thane, he lacked the experience to be a commander and had gladly let the Storches Hundred men join another company. His duty was to remain with Gyrth and Leofwine, to help them in case either one should fall or be disarmed.

He did not know when he first drew his sword—it was in his hand when he followed the first company of House Carls

202

rushing with raised battle-axes to engage the enemy. He heard someone shout that the river was too deep to be forded, that the bridge must be taken before the main encampment could be reached. The Viking defenders were shouting, "Thor for our swords!" and the English roared defiantly, "Out! Out!" Wave after wave of the King's troops streamed into battle, but still the bridge held. Now the House Carls, under Harold's command, were fighting the enemy hand to hand with broadswords. Suddenly Aelfred was confronted by an enemy soldier; he struck at him blindly. The soldier fell to the ground, blood gushing from a wound in his chest. His gold winged helmet fell off, and Aelfred looked down at the face of a boy no older than himself. But before he could stop to pity, or even to sign the cross, other Vikings were upon him. The enemy was everywhere, swelled by fresh detachments from the camp on the opposite bank. He must strike and strike, and strike yet again. Arrows fell about him like hailstones; a knife slashed at his wrist. Dimly he heard the shrieks of the wounded and dying; it was impossible to tell whether they were friend or foe.

Inch by inch Harold's army moved forward over ground slippery with blood. Now one lone Viking, his red hair streaming over his shoulders, berserk with the lust of battle, stood in the middle of the bridge, holding it singlehandedly against all comers. No spear or sword was strong enough to pierce his armor; forty men had already fallen under the blows of his battle-axe. Then, one daring House Carl slipped into the water. While several of his comrades engaged the berserker in front, he climbed onto the bridge in back of him. There was a flash of a knife and a bellow of pain as the Viking fell into the river, and Harold's forces, with exultant yells, streamed across Stamford Bridge to the opposite bank where the enemy waited behind the solid barricade of their shields.

Here, the King ordered them to stop. He signaled his trumpeters to sound a parley and turned to his men. "Gyrth, Leofwine—all my thanes, put up your swords. You, too, Aelfred Ansculfson. Trumpeters, sound the call again."

Aelfred slipped his sword into its holder. He was covered with dirt and his tunic was spattered with blood. He heard the various commanders tell their men to stand with bows and spears lowered but ready. The King called for a third parley to be sounded. Then he raised his voice and cried, "Tostig Godwineson, show yourself!"

There was not a sound from the enemy.

Again the King spoke, now pleading. "Tostig, show yourself. My brother—speak with me."

There was a stir, and a man in a red cloak stepped from behind the shield wall.

"Come nearer," said Harold. "Let me see your face."

Slowly, deliberately, Tostig came forward, then stopped and turned to the massed shields. At his gesture, another warrior joined him, a tall man with a cruel face, wrapped in a blue cloak, wearing a gold winged helmet on his head. Side by side they walked to Harold, until they were within speaking distance.

"I am here," Tostig said coldly. His face was blank and his eyes would not meet his brother's. "What do you want?"

"Only to speak with you," Harold answered. "Tostig, let us end our quarrel. You are too brave a man to waste yourself this way. England needs you." His voice trembled. "I need you. Come home and share my rule."

"Will you give me Northumbria?" Tostig demanded.

Harold shook his head. "You know that I cannot do that. But there are other places of honor, any one of which you might fill. My brother, you *cannot* wish to die a traitor's death."

For a moment the eyes wavered, as Tostig looked at him speculatively. "And what will you do for my friend Hardrada?" he asked.

"Hardrada?" The King's eyes flashed. "He shall have seven good feet of English earth to lie in, or perhaps a little more, since he is taller than most men."

Tostig smiled contemptuously. "Never shall it be said of me that I brought a friend to England only to betray him. Prepare for battle, Harold. We have spoken for the last time."

"Tostig!" Harold cried. But Tostig Godwineson turned on

his heel and walked back to the shield wall, Hardrada at his side. The King looked at his brothers. His face was ashen. "You saw me offer him peace," he said brokenly.

"We saw," Leofwine said grimly.

"Sound trumpets!" Harold shouted and, with a cry of fury and anguish mingled, flung his gold battle-axe with all his strength. "Out! Out!" the English screamed and hurled themselves against the shield wall.

For hours the battle raged. At first the shield wall held firm, even under the repeated blows of axes and the showers of arrows, but slowly, gradually, it began to break. The English rushed forward, again fighting hand to hand with swords and knives. The King seemed to be everywhere, commanding, encouraging—at one moment directing one company to advance on a new breach, at the next moment ordering another to stand firm against a counterattack. There was an exultant cry as Hardrada's Raven standard fell. Then Hardrada himself picked it up from the fallen bearer's hand with a cry of "Thor for us!" and urged his men to regroup for another attack. But the Vikings were desperate now. Knives whistled through the air; by some strange happenstance, Aelfred, in the very midst of the melee, saw a knife aimed directly at him. Instinctively he reached out and caught it, then flung it back with all his strength, to where it found its mark in a Viking throat. "Vengeance!" he cried, tears and sweat streaming down his face. In that same moment, Hardrada fell under a flying spear, and his men, seeing their leader struck down, broke and ran.

"After them!" Gyrth shouted, and Aelfred, obeying the command, joined the English soldiers running downriver to where the Vikings had anchored their ships, some of which they had already set ablaze. Many of the enemy surrendered as prisoners; others, determined to escape, threw themselves into the river, their heavy shields over their heads, but the English captured most of them, too, while others either drowned or were killed. The rest of the English army fought on beside the bridge against the soldiers of Tostig Godwineson, who had refused to run and who now carried on his own private war. Later it was whispered that Tostig and Harold met in single combat, and Tostig fell under his brother's sword.

At sunset, when Aelfred returned to the bridge with the prisoners Gyrth had put in his charge, the King was standing beside Tostig's body, hollow-eyed and exhausted, no slightest trace of triumph in his face. His men, seeing his heartbreak, refrained from giving the rouse that their victory would otherwise have demanded. Slowly the King's Thanes surrounded him, to receive his orders. When the King finally spoke, every word seemed to cause him pain.

"Our dead and wounded are to be taken to York," he said. "Send word by fast messenger to London that Hardrada the Land Waster is dead."

"And the enemy?" Leofwine asked hesitantly.

The King squared his shoulders. "They shall be treated according to their deserts," he said harshly. "Hardrada shall have his ground, and our brother"—his eyes filled with tears and he bowed his head—"our brother shall have a soldier's burial."

"Osric, please stop pacing," Aelfred said impatiently. "Can't you be still a moment? You're driving me mad with your restlessness, and it will wear you out."

"I'm sorry, master," Osric said ruefully. "It's my arm. The surgeon changed the dressing this morning and it hurts badly."

Aelfred sighed. "I'm sorry. Forgive me. I hardly know what I'm saying, these days."

"And with good reason, considering all that has happened. You'll feel better when we return to Storches Hundred. And so shall I!"

"Yes, we will. Thank Heaven the King has given permission," said Aelfred. "Even though I must return to court as soon as my father is buried, it will be a blessed relief to go home for a few days." He looked at Osric anxiously. "Does your arm pain you constantly?"

"Yes, but I'm eager to start. I'll be able to ride with you. It was most kind of the King to say that I might ride."

"It's the least you deserve," Aelfred said warmly. "I am right proud of you, Osric, and Storches Hundred will be when they hear. From all accounts, you fought magnificently at Stamford Bridge."

"The same is said of you, master. In fact, Thurlkill is telling all the palace that you were like your father reborn."

"I'm glad for his praise, but I wish I could forget that day." Aelfred shook his head. "All I've dreamed of, ever since, is the whistle of arrows and the crash of battle-axes, and trumpets and cries of pain and blood. I hope my father never had such dreams."

"He was a born warrior," Osric said sagely. "Not all men are. To me, you are the greater because you fought well and bravely even though you are not a born warrior."

Aelfred looked away, embarrassed by Osric's praise, yet pleased. "I do not think, however, that such tributes as were given to him will honor me, when my time comes for a memorial feast," he said quietly. "He truly deserves them all."

There was silence for several moments as Aelfred gazed into the firepit, absorbed by the memory of the great feast that the King had held in honor of Baron Ansculf on the night following the battle. Thane after thane had risen to speak his commendation of him. He himself had hardly been able to swallow a morsel of food, but there had been comfort in listening to his father's comrades-in-arms. There was comfort in remembering their tributes now.

"You will be as great a baron as he was," Osric continued.

Aelfred looked at him very soberly. "That's what worries me almost to a point of fear, Osric," he confided. "I know nothing about being a baron. I attend council meetings every day now, and am expected to speak, but I cannot. I'm as ignorant as a child starting to school."

"Your time will come. I think that being a baron may even be a little like sowing a field." Osric smiled. "You should have seen me the first time I tried to cast the grain. My father had just died, and I had never worked my field by myself before. My first crop was so bad that the baron refused to take his share. He told me to keep it all, so that I would not starve."

"Oh, Osric," said Aelfred, laughing in spite of himself. "Thank you for lightening my heart. You have learned to sow a field so that you can now not only feed your family but also raise enough to pay the rent of the land. I shall learn to be a baron. I know I can."

In the nearby monastery tower, a bell tolled. "The hour of Terce," Aelfred said briskly and got to his feet. "Time for council. Wait for me here. I hope the King will say that Rafe of Birnham and I can leave for Storches Hundred as soon as the meeting is over."

He left the room in the soldiers' quarters and crossed the court to the great hall. Here the thanes were assembling. He greeted Edwin of Mercia and Morcar of Northumbria, the red-bearded brothers whose city this was, and joined Rafe near the King's seat. "Do we leave when the meeting is adjourned?" he asked.

"Yes, everything is ready," Rafe answered. "I spoke to the King a moment ago, and he says that your father's cortege will leave York at noon."

"That is a comfort to hear. And when does the King march south again?"

"He says in two weeks. It will take the blacksmiths every moment of that time to repair broken weapons and forge new arrows."

"If he'll wait three weeks, my brother and I will join him," said Earl Morcar, who had resumed his place next Rafe. "Our captains rode out this morning to call up replacements for the men we lost at Gate Fulford."

Rafe frowned. "I wonder if we should delay even two weeks. William of Normandy is still in the mouth of the River Dives with his ships."

The King now came into the hall with his brothers. He acknowledged the thanes' salutes and sat down on the high seat. "Our latest word from Normandy was that Duke William had decided to disperse his forces on the first of October, if the winds did not change," he said. "It's the second, today. He won't sail this late."

"All the same, we'll maintain a good standing army in London, I hope," said Rafe. "After Hardrada's surprise attack, I wouldn't want to see us caught napping again."

"Nor I," Leofwine agreed emphatically. "I think the people

have learned a lesson, too. You'll hear no cries to disperse after Stamford Bridge."

"Let us hope not," Harold said gravely. "We were very lucky five days ago. We might not be, a second time."

"Do you know definitely that William has dispersed his army?" Rafe asked.

"No. There'd not have been time for a message to reach us. But all seems quiet across the channel."

"Too quiet," said Gyrth. "When Normans are quiet, that is the time to be most wary."

Aelfred nodded gravely with the others. "Gyrth Godwineson speaks well," he said. Then, out of his own experience, he added, "Normans cannot be trusted."

"And we shall not trust them," the King answered just as gravely. "Now, to the business to be decided here. First, we must settle the terms of ransom for the Viking prisoners of war. It is my advice that we not make them too harsh. They are honorable men, if misguided, and they fought bravely. Also, winter is coming. They have lost a battle in a foreign land, and we could accomplish nothing except to antagonize them if we make them desperate by impoverishing them or their families."

Before the debate could begin, the sound of running feet and a frantic hammering at the door interrupted him. The door was opened, and soldiers burst into the hall. One, the leader, rushed to the high seat. "Your Majesty!" he cried. "I bring grave news! That scoundrel! That Norman who calls himself an honorable man—"

"Speak. Waste no time," Harold answered. "What is your news?"

The soldier raised himself from his knees. "Sire, it is terrible news. William of Normandy has landed at Pevensey."

The thanes looked at him and at the King, dumbfounded. "When?" King Harold demanded.

"On Michaelmas Eve. He's garrisoned Pevensey and is ravaging the countryside," the soldier answered. "His army is so great that no one can stop it."

The King's face was white, but his voice remained calm. "I shall regret to my dying day that we were not there to prevent his landing," he said swiftly but evenly. Then, to his thanes, "What is your counsel, my friends?"

Leofwine drew his sword before the King's words were out of his mouth. "He has asked for battle, Sire. Let him have it!"

Swords flashed all over the hall as every thane shouted, "Battle! Battle!"

"He will rue the day that ever he set foot on this land," Gyrth cried above them. "When has the lion ever conquered the dragon?"

Derisive laughter and cries of "No Normans!" answered him as the thanes stood ready. In that moment they spoke as one. The King rose solemnly.

"Ready your companies," he said. "We march before dawn." Drawing his own sword, he saluted them and left the hall, Gyrth and Leofwine following. The others, talking vehemently together, hurried away, leaving Aelfred and Rafe alone.

Slowly Aelfred replaced his sword. A moment ago he had shouted with the rest, but now his heart sank. "We cannot go to Storches Hundred," he grieved.

"No." Rafe tried to comfort him. "Your father must lie here, Aelfred. Later, perhaps, when the world is quieter." He paused, then added, "Maybe that is what he himself would have wished, to lie where he fell."

"You will ride with the King, too?"

Rafe shook his head. "It was only because the trip to Storches Hundred would be a quiet one that the surgeon allowed it. My wound is not yet healed. I shall go with Edwin and Morcar. I hope the King can delay battle until we arrive."

"He must," Aelfred said intensely. "Oh, Rafe, I am sick at heart. Why could this not have happened last August, when we were so powerful and strong? When I saw our King standing there just now, listening to the messenger and then asking for our counsel as though the might of the land was his to command, I wanted to cry curses on all those who insisted that we disperse. Some of those who cried loudest were in the hall today. I wondered how they could look him in the face. Yet he said not one single word."

"He is a great man," Rafe said simply. "He can forgive his friends as well as his enemies."

"Do you call the men who left the south undefended friends?"

"Hush, lad. Don't waste yourself in reproaches. Follow your King's example."

"I know. Words seem useless, but they are not always. And I cannot help thinking that, if we had stood fast, Hardrada might never have attacked."

"Perhaps not. Still, I say that the strength you are using now would better be saved for the Normans." Rafe cleared his throat. "You know yourself—none better!—how cruel and covetous they are. They may strike at the London Road. What provision have you made for Adelaide's protection?"

"I told Siward to take her to Berkynge at the first sign of trouble," Aelfred answered.

"Let us pray that she is safe, then." Rafe's eyes were misted. "The battle will be fierce and terrible, my son. And we must face the prospect that we may lose. So, I tell you this for your comfort. There are some among the northern thanes who will not march to London. Harold has ordered them to fortify Durham, in case he must make a swift retreat. If he does not live to retreat, you must make your own way to Durham and seek out a man called Gospatric. He is the leader."

"The King thinks of everything."

"He is the King. He must—including the fact that one battle does not necessarily conquer an entire nation," Rafe said steadily. "No matter what destiny has decreed for him, he is determined that the fight against the usurpers shall continue. Of course, Duke William might give amnesty to the English, once he had his crown. In that event, you would be free to go home. The King's death would absolve you from your oath of fealty."

"Never!" Aelfred said sharply.

"Don't be too sure. You have never experienced the loss of

a leader. You have a wife to consider and your lands. Events may force you to be practical, and no one will blame you for it."

"No!" Aelfred insisted. "Please don't speak so, Rafe. King Harold will conquer and live. After Stamford Bridge we cannot possibly fail."

"So it seems now. But it is well for you, too, to think of everything." Rafe put his arms around Aelfred in a strong embrace. "Godspeed, my son. Tell Adelaide nothing of my wound, if you please. She will be anxious enough about her husband without worrying about her father, too."

"I shall tell her that the King himself says that you are the bravest in all England, and that she will see you soon in London," Aelfred answered, hoping that the words were not false. Rafe's heavily lined face was gray and drawn, and his wound was doubtless graver than he would admit. But those resolute eyes would permit no indulgence. Rafe, too, was a born warrior.

The next morning, King Harold led his army out of the gates of York. Down the great North Road came the long line of men, on horseback, on foot, some marching, some limping. Many had bandages on arms, legs, or head, for every man who could move was determined to go with the King. Along the way they were joined by farmers with pitchforks on their shoulders, merchants and artisans from the small towns, and numbers of churls carrying stone axes, wooden pikes, and clubs. The King welcomed them all without exception, much to Gyrth's distress.

"Churls!" he exclaimed, after an especially motley array of volunteers had made the entire line halt in order that they might be assigned to various companies. He looked at Aelfred in exasperation. "What good will they be? They've never learned the ways of fighting men."

"The King said once that every man in England would be needed to stand against Duke William," Aelfred answered. "You were there. Don't you remember?"

Harold had heard them and turned in his saddle. "On the

day they stand against the Norman, they will fight for England," he said. "Men who fight for their land learn quickly and are worth double their number. You will see."

"I hope so," Gyrth sighed, unconvinced.

Aelfred did not speak. This forced march was harder for him than the one to York had been, partly because he was still suffering from the effects of the battle but even more because he was in agony about Adelaide's safety. Reports reached them all along the line of march that the Norman armies were moving north from Pevensey, that Sussex had been pillaged without reason or mercy. It was probable that Duke William was planning to strike at London, and certainly he would devastate whatever lay in his path before he reached that city. Bad enough that Storches Hundred should be ravaged and burned, but the thought that Adelaide might still be there, alone and defenseless except for the demesne people, made his mouth dry and his hands tremble so much that he had difficulty in holding the reins. He had seen his people confronted by Norman soldiers; their courage would be unquestioned but, without weapons, useless before Normans who used the sword for sheer pleasure. Then he suddenly knew his greatest, his real fear: Tancred de Belleme might be in William's company. The subjection of Storches Hundred would be a task that he would relish. All the fear, the hatred he had once borne Tancred, that he was so certain he had conquered, engulfed him like a thick blackness that he could not pierce. He could neither eat nor sleep; he welcomed the night marches and longed for the battle that would bring him face to face with his enemy. He had fought to avenge his father at Stamford Bridge, but that fight would be nothing compared to what he would do if Adelaide were—he could not bring himself even to think that word.

Five days after leaving York, the army, increased to the number of thirteen thousand men, reached London. The city welcomed them as though it were a festival. For a brief hour, Duke William might never have planted the Red Lion on English land, as Londoners thronged the streets, hailing the heroes of Stamford Bridge. King Harold was triumphantly acclaimed; taking fire from the enthusiasm, he even smiled as he acknowledged their tumultuous welcome. The soldiers in the ranks quickened their pace, as though victory over the Normans was already theirs. But Aelfred could not share their spirit; all his thoughts were for Adelaide. Finally he could stand it no longer. Abruptly he broke ranks and rode up to the head of the procession beside the King.

"Sire, I beg of you," he pleaded. "Let me go to Berkynge now and then follow you to Westminster."

Harold looked at him kindly. "You are concerned about your wife, I know. Nor are you the only one, Aelfred Ansculf-son. I shall not know until I reach Westminster whether the Queen was able to leave Winchester in safety."

Ordinarily such a reply would have shamed him, but by now Aelfred was too distraught. "Sire, please," he begged, his voice dangerously near the breaking point. "I wish I had your strength, but I have not, and you know it well. I must go. I must."

The King smiled. "Your strength will come with years," he said. "I give you leave to go to Berkynge. Take it as a reward for your bravery at Stamford Bridge. We shall not require your attendance until council meeting tomorrow."

"Thank you." Aelfred could say no more.

"My greetings to your wife."

The King rode on, and Aelfred wheeled his horse to the left. Here he was confronted by a crowd of people, who insisted on his waiting until they had cheered him and were loath to let him go. Finally, however, they cleared the narrow lane, and he rode as fast as his horse could carry him to Berkynge.

The priory was quiet behind its wall, untouched by the tumult of the city. A bell in the chapel tower sounded the Angelus; Aelfred crossed himself and murmured the prayer. He had been long away from such things. He tethered his horse to the hitching post and knocked on the gate.

It was opened by an elderly nun, startled to see a disheveled, unshaven soldier on her doorstep. But she gave him courteous greeting and asked his name.

"I am Aelfred Ansculfson," he said, then repeated it more loudly, for she was obviously hard of hearing.

Her wrinkled face broke into a smile. It was almost as though she knew him and had hoped to see him. "Come in," she invited and led the way to the portress's lodge. "Sit here and wait. There is wine, if you wish it."

Exhausted, Aelfred slumped onto the chair. But he had seen the nun's smile and that smile kept his eyes straining towards the door. His heart pounded. Adelaide was here, then, safe within these walls. In a moment, he would look on her beauty again. Relief and gratitude welled up in him; he wanted to laugh and sing with joy, but he was so tired. He could only wait until the miraculous moment when the door opened, and she stood before him with arms outstretched, smiling and weeping together, saying over and over, "Aelfred! Oh, Aelfred!"

He went to her swiftly and took her in his arms. "Adelaide," he whispered, holding her tightly. The horror of the past days was obliterated—as though it had never been.

Gently she took his hand. "My dear love," she said softly. "Sister Portress says that you are too exhausted to stand. You need food and rest."

"But this is a convent," he said diffidently. "I cannot enter the cloister. Sister told me only to *wait* here."

"When I came, they gave me a chamber in the guest hall," she answered. "It is not in the cloister, and Mother Abbess has given you leave to stay there. Unless you must return immediately to the King?"

He shook his head. "Not until council, tomorrow," he said heavily.

She looked at him with what seemed to him must be all the love ever known in the world. "My dear love," she whispered. "Oh, my dear love."

The thanes were gathering for the council meeting. As Aelfred walked through the door of the Painted Chamber, he found Gyrth waiting for him.

"Well, a smile from you at last," Gyrth said cheerfully. "I take it that you found Adelaide safe and well?"

"Yes, thank God," Aelfred answered. "Safe, though worried and wan, but my heart is more at ease. I feel ready for anything, now."

"Anything is probably what you'll get, too."

Aelfred turned to greet Esegar the Staller, who had remained behind on the march to York to command the defenses of London. "All has been quiet here?" he asked.

"So far," Esegar said grimly. "We're all relieved to see the King, I can tell you. Why William hasn't marched on London by now, I'll never know."

"I can tell you." Leofwine had joined them. "He doesn't dare get too far from his ships. He may need them to get back to Normandy in a hurry."

The others laughed. "We'll see that his foresight is rewarded," said Gyrth. "Where is the King? It's long past Terce."

"Talking with our uncle," Leofwine answered. "He arrived half an hour ago from Winchester. By the look of it, he's brought his entire monastery with him!"

"I'll drink the health of Uncle Aelfwine after this meeting, at first opportunity," Gyrth chuckled. "And the Queen? What about her?"

"She decided to stay in Winchester," Leofwine answered.

Gyrth raised an eyebrow but made no comment. "Have the Welshmen come?"

"Some. The rest are on march," Esegar answered, "and the Dorsetshire men have arrived in full muster."

"Now, if only Edwin and Morcar will hurry," said Leofwine.

"A familiar refrain, brother!" The King had entered the Painted Chamber. "Good morning, my friends. Be seated. We have much to decide in this hour."

The wooden benches scraped on the stone floor as the thanes sat down at the long council table. The King waited; his eye caught Aelfred's and he smiled. Then he took the high seat, under the suspended sword.

217

"We have definite news of Duke William," he began. "He has withdrawn to Hastings and fortified it. His hope seems to be to draw us into a battle, and I do not think any of us purposes to disappoint him."

There was a ripple of laughter, and Esegar asked, "Why Hastings?"

"Good harbor for his ships," Leofwine answered. "Do we lay siege?"

"Not a siege," one of the older thanes objected. "A swift, surprise attack, I say, and soon. Think of all those poor souls in Sussex who have had their homes destroyed."

"The Normans are devils," another said angrily. "They know we will not stand idle while they ravage the land. But, my lords, are we ready—would it be wise to fight now? Should we not delay until Mercia and Northumbria can join us?"

"If we wait for Mercia and Northumbria, we may wait until Doomsday," Gyrth retorted. "A surprise attack would give the Normans less time to entrench themselves at Hastings and would need fewer men."

Esegar pursed his lips. "They are already entrenched at Hastings. I speak for caution, my friends. It is a pity that so many have lost their homes, but nothing we can do will help restore them if we move with too much speed. We stand to lose everything if we do not plan carefully."

"I agree," Leofwine said firmly. "Esegar, you know the land around Hastings like the palm of your hand. Wouldn't it be possible to keep William penned up in the town with a few troops camped on Telham Hill?"

"We could keep him there indefinitely," Esegar replied. "Telham Hill commands the London Road."

"And then the attack could be delayed until our army is at full strength," Leofwine continued. He faced Harold directly. "I urge you to adopt this plan, Sire. We have everything to gain by waiting, and William has everything to lose."

"Still, the idea of a swift, immediate attack has its merits," Gyrth insisted. "The longer William stays at Hastings, the less easy it will be to dislodge him. I know these Normans. They thrive on siege."

"They won't thrive when food supplies run short," Leofwine retorted.

For over an hour the debate continued; one plan after another was considered and discarded. The consultation was at its most vehement when the door to the Painted Chamber suddenly swung open and a company of soldiers, who had pushed back the guards, entered and walked towards the King. They wore Red Lions on their tunics, and their leader, a black-robed monk, carried a white flag.

Harold looked at them in haughty surprise. "Who are you? How dare you interrupt our council?" he demanded.

The monk did not even incline his head. "You know me, Harold Godwineson," he said arrogantly. "I was at Harfleur when you gave your oath."

Harold nodded. "Yes. I recognize you now, Hugh Margot. What do you want?"

"I come as Duke William's envoy of peace."

"Peace? That word sounds strange from any messenger of William the Norman."

"Do not speak so mightily, Harold Godwineson—"

"And do not dispute England's crowned and sacred King, Margot." Harold's voice was like ice. "It does not become your habit. You are here as a peace envoy, you say, so behave like one."

Margot's eyes flashed, but he modified his tone. "William of Normandy offers peace. Will you hear him?"

"He offers peace? We will all hear. Speak."

"Duke William does not want war—"

"So he comes with ships and armed men," Harold finished ironically, "and ravages and burns the land."

"He wishes to shed no more innocent blood of men who misguidedly follow you," Margot persisted. "He asks you to accept a challenge to single combat with him, the winner to take the crown."

There was an angry murmur of protest from the council. "Why not throw dice for it?" Harold retorted. "The crown of England is not a trinket to be staked on any sword. Besides, even if he won, does Duke William actually think that he could take the crown without a struggle? England would not abide by such a decision. The answer is no!"

"Duke William offers a second choice," Margot said impassively. "Will you submit the entire dispute to Rome for judgment?"

Harold rose and the thanes rose with him, murmuring urgently, "No—no, never!"

The King's face was like stone. "I have not really been angry with your master until now," he thundered. "I am King of England by the laws of this land. No other laws, no other courts can judge my claim. It has been judged."

"Do you fear that the Holy Father will be prejudiced?" Margot sneered. "I can assure you that he will not, even though he has blessed our cause."

"How dare you vilify and misrepresent a holy priest who has been deceived into believing what is untrue? Your words speak for themselves. I will say only that the Holy Father has acted in innocence of the realities."

"You dare to say so?" Margot gasped.

"Margot, in matters of religion, the Holy Father's decrees rule me and my land. In matters political, he is bound to abide by the decrees of our courts." Harold looked at him piercingly. "Go back to your master, the Norman William. Tell him that I offer him my brotherly affection and a royal gift, if he will leave England and never return. In spite of his threats and insults, my people and I do not wish for war. But if he is determined to fight, I shall meet him in battle this Saturday next. He is eager for judgment? Then let God judge between us."

There was a moment of silence. All the thanes looked at each other, trying to conceal their dismay. Harold turned to Leofwine. "My brother, take these men to the soldiers' hall. See that they are given food and courteous treatment. Then give them safe-conducts and set them on the road for Hastings."

Leofwine bowed and went to Margot, gesturing him to follow. The Normans marched stiffly out of the Painted Chamber. Only then did Gyrth raise his voice. "Sire," he said painfully. "Saturday! We cannot!"

"We must," the King said proudly. "I have given my pledge." He looked at the thanes. "We shall meet again, after we have dined," he said and, thus dismissing the council, walked swiftly from the room.

In twos and threes, talking earnestly together, the thanes withdrew. Gyrth, still standing at his place, struck the table with his fist. "Destiny is against us!" he cried. "The one thing I prayed would not happen has come to pass. Saturday!"

Aelfred looked at him wordlessly. Thoughts tumbled over each other in his bewildered brain, but there was nothing he could say. Then, a faint grating sound made him turn.

"No!" he whispered, crossing himself frantically, as he watched the great sword suspended above the throne sway on its chain.

IT WAS an hour after midnight on the thirteenth of October. In the King's tent, pitched on the heights of Senlac, the thanes had gathered that night for final orders. They were weary from the march, for the King had waited in London until the last possible moment, to enable as many men as possible to join him, and had finally left the city only three days before. Even so, the armies of Mercia and Northumbria had not yet arrived. But the thanes were optimistic; thousands of men had been moved into position under cover of darkness, and the battle plan had been drawn up during this last council meeting. The strategy was to make a two-pronged attack down both slopes, bypassing Telham Hill across the valley and encircling Hastings, so as to cut the Normans off from both the London Road and their ships.

"Is there any more to be said?" Harold asked. His eyes were like burnt holes in his drawn face, but his voice was firm.

"This—that you let me stand in your place tomorrow," Gyrth pleaded.

"I've already said no to that three times," his brother answered. "I promised to meet William in battle. I shall meet him."

"Sire, if you do, you risk your life, and the safety of all England depends on you," Gyrth insisted. "Suppose I meet him and win? That will be our gain. But if I lose, it is no one's loss. You will still be here to raise another army and avenge me."

"It's a brave plan and a good one," Esegar the Staller approved, and the others nodded their heads.

"Meanwhile, Harold, you could send some of our men to harry the land between here and London," Leofwine suggested. "Make the land a wilderness. Then, whether William wins tomorrow or not, in the end he will lose. He cannot maintain his army in a wilderness."

"What do the rest of you say to that?" Harold asked. "Some of you have lands between here and London. Aelfred Ansculfson, shall I order the torch to be put to Storches Hundred?"

Aelfred, weary and leaden-eyed, stared at the King in mute dismay. The idea was so shocking he could hardly find words. He had seen the devastation that the Normans had already wreaked in Sussex—fields blackened, houses reduced to ashes— it sickened him to remember. Could he bear to know that his own hall had become a smoking ruin? Yet he had promised to serve the King with all he possessed.

"If there is no other way, Sire, do what you must," he said woodenly. "But I cannot think our situation is that desperate."

The King smiled reassuringly. "It is not that desperate, nor will we permit it to be. For no matter how desperate we become, that is one order I shall never give. How could I possibly harm innocent people whom I am vowed to rule in peace?"

He looked at Gyrth.

"As for your question, my brother, the answer is again and again, and finally, no. I need you where you are. I need all"— he corrected himself swiftly—"*both* my brothers where they are."

With that, he dismissed them, and the thanes went to their tents to sleep. Aelfred walked with Gyrth and Leofwine to the one assigned to them, not far from the King's. Leofwine looked up at the sky.

"There's a mist on the moon," he said worriedly. "I hope that doesn't mean rain tomorrow. It's Harold's birthday, too."

"A good omen, I hope." Aelfred smothered a yawn. "But it's also Duke William's. Strange that they should meet on that day."

"Do you think someone should have stayed with the King tonight?" Gyrth asked.

"Why?" Leofwine demanded.

"Because he misses Tostig so greatly."

"Tostig was a good commander," Leofwine replied somberly. "If he were here, I'd say we were invincible."

"We were invincible at Stamford Bridge," Aelfred reminded.

"Yes, but the battle heat was on the King there because of Hardrada," Gyrth answered. "Now he's had time to think and to remember, and to regret that his sword killed his own brother."

Aelfred sighed. "Everyone loses in a war. Didn't you say that, Leofwine?"

"I did. But it's best not to say it now," Leofwine replied. "Here is our tent. Sleep is what we need, so no more talk. Stamford Bridge was a hard battle, but I know no words to describe what I think tomorrow will be."

Long after Gyrth and Leofwine were sleeping, Aelfred lay restlessly awake. Once more he envied the apparent calm of those two men that could permit them to sleep on the night before a battle. He would never possess it, no matter how many battles he might see, any more than he would ever be called a born warrior. Nor did he have any yearning ambition for such distinction. He would fight tomorrow as he fought at Stamford Bridge, to the best of his ability and with all his strength, for the sake of the land he loved and the King he served, above all for his home and especially for Adelaide, whose farewell three days ago still wrung his heart.

We must win tomorrow, he thought determinedly. We must! He could not bear the thought of what lay before him if the battle was lost, for, warrior or not, he was bound to fight for his country. He had so vowed. The Normans must be conquered, Harold had said, if not tomorrow, then another day—

if not under himself, then under another leader. Aelfred turned on his side and closed his eyes, but all he could see was Adelaide's grief-stricken face. He remembered his father; he thought of his grandfather whose ring was heavy on his hand. "Great God, let us win," he prayed over and over. "Help us, help us." Finally he fell asleep.

When he woke next morning, Gyrth and Leofwine had already left the tent. He sat bolt upright on his pallet and shouted for Osric, who came at once with a ewer of water.

"You should have called me hours ago," he scolded. "Quick, hand me my fresh tunic and help me into my armor. The battle will start before I'm ready."

"No hurry, master," Osric said with a good-humored grin. "The King said that everyone was to sleep an hour longer this morning because of the march."

"Where are Gyrth and Leofwine Godwineson, then?"

"At breakfast with the King. Some new recruits arrived early, and they had to see to them. Here, master, let me help," for Aelfred, struggling into his tunic, had gotten his head into a sleeve. "Now, let me wind your breeks."

Aelfred smiled at him. "You're ready and eager, I see."

"So are we all. It's a good day, too."

"Now, if only Duke William's spies have not found us out."

"How could they last night? And the sentries say that there's not a sign of life in the town."

"They can't know much about that. Telham Hill blocks the view. Get me into my byrnie, now."

Deftly Osric put on the metal-plated leather vest and buckled the straps. "You're to go to the King," he said. "I must return to my company."

Aelfred looked at him, suddenly filled with the terrible realization that he might never see him again. "Osric, I am an ingrate," he said urgently. "All these months, I've meant to say this and have not. Take your freedom. You deserve it. You are a demesne churl no longer."

Osric's face shone. "I thank you," he said with grave courtesy. "But I shall be your man then, Aelfred Ansculfson. What would my life be without you?"

Aelfred took him by the shoulders and embraced him. "If anything happens to me today, you will go at once to Lady Adelaide," he said in a low voice.

"At once. My life is hers to command, as well as yours." Osric handed him his sword. "Godspeed—my friend."

At the scarlet tent, Aelfred found the King and his brothers enjoying a hearty meal. At their invitation he sat down and cut himself a piece of meat. "What is the news from Hastings?" he asked.

"None yet," Gyrth answered. "The patrols have not come back."

"I'm worried," Leofwine grunted. "We should not have delayed so long. It is long past Prime and we have not even begun to form ranks."

"The men needed their rest," the King said quietly. "Didn't you see them last night? Some could hardly stand."

"Good morning," a conversational voice interrupted, and, to everyone's surprise and delight, Captain Gryffin paraded into the tent.

"Gryffin!" Aelfred exclaimed, jumping to his feet and extending his hand. Gyrth and Leofwine did the same, then the Welshman made a ceremonious bow to the King.

"My greetings, Harold Godwineson, King of England," he said solemnly, in the same manner he would have employed at a feast.

"And mine to you, Gryffin ap Gryffin ap Llewellyn, Prince of Powys," Harold replied, returning the bow with equal flourish.

"You're improving," Gryffin barked. "All except the 'Llewellyn.' You still don't pronounce that very well."

"My unskilled tongue does not lessen my pleasure at your company," Harold said blandly. Then all five men laughed, and Gyrth called for more ale.

"I've brought you two hundred archers," Gryffin announced. "They're the best in Wales. I've proved them myself. Each is worth at least three Englishmen."

"Where are they?" Leofwine asked.

"Breakfasting with Thurlkill's company. As soon as they've finished, if you'll point out any particular Normans you'd like shot, they'll be delighted to oblige you."

Aelfred chuckled. "I can think of several. Or any I'm not thinking of, for that matter."

Gryffin nodded. "If one you think of is called Tancred, he's mine. I'm looking forward to meeting him again. Unless, of course, you see him first," he amended politely.

"If all our men are as eager as yours, the battle should be over by noon," said Harold.

"So said the Kentishmen when they arrived this morning." Leofwine actually smiled. "And do you know what our Abbot uncle is doing, between hearing confessions? Putting his monks through a final sword drill!"

"It's a strange time, when monks must fight," said Gryffin, smoothing his beard. "When I see Abbot Aelfwine, I'll tell him so."

"Watch out that he doesn't lay the flat of his sword to you," Gyrth warned drolly. "Harold, when do we begin?"

"As soon as the patrols return," the King assured him. "What's all that noise?" For the sound of shouting and running men now broke the quiet.

"It sounds as though the patrols have already returned," said Leofwine. "I hope there's no trouble."

"With the Norman, anything is possible," said Harold, and rose to greet Esegar the Staller, who rushed into the tent and fell on one knee.

"Sire," he gasped. "The Normans! They're advancing from Telham Hill."

"Now?" Gyrth asked incredulously.

Esegar nodded. "They're in full force and ready to attack."

"I see." Harold flashed a wry smile at Leofwine. "You were right. Our arrival was discovered after all, and we should have moved earlier. Now we shall have to defend ourselves."

"Well, we couldn't be better positioned for defense," Leofwine said briskly. "How are the men taking the news, Esegar?"

227

"They are waiting orders," Esegar said proudly.

"Have them form the shield wall at once." Harold was now fully in command. "Let the House Carls protect the flanks. We won't use our cavalry—have the horses taken to the rear. My standards will stand above on the highest ground. Gyrth, Leofwine, your companies will be stationed just below them on the ridge."

"What about my Welshmen?" Gryffin demanded.

"They'll be in the first position immediately behind the shield wall. They'll have raw churls to their rear and on their flanks, so they will bear the brunt of the attack."

"They'll bring their thanks as soon as this little fracas is over," Gryffin promised, already on his way to them.

"To your posts, all of you," said the King. "Esegar, have my horse and two others saddled. There will be time for me to show myself to the men."

The four men left hurriedly, putting on their helmets as they ran. Only Aelfred remained. He waited a moment, wondering whether to stay or to go with Leofwine. Then the King spoke.

"In other battles, I had three brothers," he said quietly. "Two commanded the House Carls that protected me, and the third remained at my side to carry my orders as needed. Gyrth and Leofwine must be the commanders today. So you, I think, must be the third."

"Sire!" Aelfred gasped. He fell on his knee and kissed the King's hand.

"First, however, you will ride with Esegar behind me as I show myself. You shall carry the Golden Man." Harold smiled faintly. "It will be a most dangerous post, Aelfred Ansculfson. Are you sure you wish it?"

"With all my heart," Aelfred answered.

"Then put on your helmet and lift the standard."

Outside the scarlet tent three horses were saddled and waiting. The King mounted his black stallion; Aelfred and Esegar took the others. Then they began the slow ride uphill to the highest point, where Harold would direct the battle. Aelfred, holding the Golden Man aloft, followed Esegar, who carried the Gold Dragon. To his amazement, he discovered that he was not afraid, and he knew why—because the King rode so majestically, not even deigning to look across the valley at Telham Hill where the advance guard of the Norman attack was already plainly visible.

By now, the troops stationed on the heights below them had seen their king, and a tumultuous roar greeted him. Rank upon rank of gold helmets turned to look at him; the sun glittered on javelins and axes. The wall at the foot of the hill, formed by men overlapping their shields, looked even more formidable than Hardrada's at Stamford Bridge. All was not completely ready; heavy pointed stakes to provide a further hazard for the attacking army were still being driven into the ground between the ranks of soldiers, and some of the churls and shiremen had not yet found their places. But the spirit was so plainly one of victory that Aelfred thought even Duke William must hear the cheers and shouts across the valley.

King Harold dismounted and took off his helmet. At that, an even louder cheer broke the air and he smiled. "Raise the standards," he said.

Esegar and Aelfred obeyed, and the King lifted his hand. At once there was silence. "Men of England!" he cried, his voice ringing like a clarion. "By all you hold dear, stand where you are! The Norman will use every trick to draw you from the hill, but do not be deceived. Stand, I tell you—stand for England, and the might of the world cannot conquer you."

"God save King Harold!" came the answering roar.

"We left Hardrada's men twenty ships to get back to Norway," Harold called. "How many for William?"

There was a burst of laughter and a voice shouted, "Let the Bastard swim!"

"Agreed! Let them all swim," Harold answered. From across the valley came the peal of a trumpet. "Now, show the Normans what free Englishmen are worth. Stand fast, and God send us victory!"

Men adjusted their helmets and took up their weapons. Aelfred, having dismounted, still holding the Golden Man, drew his sword and looked down the hill into the valley. His blood ran cold at the sight. Coming inexorably towards them was a mass of moving men, some on foot, many more on horseback. Every horseman carried a banner; over and above them all waved the Red Lion of Normandy. His heart beat wildly. How could their army stand against so great a host? Now he could distinguish the archers, led by a man riding a black horse. He squinted; something about that leader was familiar, though he could not see his features. But his bearing—the way he sat his horse—Aelfred's blood surged to his head. Tancred de Belleme! He would know that arrogant figure anywhere.

"Sound trumpets," King Harold commanded. "Retire standards ten paces."

Aelfred saw Esegar give the Gold Dragon to a soldier who stood behind him. He turned to follow suit and, to his surprise, was met by Osric.

"How do you happen to be here?" he asked. The sight of his friend was a needed comfort at that moment. The glimpse of Tancred had been strangely unnerving.

"I was sent for," Osric replied, as he took hold of the Golden Man. "God be with you! Strike to kill, Aelfred Ansculfson. I recognized him, too."

The trumpets sounded the signal to prepare for the first assault. A single rider advanced from the Norman line. Dressed in blue, bareheaded, he sang as he rode, tossing his sword in the air and catching it again. The archers followed close behind him; there was a sound like the rushing of a thousand wings, then a thundering crash as the first volley of arrows struck the shield wall. A moment later, the Norman minstrel fell from his horse, struck by an English javelin. The battle had begun.

Now Norman foot soldiers tried to make their way up the hill, battering their swords against the overlapping shields. Many were struck down by the Welsh archers or were impaled on the horrible stakes as the English jeered, "Out! Out!" and the first detachment fell back.

Again the Normans re-formed and tried to scale the hill, throwing themselves against the shield wall, shouting, "God with us!" But the English, obeying Harold's command, held firm. Battle-axes, javelins, lances, clubs, as well as arrows, kept the enemy from gaining even a toe hold. "Out! Out!" the shiremen shouted, and the House Carls thundered, "No Normans!" Finally, after several hours of bloody fighting, Norman trumpets signaled the retreat.

King Harold turned to Aelfred. "Go to Leofwine; tell him we need twenty more men on the right flank. Hurry!" He looked across the valley. "Tell Gyrth to send thirty of his men to strengthen the center."

"Whom shall I tell first?" Aelfred asked breathlessly. He had been taking messages back and forth between the King and his brothers all morning.

"Both at once," the King said shortly. "No—not Leofwine. He's seen what's to be done. Tell Gyrth."

Aelfred ran to where Gyrth was stationed and gave the message. As he returned, he looked down the hill, wondering why Gyrth had looked so anxious and the King so grim. What he saw made him stop stock-still in horror. The Normans had sent in their cavalry. They galloped in perfect formation across the valley, banners flying, lances lowered to strike the shield wall. "Stand!" the King shouted. And the English stood. The House Carls moved into position, axes raised. Horses screamed as the iron clove into them; Norman soldiers, their horses killed under them, drew their swords. All over the hill men fought hand to hand; javelins and arrows whistled through the air. Another wave of cavalry charged, then a third, then a fourth. Still the shield wall held, and above the din came the defiant cry, "Out! Out! No Normans!"

Suddenly a detachment of horsemen turned and raced pell-mell across the valley. Their panic spread through the enemy ranks, and within minutes the entire Norman army was in disorderly retreat. The English jeered and yelled after them; in that moment, the battle seemed won. The trumpets blew the call to stay action, and the various company commanders hurried to the King for further orders.

"Let all the wounded be carried to the rear," Harold said. "How many men have you lost, Leofwine?"

"Very few, and the wounded don't want to retire," Leofwine said with a broad smile.

"Mine say the same thing." Gyrth shook his head. "Never again will I speak against churls. They fought like veterans."

"I saw one go after a Norman with his bare hands," another commented.

"See that weapons are replaced where needed," the King directed. "Impress upon your men that they must not be lax. They must continue to stand."

"Indeed they must!" Abbot Aelfwine, a byrnie over his habit, joined the group. His face was white. "I have sad news, nephew. Some of the Kentishmen went berserk and started after the Normans when they retreated. They'd hardly gotten into the valley when somebody—Duke William himself, I hear —rallied a company and cut them to pieces." He shuddered. "Horrible!"

There was a moment of shocked silence. Then Harold said grimly, "Tell this to your companies. They must stand!"

A trumpet sounded. "Here they come," Leofwine said gravely. "I think it's William leading the charge this time."

"Move to the rear, Harold," Gyrth said brusquely. "He's riding hard.

But the King shook his head. "Advance standards," he ordered.

With shaking hands, Aelfred took the Golden Man from Osric. His knees were trembling. Up the side of the hill, despite all attempts to stop him, rode a Norman in blue. A gold crown circled his helmet; the Red Lion blazed on his shield. In his hand he carried a terrible mace, which he swung back and forth, felling men on both sides of him as he made straight for the King.

"Harold! Give ground!" Gyrth shouted. He rushed into the duke's path, hurling his javelin. The horse crumpled to its knees, as the weapon missed its real target by inches. In that same instant, the terrible mace flailed the air, and Gyrth God-wineson lay dead on the hillside. A shower of English javelins forced the duke to retreat, but the Norman spearmen who had accompanied him struck out wildly on all sides, and a flying weapon struck Leofwine in the thigh.

"Sire!" Aelfred cried, tears streaming down his cheeks. He passed the Golden Man to Osric and drew his sword. The King's face was like a stone mask. The bodyguard of House Carls, deprived of their commanders, looked at him.

"Stand!" the King shouted. It was a cry of agony.

For six long hours, the battle raged, and still the English stood, with their reverberating cry, "No Normans!" Every advance was cut down; the Gold Dragon still waved proudly on the hilltop. Then, suddenly, there was a pause—the length of a heartbeat. Aelfred, at the King's side, watched how Duke William raised himself in his stirrups and turned to shout at the men behind him.

"They will parley, Sire," he said hoarsely. "Surely they will parley?"

The answer was a hail of arrows, shot not against the shield wall but into the air. They fell on the bare heads of the shire-men, piercing eyes and throats. Screams of anguish tore at Aelfred's ears. He watched in horror how the men tried to protect their heads with their shields, breaking the shield wall, exposing their bodies to Norman swords. Again came the pitiless barrage. Three arrows fell within a foot of where he was standing. Enemy foot soldiers and cavalry were advancing easily up the hill, now; the House Carls moved to attack and Aelfred joined them, striking blindly with his sword. He had killed three Normans before he heard the terrible cry. He turned to see Harold Godwineson crumple to the ground under a Norman spear.

"Sire!" he screamed and ran to the King. But before he could reach him, someone grasped his arm. It was Abbot Aelf-wine, his habit torn and stained with blood, a gaping wound in his shoulder.

"Let me go!" Aelfred cried. "The King—"

"No," the Abbot said firmly and pressed something into his hand. "Ride to Westminster. Give this to Archbishop Stigand. It's the great seal of England. He'll know what to do."

"The King is dead," Aelfred insisted. He stared at the Abbot numbly. The words made no sense.

The Abbot shook him roughly. "You can do nothing for him here. Get to Westminster. Quickly!" He turned to Osric, who had come running to them, still holding the Golden Man. "I'll take that. You ride with Aelfred Ansculfson."

"I'm his man. I'll take care of him," Osric replied. He took Aelfred by the arm. "The horses are on the other side of the hill."

Dazedly Aelfred allowed himself to be led away. They found horses quickly enough, but he could hardly mount. Osric boosted him, then sprang onto another horse that a frightened churl was holding. "We must ride fast," he said.

"Yes," Aelfred said dully. The shouts of the Norman victors were very near. He shuddered violently. He did not know when or how he wheeled his horse round and set off at a gallop beside Osric. All he could ever remember of that moment was his sense of complete exhaustion and defeat when he saw how, at the top of the hill where the Gold Dragon had flown so proudly, the enemy had implanted the Red Lion.

IN THE soldiers' hall of Westminster Palace, Tancred de Belleme was putting on his finest clothes. That morning Duke
William had entered London in triumph, the elected king of
England. Despite the winter cold, for it was only five days
until Christmas, the streets had been crowded with people ac-
claiming the new ruler—the same people who, only a few short
weeks ago, had sworn to resist him with their last breath. But
the swift Norman advance from Hastings to Winchester to
London Bridge had made them realize that a conqueror had
come who would not be gainsaid. Oh, the Londoners had
fought at the bridge that day, but the duke's forces had
beaten them easily and had fired Southwark to make his
victory complete. Then, in a lightning move, William had
crossed the Thames and reached Berkhampstead. The south
of England was in his hands; the Norman army blocked all
access to the north. Isolated from the rest of the country,
London had waited only a few days and then had surrendered.

And not only London had capitulated, though the submis-
sion of Edgar the Atheling and Archbishop Stigand had been
momentous enough. The earls of Northumbria and Mercia
had also come to Berkhampstead, offering William peace and
the crown. With their powerful influence, the hastily assembled

witenagemot had readily agreed, having received the duke's assurance that there would be no reprisals against them. The red-bearded brothers had ridden in the procession this morning and had sat at the council table where William had announced his intention to govern England by English law. But he had already told his Norman supporters that he would be generous in rewards to them, and Tancred had determined not to delay in asking for his.

"The demesne of Storches Hundred and the hand of Adelaide of Birnham," he crooned, as he adjusted his gold chausses. That he would receive both, he had no doubt. William had said that his followers might choose their lands from those of English thanes who had died in battle, provided there were no survivors to claim them—a nice meticulousness, Tancred sneered, that did not apply to him. He had learned from Earl Morcar of Northumbria that Baron Ansculf had died at Gate Fulford, and he himself, by lucky chance, had seen Aelfred fall at London Bridge. A small doubt nagged at him that his stepbrother might have survived that action too, but he dismissed it. By general account, none of Edgar the Atheling's pitiful army had lived through that day. As for Adelaide —well, even under English law a wife's claim to her husband's land depended upon the King's favor, if there were no children. He smiled complacently as he put on his cloth-of-gold tunic. He had no doubt of his ability to get her, or that the new King would approve the match.

For had he not performed the impossible and won over William completely? During those months when the Norman fleet had waited in the mouth of the River Dives, he had insinuated himself into the duke's confidence by conducting himself so irreproachably that even he was amazed. Wherever William was, he was first to offer service and last to leave. His position as captain of the archers, the reward of his prowess at the contest, which he had won as he had known he would, gave him an enormous advantage. He was allowed to speak in council meetings, and the devotion of his men, which he had assiduously courted, increased his reputation as a commander. The sight of him on the drill field, putting the archers through their paces or practicing by himself, had done him no harm either. Of course Duke William could not know that his dedicated captain had been kept constantly apprised of his master's coming and goings. Tancred's being constantly under his eyes had seemed altogether natural, as Tancred intended it should. His image as a soldier devoted wholly to his duty had increased the duke's good opinion of him, and, by the time the Norman fleet sailed, his position was secure. It had needed only his suggestion at Hastings that the archers shoot into the air instead of at the shield wall to make William look on him with the kind of gratitude that inspired the most munificent rewards.

He had managed one other coup that made him chuckle with glee whenever he thought of it. Almost overnight he had begun to praise his uncle to the skies, to any ear that would listen, especially William's. Daily he remarked on Guilbert de Belleme's prudence and judgment and on his ability to manage men. His uncle had basked and purred under such attention; even more important, the duke had listened. And, when the time came to sail, Guilbert de Belleme had been one of the men commanded to remain in Normandy to secure the peace of the realm during the ruler's absence. Tancred smiled, recalling his uncle's face when the announcement had been made. De Belleme had wanted desperately to go to England, but he had been outwitted at the last, and now the benefits of victory to the house of Belleme would not have to be divided. Tancred would reap them all.

He adjusted his cloak and clasped his sword to his belt. Then he took the scroll on which he had written the names of his archers and the bounties he felt each one was entitled to; this would provide his excuse for an interview with William. Not that an excuse was really necessary for a man who had already been chosen as one to hold the canopy over the new King at his coronation! But bounties for archers could easily lead the conversation to his own reward, and he was not going to leave one detail to chance. He had learned that much from his Uncle Guilbert.

He found the duke alone in his study, poring over some

dispatches. Standing in the open door, he made his most flourishing bow and murmured, "Your Majesty."

"Oh, Tancred," the duke said cordially. "Come in. Close the door, please. The drafts in this place are infernal."

"You must teach the English how to build proper palaces." Tancred smiled.

"All in good time. I'll have to teach them to accept me as King, first."

"Surely there's no doubt that they accept you?"

"Their earls do, but that is because they are practical, reasonable men, who prefer to accept situations as they are." The duke motioned to him to be seated. "The people—ah, that's another story. There's already trouble in the north. Some upstart called Gospatric has taken Durham."

"We'll settle with him, Sire."

"Yes, and without too much bloodshed, I hope." The duke raised an eyebrow. "That surprises you? Well, you'll learn as you grow older that violence can only do great harm. I want order and harmony in England, not discord. That's why I've insisted on ruling here by English law and expect my vassals to do the same."

Tancred nodded gravely. "We are yours to command, Sire."

"I hope so," William said bluntly. "What's that in your hand?"

"The list of archers and their bounties." Tancred laid it on the table.

"No wonder your men sing your praises so highly. You constantly think of them. That's good." He leaned back in his chair. "Is your own reward included?"

"Oh, no, Sire," Tancred protested.

"I can't believe it! Do you know that you're the only one of my commanders who hasn't hinted about lands and women? They've been pecking about like sparrows."

Tancred laughed. "Some act as though England will not be here tomorrow, and they must take what they can while they can."

The duke chuckled. "You're wise, my friend, and astute. Well, suppose you tell me what you would like? You certainly are entitled to a handsome reward, especially since you've never claimed the prize of your own choosing from the archery contest. What can I give my faithful liege and servant, eh?"

How easy, Tancred crowed inwardly. How very easy! "If you will agree, Sire, I ask for the demesne of Storches Hundred and the hand of the Lady Adelaide of Birnham," he said diffidently. In another moment, he would have all he wanted.

The duke, however, frowned. "That's your foster-father's estate, isn't it?"

"Yes. But Baron Ansculf died at Gate Fulford."

"After Gate Fulford. And his son is still very much alive."

"What?" Tancred stared at him dumbounded. Then, noticing the almost imperceptible look of surprise on William's face, he lowered his voice and said with as bland an expression as he could muster, "I am amazed, Sire."

"And not too rejoiced, I take it?"

"Of course I am happy at the news," Tancred said quickly, worried to hear the slight chill in the duke's voice. "Where is he? I must go to him."

"He's well taken care of, but not well enough to see visitors."

"And—has he sworn the oath of fealty to you, Sire?" Tancred asked.

"Not yet. But I want him to swear. I sent de Warrene's son to invite him to take the oath, and do you know what he did?" The duke laughed. "He took hold of the young man with his good arm and all but threw him out of the room. That's the kind of spirit I want in my court. To be truthful, I don't like these mealy-mouthed English thanes who change their coats so easily. Aelfred Ansculfson is honest."

"I—I know only good of him," Tancred stammered, appalled at the turn of the conversation.

"So, I can't give you his lands. At least, not now. I want to ask him for his oath again, when he's completely recovered from his wound."

"You are gracious indeed, Sire. But what if he will not swear?"

"Oh, in that event, Storches Hundred is yours. You have my word for that. If he does swear fealty, however, console yourself. There are other lands."

"Yes," Tancred murmured. William's words carried such an obvious tone of dismissal that he rose and bowed, despite his longing to speak more. Suddenly a thought came to him.

"Sire, Storches Hundred is only a short distance from London. May I have leave to ride there tomorrow, to see that all is well? I have been anxious. And now with my—my brother" —the word came with difficulty, but he spoke it—"unable to attend to his lands—"

"A most considerate thought," the duke said quietly, his eyes on the papers before him. "By all means, go. You may be able to set the Lady Adelaide's mind at ease about her husband, as well."

Is there nothing he does not know? Tancred thought furiously. But he made his voice calm and even. "I shall, Sire. Thank you."

He was almost to the door when the duke called sharply, "Tancred?"

"Yes, Sire?"

"It's a small matter, but I think I'd better ask. Did you ever swear an oath of fealty to Baron Ansculf?"

The unexpectedness of the question took his breath away, but only for a moment. He pulled himself to his full height, looked the duke boldly in the eye, and said, "No, Sire. Never."

"*Bien.* Just this matter of English law, you know." With a charming smile, William dismissed him.

Outside the royal apartments, Tancred leaned against the wall. For a moment, he thought he was going to be violently ill. Had the duke believed his "No"? Even more important, were there any witnesses whom, if the matter was raised, the duke might believe against him? Aelfred would never swear fealty to the Norman, of that he was certain, and that removed him as an immediate danger. Without that oath, no matter what he said, William would not give it credence; he probably would not even see Aelfred, for Englishmen who refused to swear fealty to him were not included in the general amnesty. Many had already fled to the north. Aelfred would doubtless be imprisoned, perhaps executed.

He walked towards the soldiers' hall, trying to think coherently. Baron Ansculf and Rafe of Birnham were both dead; Adelaide had not been present, so her words would have no effect. Guilbert de Belleme was safely in Normandy. Then he remembered. Siward! Yes, the reeve had witnessed his oath and was exactly the kind of witness that the duke, in his urgency to rule by English law, might believe. And Siward could testify how he had broken his oath even before the baron's death.

He walked faster. Siward must be removed, and quickly. Among his company were a few he counted as his most trusted friends, men who would do what he commanded without question. They would ride to Storches Hundred tomorrow. He smiled grimly. "No violence," the duke had said, but those were easy words for him. William had already obtained his objective, but Tancred had not yet reached his. And he had no intention now, after all his conniving, of letting it slip out of his grasp.

It was the day before Christmas. Adelaide stood before her window in the guest hall at Berkynge, looking at the snow-covered streets. She tried not to see the houses, decked with banners and tapestries for the coronation procession tomorrow, for the thought of anyone but King Harold riding past them made her ache with pain. During all those weeks since the battle at Hastings, she had waited, torn between hope and dread, trying to sift fact from story in the hundreds of rumors that bombarded London while the Normans slipped their noose around the city. Up to a few weeks ago, waiting had been endurable, for Aelfred had come to her soon after Hastings, and she knew that he was alive and well up to the battle at London Bridge. But from that day on, there had been no word from him at all. She had lived like a mazed thing, unable to sleep or eat. She could not make herself believe that he was dead, though she heard continually that no English had lived through that day.

Then Edgar the Atheling had surrendered to the conqueror. It was inevitable; what could a child do against the might of Normandy, especially when city after city in his own land had submitted? Adelaide had wept the day when Harold's Queen had handed over the keys of Winchester. Winchester was a strong fortress, and the Queen's troops could have defended it for months; yet she had capitulated without a blow. Edwin and Morcar, too—all Harold's thanes had deserted him. And tomorrow, William of Normandy would be crowned King of England in the Abbey Church of Westminster. Those who, a year ago, had shouted for Harold Godwineson were making a festival on what ought to be a day of mourning.

She turned from the window, tears blurring her eyes. What was to become of her? She knew that William had announced a general amnesty for those who had fought against him, provided they would swear fealty; and she waited eagerly, hoping that Aelfred would send some word to her, even if he refused to take the oath. But no word had come. She must face the terrible fact that she was both widowed and landless, for the conquerors would take Storches Hundred, surely, and probably Birnham, too. Even worse, her child would grow up landless as well as fatherless. She bowed her head in her hands. What malignant fate had destined that she would know too late to tell Aelfred, so that he had had to die in the bitter supposition that his line had ended? But she could not give way to weeping; she must make some provision for herself. She could not bear her child within the convent walls; the nuns had sheltered her kindly, but they must live by their Rule, and it was doubtful, too, that the Normans would allow them to give the widow of an enemy indefinite sanctuary. Oh, not that they would come with drawn swords, but there were ways of coercion that could be used against Berkynge. She must leave, but where could she go? Her father was dead and so were most of his friends. Some women in her same plight had thrown themselves on William's mercy, but the very thought of that repelled her. No, she must make her own way. The son of Aelfred Ansculfson must be born free. It was little enough, but that much she could do for him.

There was a knock at the door. "Come in," she called, brushing the tears from her cheeks.

A young man came into the room. He bowed awkwardly, then stood before her, obviously expecting her to recognize him. When she did not, he said diffidently, "I am Wilnoth son of Elred shepherd, my lady."

"Wilnoth!" She rose to greet him. "You must forgive me. I did not know you for a moment. You are greatly changed."

"A few gray hairs, my lady. But you have not changed."

She smiled wearily. "You see me with too kindly an eye. Sit down, my friend. What is the news from Storches Hundred?"

He pulled a stool close to her chair. "The news is terrible."

"It can be no worse than news here," she sighed. "What has happened?"

"Tancred came three days ago with a company of Normans."

She closed her eyes. "He always wanted those lands. He has wasted no time."

"He took the baron's money chest, then he sent for Siward. They talked together in the baron's bower. A little later, he rode away." Wilnoth swallowed hard. "When we went into the bower, we found Siward. Ten stab wounds, my lady."

She looked at him woodenly. "He was dead?"

"Not before Father Owain confessed him, thank God. And before he died, he told us why Tancred had murdered him. It was because he had witnessed Tancred's oath to Baron Ansculf."

"Which Tancred has broken again and again," Adelaide said bitterly, "and we could do nothing. We can do nothing now."

"Your pardon, my lady, but there is much we can do," Wilnoth said earnestly. "Father Owain wrote down what Siward told him, in good Latin, and Siward put his mark to it. We all witnessed. I have the parchment with me. You must take it to Duke William."

243

"What good will that do? He is a Norman, like Tancred."

"He has promised he will rule here by English law. There has been murder done, my lady. Also, the duke has said that above all men he hates an oath breaker."

Adelaide rose and went to the window.

Wilnoth spoke again. "You must do this," he said solemnly. "You must lay claim to the lands in the name of Lord Aelfred's son."

She turned swiftly. "How do you know?"

"The Sister who admitted me told me," he answered, blushing.

"Even if I went to Duke William, I doubt he would listen to me. Lord Aelfred died fighting against him. His lands are confiscated."

"Only if there is no claimant, my lady."

She looked at him in amazement. "How does it happen that you know so much that I do not?" She smiled faintly. "How, for instance, do you know that my child will be a son?"

"He will be. There must be a baron," Wilnoth said stoutly. "My lady, will you go to the palace now?"

"You really believe that we will find justice there?"

"Duke William has promised to rule by English law," he repeated doggedly.

There was silence for a moment. Then Adelaide said slowly, "Go back to the Sister Portress and ask her to have the char readied. I shall not be long."

As Wilnoth left her, she hurried to her clothes chest. If she was to go to Westminster, she must not appear in dingy black. Swiftly she changed into a blue silk kirtle and fur-lined cloak. She put on her pearl necklace, her mother's rings, and the silver butterfly brooch that had belonged to Aelfred's mother. Over her white coif, which hid her hair as became a matron, she draped a black veil. Then she hurried to the gate, where the char, an open wagon drawn by two gray horses, was waiting. Wilnoth helped her in and took the reins. He was an expert driver, even in the narrow city streets, so, within an hour, they reached Westminster Gate. Here the Norman soldier on duty halted them and ordered them to name themselves.

"Adelaide, wife to Aelfred Ansculfson of Storches Hundred and Lady of Birnham," she answered in French. "I wish to see Duke William."

The sentry, though impressed by her splendor, shook his head. "Impossible, my lady. No one may enter Westminster until after the coronation tomorrow."

"Could you not take a message to him?"

"No, my lady. In fact, I do not even know where he is at this hour."

Adelaide took a silk purse from her girdle. "Perhaps you would know someone who could tell me his whereabouts?"

The soldier was very young and, by now, quite overwhelmed. His struggle between duty and the purse was so apparent that Adelaide, for a moment, felt sorry for him. She even felt a little guilty at offering the bribe, but she continued to wait. At last he sighed.

"I do know, my lady," he admitted. "He is in his apartments."

"Good. Then I can find my way." Smiling she dropped the purse into his hand. "I was often here in the time of King Edward."

He bowed. "I shall escort you, my lady. There are other soldiers. You will need me, in order to pass them."

He called to one of his companions to replace him, then went to one of the horses and took hold of the bridle. Adelaide, still smiling, turned to Wilnoth, who was looking at her in open-mouthed admiration.

"We're past the gates, at least," she said in English.

"I would not have thought to give him money," he answered.

"It would not have been necessary before now." Suddenly she put her hand on his arm. "Wilnoth, I just thought. Suppose we meet Lord Tancred?"

Wilnoth touched his knife. "I hope we do," he answered grimly.

At the great hall, the soldier helped her from the char, and the sentry stepped aside to let them pass. She turned to Wilnoth. "Give me that parchment. Wait for me here."

The hall seemed full of soldiers who stopped their drinking and dicing long enough to stare, but no one stopped them. The soldier led her to a door and knocked. A thin, stooped man in a monk's habit opened it. "Yes?" he asked coldly.

"I am Adelaide, wife of Aelfred Ansculfson of Storches Hundred and Lady of Birnham. I seek justice of Duke William for murder done on my demesne," she said in a clear high voice.

The monk frowned. "His Majesty, the King," he corrected, "can see no one. You must wait until after tomorrow."

"In England, the King's door is always open to a plea for justice," she replied firmly. "William of Normandy has said that he will rule by English law."

The monk looked at her uncertainly; then a voice called, "Admit her, Rannulf." Head high and smiling, Adelaide swept into the presence of Duke William.

He did not rise. He sat behind the table, looking at her impassively. He was a powerful man, she thought swiftly. Indeed, power cloaked him. He was handsome, too, and strong with a brute strength that disconcerted her. Instinctively she dipped a slight curtsy. The man, by his very character, demanded respect.

"Sire, I come seeking justice." The title came to her lips easily. He was King, no matter how he had gained his crown. And England had made him King.

"You speak French, I see?" She nodded and he turned to his secretary. "Take this down, Rannulf. You seek justice, Lady Adelaide? You shall find it here." He gave her eye for eye. "What is your grievance?"

"Murder has been done on my demesne. Three days ago, Norman soldiers came to Storches Hundred and left my reeve, Siward son of Sihtric, dying of ten stab wounds. I have his accusation written down by the priest and witnessed by his mark and those of others who found him."

"You were not present. How do you know murder has been done?"

"My people are not liars, Sire," she said coldly.

"H'm. And the names of the murderers?"

"I do not know them all. The leader was Tancred de Belleme."

William's eyes flickered. "Tancred de Belleme is one of my most valued commanders," he said evenly. "Why should he wish to kill your reeve?"

"Because Siward was the only living witness to Tancred's oath of fealty to Baron Ansculf, my husband's father."

"Baron Ansculf is dead."

"Under English law, the oath is to a man's household, as long as his line shall last," Adelaide countered swiftly. "I charge Tancred de Belleme with oath breaking to my husband and to my son."

"Your son?" William was visibly startled. "I was not told of this."

"My husband does—did not know before his death." The room was beginning to spin, and she gripped the edge of the table to keep from falling.

William rose. "A chair for Lady Adelaide, Rannulf," he said. "Quickly! Then find Lord Tancred. Tell him to come at once. And not a word about our visitor. We shall surprise him."

As Rannulf left the room, the duke poured two glasses of wine and handed one to Adelaide. "It will do you good." She hesitated and he smiled ironically. "Don't worry. It is safe. Drink it."

He waited until she had taken a few sips, then sat down beside her.

"Now, I want to hear everything you wish to tell me about Tancred de Belleme," he said quietly. "Take all the time you wish. Do not omit one detail."

Adelaide told her story, beginning with Tancred's oath at the Twelfth Night feast. She told of the folkmoot and Mab's death, of Ellen's suicide and her own escape, of Aelfred's flight to Walsingham and their marriage, and repeated Wilnoth's account of Siward's murder. The longer she spoke, the darker grew William's face. When she had finished he returned to the table with her parchment and read it through carefully. Then he looked at her.

"Your story is either the most fantastic lie or the most fantastic truth ever told," he commented.

"It is all true," she said shakily.

He replenished her glass. "Two things I know are true. Tancred *had* asked for Storches Hundred, and I gave him permission to ride there three days ago."

"He cannot have Storches Hundred. I claim it for the son of Aelfred."

"What if the child is a daughter?"

"Under English law, a daughter may inherit," she answered. "I hold Birnham in my own right—provided my claim is honored there."

"Rest assured, it will be!" he said fervently. "You are your father's only child?"

She smiled. "Yes, Sire."

"I wager he never felt the need of a son," William commented. "Well, to your grievance. First, let me remove a sorrow from your burden. Your husband is alive."

Joy flooded her. "Alive!"

"Yes. I've had him rather closely confined, partly for his own good. I became aware recently that his stepbrother has little love for him. Also, I've been waiting for him to come to his senses and swear fealty to me. If he does, he returns to Storches Hundred. If he does not, he forfeits the lands for himself *and* his heirs. That, too, I believe is English law." He looked at her soberly. "Perhaps you will be able to persuade him."

The news had so overwhelmed her that she could hardly speak. "I shall try, Sire," she breathed. "Oh, I shall try."

"Good. I saw him at Hastings, and I want him. Now, as to Tancred de Belleme—a broken oath, murder, and theft, you say?" She nodded. "A neat catalogue of crimes. But let me warn you, it's not going to be easy to prove them against him. His kind always seem to manage to stay within legality. I have promised redress today to all Englishmen who can prove that they have suffered at Norman hands apart from in battle. Prove, I said. It will be your word against his."

"I am speaking the truth, Sire. I will take the oath in the church. I will"—she thought wildly for a moment—"I will submit to ordeal."

"That won't be necessary." He extracted a parchment from the pile on the table. "There is still one pawn on the chessboard."

The guard opened the door and Tancred de Belleme stepped over the threshhold.

"Ah, Tancred," William said. "Come in."

Adelaide turned to look at him. Tancred looked only at the duke as he entered the room, his expression blandly confident. Then he saw her, and his entire face changed. Anger, hatred, fear rushed across it before it settled into its accustomed mask. He bowed, but without much flourish.

"Lady Adelaide!" he exclaimed, trying to smile. "What a delightful surprise! What brings you to Westminster?"

"Murder," William said unequivocally.

"Murder?" Tancred blanched.

"One Siward son of Sihtric, reeve of Storches Hundred." The duke looked at him coldly. "You were there three days ago, weren't you?"

"Yes, but— but—" Tancred was shaking. "It was not murder! He drew a knife first."

"Siward never drew a knife on a man in his life, unless he was attacked," Adelaide cried scornfully.

"You admit that knives were drawn," the duke continued. "And you left without a scratch, after you'd stabbed him ten times. Wasn't once enough for you?"

"Sire—Sire, I protest," Tancred insisted. "They are lying, all of them. And Lady Adelaide was not even there. How can you believe me a murderer?"

"Talk behind closed doors and a powerful man left dying while his visitor rides away unscathed would point to murder, even under Norman law," William said calmly. "However, we'll put that by for a moment. Answer me this. Did you not

249

tell me, in this room, that you never swore fealty to Baron Ansculf?"

"I did." Tancred's mouth was like a slit in a block of stone.

Solemnly William took a large medallion from inside his tunic. "I should like you to swear to that, now. This is a relic of St. Louis. Place your hand on it."

Trembling, Tancred stretched out his hand.

"Be careful," the duke warned. "Don't add sacrilege to perjury."

Tancred gasped. His arm fell limply at his side.

"I see," the duke said quietly. "Your uncle was right."

"My—my uncle?" Tancred stammered.

"I had a letter from him while we were at Berkhampstead. In fact, he sent me quite a dossier. He was at Storches Hundred the night you swore. Had you forgotten him?"

Tancred fell to his knees. "He lies!" he shrieked. "He is angry because he can claim no English lands."

"Of course. But his anger does not preclude his telling the truth about you. No, no protests! Have you also forgotten how you praised him, after damning him with faint praise before? Did you think I had not noticed your change of tune? You are a fool, Tancred de Belleme!"

"I have served you well, Sire," Tancred whimpered.

"With murder, theft, and a broken oath! I went to war with Harold Godwineson over a broken oath. Am I to treat yours differently from his? Get up!"

Slowly Tancred rose and faced him.

"You will pay the wergild of Siward, five hundred ecus in gold. You will return the money chest. And you will take the first ship leaving for Normandy," William said calmly. "Never show your face in my presence again, and count yourself fortunate that nothing worse has happened to you. But remember—I shall be watching you, and my arm is very long. And quick, too, when I am angered. Now, go!"

Tancred stumbled out of the room.

Breathing heavily, William leaned back in his chair for a moment. "So much for him," he said. "He will hold no English land."

"Sire, I cannot tell you—" Adelaide began, but he silenced her.

"Don't," he said shortly. "I've never trusted the Bellemes, though I've used them. One of them cursed me in my cradle. I owe you a debt of gratitude. You've rid me of that one." He drained his glass and set it on the table. "Now I am going to send for your husband. He must swear fealty to me, my lady. Try to make him see the sense of it."

"I will try. I promise. I think he will, when I tell him that you truly rule by English law."

"Good. He'll come here. You'll be quite alone. Tell him about the child. That should convince him, if nothing else can."

Adelaide rose and faced him. She had come to Westminster prepared to demand justice but equally prepared to hate William of Normandy. In this short hour, her feeling about the man had undergone considerable change. She must see if she could not make Aelfred regard him as she did, now.

"Remind him that Harold is dead. He is free to swear fealty where he will," the duke said, almost pleadingly. "Tell him that I am ready to give him double recompense for Tancred's injuries."

"I shall persuade him. I love him, Sire," she answered. She dropped a deep curtsy and kissed his hand.

He smiled gently. Then he left her alone.

"AELFRED Ansculfson, the doctor says that you should rest."

Aelfred paused midway to the door and turned to look at Osric, who sat on a low stool near the bed, watching him anxiously. "Don't worry so much about me, my friend," he said quietly. "My wound is almost healed."

"But it's the same leg you injured on the way to Walsingham. Please sit down. You've been walking up and down for the last half hour!"

"I can't seem to help it. I'm restless, Osric. I know now how you felt, the time I chided you for being restless when your arm hurt so badly. And I'm worried about Adelaide. If I could just see her! I have a feeling that Duke William is going to demand an aye or nay from me very soon, and I'm just as perplexed about what answer to give him as any mortal could be."

Osric smiled. "You were sure enough when you pitched young de Warrene out the door."

"Yes, but since then I've had time to think about what he said, as well."

"Maybe you should not think so much," Osric said sagely.

"That is easy for you to say," Aelfred retorted almost angrily. "The decision isn't yours to make. I don't have Solomon's wisdom, but as far as I can see, anything I do will be hurtful. If I swear fealty to William, I keep Storches Hundred but I break my oath to King Harold and to England. If I refuse, I keep my oath, but some Norman—Tancred, most likely—takes over our lands. But if I swear fealty to William, my lands won't really be mine anyway excepting on Norman sufferance. And I swear all my demesne—my people—to abide by Norman rule. The duke says he will rule England by English law, but that is not the way he conquered us."

He sank into the chair and rested his head on his hands.

"I never wanted anything so much in my life as to see Adelaide." He sighed. "I wish time could roll back to the days when all I had to decide was whether or not to become a monk. When I accepted sake and soke of Storches Hundred, I did not know what it would mean. Duke William will not wait forever for his answer. I know that much."

"Well—King Harold is dead," Osric offered tentatively.

"But his cause is not. Many men have already gone north to Gospatric. Not every loyal Englishman fell that day at London Bridge, and there were hundreds in Mercia and Northumbria who did not even fight at Hastings."

"Edwin and Morcar have gone over to William, though."

"They're fools," Aelfred said bitterly. "If they had ever had to battle with the Normans, they'd know that Normans need to be fought the same way tomorrow. We can't let them have England so easily."

"I wish I had been at London Bridge that day."

"Be glad you were not. It was horrible."

"And you still want to fight again?"

"No. But I feel I must, if that means keeping England for England."

There was silence as Aelfred resumed his pondering, thinking again of those dark days after Hastings, when at the Abbot's bidding he had taken the great seal of England to Archbishop Stigand, who had promptly proclaimed young Edgar the King. In that desperate hour, London had vowed to withstand the conqueror and hailed their new ruler with complete sincerity—a pathetic boy who could not even hold the gold orb, much less wear the crown. Hard upon that, the swift Norman advance had come, bringing blight to all it touched, and the news that city after city had surrendered struck terror to everyone's heart. Then, the battle at the bridge—a few hundred Englishmen against the enormous Norman host which trampled them down. Aelfred writhed inwardly, recalling the cavalry charge, the carnage, the sickening blow on his own thigh, and finally, so that he could continue, wounded or no, his attempts to pull the javelin out with his own hands until he had fainted from loss of blood and pain. For days he had lain on a bed in a small room in the soldiers' hall, oblivious to everything, and had finally awaked to hear that London had surrendered. That had been the worst time of all; he was ashamed now to remember how he had raged against the cowards who had betrayed their King. People had only laughed at him and whispered that he was mad.

And then, Duke William had entered the city and demanded an oath of fealty, which, in most instances, was given gladly in exchange for amnesty and promise of recompense for injuries done by Normans. Even the thought of such weakness had revolted Aelfred to his soul, and he had hotly refused. But now, as he had told Osric, he had had time to think. Over and over, the words, "My wife, my lands," pounded at him. What would happen to them if he did not swear? During these past four days, he had wondered again and again what his father would have done, faced with such a decision. Baron Ansculf would have refused, he thought; yet other thanes, like Edwin and Morcar, had complied. Still, he recalled now, the two cases were not exactly the same. The red-bearded brothers had never been as wholly committed to Harold Godwineson as his father had been. They did not find William's personal ambitions and means of realizing them, weighed in the balance with Harold's love for England, greatly wanting. All the thanes who had stood with Harold and really loved him were dead—at Gate Fulford, Stamford Bridge, or Hastings. Except for a shadowy figure named Gospatric, there was no one left of that company which King Harold had inspired with his vision. And, in all this, where did his own duty lie?

"No one will blame you for swearing fealty to William," Osric ventured.

"No," Aelfred answered, "except, perhaps, myself. There was more in my oath to Harold than a pledge to a man. He was really too good for England, considering what they did to him."

Osric nodded. "I know. I saw little of him, but he made me love this land more than I'd have believed possible."

"Yes, he could do that." Aelfred looked at him searchingly. "What will you do, Osric, if I do not swear?"

"Go with you," Osric said promptly. "I am your man."

"But the others on the demesne—they could not go with me. Can I leave them to the mercy and rapacity of the Normans?"

Before Osric could answer, the door opened. Ever since the duke's arrival at Westminster, a guard had been posted there, but he had never spoken and neither had Aelfred, except to say once that no guard was needed. He had no wish to go into the palace and see Red Lions where once Gold Dragons had been blazoned.

"The King wishes to see you," the guard said brusquely.

Aelfred rose. The moment of decision had come, and still he did not know what to do. But, he thought ironically, had not every important encounter of his life come upon him unprepared? He smiled slightly and buckled on his sword.

"Take me to Duke William," he said to the guard, who glared at him but did not answer. He followed his escort out of the soldiers' hall, across the court, and into the great hall. He had half expected to find William enthroned on the high seat, but it was empty on its dais, and the Gold Dragon on its back had not been removed. Well, he thought, it was too deeply carved to be removed, and that was good. They would have to get a new high seat for the conqueror. He stopped for a moment to look at it. What would Harold Godwineson say to him, if he were here? He walked through the Princes' Court and the Painted Chamber; ghosts of the days so briefly past thronged about him. He could almost see Gyrth, Leofwine, his father—above all, King Harold, in that moment when he had issued his challenge to the Normans. Harold was dead, but had his dream of England's greatness died with him? Should not at least some men try to carry it on, if not fulfill it? Vividly he seemed to see that moment in the Abbey when the King had taken his coronation oath, "that England may be great." For a few short months, England had been really great. Must even the memory of that greatness die, and England eventually become a fief of Normandy? He raised his head a half inch higher, and his shoulders straightened.

The guard pointed to the door leading to the royal apartments. "In there," he said.

Aelfred kept looking at the door as he walked towards it. Once, long ago, Mab had told him that he would know what to say in a time of need, and he prayed that the right words would come to him now. With firm step, clasping his sword hilt, he strode into the chamber. But Duke William was nowhere to be seen. Instead, it was Adelaide who stood before him. He stared in stunned amazement. Surely she could not be real. This was some trick of the devil on his imagination and longing, to send him into wansickness or madness. Then she spoke his name, and went to him, and put her arms around him. He could not speak for a moment, then only murmured her name as she clung to him.

After a little, she led him to a bench and sat him down beside her, her cheek on his. "I cannot believe it," he said huskily. "It is true, isn't it? But I cannot believe it. I never thought to see you."

"Sh-h," she said softly, kissing him. "I have much to tell you, and that you must hear."

For the next quarter hour, she talked to him, telling him things he could hardly believe had happened. Grief, shock, and anger made his head reel. Siward's death, Tancred's banishmen, the duke's promise—

"It does not seem possible that so much can have happened to change our lives so completely," he said dejectedly.

"I know. I watched much of it happen, and I can hardly believe it," she assured him. "But it is true. Storches Hundred is yours. Tancred is gone."

There was a pause. Then Aelfred said painfully, "Storches

Hundred is mine, provided I take an oath of fealty to William."

"Yes, of course." She smiled. "Is that so hard? Look what we will gain."

"You make it sound as though you think it very easy."

"It *is* easy. King Harold is dead. William is King, or will be tomorrow. He wants you in his company; he told me so himself. He says he will rule by English law, and I think his judgment against Tancred proves that he is to be trusted." She looked at him questioningly. "What are you pondering so gravely?"

"Perhaps about the many other Tancreds, who may never come to his notice," he admitted.

"Need you worry about them?"

"If innocent people suffer because of them, someone should. Particularly someone English, if they are English."

"Well, could you not do more for them as a member of the King's court?"

"I don't know. They might never come to my notice, then. Such people do not always speak their woe to men in high places."

"Then why do they not? I did," Adelaide said exasperatedly. "Aelfred, you are not thinking of refusing to take the oath, are you?"

Never had he felt a greater desire to take her in his arms and tell her that he would do as she so plainly wished. But, in the back of his mind, he could still hear King Harold's words. Slowly he nodded his head.

"I—I don't understand," she cried.

"I don't understand myself." He looked at her helplessly. "I only know that I should despise myself for the rest of my life, if I accepted my own life and all it means to me—my lands, my own dear wife—as largesse from William of Normandy. Which is what it would amount to, if I swear fealty to him."

She rose and walked swiftly away from him to the center of the room. Her eyes were blazing with anger. "Can you want your son to grow up landless?"

For a moment, the words made no sense. When they did,

he went to her, shaking in every limb. "We are to have a child?" he asked wonderingly.

Her anger left her as quickly as it had come. "I had not meant to tell you this way."

Joy overwhelmed him, and once more he took her in his arms. She rested her head upon his shoulder and whispered, "He must not grow up to learn that his father willingly left him landless."

Her words twisted his heart. In a voice he hardly recognized, he answered, "Neither must he grow up to learn that his father was a nithing."

Her arms dropped to her sides. "I see."

"No—no, you don't," Aelfred said urgently. "To you, my dearest, it is very simple. A matter of a few words. But for me, it is breaking an oath I made to follow a liege to death and beyond. What good will Storches Hundred bring me, if in my own heart I know I am furthering the ambitions of England's conqueror? And, in the end, the lands will be his, not mine. He looks on all England as his demesne."

"But have you no thought of me?" she asked dully.

"My every thought and breath is yours, Adelaide. But I could not ask you to love a nithing."

"I could not! I don't!" She started to weep. "You are *not* a nithing! You are foolish—rash—you will die for this dead liege of yours, and then what will become of me? I'd rather have you with me, alive, on the land we love, no matter where your allegiance would be, than remembering that you died for a cause that you had no chance of winning."

He quailed before her. "I wish I could speak better, Adelaide. But perhaps, here, fewest words are best, since in this your heart does not answer mine?"

She wiped her eyes. "If King Harold were still alive, I might understand—I think. But it seems to me that you have done enough for him, without seeking your own death." She struggled against another storm of sobs. "However, since you will have it so, I shall stay with you."

"Oh, Adelaide!" He clasped her tightly. "No, my love. You shall not. You shall go back to Birnham and bear our child.

258

And when he is old enough, you shall tell him that his father fought to his last breath for your right and his upon his coming of age to hold that land and ours freely and without duress. So that his mother could hold her head as proudly as any Norman-pledged woman in all Duke William's domain."

He kissed her tenderly.

"Now, go, my dearest. My resolve will surely melt, if I see you weep much longer."

She shook her head. "It will not. I know you better than that." Her arms tightened in a last embrace, and he led her to the door. He kissed her again before he opened it for her. She did not look at him. Sobbing unashamedly, she fled through the hall.

I must not weep, Aelfred told himself savagely. I must not! What would happen to him now, he did not know. William might order him imprisoned or executed. One thing was certain. It would not be long now before he knew. The Norman was never slow to act.

The door opened. He hardly noticed. Until he noticed indeed that the duke stood before him. For several minutes they took each other's measure in silence. Then William took the chair behind the table and motioned Aelfred to be seated.

"The Lady Adelaide failed to persuade you." It was a statement, not a question. The duke's voice was quiet, but there was a powerful quality in it that reached Aelfred's distracted ear, and it reminded him somewhat of King Harold's.

"She did not persuade me," he answered, just as quietly.

"So. I suppose you are expecting me to try to persuade you?" Now the voice held challenge.

"No, my lord. Why should you?"

"I don't know. Perhaps you can tell me. I think you're a fool, Aelfred Ansculfson. I've offered you complete amnesty, your lands, and recompense for the wrongs that Tancred de Belleme has done you. I add my firm promise that you will live in peace and honor for the rest of your days."

"Honor?" Aelfred asked sadly. "Perhaps we have different ideas about that, my lord. I should not consider it honorable to accept my father's lands as the price of peace from a Norman. You should not consider it a right or privilege to 'give' me my own lands."

"Nevertheless, honor is an empty word when death stares you in the face."

"Oh? Then honor was not the reason for your battle with King Harold?"

William's eyes smoldered. "Harold Godwineson was an oath breaker."

"Precisely." Aelfred smiled. "So, you went to war to defend your honor. Was honor an empty word then? He broke the oath you had forced on him for love of England. You made war on him to satisfy your own ambitions."

"Don't bandy words with me, young man," the duke threatened. "My honor is quite safe, and yours is not. Let us keep to the point of this conversation. I am asking you what more you want, before you will behave like a practical, reasonable man. Your wife is with child—your heir! Are you made of stone?"

"No, my lord."

"I thought you English looked on landlessness as a great disgrace."

"We do."

"Well, then?" He waited for Aelfred to reply, but when no answer came, he continued, "Also, I believe that, under English law, if a man's liege dies he is free to pledge fealty where he will."

Aelfred looked at him quietly. "I did not give my oath to King Harold alone," he answered. "I pledged my fealty to England. Do you, who hate—as you say—above all things an oath breaker, now ask me to break mine?"

"The question is irrelevant," William said shortly. "I am England, now."

"No! No, you are not!" Aelfred faced him boldly. "You are England's conqueror, but you are not England. Never as long as I have breath to fight. Do you think it is easy to forego a life of ease? But as long as men like me exist—and there are more of us than you realize, I think—you are *not* England!"

"Then I shall be, in time."

"By working to destroy us?"

"Not unless you insist upon being destroyed. Hear me, Aelfred Ansculfson. I want to go down in history as a good ruler and to make a nation of this land. To unite her under one head, as your kings up to now have never been able to do, for all your fine talk about honor and loyalty. I have the power and the means and my own men. But I want the English with me, too. For England's sake."

The words were so plausible that, for a moment, Aelfred almost believed them. Then, slowly, he smiled. "You *need* us with you, you mean."

William's face grew purple. "I do not need you!" he shouted. "No more of this. For the last time, what do you want?"

Aelfred caught his breath. The words came to him. There was one thing that he could accept. "You promised to recompense those of us whom the Normans have injured," he reminded, slowly and distinctly.

"I did. I've offered you recompense."

"I ask that the recompense be given to my son."

There was a long pause. "I see," the conqueror said quietly.

"And I want your assurance, on your honor, that my wife and my child and all my demesne and hers will always be free of any Norman interference. Forever! That is the recompense I ask."

"Nothing for yourself?"

"Nothing. Unless a safe-conduct to the north."

"To join Gospatric?"

"To join Gospatric." Aelfred smiled. "You know about him, I see."

"It's my business to know such things," William said shortly. "So you insist upon casting your lot with them. The losers! The conquered! Why?" His voice rose in exasperation. "In Heaven's name, man, tell me why?"

"Because they are not losers. They are not conquered. I had rather cast my lot with men who fought beside Harold Godwineson than with you, the conqueror."

"That's a fool's answer," William snorted. "Speak sensibly."

"I shall try. It's not that I hate you—especially now, since I've spoken with you, face to face." Aelfred spoke in all sincerity. "In another time, place, and circumstances, I might have served you, and served you well. But you are only one Norman—and I saw what was done here by Normans before you came, to influence the people and to prepare the ground for your victory."

"You also know that they've done many things that I do not approve. And that your own particular Norman has been banished."

"Yes. But as you say, it is your business to know and attend to all things. And there were many others whom you could not have won without, either. Nor will they allow you to forget them. And what will they do to England now?"

William looked at him somberly. "Still, Harold Godwineson is dead. England has no one else but me. What good will it do you to fight me? Why lose your life in a lost cause?"

A wave of longing swept over Aelfred for the land he would never see again. Adelaide's face drifted before him, and his heart contracted. What good, indeed, was it to fight against the inevitable? Then, strong and sure, the answer came.

"So that you will not forget us," he said quietly. "So that your Norman armies will not ride roughshod over this land and impose your will on us too easily. Because, for all you say, King Harold made us a nation. His love for the country and his people was contagious, and *we* are England, because of him. If all the English join with you, they will become Normans. And the chief reason they join with you is because you give them lands and money which cost you nothing. But if some of us oppose you honorably, we can make your victory longer and harder in coming, so that there will still be an England for our children, and not a Norman fief, no matter how many go over to you for what you give them!"

William, who had listened intently, shook his head. "You are the maddest of men, Aelfred Ansculfson. Does it not matter to you that all practical, reasonable, ambitious men will call you a fool?"

"No!" His steadfast eyes never wavered. "You will have many ambitious, practical, and reasonable men with you, and you will need them, believe me. But England needs men like me—and Gospatric—to fight against you. To stand. And I promise you, we will stand. I promise this to my wife and child, even more than I do to England."

"I'd rather have you stand at my side," William said crustily. "But I know that is impossible. I could not have you fighting against me right next to me, as I know you would. It rather keeps my faith in mankind to know it. And I'll speak honestly to you, now, since this is probably the last time we'll speak together. I dislike turncoats as much as I do oath breakers. Some of your English thanes make me ill with their fawning. Bah! Do they think I'm a fool?"

"No. They are only ambitious, practical, reasonable men."

William threw back his head and roared with laughter. "*Sainte Marie*, how I wish I could keep you here!" he said, wiping his eyes. "But, be it as you have asked. The Lady Adelaide of Birnham shall hold sake and soke at Storches Hundred, until your son is of age. I'll make the child a ward of the crown, so even if you die in battle and your wife marries again, he and your lands will be safe. Because"—he grew very sober—"you'll not be returning here again, unless I'm driven out, which is unlikely, or you come in chains as a prisoner of war."

He took a parchment from the pile on the table.

"Here is your safe-conduct to the north. Your man Osric is waiting in the court with two horses. My advice is to start riding and not stop until you reach Durham."

Aelfred's hands were like ice as he took the parchment. To his amazement, he saw that it carried the duke's seal. "You had it there, all the time!" he cried.

"I took your measure the first time I saw you," William answered. "It was at Hastings. You carried the Golden Man. Nevertheless, as an ambitious, practical, reasonable man, I had to try to make you change your mind."

"Thank you—Sire."

"No thanks, and not that word from your lips either.

Though I think you mean it well. There is only one King for you." William smiled. "One word more—don't grieve too much about your wife. Actually, she is very proud of you. You should have seen her when I called you a fool a little while ago. Apparently that is her privilege, but definitely not mine. There will be a way to send you news when your son is born."

"Thank you for that comfort, too." Slowly Aelfred raised his hand in salute. "I wish we did not need to be enemies, Sire." He smiled. "You see, since I took no oath, I need not deny you!"

He turned quickly on his heel and hurried from the room. He ran through the hall and into the courtyard where Osric was waiting.

"You came!" Osric said jubilantly. "I knew you would. Let's be off! Duke William might change his mind."

"No," Aelfred said decidedly, as he mounted. His horse, he noticed, was superb, one of William's best. "He will not. He's a good man, Osric."

Osric snorted. "He's a Norman."

"The Lady Adelaide and I have learned today that not all Normans are like Tancred de Belleme," Aelfred replied, as he turned his horse towards the gates. "He's good. I'll hear nothing against him, even though I fight against him to my last breath."

"We ride north," Osric shouted exultantly.

Aelfred smiled, a little sadly. Everything was very simple for Osric. In his way, he, too, though not in the least politically ambitious, was a practical, reasonable man. And, better than that, a loyal one. England had need of his kind. For himself, all possible excitement was engulfed in the heartbreak of leaving. He dared not even think of Adelaide, now. Perhaps one day she would understand that this was best, but it would be expecting a great deal. A very great deal!

"To the north! To Gospatric," he answered, and resolutely guided his horse up the great North Road.

Rosemary Sprague, whose highly acclaimed *Forever in Joy: The Life of Robert Browning* was published in 1965 by Chilton Books, was born in New York City. She moved to Cleveland, Ohio, when she was about a year old. She admits that she was not overly fond of school. Her parents were aware of this, although they never let her know that they knew until she was in college. She learned to read before she entered the first grade, a discovery which surprised her father and mother as greatly as it annoyed the teacher!

With Cornelia Otis Skinner, she feels she shares the honor of being the most innocent freshman ever to enter Bryn Mawr College. There, she majored in English, took all the languages and history she could and was an active member of the Dramatic Society, choir and glee club.

Following her graduation from Bryn Mawr, she spent a year in New York studying acting with the late Frances Robinson-Duff. Then she entered graduate school at Western Reserve University, where she took her M.A., and was a Fellow-in-English during her last two years' work on her Ph.D. Since receiving her doctorate, she studied at the Shakespeare Institute at Stratford-on-Avon, England, and the University of London. She has been a delegate to the Conference on English Literature at Oxford University in England and to the Conférence Sur des Auteurs Francais at Brussels. She was also a member of the first School of Letters (New Criticism) at Kenyon College.

In 1962 she attended the Shakespeare Seminar at Stratford, Ontario, and delivered a lecture there on "The Men Who Were Not Shakespeare." She has also lectured extensively on children's literature; on Robert Browning; and on Queen Elizabeth I at the Thomas More Institute of the University of Montreal.

She has taught at Western Reserve University; Fenn College, Cleveland, Ohio; The Cleveland Institute of Art; and was director of dramatics at Notre Dame College, South Euclid, Ohio, where she staged the North American premiere of Paul Claudel's *The Satin Slipper*. She is now professor of English at Longwood College, Farmville, Virginia, the oldest women's college in the United States, where she teaches her two specialities, the Victorians and Chaucer. In her spare time, she plays the piano, experiments with gourmet cooking, continues to read incessantly, and goes to the theatre.

Miss Sprague has carved a distinguished career for herself as the author of many historical novels for young adults. *Northward to Albion* was the first and was followed by *A Kingdom to Win*, and *Heroes of the White Shield*. *Heir of Kiloran* grew out of her love of the theatre and the *commedia del' arte*, in addition to her fascination with the outcome of the intrigues surrounding Mary Stuart. It was named one of the 100 Best Books of 1956 by the *New York Times Book Review*. This was followed by such books as *Conquerors of Time, Dance for a Diamond Star* —concerning Maria de Camargo, the eighteenth-century ballerina—and *The Jade Pagoda,* set in Salem, Massachusetts, in the days of the China trade.

In addition to writing her life of Browning, Rosemary Sprague has recently edited *Poems of Robert Browning.*